THE ATOMIC WEIGHT OF LOVE

After you've read this galley, we'd love to hear what you think.
Please contact us by e-mail at marketing@algonquin.com.

The ATOMIC WEIGHT of LOVE

A NOVEL BY

Elizabeth J. Church

ALGONQUIN BOOKS
OF CHAPEL HILL
2016

Published by
Algonquin Books of Chapel Hill
Post Office Box 2225
Chapel Hill, North Carolina 27515-2225

a division of
Workman Publishing
225 Varick Street
New York, New York 10014

Printed in the United States of America.
Published simultaneously in Canada by Thomas Allen & Son Limited.
Design by TK.

LIBRARY OF CONGRESS CATALOGING-IN-PUBLICATION DATA

[TK]

10 9 8 7 6 5 4 3 2 1
First Edition

To Frances Salman Koenig,
this novel's strongest champion,
and
To my brother Alan A. Church,
for his steadfastness.

How have all those exquisite adaptations of one part of the organisation to another part, and to the conditions of life, and of one distinct organic being to another being, been perfected?

—CHARLES DARWIN, *On the Origin of Species*

Los Alamos is in a restricted airspace reservation covered by an Executive order, dated May 23, 1950. This airspace cannot be penetrated except by authority of the AEC [Atomic Energy Commission]. Historically permission has been refused except for the chartered [AEC flights of official visitors and project personnel].

—from the report of the Hearing before the Subcommittee on Communities of the Joint Committee on Atomic Energy, Congress of the United States, Eighty-Sixth Congress, First Session on Community Problems at Los Alamos, December 7, 1959

THE ATOMIC WEIGHT OF LOVE

Prologue

In early January of 2011, forty-five hundred red-winged blackbirds fell dead from the Arkansas skies. A few days later, five hundred more birds plummeted to earth, and their broken bodies covered an entire quarter-mile stretch of the highway near Baton Rouge, Louisiana. Some thought that one bird, confused by bad weather, led the others to their deaths; others blamed pesticides. I suspect there were also those who felt God had struck the birds from the sky in some sort of apocalyptic fever. Eventually, wildlife experts determined that the birds had died of blunt force trauma. Startled by the explosion of celebratory New Year's fireworks, the birds—who had poor night vision—flew into power lines, telephone poles, houses, mailboxes, and tree branches. Our exuberance killed them.

I'm watching the birds, still. Paying attention, observant—ever the ornithologist. Stories such as these keep me awake at night when I cannot escape the beating of my eighty-seven-year-old heart, the constancy of it, the weariness of it. I cannot say with scientific certainty how many times over these many decades it kept or deviated from its rhythm, how many times it catapulted with love or capitulated in grief. Maybe Alden could have calculated those numbers for me. Across the universes of so many academic blackboards he flung like stardust numbers and symbols, the language of mathematics and the elegant formulae of physics. He dissected unseen worlds, galaxies I could only begin to imagine. One of the scientists who created the first atomic bomb, Alden knew the weight of invisible neutrons, could predict the flight paths of escaping electrons. He could conceive of the existence of such phantasms and then release their formidable, destructive power.

But Alden never knew how to measure the weight of a sigh. He could not predict the moment when the petal of a spent rose would release and descend. Alden could not tell me when a screech owl would cry out from a darkened pine bough outside my bedroom window and insinuate itself into my dreams.

I first loved him because he taught me the flight of a bird, precisely how it happens, how it is possible. Lift. Wing structure and shape, the concepts of wing loading, drag, thrust. The perfectly allotted tasks of each differently shaped feather. The hollowness of bones to reduce weight, to overcome gravity. I was too young to realize that what I really yearned to know was *why* birds take flight—and why, sometimes, they refuse.

This is not Oppenheimer's story. It is not that of Edward Teller or Niels Bohr, Fermi or Feynman. This is not the story of the creation of the atomic bomb, or of Los Alamos, the birthplace of the bomb. It is not even Alden's story. Someone else has told their stories—will tell their stories. This is my story, the story of a woman who accompanied the bomb's birth and tried to fly in its aftermath.

A Parliament of Owls

1. A solitary, nocturnal bird of prey characterized by its small beak and wide face.

2. A farsighted bird, the owl cannot clearly see anything within a few centimeters of its face.

He was a giant of a man. You had to be, to win on the battlefield. Over six foot seven inches tall. A mountain of a Scotsman." My father held the carving knife suspended in the air over a Sunday roast chicken. "Brown, curly hair, piercing eyes that could spot treachery and deceit one hundred yards away." He freed a drumstick. "Meridian, pass me your plate."

I felt relieved. Sometimes Daddy purposefully denied me a piece of dark meat; he thought I should learn to make do with whatever was offered. Caught up in his Scottish lore, he must have forgotten for a moment about building my character.

"Guns are a great equalizer. You don't have to be physically strong to shoot someone, not like close-quarter combat," he continued. "Wallace had to be a true warrior. Still, he carried a Psalter with him, knew the psalms of David by heart, even quoted them as the English tortured and killed him."

"Grahame, no. Stop now." My mother forced his gaze to meet hers across the supper table.

"Why would he carry salt?" Eight years old, I was wholly enamored of my father and his stories.

"They're facts, Jennie. Meridian shouldn't be afraid of facts. That's life." My father turned to me. "A book of psalms, not salt."

"He took a book?"

Fingering the salt shaker rather than passing it my direction, my mother interrupted him again. "No. No dirks. No broadaxes or longbows. We're not going to list the ways in which William Wallace was tortured. Not at Sunday dinner."

A high school history teacher with thinning brown hair and a deep cleft chin, my father loved outlandish tales of wildly self-destructive Scottish courage and the brilliant defeat of the English by Wallace during the Scottish Wars of Independence. Grahame Alan Wallace could not prove it, but he was certain we were descended from Scotland's greatest hero, a man whose unconventional tactics let the Scots win against all odds. *Stirling Bridge. 1297.* My father hammered those facts into me, a litany more powerful than any I ever heard in Sunday school.

"God comes in handy in a war, that's why he carried the book of psalms," my mother pronounced, tugging at the cuff of her sleeve. She made all of our clothes then. It was 1932, and the Great Depression was heavy upon us. To my enduring shame, I had to wear a neighbor girl's dresses made over by my mother to fit me. My soft, fine, dark blonde hair hung lank to my chin, just the tips curling inward, as if seeking protection beneath the angle of my jaw. Omnipresent dark shadows dwelt beneath my eyes, maybe because when I could get away with it I stayed up late into the night, reading.

"God picks sides?" I asked.

"What?"

"Is one side in a war always right and the other wrong, is that why God picks sides?"

"This is what your conversational topics are doing to us, Grahame." My mother held out her plate for her serving of chicken.

"Brave men win wars, Meridian. And God makes men brave." My father lay to rest the carving knife, along with his favorite topic. "Now, your mother wants to discuss other matters. You choose."

"Oh, birds! I choose birds." I maneuvered my peas to the side so that they wouldn't contaminate any of the good food on my plate.

"Such as the one you're eating?" My father teased, waving a fork loaded with tender chicken in my direction. "Don't you just *love* birds?" he said, sighing like a girl in love.

"Daaaaddy," I pleaded, and he laughed, closed his eyes in mock rapture as he chewed.

I looked at my plate, my love of birds battling with my salivary glands.

"Don't torture your only child," my mother said, accurately reading my consternation. "Go ahead and eat your chicken, honey."

"I'm not torturing her. She's asking questions about the morality of war, right and wrong. She's a smart girl, capable of resolving this dilemma for herself." My father's rigorous expectations permitted no softness—nothing he viewed as weakness. I owed all amelioration of his stringencies to my mother's compassion, her sensitive barometer.

"She's a very smart girl," Mother smiled at me. "Very," she said, this time smiling at my father, who then winked at me.

I bit into the drumstick, my hunger having won the battle.

ONE CHRISTMAS, MY PARENTS put a precious, rare orange in my stocking, along with a wooden pencil box. The other kids in my

Greensburg, Pennsylvania elementary classroom had long showed off their pencil boxes, with lids that slid perfectly open and closed, and I had so longed for one—in those days, in my family, an outright extravagance. The box was made of pecan wood—smooth beneath my awestruck fingertips, with the sharp scent of varnish. My mother then took me to purchase the rest of my gift: a pair of Educator shoes from Kinney Shoes on Main Street. An advertisement in the store's front window featured a black and white drawing of two children with schoolbooks and lunch pails, and the caption: LETS THE CHILD'S FOOT GROW AS IT SHOULD. My father taught me how to polish and buff the deep chestnut leather, and then it became my job to polish his shoes as well on Saturday nights, before Sunday morning services.

My parents knew better than to give me dolls—something that held no appeal for me, but that seemingly every single one of my friends shamelessly coveted. I felt no affinity for long-lashed glass eyes that stared blankly or miniature outfits with tiny buttons and bows, and I didn't want to feed them or change diapers. Dimpled, stiff dolls couldn't converse with me, not in the way I longed to talk. And my true love was nature, the outdoors. There, in the solemn patience of a doe or the swift flight of birds, I found the kind of companionship that made me wonder, that challenged me.

When I was ten years old, my father gave me *The Burgess Bird Book for Children*. In the book's precious color plates I discovered open-beaked Carol, the Meadow Lark, with a black bib over his yellow chest; Chippy the Chipping Sparrow, Sammy Jay, and Speckles the Starling. I would take the book down to the fields by the train tracks at the edge of our neighborhood, and there I would lie in the grass, smell the fecund earth, and cradle my head on an arm while reading. Trains would rumble past, clouds of tiny flies would aggravate me, and eventually Daddy would be sent to bring me back for chores and supper.

I had to sweep both porches, front and back, and it was my job to dust Mother's hand-painted china cups and saucers. While I worked, I would go over the various bird attributes in my head: beak lengths, feather coloration, foraging behaviors, and nesting composition—all in preparation for much-anticipated questioning by my father.

That's where my career as an ornithologist began—at the dinner table, beside the train tracks, in the late-night hours while my parents slept and I read lying in the empty bathtub. When I found a dead goldfinch on the walk home from school, my father applied the balm of Darwin to my broken heart. I had *On the Origin of Species* in hand by my eleventh birthday.

SIX MONTHS LATER, I awoke to my mother's frantic voice as she begged my father to awaken. He did not. He was dead of a massive heart attack at age forty-three.

It was impossible that the exuberance that had been my father—his riotous laughter, his dogged perseverance of knowledge and truth—had simply dissipated. Where did all of that energy go? Vaporized, maybe—but into what, and where? What happened to the bounty of his being, his love for us, for me?

I tried to remember every second of my last exchange with him—the good-night peck, the tingle of his whiskers against my cheek, his breath scented with onions. The times he'd let me climb onto his lap and circle his neck with my arms, before he began telling me I was too heavy, when I held my breath hoping to be less burdensome. I closed my small fists about the memory of his telling me how soft my hair was, that if he weren't careful, he might fall into the waters of my blue eyes.

It was the first time in my life my heart crumpled, caved in on itself. I developed stomach pains that kept me up at night, pains no doctor properly diagnosed as intense, internalized grief. My mother would let me crawl into what had been their bed, now her lonesome bed, and despite her own deep misery she would stroke the hair at my temples, a small gesture that eased the pain enough to let me sleep. Mother was my ballast. She held fast—to life, to me.

In the wake of my father's death, I found focus and meaning in schoolwork. I doubled and tripled my efforts to be the best. Math was perfection—for me, it flowed and held a hint of magical, unseen worlds and concepts. I kept my pencils sharp, gloried in writing out neat algebraic equations and discovering the hidden values of x, y, and z. My teachers conferred, and when I was twelve they gave me a few intense tutorials and then promoted me a year ahead in math classes. I felt odd, singled out, the object of conjecture and some envy among my classmates, but I could also see the pride in my mother's face, imagine my father's hearty approval.

Primarily, though, I cared about science—deciduous versus evergreen, monozygotic versus dizygotic twins, and the colors of Mendel's pea plants. When I finished high school, I knew the world would only get bigger for me, that I would be challenged to comprehend the exquisite perfection of adaptation; the myriad, vast ways in which living organisms achieve life and death.

HOW MANY STRANGERS' TOILETS did my mother scrub, how many floors, how many linens did she launder to supplement my meager scholarship to the University of Chicago? At age seventeen, I was a younger-than-average college freshman in the fall of 1941, buoyed by my mother's faith in me, and I set about obtaining a biology degree with a focus on avian studies, and a plan to earn an advanced degree in ornithology.

The whole enterprise was far bolder than I. I concealed fears: near-certainty of my dire lack of qualifications and absolute certainty of my inability to fit in. The first day of classes, I rushed between buildings, the heavy, costly textbooks in the book bag bouncing off of my hip. In a gloomy, bell-jar-lined classroom in the zoology building, I sat near the front and watched men—all men—file in to join me. A few of them met my eyes, smiled tentatively. I saw clean-shaven cheeks and starched shirts, hastily tied Windsor knots. Some nodded, but none sat next to me.

Instead, they filled the back rows, as if to warn the professor that he'd have to work for their attention. I wondered if I should temper my eagerness, but I could not bear the thought of wasting a morsel of what was offered. I tugged at the collar of my plain, white blouse while two fraternity brothers sat behind me.

"What do you think?"

"Her?"

"Who else? She has great eyes."

"Church mouse."

"Maybe still waters run deep."

"Not with that one."

I soon learned that my classmates preferred to entangle themselves with sophisticated sorority girls whose teeth were perfectly aligned and whose clothes had not recently hung on the racks of a second-hand store. Girls who were *fun*. I told myself I didn't mind. They left me alone to prove my mother's efforts were not in vain.

On weekends I lived in the musty rooms of the Field Museum, letting my mind wander through the library's collections of botanical and natural history illustrations, focusing on evolutionary biological contexts. Through the museum windows, I watched the fall leaves, puzzling over why it seemed that the last leaf on the tip of a limb was usually the first to change color. Did the tree pull back its sap from the limbs first, focusing its energy at the core? If a leaf's change is due to a reduction in chlorophyll, to altered light duration, why would the leaf on the end of the limb turn first? And why didn't the entire tree follow that pattern with leaves turning in order, from limb-tip to trunk? Why instead would the remaining leaves turn in a random fashion?

To question, to ponder, to ask, and to learn. Education was my drug of choice—classrooms, books, lectures, pushing myself to understand. Forever trying to win my father's approval, never quite grasping the fact that a dead man cannot applaud.

Through those same windows, I watched the first snowfall begin as a light, dry powder and morph into those luscious, fat, lazy flakes that sashay downward and accumulate into weighty drifts. Once, I stood shivering in a neighbor's yard, reluctant to frighten away a dark, rough-legged hawk that sat atop a wooden picket fence, huddled and motionless while snow blanketed him in disguise. His humped shoulders beneath the white shroud made me think of old men on park benches, waiting for someone or something to move them from their torpor. On my walks between Mrs. Hudson's boarding house and the campus, the snow sifted in over the tops of my galoshes, melting into rivulets that pooled, lukewarm, beneath the soles of my feet. My legs, clad only in thin stockings beneath my skirts, were red and numb by the time I reached the school buildings. Radiators clinked and hissed, and windows fogged. The stars were bits of ice in cold, clear skies.

At night, I closed my eyes in my narrow single bed and prayed a godless prayer of gratitude for every moment, every opportunity of each day.

EVEN IN CLOISTERED ACADEMIA, we knew the war was coming. With Germany threatening to blur all recognized lines in Europe, it was clear the United States would be compelled to fight. In the evenings after dinner, I joined the other boarders to sit in Mrs. Hudson's parlor drinking coffee, darning socks, and listening to the radio's news programs. When the Japanese attacked Pearl Harbor on December 7th, we were all in a state of shock. As much as we'd known that Great Britain was vulnerable, the idea that America—all the way across the Pacific—was exposed to attack . . . well, it was incomprehensible. We listened to a recitation of the numbers of dead, the horrendous loss of ships and planes. Four days later, Nazi Germany declared war on the U.S., and the U.S. replied with declarations of war against Germany and Italy.

It was like a stealthy fire, one that glows quietly, secretively, for ages, and then *whoosh!*—is suddenly ablaze. When I looked at maps in the newspaper, talked with other students in the commons, heard the boasts of boys not yet war-torn, all I could think was *conflagration*.

And yet, we attended classes, professors lectured. We still laughed. We still fell in love.

He leaned on the lab countertop, fingered a glass beaker, and said, "There's a dance on Saturday."

It was Jerome Bloom, my biology lab partner. Jerome. Jerry. *Jer!* Why did he think he needed to tell me about the school social calendar? It didn't even enter my mind that he might be asking me out. I reached into the pocket of my lab coat for my mechanical pencil.

"Are you going?" he asked.

"Oh, I doubt it. Those things really aren't for me." I delicately sandwiched a drop of pond water between two glass slides and slid them beneath the microscope lens.

"You don't like to dance?"

"I love to dance. I really do. It's just that . . ." I looked through the eyepiece, began adjusting the focus.

He waited until he could tell I wasn't going to add anything more.

"Meridian, you should get out more, meet more people. Have some *fun*."

"I suppose I should, Mother Dear."

"Just come with me. Let me take you."

"On a date?" I gave up trying to focus on the slide and looked up at him.

"Is it that too awful to contemplate?"

It wasn't awful. I just couldn't believe he'd ask *me*. What I knew about Jerome was that he was making his way through the girls in the nursing department. I'd seen him walking the campus sidewalks, and I'd noticed his carefully pomaded hair, his houndstooth checked jacket and—the true *Jer!* on-the-make touch—his red and white polka-dotted tie. He was a bit on the short side, but with a speedy walk that reminded me of a frantic piston. His lips were plump and sensual, and he wore wireless eyeglasses so that nothing obscured the breadth of his brown eyes. He was way out of my league.

"Don't tell me you have to wash your hair. None of those fake excuses." He touched my elbow. "If you don't like it, I'll walk you home. Safe and sound."

I'd heard he was a good dancer. He knew how to lead so that even the clumsiest of girls could follow.

"Oh, all right. Yes. Yes, I'll go to the dance with you on Saturday." He let go of my elbow. "Now, if you don't mind, let's get back to the paramecium." I bent over the microscope once more and hid my smile behind a curtain of hair.

"You say the naughtiest things," he said, his low baritone an intimate whisper. I felt the frisson of fear and adrenaline I'd read about in my purloined copy of *Lady Chatterley's Lover*. I was way out of my league. Way.

KITTY, ONE OF MY FELLOW BOARDERS, conspired with Mrs. Hudson to tutor me a few evenings before my date.

"What do you plan to talk about?" Kitty asked over the dinner table.

I reached for the butter dish. "Talk about?"

"Conversation," Mrs. Hudson piped in.

"I don't know. Whatever comes up."

"No no no!" Kitty let out an exasperated sigh. "No wonder you have trouble getting dates."

"I'm not here to date."

"You can do both, dear," Mrs. Hudson said. "Learn and find a husband."

The lamp behind Kitty turned her frizzy red hair into a thick halo of bright copper wire. She put down her silverware, leaving the gravy on her pork chop to congeal. "You can't just talk about any old thing, Meri. Knowing you, you'll end up lecturing him about the composition of eagles' nests or the migration patterns of some obscure bird species."

"What's wrong with that? He's in my biology class."

"You have to flatter them," Mrs. Hudson said, blowing a strand of hair from her forehead. "Pick a topic they know, something they like talking about."

"Which is biology," I said with a degree of certainty I hoped would put an end to the conversation. "Why are you two ganging up against me?" I teased and took a bite of carrot.

"Because . . . well . . ." Kitty looked to Mrs. Hudson.

"You could use a little help when it comes to flirting."

I laughed.

"We're not joking."

"Mrs. H is right. You have to ask him about things he knows, let him know you're interested. To hook him, I mean."

I closed my eyes briefly.

"Ask him questions you know he can answer—let him think he's smarter than you," Mrs. Hudson said, and took a sip from her water glass.

"Yeah, you scare them away with your brains."

"Oh, honestly." I wiped my mouth and got ready to push back my chair and retrieve the coffee pot from the stove. "You two want for me to lie, to pretend I'm stupid so that some man will like me? Maybe Jerry likes me precisely because I am smart."

I saw them exchange another look. "Oh," Mrs. Hudson said.

"You are intimidating, Meri, whether you know it or not," Kitty said. "You're not exactly approachable. Just make sure you prop up Jerry's ego a bit, that's all we're saying."

"Oh, he's fine without my building some sort of scaffolding for him," I said and finally ended things by taking my cup and saucer for a refill.

"Just think about it," Kitty begged.

ON SATURDAY, I TRADED my sensible dark wool skirt and scratchy crew-necked sweater for an evening dress, the only one I owned—a brown, cocktail-length dress made of a shiny synthetic material. It was gathered at the waist with a pleated belt that tied into a bow on the side, and there were three fabric-covered buttons that I managed to convince myself elevated the dress to near elegance. I added black pumps, the string of pearls my mother had given me for high school graduation, and a muted red lipstick.

I had a fresh face, a pretty face. I have always been small, my wrists fragile, like fireplace tinder, easy to snap. I have an open, heart-shaped face with high-arching eyebrows, insistent cheekbones, and Scottish skin that blushes and pales like an ever-changing weather map. Genetics have given me a tongue I can roll, unattached earlobes, and the recessive trait of clear, light-blue eyes.

That night, my youth was all the makeup I needed, but looking in the mirror and brushing my dark blonde hair back from my face, I felt so plain, anticipating the stylish coifs of the popular girls. I didn't own a lace collar that could be attached to different dresses to spice them up. I lacked the crystal-studded pins girls added to their coats or hats, and the clips that held my hair in place were only a facsimile of silver. My plumage was not the kind that would attract a mate, that would let me stand out from the rest of the flock.

Jerome's breath on my cheek sent shivers along my spine as he pinned a corsage of generous white mums onto my bodice. His fingers were careful, practiced, and I liked the way he tucked the pearlescent head of the pin beneath the greenery of the corsage. I smelled the sharp scent of whatever it was he used to try to dissuade his curls, and the collar of his shirt was starched a perfect, crisp white that made me want to tap it with my fingertips to see if it would sound like the taut head of a drum. Two tiny moles perched just above his collar, on the left side of his neck. Part of a constellation?

The first thing I noticed was the heat of the room. I couldn't imagine how we could dance for long or how my dress would hold up. Jerome's suit coat had to be ridiculously hot. He got us each a glass of sweet red punch, pulled a flask from his breast pocket, and poured a splash of amber liquid into the cups. He smiled lopsidedly and shrugged his shoulders.

We touched our glasses. "To victory!" I shouted, and felt the heat magnified as the alcohol spread its warmth across my chest. Shyly, I put the back of my hand to my mouth and smiled. It was my first-ever taste of alcohol, and in that moment I was, at last, part of the true college life. He took the glass from my hand and set it on a nearby table.

"A Pennsylvania girl has got to know how to polka." He steered me toward the dance floor.

Oh God, I prayed silently to the God who had never shown his face to me in any kind way. *Don't make me do this.*

But I did do it. And Jerry was a dream of a dancer, as advertised. We stopped dancing only twice all night—to soak up more punch and later to permit me a trip to the ladies' room for an assessment of the state of my declining composure. The face in the mirror grinned back at me, despite her awry and wilting hair. Nothing mattered but that I was alive, dancing, at college, with a desirable date. Sorority girls be damned!

At Mrs. Hudson's door, Jerry leaned in to kiss me. Reflexively, I turned my head to the side at the last moment and he kissed my ear. Later, as I lay awake with the music in my head, cigarette smoke permeating my hair and pillowcase, I wished I'd touched the tip of my tongue to each of those tiny moles, in succession.

"FLIGHT REQUIRES DEFIANCE OF gravity and is really, when you think about it, a bold act."

The professor at the front of the lecture hall paused for dramatic effect, but as far as I could see, I was the only fully engrossed member of the audience. I wasn't enrolled in the class but had instead taken a seat at another professor's suggestion. I was enraptured not only because I felt I was looking at a wild man, someone whose long, tousled hair intimated that he had rushed in from a hike along some wind-blown cliff to lecture to a bunch of physics students—but more so because I knew he could explain mysteries to me, decipher Newton and the others and render them comprehensible on a practical level. My expectations were high, and Alden Whetstone met them.

"We think about vertebrate flight as falling into four categories:

parachuting, gliding, actual flight, and soaring. If a bird can soar, generally speaking it can also perform the three lower forms of flight." Alden paced the stage. "Don't confuse gliding and soaring. To soar, an animal must have evolved to possess specific physiological and morphological adaptations, and soaring birds must know how to use the energy of thermals to maintain altitude."

Oh, lord, he was speaking my language—a physicist employing Darwin. Professor Matthews had been right to send me here. The smell of wet wool brought about by January snow permeated the room.

"We'll see, over the course of this and the next several lectures, that the soaring form of flight has been achieved by only a few animals over the entire course of evolution. We'll examine concepts of drag, thrust, vortices created by the flapping of wings, and the evolution of the flight stroke, without which there is no flight."

Baggy corduroy pants. A broad red, blue, and white tie of abstract design, loosely tied as if in begrudging compliance with a dress code. Frayed cuffs beneath his suit coat sleeves, and an audacious mustache that was bushier than most men's entire heads of hair. He was the quintessential absent-minded professor, which thoroughly intrigued me. This was not *Jer!* on the make; the professor's attire was not calculated to attract, to stand out. This was a wholly intellectual creature barely cognizant of the physical world and its requirements. I felt myself longing to soar along with him in the realm of pure ideas, of complete and total academic isolation. *I bet* he's *never worn a polka-dot tie*, I thought with smug satisfaction.

There was a loud knocking noise. It persisted. The class grew restless, and the noise was sufficiently distracting so that none of us was listening to the lecture. Alden continued longer than anyone might believe possible given the noisy competition, but finally he returned to earth.

"What's going on?" He faced his students. "No one knows?"

Feet shuffled, but no one responded.

"It's coming from upstairs. What are they doing? Moving furniture or something?" Alden left the stage and went out into the hallway, apparently to confront the person or persons who were interrupting his flow of thought. Now, there was outright laughter among the students, all of whom were male. I looked about, trying to understand the joke.

One of the boys caught my eye. "You don't get it, do you?" he asked me.

"What is there to get?"

"This is the top floor. Whetstone is headed God knows where."

I was immediately embarrassed for the man who'd been speaking so eloquently. I, too, had believed that someone was dragging furniture across an attic floor overhead.

The classroom door opened, and Alden was back. Although the volume subsided, the laughter remained.

"So, no one wanted to tell me that there is no upper floor?" He stood facing us, his hands on his hips. "Top secret?"

Nothing but nervous silence greeted him. I wondered how long he'd been teaching in this particular room.

"Doesn't matter," he said, running a hand through his unruly hair. And then, without missing a beat, he returned to his lecture.

I liked that he was unembarrassed. It bespoke a level of confidence and maturity that I longed to stand beside.

It was known that Alden Whetstone had a reduced teaching load that year because he was working with other scientists on some hush-hush war project. How different Alden was from college boys, how I envied his ability to ignore social convention—or to be so entirely unaware of it so as to have no need to ignore it. Although he was twenty years my senior, he was still young, fired by the practical applications of his hard-earned knowledge and the associations he was forming through his war work with other world-class scientists.

I approached him after that first lecture and accepted an invitation back to his office. After nearly an hour, we left his office to continue talking over coffee. We spoke about what we believed in, what was happening in the world, and what the world might become. It was as though we'd both been starving for that kind of easy conversation and comradeship. When I was with Alden—discussing, listening, leaning across tables and fully animated—life was painted in more vibrant colors; birdsong was more elaborate, rococo.

If I'd played Mrs. Hudson's recommended fawning, dumb girl's role, Alden wouldn't have paid me a moment's notice. I never once thought about feigning stupidity in Alden's presence. Rather, I felt called upon to stretch my mind, to show him I could run alongside him.

Still, I kept dating Jerry. Alden was so high above me—he was such pure intensity and demanding, hard work—work I was not afraid of, but work nevertheless. Jerry was someone with whom I could let off steam, laugh, and maybe even be silly.

IN THE SPRING OF 1942, newsreels that played prior to the start of films at theaters showed us the bravery of our fighting men and touted U.S. victories. *It won't be long now*, we all thought as we sat in the dark, watching and hopeful, and Jerry squeezed my hand. Mother sent me clippings from the Greensburg paper and filled in details gleaned from her friends at church: Doc, Eddie, Mickey, Dean, Lester, Gabby, Rusty, and Tom Kilgore—Dot's husband—all of them dead or wounded. Mother told me Lisa Jackson, a friend from Girl Scouts, had married Buck Pemberton, who had joined the navy and was about to ship out. *I signed your name to the card*, Mother said, *and I embroidered a nice pair of pillowcases for them.*

Corregidor fell to the Japanese on May 6, 1942, just as we were finishing final exams. Jerry was horrified by the number of ships sunk by the Japanese, but even more so by the number of ships our navy scuttled or destroyed over the course of just two days, all to keep them out of the hands of the enemy. Corregidor floated just south of Bataan, and we knew that the U.S. had surrendered Bataan about a month earlier.

I could understand numbers—so many dead or captured. I could look at maps, gauge distances, try to contemplate vast oceans or ships' holds packed with sleepless, sweaty, frightened boys on their way to face death. I could talk with Jerry and other students about the war—the fiery, insane world at war—but I could not *know*. I could never know what it felt like to face mortality.

ALDEN AND I DIDN'T really date—I think we fooled ourselves into thinking we were just spending time together. I didn't tell him about Jerry, and while Alden once referred to an ex-wife, I didn't know if he had a current romantic interest in his life. Nothing so mundane entered our orbit.

I was in awe of Alden. I could only sense the very fringes of concepts that his intellect grasped with such easy, ready fingers. I worshipped his knowledge, his aloof independence and greater world experience. He was my teacher; he led me, and I followed gladly.

We often walked together between or after classes, when Alden wasn't committed to secret work in his laboratory. I remember an ozone-scented April afternoon when he pulled my hand from my raincoat pocket and held it in his hot, enveloping hands. Abruptly, suddenly aware of his own gesture, he paused in his description of atomic half-life, radioactive decay. We stood on the rain-darkened campus sidewalk, looked at each other, and I used my free hand to tuck a curl of his hair behind his ear. I felt so calm with Alden. Jerry always felt precarious, but Alden gave me sure footing. *He's solid,* I thought as, wordlessly, we began walking once more.

My thoughts surprised me. Unconscious, unbidden, I was falling in love.

THAT SUMMER, I BOUGHT a red swimsuit with money from my job at Davidson's Bakeries (honey and sponge cakes, butter cookies, birthday and wedding cakes, challah). Jerry and I packed a picnic basket with day-old pastries and headed to the lagoon in Jackson Park.

Sun-drunk, I lay on the enormous, rectangular boulders beside the water and waited for the heat to rid my bones of every vestige of the brutal Chicago winter. Jerry towered above me, taking pictures.

"Tell me again. The name of your high school swim club," he said, clearly planning to tease me.

"The Mermaids."

"Perfect."

"My mother has my annual at home. There's a photo of the seven of us, arranged quite attractively on the diving board and ladder."

"With some never-married, male-looking girls' swim coach, am I right?" He settled onto the rock next to me and lit one of his Old Golds.

"Miss Berenstein."

"She never stood just a tad too long, watching you in the shower?"

"Jerry, stop!" I sat up and shook out one of his cigarettes for myself. "I didn't know about those sorts of things then. Not until you."

"Stick with me, baby. I'll show you the world." He paused. "Not like that old man you're stringing along."

I shaded my eyes from the sun, tried to see Jerry's face.

"Professor Whetstone?"

"Yeah. The old guy."

"He's not old."

"Too old for you."

"He's brilliant."

"Maybe," Jerry began tickling me, "but does he make you laugh?" I squirmed beneath his fingers. A rough patch on the boulder scratched my thigh and drew blood. When Jerry noticed, he bent until his lips touched my skin, and beneath his soft touch I took a deep breath. He lifted his head, looked into my face, and grinned. "There's more where that came from." He let his palm hover over the spot where his lips had been. "Whenever you're ready."

But I wasn't ready. I felt that if I let Jerry pursue his lovemaking past the kissing we'd already done, I'd lose my hold on things, become another box checked "Done" on his to-do list of college girls. I didn't really trust Jerry—at the same time as I feared losing him.

IN CAFÉS OVER STRONG black coffee, Alden told me of his childhood, of the curiosity he'd had for the way objects moved.

"It's all energy, Meri. Energy! Energy is never created or destroyed. Never! Think about it!" Other patrons looked in our direction, but Alden didn't care. If his enthusiasm disturbed them, then they should find other tables or leave. "We don't necessarily know what the total amount of energy is in any given environment—say, a room, or the universe." He used his index finger to draw an imaginary boundary on the tablecloth. "We can measure changes in energy, know when energy transfers have taken place. If energy comes from outside of a boundary, is transferred into that closed environment, we can measure that change. But what's most exciting," he took my hand over my plate of chicken-fried steak, "is the fact that there are so many different ways in which energy can manifest itself."

Alden's energy held me entranced. I could not drift in and out of conversations with him; I had to listen, follow where he led. His demands, his challenges, were exactly what I'd always gravitated toward.

He paused, and in silence we watched a mother at a nearby table as she spooned mashed peas into her baby's mouth. The woman gently wiped the infant's chin with his bib and cooed until the baby responded with a gummy smile.

"My ex-wife miscarried. Twice," Alden said, thoughtful, still focused on the mother and child. I said nothing—the last thing I wanted to hear about was a tragedy they'd shared. I was intent on avoiding comparisons, leery of failing in competition with the shadowy former Mrs. Whetstone—although for all I knew she was shallow, maybe a debutante of some kind, a woman who lacked curiosity. "What do you think?" Alden asked, now turning to face me.

"About children?" I folded my hands on the tabletop. "Maybe later in my life," I said. "Much, much later," I said with emphasis. "There are too many things I want to accomplish first."

I didn't reveal the full breadth of my ambivalence, my sometimes disconcerting lack of any biological yearning for children. As a girl, I never babysat; I hadn't had to care for any younger siblings. My life hadn't included diapers, burping, the joy of first words or miraculous first steps. I had so long ago taken children off of my plate, removed them from the realm of probability, if not possibility. I looked at Alden, wondered if he were asking me for more of an answer than I was willing to give. Was he considering my viability as a candidate for his next wife? Was I about to remove myself from the running?

I felt a furrow form between my brows, struggled with the part of me that wanted to please him, to assure my place at his side by giving the right answer. But while I circled, caught in a spinning eddy of thought, Alden moved on. "The greatest discovery of this century. Of *several* centuries," he said, now lowering his voice. "We're on the verge of just that." He closed his eyes, shook his head not in disbelief but as if he, too, were having difficulty grasping the enormity of what lay ahead. "Earth shattering," he said, finally opening his eyes and looking deeply into my face. He smiled broadly and lit a cigarette. "Now, shall we talk about flight?"

I felt a wave of relief. Alden wasn't asking me for a definitive answer on motherhood. Perhaps he shared my ambivalence about children. Still, I was unsure.

Jerry was just so much easier. But when had I ever chosen *easy*?

RATIONING BEGAN IN EARNEST that summer—sugar, gasoline, even typewriters could only be purchased by using ration coupons. Every man, woman, and child was issued a coupon booklet, and along with the other boarders, I turned mine over to Mrs. Hudson.

Omnipresent advertisements in the school paper (and magazines, posters in store windows, telephone pole notices, advertisements in theaters and buses and trains) pushed us to purchase war bonds and stamps. We should buy as many as we could afford, see how many luxuries we could do without. Boys should buy their girls war stamp corsages from the "sweet YWCA girls" who sold them every Thursday in the student commons. We probably "tossed away at least a buck a week on unnecessary things"; at that rate, the paper's editor argued, we could buy a bond almost every semester. Upon graduation, we'd have accumulated eight bonds, with a maturity value of $200.00—an amount that we could apply to our "kids' college educations."

I couldn't afford to buy a war bond outright, so I began collecting the red, ten-cent war stamps that pictured the stalwart minuteman, rifle in hand. By the end of college, I had filled three booklets, worth three $25.00 war bonds. I sent them all to Mother.

"I NEED TO TELL you something," Jerry said.

"All right."

"It's not easy."

Seated next to him on a park bench with tired, dry November leaves beneath our feet, I waited.

"I met with a recruiter, passed the exams. For the army." He pressed my hand, refused to raise his eyes to meet mine.

"Oh." The sudden exhalation was involuntary.

"I had to, Meri, with what's been happening in the Pacific and all. I had to. I can't keep hiding here."

I couldn't catch my breath. *Maybe this is what hyperventilation feels like,* I thought. I cupped my hands about my nose and mouth, trying to breathe in the dark, warmed air.

"I'll write. I'll be back. This isn't the end of us."

"When do you go?"

"I leave for boot camp in three days."

"Oh, Jesus."

"Meri, I'm sorry. I'm so sorry."

I wanted to tell him that words are cheap. I wanted to tell him that I didn't want for him to die. I wanted to keep him in Chicago, safe. Nothing I wanted mattered, though.

And he'd confirmed my decision for me. It would be Alden, not Jerry. Alden.

ALDEN TOOK ME TO the Monte Cristo on St. Clair Street, where an eight-course dinner could be had for $1.25. I consumed a huge dish of sautéed mushrooms, making every effort to keep the butter from dribbling down my chin. Preoccupied, Alden cut his porterhouse into thin strips. At last, he took his napkin and folded it precisely before placing it next to his plate and patting the material smooth. He lit a cigarette, looked at me across the tablecloth, and I saw a distance in his eyes I'd not seen before. The waiter brought our coffees.

"Meri," he sighed out a lungful of smoke. "I want to ask you something, and I don't want you to take offense."

"OK . . ,"

He moved the obligatory tabletop candle to the side and reached for my hands. "I got us a room."

I wanted to pull away but didn't. In the span of that short dinner, Alden had accelerated our relationship far beyond the place of easy familiarity where it had lingered for months.

"Meri?"

"OK," I said. "OK."

"You're sure?"

I took my hands back, discreetly wiping them on my napkin. His palms were sweaty, nervous.

"I don't have anything with me, though. No toothbrush, no toothpaste."

"The hotel has them. It's a nice place, Meri. It's not a dump. I wouldn't do that to you."

"All right, then." I reached for my purse. "Let's skip the apple pie."

I DON'T BELIEVE WOMEN lose their virginity. It implies they can find it again. Nor do I believe people lose their lives—"*Whoops! Now where did I put my life . . . beneath a cushion on the couch? Maybe I left it on the kitchen counter . . . Honey, have you seen my life? I know I had it a minute ago . . . .*" So, I did not *lose* my virginity in that hotel room. Boys I knew did not *lose* their lives in the war.

Lying in bed with Alden, I longed to set myself free from constant analysis, but I could not. It was as if a part of me were suspended above the bed making observations. And so the physicality of the act, the sensations, were diminished—even more so than they naturally would have been because of my newness. Alden was respectful, careful of me. Perhaps too careful—there was definitely a part of me that wanted for him to be masterful and in charge, to help me transcend omnipresent thought.

It hurt. Alden seemed to know or care little about lubrication or taking his time, about the delight of suspension. Granted, he was as anxious as I, and so while we both put forth great effort, we were nervously taut. Still, there is no escaping the closeness of skin against skin, and I felt my senses engage: touch and warmth, the smell of his sweat and, afterwards, the smell we created together, tangled beneath damp sheets. The taste of salt and scotch. Street noises rising from below, the occasional rasp of a bedspring as we shifted our weight. The light I'd left on over the bathroom sink as it slanted into the room, crossed the carpeting, and highlighted my purse on a chair. Alden's pants neatly folded over the back of the chair.

That single careful gesture—the controlled placement of his pants. It told me something I refused to acknowledge: Alden would always be too careful. There would be no transport for me, not with a man who was that precise in the face of impending passion. Passion walks the edge of control, teasing. It looks down at the rocks in a canyon and contemplates plunging, taking one fatal step to the right. It soars, having released the weight of consciousness of all but the moment.

At half past midnight I woke him.

"I have to get back. I can't stay out all night."

He was groggy—the scotch, no doubt, combined with the relief of having accomplished what he'd set out to do. He fell back asleep, and I was sorely tempted to do the same.

"Alden."

"All right." He sat up on the edge of the bed and turned on a bedside lamp. The light was painful, harsh in its revelations. I reached over and touched the bones of his spine, ran my fingers lightly across his shoulders, pinched the nape of his neck.

"Don't start something we can't finish."

I tattooed my fingers across his back, imagining that my fingertips were raindrops, gently pelting his skin.

"Meridian, we need to get dressed." And with that he was up, across the room, quickly thrusting his legs into those perfectly creased trousers. When he finished buttoning his trousers, he crossed the room, knelt on the carpet, kissed my knees. "You're beautiful," he said, and I could see that in his eyes, I was.

I made my way to the bathroom and wet a washcloth to clean up the blood and semen I found adhered to the insides of my thighs. I wondered if the maids counted how many post-deflowering washcloths they tossed into the laundry each week.

The next morning, I sent Jerry a letter full of campus gossip and cheerful news. I signed it "Fondly" and told him to keep himself safe, alive. Then, I sat back and wondered what Jerry would have done in that hotel room.

A Watch of Nightingales

1. A brown bird with a reddish tail, slightly smaller in size than a robin.

2. Unlike most birds, the nightingale sings at night as well as during the day.

Lionel Hampton's drums and the singer's world-wise, penetrating voice expanded in my chest as I sat beside Alden in the Regal Theater in late December, the mouth of my cigarette case spilling Chesterfields across the immaculate white tablecloth. She was Ruth Jones, recently reinvented as Dinah Washington, the queen of the blues, and she sang of her need for caviar at breakfast, champagne at night.

I leaned into Alden's shoulder, whispered: "Are you listening? Shall I make the same demands? Are you ready for that?" He pulled back to look at me, and in the nightclub's gloom the miniature table lamp cast shadows like war paint beneath his eyes and across his cheekbones. How fitting, I thought—with Alden on his way to participate in some top-secret mission somewhere in the Southwest. Alden, impossibly, a University of Chicago physics professor about to become a warrior. He ran the back of his thumb along the curve of my jaw.

"Are you saying yes, then, Meri? Is it yes?"

I took another pull of my cigarette and felt my right leg instinctually keeping time with the music. Even at age nineteen I knew it was a moment I should take in with all of my senses.

"That's what I'm saying. Yes." For emphasis, I crushed the last of my cigarette until it lay like an accordion in the ashtray.

His lips were on my neck, a quick brush designed to preserve my Revlon Red lipstick. I touched his shoulder briefly, lightly.

He was leaving his university position, his office and desk, his lab and me, to participate in some unspecified way in the war effort. Almost reflexively, I had said "yes" to his marriage proposal, thinking of it primarily as a way to keep him close.

The band broke, and I watched Dinah Washington put her hand on the pianist's shoulder while she reached for her glass with her other hand. He looked up at her, wiped the sweat from his forehead with a handkerchief, and I swear I could see the black beads on her dress shiver beneath his gaze.

I wanted to feel that with Alden. I was waiting for it. I took a sip of my champagne cocktail and curled my hands, one within the other, on my lap. Alden cupped the bowl of his pipe in his hand, and the match flared. He had beautiful hands, the hands of an artist, and I liked to see how carefully, with what natural grace, he held even the most mundane object.

The lights came up, and several of the patrons formed a conga line. Drunks too inebriated to stand used their silverware to beat out the necessary rhythm—*boom boom boom boom boom, BOOM! Boom boom boom boom boom, BOOM!* We were all suddenly united in our need to forget the war, instead insisting on life and possibility.

One woman stood out, leading the conga line like some kind of deranged toucan, her nose just a bit too big and her black evening dress slashed with caustic stripes of green, yellow, and red. *Boom boom boom boom boom, BOOM!* She thrust out a hip, her mouth stretched into a giant O. I could see crescent sweat stains ruining her dress as she waved her arms with the drumbeats, and when the line snaked past our table, I smelled Evening in Paris cologne.

The toucan woman caught my eye, waved for me to join her. I envied the fun she was having, but something about this evening, about Alden's impending departure and the way he frowned at the conga line, stopped me. Wanting to avoid displeasing Alden, I mouthed "No, thanks," and smiled as the woman moved on.

When he kissed me good night, called me his beautiful fiancée, I cried into the buttons of his overcoat, already missing him.

The next morning, shafts of sunlight beat into Union Station, and I watched golden dust motes dance in response to my breath.

We stood in the train station, Alden and I. My cheap cloth coat, the lining of the right pocket torn, his minimalist bag at his feet. He looped a locket about my neck, promised me an engagement ring "down the line." The book-shaped locket was empty—meant to be filled with our future.

Alden's hand on the small of my back was warm through the material of my insubstantial coat. He couldn't tell me where he was going or what he was going to do—just that it would be in an isolated location in the Southwest, that he would contact me as soon as he was permitted to do so. We parted with me feeling tearful and angry, already regretful that I could not force myself to be more mature. I was sad at his leaving, at my being left out, at the delay this secret war assignment meant to our life together. Angry that he could find it in himself to leave me with such barely disguised excitement. Whatever he was going to do, it flipped all of his mental switches; he glowed secretly like the vacuum tubes settled in the dark interior of the radio beside my bed.

When the whistle blew, Alden eagerly hopped up the stairs of the coach car, removed his hat, and then disappeared into the dimly lit interior.

Before heading back to Mrs. Hudson's, I bought myself a medicinal chocolate malt at Fred Harvey's, watched the Harvey Girls comport themselves with perfection, and wondered if there were Harvey Girls where Alden was going. I purchased a picture postcard of the train station and addressed it to Jerry. I told him I was engaged to Alden, wished him a happy new year.

I dropped it in a trash can on my way home.

THE LONG-AWAITED WESTERN UNION telegram from Alden was brief: "PO Box 1663, Santa Fe, New Mexico. Alden." I found the place on a map and wondered what on earth such a place with so few cities or centers of commerce and industry could possibly have to do with the war effort. And I was disappointed—Alden sent not a word of his love, despite the fact that we'd been engaged to be married for less than two weeks.

PROFESSOR MATTHEWS WAYLAID ME in the hallway outside of his third-floor office in the zoology building. He'd taken me under his wing and was helping me map out the remainder of my undergraduate studies.

"Come sit for a bit." He fished in his pants pocket for his keys and unlocked his door, motioning for me to precede him. Overflowing ashtrays ruled every flat surface. He tossed a pile of library books onto a chair, and a cloud of dust rose from the cushions. The single overhead light fixture sputtered and then the light bulb popped, leaving us in a gray twilight.

"Ridiculous," he said, crossing to the windows. He struggled with the cords of the venetian blinds, raised them several inches, and emptied the nearest ashtray into his trash can, finally pushing it toward me. We lit up while he leaned against the edge of his desk.

Professor Matthews was soft all over and gave every sign of being headed for unbridled corpulence one day—perhaps sooner rather than later. The heels of his shoes were worn at odd angles because of his heavy, awkward gait. I guessed he was in his early sixties, and that he'd likely been in the same office for a good thirty-five years or so—enough time to accumulate layer upon layer of solidified geologic time.

"I want for you to find your focus." He exhaled smoke. "You can graduate in under four years—maybe as little as three, by my calculations. But I'd like to see you use your time and abilities to begin an area of specialization. It will help when it comes time to apply to graduate school."

I looked at the glass display case that ran the length of one wall and included at least fifty specimens of stuffed birds, from cardinals to nuthatches. Over time, dust had made its way into the case, and now the poor creatures bore a patina of gray that dulled their feathers and filmed their glass eyes. It reminded me of what I'd read about the Victorians' proclivity for killing and collecting every plant or animal species they encountered—Darwin included. I imagined pinprick openings appearing in the bellies of those preserved birds and then envisioned how the sawdust stuffing would sift downward like the sands of an hourglass until each of the dead bodies was nothing but a depleted small sack of tanned skin, a sad coat of former glory. It made me want to weep.

"I'm suggesting that you think about disciplines such as acoustic networks, songbird communities, counter-singing. Mating systems, social and reproductive behaviors. Or, there's navigation, migration patterns." He tapped the ash from his cigarette. "You could also take another approach, focus on a specific species."

"I think that's where I'm headed," I said, sending a stream of smoke ceilingward.

"What direction?"

"Species. Focus on a species. *Corvus.*"

"Excellent choice. But tell me why."

"Their intelligence. We've just begun to scratch the surface when it comes to understanding crow and raven behavior."

"Agreed. Is there a particular aspect of their behavior that interests you more than another?"

"Their seeming use of tools, since that runs counter to all current assumptions about what separates humans from other animals."

"Perfect. Just the sort of analysis I'd expect from my best student."

"And, I like them because so many people dislike them. All of the myths, the negative associations—carrion birds, birds of war. I was reading recently about a Tibetan funeral ritual involving crows and ravens. The deceased's body is cut into small pieces and laid on an altar, and then the birds carry the departed, albeit in pieces, to the next life."

He stubbed out his cigarette and stood, dismissing me. "Be a scientist, Miss Wallace, not an English major."

"But I beg to differ, respectfully. Rachel Carson talks about this. I don't want to write solely for the scientific community." Aged cigarette smoke filmed his windows, turning the late afternoon light a sickly chartreuse.

"Listen to me: your thesis committee, the academics who hold your professional future in their hands, are not the Rachel Carsons of this world. They are old school, and you have to be ready to jump through all of the hoops they require of you."

I thanked him, gathered my coat, and shifted my books to one hip. When I entered the staircase, I thought about crows. Why they compelled me. The affinity I had for them and their mythology. I wanted to know everything about them—these dark birds that seemed to me to be so misunderstood, so underestimated.

To:	From:
Meridian Wallace	Alden Whetstone
1225 Wayland Ave.	PO Box 1663
Chicago, Ill.	Santa Fe, N. Mex.

January 25, 1943

Dear Meri,

I'm sorry for the long silence, but it couldn't be helped. Someday we'll be able to sit and have one of our luxurious conversations, and I'll be able to tell you about all of the myriad personalities, the turf wars, the GIANT egos at work here. And maybe I'll be able to tell you how much I am learning from these men, how exciting the ideas, the potentialities.

I am proud to be engaged to you. I never thought I'd meet someone like you, have a chance to share your sweetness, your youth.

Do you remember my mentioning ██████? I think I told you he and I worked on ████████████████████ ████████████. Do you remember? He's a █████ █████. Anyway, he and I are ██████ again, and that alone is worth the trip to this place.

Tell me of your studies. Tell me you are not dancing with boys. Tell me, tell me, tell me, Meri. Tell me everything. I want the freshness of your voice, your enthusiasm.

And I want for you to think about my coming to see you just as soon as I can get a break. I need to ██████████████ ███ and to smell your hair.

I love you.
Alden

It was difficult to respond to his letter, as I really had no idea what he'd tried to tell me. Still, I had the words that mattered most to me—evidence that he missed and loved me, that he was alive somewhere.

To:	From:
Alden Whetstone	Meridian Wallace
PO Box 1663	1225 Wayland Ave.
Santa Fe, N. Mex.	Chicago, Ill.

February 6, 1943

Dear Alden,

First things first: I miss you.

Secondly—you should know that a good deal of your letter consisted of elongated black rectangles. What are the censorship rules?

I haven't been dancing with anyone except Newton. We're on his Second Law of Motion, and so I'm trying to understand gravitational fields—something you can do in your sleep, I know, but for a lowly biology major, it's a challenge.

What I'm finding fascinating is the complex relationship between the gravitational fields of two masses. One force pulling at the other, each separate gravitational force or power pulling at the other. Grace à Newton, I know that because your mass is greater, you must exert a stronger pull on me than I can on you. Or do you just shake your head at me for trying to make human relationships follow the rules of physics? Surely by now you recognize that as part of my allure, right?

Yes, I'm eating.

Yours—Meridian

MOTHER HAD ALREADY BEGUN sewing linens for my trousseau, and Kitty offered to come with me to look for a cedar hope chest.

For some reason, the war had made cedar chests scarce, so we couldn't find any amongst the stores we searched. Finally, we stopped for ham salad sandwiches and pickles at Alderman's Soda Shop.

"Did you hear?" Kitty asked. "Red's coming back." Red had lived in the boarding house with us, before he joined up. Kitty's sapphire and diamond ring caught the light, reminding me of her story about how during the Depression her grandmother had hidden it, kept it secret so that it would not be sold.

"When?" I asked, trying to talk around a bite of sandwich.

"Mrs. Hudson said next week some time."

"Is he OK?"

"Something happened to his leg. With the Marines, at Guadalcanal."

"God."

"Amy and Gretchen have agreed to share a room so he can have his old room back."

"That's nice."

"Yeah, they're swell gals." She fiddled with her straw. "Do you ever hear from Jerry?"

"A short letter last week," I finished my pickle and smiled at a boy in uniform who did a double take when he passed our table. "Jerry doesn't say what's going on, just superficial things, like jokes the soldiers play on each other."

"Have you told him about Alden?"

"I will. My next letter."

"Will it be hard?"

"A little."

"Do you want to know something that will make it easier?"

"Sure."

"He's writing to at least three other girls." Kitty's fingers circled her soda glass, and her cheeks flamed bright red. "Sorry," she added.

"I'm not." It was a relief—a huge relief—and it sounded exactly like Jerry. "Kitty?" I smiled at her. "I'm sure they're all *just friends.*" We burst out laughing, and I thought about how I'd sign my next letter to *Jer!*

As I finished my Coke, I looked at a poster tacked to the wall behind Kitty: SHAVE HITLER AND SAVE AMERICA: BUY WAR STAMPS. The cartoon showed Hitler with his small mustache, and a disfigured swastika tumbled across the drawing. Next to that, an advertisement for Coca-Cola read: ASK THE FLYING TIGER FROM CHINA—"Scratch one zero," the soldier in the drawing said, "Out there we'd give a buck for a Coke. They're still a nickel here."

"I have an idea," I said. "What if we do a scrap metal drive, in Red's honor? As a welcome home?"

"I like it!"

"Maybe next weekend? We can make some flyers, see what we can bring in."

"We can make it into a party," Kitty said, and the intensity of her blush made me wonder if she didn't have her sights set on the returning Red Palmer. The marriage of two redheads, I thought, and smiled while picturing the porcelain skin of redheaded babies.

ALDEN PAID THE CABBIE and helped me out of the taxi. Although it was April, stubborn traces of winter clung to gusts of spring wind, and I pulled my coat closed and shivered. We stood on the sidewalk in front of Malnekoff Jewelers—and the mood I was in was not how I'd imagined I'd feel moments before choosing an engagement ring.

"I'm saying that you're driving the censors crazy. You've got to stop talking about or asking any questions having to do with science."

Why was it my fault that the censors couldn't distinguish between science that might be top-secret, nuclear science, and my brand of biology? Why was Alden angry with *me*?

"Don't pout. Just stick to topics that get nowhere near anything that might be censored."

"I still don't know what those topics might be, really I don't. I don't know the rules, and I'm not a fortune teller, Alden. I'm not that kind of supremely intuitive woman."

"Your sarcasm is quite attractive. Really a nice quality. Very."

"I don't want to fight. I also don't want to be blamed for something that's not my fault. It's not fair."

"Nothing about this is fair, Meri. And if you're waiting for 'fair' to show up, I suspect you'll have to wait until long after this war is over—and that's if we win."

Alden's soft green eyes were bloodshot. I brought his hand to my mouth and kissed his nicotine-stained fingers.

"Sweetheart, I'm sorry," he said, "but I can't even tell you how many houses are being constructed because then you'd have an idea as to the scope of the project. I can't give you any estimation of how long my job will last, other than to tell you that it will last 'the duration of the war.' That's the official, prescribed language. The degree of censorship is absurd but maybe necessary. I don't know. What I do know is that most of your letters are almost completely excised, and this whole issue is coming between us on the first days we've had together since January. Now, that's even more absurd than the regulations I'm telling you about—the ones I'm not supposed to tell you about."

A light rain began to fall. I let the drops hit my face and felt a wide moorland of loneliness stretching between the two of us. The war cast a pall over everything, wore us all down to the nub.

I ended up choosing a simple, square-cut diamond accompanied by two small diamonds perched on either side of the large stone. There was something about the number three—three diamonds—that appealed to me. When I told Alden how I felt about the number, he waxed eloquent about the solidity of triangles, the power of four triangles combined to form a pyramid. And then, like a cherry atop a sundae, he threw in a small discourse on Euclidean geometry.

I took his arm. Walking beside Alden was like having a set of the *Encyclopaedia Britannica* at my disposal, always at hand to satisfy my curiosity.

Our foreplay that night consisted of piling one idea on top of another, drawing connections, extrapolating while we lay beside each other, naked. Finally, Alden rolled to face me. He leaned on an elbow and used his other hand to trace the line of my nose, to twist my hair amongst his fingers.

"What's different about your hair?"

"Kitty gave me a permanent wave. It gives it body—my hair's so fine, otherwise it just lies flat, boring."

"I like it." He moved his weight onto me, laid his body the full length of mine. "Meri," he twisted my hair in both hands and sighed. "Meri."

His mouth tasted of cigarettes and after-dinner coffee. "Open your mouth," he said. "More." I closed my eyes and breathed in his commanding tone. Our teeth clicked against each other, and we laughed. He wet his fingers in his mouth and probed inside of me, commanded that I look at him, that I unflinchingly meet his gaze. "Don't ever be sorry," he breathed into my ear. "Don't ever be sorry about us, no matter what." He entered me, and my back arched, my pelvis rose to meet him. "Promise me, Meri."

"No," I said reflexively. "Never." And I wondered what he might be predicting that would lead him to extract that promise.

At the train station the next morning, he kissed the back of my hand. We stood there wordlessly, and all I could think about was departures, always departures. Whenever Alden left me, it felt like my tissues were being torn, like old wounds reopening.

ALDEN SENT ME A packet of black and white picture postcards. I was surprised by the climate revealed in the images—dust, dust, and more dust. He'd written descriptions on the backs of the cards—none of which, to my amazement, were censored.

I saw soaring rock cliffs pockmarked with holes Alden described as being a mix of wind-altered stone and stone purposefully carved by ancient Indians—handholds and footholds for climbing the sharp cliffs. There was a photo of an Indian woman with a woven blanket draped over her head. Her cheekbones were forthright, beautifully angled, her smile that of a bemused Mona Lisa. A close-up picture of a donkey he identified as a "burro, the most common New Mexico resident, although all of them are friendly." It made me smile. There were several images that he said typified the local architecture—low-slung homes made of adobe mud bricks; bleak, bare courtyards; thick, twisted cottonwoods growing in flood plains along a river. At his altitude, which he said was nearly 8,000 feet, there were aspens.

How primitive it all appeared—as if it were another country, certainly not the United States. Despite having been designed for tourists, the postcards showed an impoverished swathe of a nation that at the same time incongruously strode the world stage, spending so much money each day, each minute, in war. How abjectly poor must one be to build a house of mud, cow manure, and straw? Alden described the climate as "high desert," meaning that the winters were cold, with snow. How on earth would a mud house provide adequate shelter in wintertime, and why didn't the walls melt into mud when it rained?

I wondered how many questions might escape the black pen of the omnipresent censors. I decided to play it safe.

To:	From:
Alden Whetstone	Meridian Wallace
PO Box 1663	1225 Wayland Ave.
Santa Fe, N. Mex.	Chicago, Ill.

May 10, 1943

Dear Alden,

I wrote to Mother about my beautiful ring, and she's asking when she will be able to meet you. Don't worry—I won't make promises I can't keep.

I've been thinking about my father. Did I tell you that he used to call me "my wee brown sparrow"? I wish he could be here when you and I marry.

I won't tell you about any of my initial crow research. No need to tempt the censors. The postcards were grand, although honestly they were also unsettling. I cannot fathom this place where you are living, the bleakness of it all. Am I wrong? Is it as bleak as it appears?

I was thinking about this: We believe in lovebirds. Not lovehorses or lovecows, or even lovebutterflies. Lovebirds.

I believe in you, Alden.

Yours—Meridian

To:	From:
Meridian Wallace	Alden Whetstone
1225 Wayland Ave.	PO Box 1663
Chicago, Ill.	Santa Fe, N. Mex.

May 31, 1943

Dear Meri,

Do NOT taunt the censors. It doesn't do anyone any good. I don't want to have to repeat myself ad nauseam on this topic, and I think I've been quite clear. If that's your form of humor, alter it.

I'm returning your draft tax return. Are you certain there are no additional sources of income, other than your work as a teaching assistant? You'll see that I've checked your math and noted several errors.

The landscape is desolate. However, I'm told the wildflowers are spectacular and that the mountains are much cooler and more pleasant than are the valleys in the summer months. Remember, too, that many people come to New Mexico precisely for the arid climate—as a curative for tuberculosis. So, it has its advantages.

I'm working ████████████—we're all ██████. Still, I will try to get in some hikes, to explore some more of this land. Will pick a bunch of posies for you.

Tell me how many men you snub daily on my behalf.

Always—Alden

He enclosed my tax return with corrections and commentary written in his succinct draftsman's printing: "Where did you get this number? It should be X." and "No!—the instructions said ADD this amount, not SUBTRACT this amount!" I was hurt and a little ashamed to have made so many errors—it was my first-ever tax return. I'd failed to live up to Alden's expectations. I'd have to do better.

IN THE SUMMER OF 1943, I worked as a lab assistant for Professor Matthews, learning the basics of field research. It surprised me, given his girth and complete lack of visible muscle tone, that he had the stamina to climb trees or ladders to blinds and to sit or squat for the hours of observation. Sometimes, all I could think about was how I'd never be strong enough to drag him miles back to civilization and medical care.

I found a good pair of used boots that I could muck up, and I bought two pairs of sturdy men's pants that I could cinch with a belt and roll up at the cuffs. The summer humidity made the work even dirtier, but I didn't mind. I loved the sensation of thorough physical exhaustion and the aftermath of deep sleep. Fearful I might lose it, I left my engagement ring in its burgundy, velvet-lined box on top of my bureau. Sometimes, several days would go by without my wearing it so that when I did have it on, I felt its weight and how it encumbered the movement of my fingers. I could also see Mrs. Hudson notice its regular absence.

It was thrilling to hold in my heavily gloved hands a newly banded juvenile Cooper's hawk, to be in such close proximity to a creature so wholly wild, so perfectly free. His distress call distressed me—a rapid-fire *bikbikbikbikbikbikbikbikbik*, silence for a beat or two, and then repetition: *bikbikbikbikbikbikbikbikbik*. Professor Matthews taught me how to hold the raptor by its legs, raise it above my head, and simply let go. Just before letting go, though, I watched the bird's eyes, vigilant, rapidly flicking to the left, right, above; the short, fine facial feathers lifted by a breeze. Once released, how quickly the bird recovered, immediately executed several powerful wing flaps, and spirited itself away. I was humbled by the thought that our lives, however briefly, had touched.

I thought about how lives bump up against each other, whether for moments of superficial conversation in line at the post office or a deeper enmeshment, such as that I had with Jerry for those few months. How much meaning should I ascribe to knowing a stranger for the moments it took for me to donate to a V-book campaign? What are the evolutionary implications of kindness? I missed Alden, longed to talk about these sorts of things with him, wondered how he'd frame the matter.

When I finally wrote to Jerry of my engagement, his letters ceased. Through Kitty, I knew he was still alive. He just let whatever it was we'd had die a merciful death.

Meanwhile, Professor Matthews was unrelenting on the subject of my academic career. "Talk to me about your progress, Miss Wallace. Update me on your current research leanings."

The autumn of 1943 had come and gone, and Professor Matthews and I were sharing a sandwich early in the spring semester. He'd decided to lose weight, and so we often split the lunches his wife made for him.

"Foremost, that crows understand cause and effect."

"Be more specific," he said, eyeing my half of the sandwich resting on a rectangle of waxed paper. Soft white bread, liverwurst, and a generous layer of mayonnaise. The paper had been intricately folded, making me think his wife was perhaps unwittingly practicing origami.

"Do you want my half?" I asked, sliding it toward him across the tabletop.

"No, no." I could tell he was trying to convince himself.

"I'm not all that hungry, really. I've had about six cups of coffee this morning," I said.

"If you're sure." He hesitated for only a second before pulling the food close to him.

I lit a cigarette, realizing that later I'd have to find something to eat. My clothes were hanging loosely on my frame.

"Keep going, Miss Wallace," he said in between bites and motioned with his hand.

"OK. Well, one of the first North American ornithologists was an army major, Charles Bendire."

"Of course. Yes." One more bite, and the sandwich was gone.

"OK. Well, he recounts the tale of a crow named Jim. Some idiot taunted Jim with a knife kept just out of Jim's reach. Finally, Jim bit the hand that held the knife, causing the tormenter to drop it. Then Jim flew off with the knife, hiding it and putting an end to the teasing game. Cause and effect."

"What else?"

"I just now thought about it. Jim Crow laws. Hunh." I paused.

"Stay on topic. Please." He folded the waxed paper into smaller and smaller rectangles. "None of your peregrinations."

"Oh, bird humor. I love it!"

He sighed meaningfully.

"Crows know to soak hard food in water to soften it. They know to put a nut, a walnut or whatever, on the road and wait for a car to run over it, to crack the shell."

"Right, so that's causation." He wiped his mouth and reached for his pack of cigarettes. "What else?"

"They have an astounding number of calls, an intricate system of communication."

"Exactly. And, while you've not asked for my opinion, I'm going to give it to you. That's where your focus should be—on crow language. It's rich and ripe for in-depth research, and no one has yet done a thorough study. I truly believe you could make a name for yourself there—that's the place to put your energies."

I smiled. This man who I so respected said without hesitation that I could make a name for myself. *Me.* I could become the first female expert in crow language. I closed my eyes with pleasure, savoring my foodless lunch.

To:	From:
Meridian Wallace	Alden Whetstone
1225 Wayland Ave.	PO Box 1663
Chicago, Ill.	Santa Fe, N. Mex.

February 10, 1944

Dear Meri,

Happy Valentine's Day, my girl.

Just to be certain: Will you still marry me?

Will you marry me on April 22nd?

I will come to Chicago or Pittsburgh, so as to make things easier for your mother—you tell me, and I will be there.

Eternally—Alden

P.S. What did you decide about the timing of your graduation? I'll explain in person.

Guess
Who???

PITTSBURGH WAS AN EASIER trip for Mother, so that's where we were married. Much to Mother's disappointment, I chose a civil marriage ceremony, not the church wedding she'd envisioned. I didn't want for her to spend one penny, and so I bought my own flowers, paid for my own cake.

I kept everything in my white leather wedding album: the receipt for our blood test (six dollars); my dried orchid corsage; and the florist's bill (fifty dollars). I used some of my summer earnings, and I was proud of having paid for things myself, although I wished Alden had offered.

He did pay for the honeymoon at the Roosevelt Hotel—three nights at five dollars a night, and long distance charges incurred by Alden when he made mysterious but "highly necessary, Meri" calls back to New Mexico (thirty-one and ten cents, respectively).

We stayed in a beautiful room with a private bath and a radio. We ate at Childs and kept eating there because we liked the food. In the Buhl Planetarium, I rested my head against Alden's shoulder while he whispered to me of the flight of electrons and the universes contained in something as small as the nucleus of an atom. Still, we were only able to hide from the impositions of the real world for two days before he had to return to New Mexico.

Mother visited a Pittsburgh cousin while Alden and I honeymooned, and she and I had breakfast together before I boarded the train back to Chicago and she boarded a bus for Greensburg. Alden had left for Los Alamos late the previous night, and I had the sensation of a hole widening in the center of my being, a darkness I'd have to hide and endure. He'd hinted broadly that work was intense, that he'd moved mountains to get even these few days to be wed.

"I want you to be happy." Mother smiled at me. Morning light intensified by the white tablecloth accentuated my mother's burgeoning wrinkles, making me even sadder.

"I am. I will be. I want to be as happy as you and Daddy were." I hoped that I'd not overstepped and quickly added: "If that's all right for me to say."

"Of course it is. I was happy with your father. But, honey . . ." she paused, "don't have unrealistic expectations."

"Happiness is unrealistic?"

"Constant happiness, yes. Contentment—that's realistic. I should have said I want for you to be content, that your daddy and I were content."

I nodded at the waitress who asked with a glance if I wanted more coffee. When she finished pouring, I said: "I want mountain peaks, Mother. I want joy. Elation."

"Well, sweetie, temper that enthusiasm with a little reality, that's all I'm saying."

I smiled, placating her. I had no intention of settling. None whatsoever. I told no one of my dream of accepting prizes for my work with crows, for my discoveries and proofs. I wanted to see Alden in the shadows of the audience while I gave acceptance speeches, wanted to see him proud, holding a glass high to toast my accomplishments. I wanted to see my name on the spine of a book on a library shelf, the preeminent authority on crow behavior. Maybe next to a volume by Alden. Whetstone, side by side.

To:	From:
Mrs. Alden Whetstone	Alden Whetstone
1225 Wayland Ave.	PO Box 1663
Chicago, Ill.	Santa Fe, N. Mex.

May 16, 1944

Dear Mrs. Whetstone,

How did you do on your exams? Were you number one on each and every one? I don't doubt it—don't really even need to ask, sweetheart.

I know we discussed your taking the full four years to get your bachelors of science, and that makes sense to me—especially in light of Matthews' recommendations about building your academic resume for application to graduate school. So, I'm fine with all of that. But I need to have you closer to me—I need you in more than writing or sporadic, rare visits to Chicago. Some of the other men have their wives living in Albuquerque. It's about 100 miles from here, so maybe a half day's drive. I could come be with you on weekends. Just for the summer, and then you can head back to Chicago for your last year.

I've made arrangements for you to rent the other half of a duplex in Albuquerque next to wife. He's a , a nice guy. I don't know her, but the two of you will be friends, I'm sure.

I've enclosed your train ticket. Pack your bags!

Can't wait—Alden

A part of me could not believe that he'd already made the arrangements, but I suppose I saw that it made sense, and I really did want to be closer to Alden. Our separate lives took a toll on me, too. So I tamped down my resentment and followed Mother's example, set about to please my husband. When Alden and I were at least living in the same state, I reasoned, we could discuss these kinds of issues, work things out. For now, I needed to understand that these were extraordinary times, calling for compassion and compromise.

I know I disappointed Professor Matthews when I told him I wouldn't be working for him that summer, that I was headed west to be with Alden. He was gracious and didn't question my need to compromise for my husband's sake. On our final meeting before my departure, he presented me with a copy of Roger Peterson's *A Field Guide to Western Birds: Field Marks of all Species Found in North America West of the 100th Meridian, with a Section on the Birds of the Hawaiian Islands.*

"You're venturing past the one-hundredth meridian, Miss Wallace—I mean Whetstone—and I think that's significant. Go west, young woman!" he laughed, but stopped abruptly. "Just come back. Finish what you started, my dear." And then he surprised me with the familiarity of a hug. I thought I smelled glazed doughnuts beneath the omnipresent cloud of cigarette smoke.

I had no idea how to pronounce "Albuquerque," let alone what I'd do there. I was guessing that none of my clothes would suit the climate I'd seen in Alden's picture postcards. He told me that summer in Albuquerque could mean several consecutive days of one hundred-degree heat. "But not that humid heat you're used to, Meri. It's different—just plain dry." I was scared and thrilled, all at the same time. And I was eager to be with my husband again.

A Party of Jays

1. Part of the crow family, jays are regarded as noisy, colorful, bold, and fearless.
2. "Jaywalking" may take its meaning from reckless, impertinent behavior associated with these birds.

The *Super Chief* luxury liner left Chicago on time at 12:01, and my love for Alden reached its fingers around my breastbone in an irredeemable grasp, dragging me across the United States, my feet helplessly bumping over rocks and sagebrush. Dodge City, Kansas; La Junta, Colorado; Las Vegas, New Mexico; and finally Albuquerque. I reveled in the crisp linens of the dining car, melt-in-your-mouth lamb chops, waffles for breakfast, and a black waiter with more practiced manners than I. A fellow diner told me the secrets of the dinnerware, which bore reproductions of Mimbres Indian designs—beautiful white pottery with simple, abstracted black designs of animals, rainbows, gods. My sleeping compartment was a girl's dream of a doll house with clever miniature soaps, a single rose in a slender vase, and turn-down service.

I savored the heavy hunks of milk chocolate fudge Mrs. Hudson had sent with me, careful to keep melted chocolate from staining my new tan rayon dress—short sleeves, belted, with a bold black geometric design running along one side, top to bottom. Kitty had given me her old imitation alligator bag, and I pulled my powder compact from it to check my lipstick. I contrasted the cocooned opulence in which I hurtled away from everything I knew to the setting outside my window, the country as it morphed from deep greens and tilled soil planted with corn and wheat to less demanding crops such as alfalfa—from lucky, fat milk cows to subsistence-level ranchland with stringy meat cattle perpetually in search of shade. It was as though the farther west I traveled, the sun leached more from the countryside and impoverished everything. At the same time, colors intensified, and the earth's palette seemed to explode with variety and subtlety, all beneath an astounding blue sky freed of the haze of humidity.

Alden wasn't there when I disembarked in Albuquerque. I was stiff, jittery, and irritable, standing there alone with my suitcase and my oh-so-stylish purse that contained what was left of my last paycheck– $6.43. Sweat began just beneath my hairline and trickled down to sting my eyes. I stood on the promenade beside the tracks in the June sun outside the Alvarado Hotel and used a cotton handkerchief to wipe the back of my neck. Before me, there was a large building with a round, painted emblem of a fantastic figure—part human, part bird, arms feathered and outstretched. A sign identified it as the Indian Building, and along the sidewalk that led to the door I saw dark-skinned women with thick, blunt-cut, blue-black hair, unbelievably shrouded in blankets in the same heat that threatened to incapacitate me. The women squatted or knelt, and on cloths spread in front of them they displayed baskets of polished stones, necklaces made of dried, dyed corn threaded on leather thongs, and careful lines of silver jewelry with bright blue stones the color of the sky. None of them met my eyes.

Indian men stood behind the women, some of them wearing heavy silver necklaces extending nearly to their navels, rich red and purple velvet shirts, and brightly colored headbands. The men's hair was drawn into single or double long braids, or sometimes loose, elongated buns at the backs of their necks. Their eyes were narrow, their skin weathered and dry. All I could think about was how harsh this place must be, how unforgiving. It seemed that the line between life and death was easily crossed here.

How could Alden possibly be late? Had he forgotten me, lost in his formulae, his misbegotten sense of the here and now? I was just about to pick up my suitcase and step into the shade of the wide veranda, thinking I'd find some food in the Fred Harvey Café, when I heard him calling my name. He half-jogged toward me, and I felt the surprising revelation that I was married to the man who approached me.

"Meri, Meri," he said, rushing to hold me and inadvertently knocking over my suitcase. He buried his face in the side of my neck and inhaled deeply. "I missed the smell of you," he said, his voice muffled. I turned my head and kissed his fat, substantial earlobe. His hair had grown even longer, curling just above his collar, and for the first time I noticed that his mustache contained some gray, along with whiskers tinged a barely discernible nicotine yellow.

"I'm so glad you're here and so sorry." He released me and instantly returned to high gear. "It was crazy getting here. We had a flat, but thank God the tube held for the rest of the trip. I don't know about the return trip. Honestly, I don't. Those things have been patched so many times."

"We?"

"I gave a colleague a ride down. He'll get another ride back, but you'll meet him one day. You'd like him—brilliant, enthusiastic, close to your age. His wife is in the sanitarium here."

"Sanitarium?"

"She's got TB."

"Oh, God."

"It's awful. But Feynman's pretty upbeat, despite it all. He tries to come down just about every weekend, and of course I wanted to help him out. He doesn't have a car."

"And you do?"

"1940 Studebaker Champion Utility Coupe."

"Wonderful," I said, feeling my eyes begin to burn in the sun's sharp glare. "But, I have to tell you that what I want right now is food and something cool to drink."

He picked up my suitcase and mimed weighing it. "Planning to stay more than one night?"

"I didn't know what to bring. And it is just for the summer."

"As long as you have your swimsuit."

"Of course."

"Then all is well with the world. C'mon, wife of mine, let's get you some food. Oh," he stopped suddenly. "Forget the name I mentioned. Damn it, I keep forgetting. I called him 'Joe,' OK?"

"All right." I held up my hand as if swearing a witness' oath. "I will look forward to meeting your friend 'Joe,' about whom I know nothing whatsoever."

THE PROMISED RENTAL OF the other half of a duplex hadn't worked out, for reasons Alden didn't say. Instead, he'd found me rooms in a Victorian-style home on Walter Street, near downtown Albuquerque. Walter, High, and a few other streets in the area had five to six Victorian homes apiece—all completely incongruous with the rest of the landscape and architecture, and all in jarring contrast to the postcard images Alden had sent me. My rooms had hardwood floors, tall sash windows, and the house was surrounded with locust trees that were in the last stages of full bloom. Alden carried my suitcase up the stairs and immediately opened the bedroom window; we could smell the heavy, sweet scent of the white-blossomed trees. I heard robins calling to each other, and I felt I would be happy here.

The furnishings were more than adequate: a brass bed, complete with an unforgiving mattress and starched white sheets that smelled of wash lines and the outdoors. A bureau with a crocheted dresser scarf, a tiger walnut armoire with a long, rectangular mirror on the inside of one door. I could see where some ancient mouse had gnawed through the back panel of the armoire; the hole had been stained over, a slapdash approach to remediation. In the sitting room were a pale pink upholstered love seat and a wonderful floral wing-backed chair with a reading lamp. A small desk stood next to a set of bookshelves, and Alden had stocked the shelves with some Southwest guidebooks and histories. He even included a best-selling novel I'd mentioned wanting to find the time to read—*A Tree Grows in Brooklyn*. I was touched by the trouble he'd taken to be sure I was comfortable.

I was also, admittedly, relieved. I know Alden had meant well when he planned to set me up with some colleague's wife as a roommate, but I preferred to be on my own. I'd never lived completely alone before, and the idea of it made me feel a kind of anticipatory joy. I wanted to challenge myself to meet New Mexicans, not other temporary, wartime transplants. I thought about having the time to read something other than textbooks, exploring on my own, how much I'd relish the chance to be so independent. I didn't want to be one of the other fungible wives; I wanted my own life, my own experiences without the prejudice of someone else's likes or dislikes. Still, I wondered about the other wives, how they felt about New Mexico.

BEFORE WE MADE LOVE, I insisted on taking a bath. I knew then that the bathroom would be my favorite room—in particular because it was the first time in years that I'd had a bathtub I didn't have to share with other boarders. The floor was tiled in small squares of traditional black and white, and there was an enormous claw-footed tub, a porcelain sink with a rubber stopper carefully leashed on a chain in case it had any inclination to roll across the floor and make a break for freedom. There was no mixer; separate spouts gave cold and hot water, and part of the pleasure of bathing or washing my face that summer was getting the temperature just right. Alden teased me, saying that my lab skills—my exactitude with measurements, beakers, and volume—were finally of some practical use.

I filled the tub with lukewarm water and immediately sank beneath the surface, feeling my hair float in loose curls, released from gravitational pull. The water felt utterly delicious. Alden brought the desk chair in so that he could sit and talk with me, but soon he knelt beside the tub, took a washcloth in his hands and the cake of Ivory soap from my slippery fingers. "Let me," he said, and he worked the cloth into a lather, began with my feet, washing between my toes, stretching the toes, the arches of my feet, releasing all of the hidden little cramps, aches, and pains. He took his time, moving up my body, and behind my closed eyelids I envisioned tenderness in his face, a veritable ministration. Instead, when I opened my eyes I saw the expression of a man intent upon a task. He was literally bathing me, as if my cleanliness were a project. His eyes showed focus, but they lacked the sweetness I'd longed to see.

The water cooled, and I felt goosebumps forming all over my body, heard the water sloshing. He reached my neck, kneaded the muscles of my shoulders.

"Do you know about wave propagation, wife of mine?"

I kept my eyes closed, held my silence.

"Wave propagation refers to the ways in which waves travel. Their speed of travel is largely determined by the density of the medium in which the waves exist."

I set myself afloat on the waves of his words, remembering that teaching sessions like this were why I fell in love with him.

"Obviously, on a molecular level, waves are created by molecules bumping into each other. And molecular movement is a result of vibration. That vibration can be referred to as 'local excitation,'" he said, letting loose of the soap, which as advertised floated rather than sank. "And, as you know, for there to be any wave motion, inertia must be overcome." He helped me to stand and wrapped a towel about my shoulders before leading me to bed.

And so it was, the seductive language of physics and a quickly repressed longing for more.

I AWOKE ALONE THE next morning after a deep, seemingly dreamless sleep. A note stuck into the frame of the bathroom mirror told me Alden had gone to get us Sunday doughnuts and coffee. I was to wear my swimsuit beneath my clothes, grab towels, and be ready to head out for my first real tour of Albuquerque. My clothes were wrinkled and smelled wet, of another land, another time. Still, I didn't bother pressing anything—just vehemently shook my cotton shift several times, as if that would render me presentable. Thinking of the heat, I slipped on a pair of sandals.

Our Studebaker was cream-colored, with a layer of gritty, pale-brown dust coating every inch of it, inside and out—the upholstery, the mirrors, the dashboard and steering wheel. I thought of the contrast of the near-black soil of the Midwest, the gentle green hills of Pennsylvania. Alden's handprints made appearances at the door handles and trunk, and I wondered if the obvious passenger-side handprints might belong to the Feynman fellow whose name I was supposed to forget. The secrecy, this truncated way of living—and all any spy had to do was to take fingerprints from the door of a car. I looked around. All of the cars were this dirty. I started to think that my entire life would soon be covered in a fine patina of transient New Mexico sand.

Alden handed me a still-warm, grease-dotted paper bag that smelled wonderfully of fat and sugar, and he waited until I was inside the car before settling a Thermos of coffee in my lap alongside the doughnuts. I could tell he was excited, happy to be showing me his new world—at least the Albuquerque part.

"OK," he said, and the engine roared to life. "Are you ready for a perfect day?"

"Absolutely," I said, wondering how car engines functioned or people with frail lungs breathed in this dust-driven expanse. I overcame a desire to cough.

"You snored." Alden pulled the car out of the parking spot.

"Did not."

"Did," he said, and reached over to squeeze my knee. "It was the second-most lovely thing I've heard in the dark for a long, long time, Meri."

I put my hand over his until he had to shift gears.

We drove down Central Avenue, through downtown Albuquerque. The tallest building was a department store, three stories tall. I saw a policeman astride a horse and block-shaped Indian women in tiered velvet skirts with deerskin moccasins that ended at mid-calf. They moved slowly, eyes downcast. The drive through the business district took less than two minutes.

I felt a lassitude emanating from the buildings, the asphalt of the street—nothing like the frenzied pace of Chicago. There were no blaring car horns, and no groups of pedestrians waited on the corners for lights to change. Instead, people just ambled out into sparse traffic, trusting that they were immune from motorists.

"Land of *mañana*," Alden said, reading my mind.

"Is it the heat?"

"Doubtful. Think about Chicago summers. It doesn't stop anyone, does it?"

"I suppose not." I held my hand out the window, thinking I could nearly see the moisture evaporating from my skin. "I'll become a leathery old woman here," I said, pulling my arm back into the car. "Dry up and blow away."

We crossed a bridge over a broad, shallow expanse of red-brown water lined by vibrantly green cottonwoods.

"The Rio Grande," he said, nodding his head toward the water.

"*That?*"

"Meri, out here, *that* is a lot of water."

I tried to look again, to reassess my first impression, but it was too late, the river was already behind us. Alden turned into a parking lot jammed with cars and pickups. A painted plywood sign read TINGLEY BEACH.

"A *beach*? Here? Is it a joke?" I realized I was gripping the paper bag too tightly, putting our fresh doughnuts in peril.

"They diverted some of the river water. You'll see."

Alden shut down the engine and came around to get the door for me. He pulled a plaid wool travel blanket from the trunk and took my elbow, steering me toward the sand. I saw men fishing along a thin ribbon of red-brown water, some of them with little boys alongside them. There were women in light cotton dresses, a few sunbathing in swimsuits. An old man dozed beneath a tented newspaper, a curly-haired black dog panting at his feet. Two little girls flicked tiny children's shovelfuls of sand at each other.

"I know how much you love to swim, and I just wanted to show you that you'll be able to do that all summer if you want." He found an open spot and spread the blanket. I watched him make sure the fringed edges lay perfectly flat. I looked at the stingy flow of water and sighed. He couldn't begin to understand what real swimming was, if he thought I could swim here.

"Time for doughnuts," Alden said, pulling me down beside him. I watched him fill the nesting cups of the Thermos with coffee, and I took off my sandals to let my toes wiggle free in the sun. There was a squeal of delight from down the beach—teenaged girls splashing teenaged boys in the shallows of the river water. The suspended droplets trapped the sun, sent shivers of sparkling water arcing into the air. I felt the colors of the day lodge in my chest, the perfectly combined scent of doughnuts and coffee, and I reached for Alden's hand, squeezed it.

I told myself this was different, that was all. I needed to adjust to this new life. My husband was trying to make me happy. Couldn't I do the same for him?

I stood and removed my shift, stalked bravely to the water's edge. The river was cooler than I expected, and I waded in until I was calf deep. I scooped a handful of water, sent it flying, and watched the glittering results. I could feel Alden watching me as I bent over; his gaze generated a pleasant warmth at the back of my neck. When I turned to wave, he smiled with his success.

AFTER THE BEACH AND my near-immediate sunburn, Alden took us on a sightseeing drive. We looked up at the 10,000-foot Sandia Mountains, Albuquerque lying supplicant below. He showed me a nearby grocer, the library a few blocks from my rooms, and—grinning all the while—several bars I was to avoid. During the night, we got up and watched a dust storm blow through town. It turned the beams of light beneath streetlamps into a deep-brown mass of whirling, stinging silica and obscured stop signs and fire hydrants. I marveled at how brutal nature could be here, how unforgiving. I held onto Alden as we stood together at the window, his body warm and solid, reassuring beside me. Despite my insistent autonomy, it felt good to lean on someone.

Alden had to leave for Los Alamos at about three that afternoon, but before he left, he handed me a small box as we sat together on the edge of the bed. Atop a cushion of cotton was a narrow, three-quarter-inch-wide band of silver, with black geometric designs and a single rough knuckle of turquoise. He stretched it around the bones of my wrist and squeezed to make it fit snugly. He kept his hand over the bracelet and gazed out the window to the locust tree where it shifted in a minuscule breeze.

"I'll be fine. Really, I will." I assured him. He didn't look at me, kept his gaze fixed out the window, wedded to the tree branches. "Alden?" I begged a response.

"It's not that." He turned to face me. "It's not you." He looked at the pile of our hands, and I felt the weight of them grow. I decided I needed to be quiet—to let him tell me whatever was bothering him. I heard the heartbeat of a sprinkler on the lawn below.

"What we're doing . . ." he began, a false start. The sprinkler measured out the time. "Maybe it will work. No one knows, really. We're all trying damned hard, using everything we've got." Again I had to resist the temptation to fill the silence, somehow to make everything all right with words. "It has the power to end the war," he said, finally looking at me. I felt my head tilt, my eyes fill. He was, in that moment, so inalterably beautiful to me with his wild hair, his tanned face, his straight, narrow nose.

"It also has the power to end life as we know it. It will change the world."

I could tell he took no joy in that possibility. That he feared his science, his intellect, were not necessarily lending themselves to positive change. I bent and kissed his hands in mine, and we sat together, both of us looking out that window. To the north, unseen by us, clouds boiled into giant castles, dark, rumbling monsters shot full of thunder, lightning, and menace.

I OPENED ALL OF my pores to what New Mexico had to offer. With a portion of the weekly seven-dollar allowance Alden gave me, I bought a clunky old tank of a bicycle. I rode through neighborhoods where the houses matched those from Alden's postcards—crumbling adobe, cardboard patching broken window panes, dispirited dogs chained in desolate yards, dust devils forming and dying in seconds.

Within a few days of moving into the Walter Street rooms, I met Jan Tilman, a nurse at the veterans' hospital who lived on the ground floor beneath me. When Alden couldn't come to town, Jan and I would go dancing at the USO. She was a bit on the chubby side, but it was the kind of chubby that is comforting, plush, not yet spilling over into excess. Her softness undoubtedly soothed the sick and hurting; she was friendly, genuine, and on the hunt for a man who could knock her socks off, she said. At the dances, we drank Coca-Colas and laughed alongside the soldiers who were blowing off steam, and Jan showed me the lucky rabbit's foot one particularly enamored soldier had given her.

There was never a moment when I didn't want Alden with me at those dances, and I think he understood that. I know he trusted me, and with good reason: I loved him so, and the proximity of him combined with the constant lack of him created a sweet sort of torture, a push-pull of palpable desire. Some nights, when Jan and I got back to our rooms after the USO dances, I'd stand in front of the armoire, pull one of Alden's shirts to my nose, and inhale.

On weekends, Alden and I went to the movies to escape the heat. D-Day happened that summer, and I remember sitting in the dark next to Alden, watching one of the United News newsreels describing the Normandy invasion. Haunting images of ready-and-waiting paratroopers, their faces blackened to lessen their visibility in the dark. Churchill with his cigar boarding invasion crafts to encourage departing troops, Eisenhower speaking to the soon-to-be-liberated population of France, encouraging "all who love freedom" to "stand with us." Bomb after bomb burst into huge, fuel-filled clouds of smoke and fire. I held on to Alden in the darkened theater, and when I saw the parachutes of so many men open and drift earthward, all I could think about was their courage, their faith. I wondered, too, where Jerry was, if he were anywhere near France. Alden leaned toward me quietly and said, "We will end this carnage."

Alden took me to San Felipe Pueblo, north of Albuquerque. With the other tourists, we sat cross-legged in the dirt along the edges of a wide, rectangular courtyard, and Indian dancers filed in from two sides, keeping time with a circle of four men who beat out increasingly intense rhythms on drum heads made of leather and sinew. Draped across the shoulders of the women were beautiful, colorful woolen weavings. The women wore white leather moccasins studded with silver buttons and fringes that curled with the pounding of their feet. Sweat ran down the faces of performers and audience members alike, and rattles made from seed-filled gourds made me think of rattlesnakes—something Alden said people regularly found in homes and yards out here.

In Santa Fe we walked down picturesque, unbelievably narrow corridors where I could not shake the feeling that we were being followed, that Alden was being watched. Surely the usual Santa Fe residents had to know something was going on just north of the old city, up on that mesa where Los Alamos grew overnight. The influx of people had to be obvious. Even I could spot probable Los Alamos transplants as they made their way through town on errands impossible to fulfill in Los Alamos: watch repairs, car parts, more liquor than your fellow scientists should know about. The scientists even walked differently, precisely, either wholly self-conscious or lost in the clouds. I saw them squatting to inspect bolo ties, belt buckles, and rings sold by the Indians who lined the shadowed portico of the Palace of the Governors on the Plaza, and I saw them seated on benches, hungrily spooning chunks of Woolworth's Frito pie into their mouths.

Maybe everyone felt as if they were being watched; everyone was on edge. Alden must have become inured to having someone look over his shoulder, check his credentials; he must be used to locking his thoughts away. Maybe he had always lived an inviolate, completely interior, intellectual life. I had a strong sense of vulnerability though, of unseen violation. I wasn't used to living that way—I lived my life on a college campus where thoughts and ideas flourished because they thrived in sunlight, in soil enriched by other theories, by challenge. I realized what a huge adjustment this wartime secrecy must be for an academic like Alden. Even on the Hill, as he called Los Alamos, conversation was circumscribed.

I took Alden's hand, willing my thoughts to enter his bloodstream through that skin-to-skin contact, wanting for him to know that while we couldn't really discuss much of his life, I honored his sacrifice. I was determined to focus on something other than the leviathan secret weighing on our marriage, our intimacy.

I fingered the wool of Navajo rugs and thought about Scottish woolen works, what my father would have said and done in the arid New Mexico heat. We ventured east of the Plaza to the cool interior of the miniscule gothic Loretto Chapel to see the wooden spiral staircase, built with only wooden pegs. Alden rested his palm on a curve of the wood as if it were a reliquary, and I inhaled the mix of incense, candle wax, and desperate prayer. Standing there, with my hands resting on the back of a pew, my eyes relaxing into the wedding-cake white of the altar, I wanted to believe in a God—a God that would end the war, the state of suspended animation in which Alden and I lived our marriage.

ONCE ON MY OWN again, I didn't return to Tingley Beach; instead, I hiked the bosque along the Rio Grande. Beavers had carved some of the cottonwoods into wasp-waisted creatures, and at times the wind on the water would create spectacles of shimmering, dancing refractions of summer sunlight. I loved encountering one big male coyote in particular. Gold, brown, and gray, he would freeze and stare back at me, his hindquarters quivering with the energy he'd need to turn and run if I got too close. In the shadows of the canopy, I found beefy flickertails and the occasional bright, tropical-colored tanagers. I also saw my first greater roadrunner—the bird's odd, warning rattle was what initially caught my attention. His beak was more ferocious than I'd imagined: long, sharp, and clearly made for spearing his prey of small songbirds, lizards. I found him disconcertingly threatening, more so than any coyote I encountered while walking alone in those woods.

I discovered that when the limbs of cottonwoods die, they slough off their bark until all that remains is a smooth, supremely touchable gray-white wood. Only then is it possible to see that beneath the skin of bark, burrowing insects have engraved the wood with trails of hieroglyphic language. I loved to touch those symbols with my fingertips, closing my eyes as if reading Braille.

Some evenings, I would sit on a downed tree carcass along the river to watch crows return from days of foraging to roost and repossess their home territories. Eventually, hundreds of crows would gather and send up a loud, raucous din that lasted until dark. I knew my master's thesis would be on crow behavior, the social aspects of the bird, but I also knew I needed to hone in on a narrower aspect of their social lives. I longed to know how, when, and why they formed allegiances and if those bonds crossed familial boundaries. I wanted to understand loyalty—to know if it derived solely from evolutionary advantage, or if it might also be motivated by something else, something akin to caring, love, and devotion.

On several occasions I observed crows acting in concert to attack another species, and my beautiful giant of a coyote was one of their humiliated victims. I saw the crows' display first from a distance, heard them cawing and shrieking at something close to the ground. My magnificent boy was standing in an open area along the river, his tail tucked beneath him, his head lowered. The crows dive-bombed him repeatedly, but why? Was it a matter of territory? Or were they merely seeking to relieve their bright minds of boredom? They reminded me of cocky young men on a street corner, hassling passersby in a display of virility.

Darwin talked about the struggle for survival being more intense between species of the same genus, when they come into competition with each other. He said it made sense that competition would be the most severe between allied forms, since they fill almost the same stratum in nature. I was thinking about crows this way—how much infighting was there? Social behaviors only survive if they increase the bird's survival and ability to reproduce, but how social were they, really? Did the degree of participation in family life vary throughout the crow's life, or did it follow a stable pattern? These were the questions I wanted to answer, and I tucked them away in my memory bank, eager to build upon them when I began my graduate studies.

FOR OUR LAST EVENING together before I returned to Chicago and school, we found our way to a little hole-in-the-wall spot called La Cocinita, and there I had my first taste of enchiladas. They were delicious, smothered in jack and Colby cheeses, heavy with onions, accompanied by *papitas*—little fried potatoes. I tasted pinto beans for the first time, too. They'd been liberally doctored with a powder made from red chiles—so hot with spices that I drank two glasses of water trying to soothe my tongue and throat. Watching me, Alden laughed.

"It's a New Mexican test, you know. How hot you can stand your chile. A measure of your *cojones*."

"My what?" I choked, dipped my napkin in my water glass, and applied the water directly to what I was sure were blisters indicative of third-degree burns, at least.

"Balls, my dear."

"Balls?"

"Your manhood, your macho status."

"Oh. And I'm supposed to want that?"

"Meri, you *are* that. You are one ballsy woman. The ballsiest I've ever known."

"I'll take that as a compliment."

"It was meant as one." Alden took a bite of his pork tamale. "You've done a good job this summer. You've made the best of things, taken care of yourself."

"Isn't that what you expected?"

"It's what I knew you could do. It's not what other men's wives have done." I let what he'd said sink in. I felt pride, but it was tinged with something else, something I couldn't identify. "And soon, Meri. Soon, maybe we'll be together permanently."

"Are you telling me something"

"No. No, I'm not. I am emphatically *not* telling you anything."

"How wonderful it would be not to have to part." I reached across the table and pulled a lock of his hair until it was straight. It extended past his collar. There were *sopaipilla* crumbs in his mustache. He kissed my wrist and then returned my hand to my side of the table so that he could continue eating. I could hear the rasp of cicadas in the trees lining the street outside.

After a few minutes, Alden pushed back from the table, and we both lit up, exhaling smoke toward the wood-beamed ceiling. "I know a purported cure for too-hot chile," he said.

"Do tell." It had been a good meal. I felt my shoulders relaxing away from my ears, and I was sure he'd say the cure was making love.

"Ice cream."

"Ice cream?"

"Yes."

"All right. I believe you."

"You should always believe me, Meri. I will never lie to you."

I knew he meant it. It's keeping promises, not making them, that is the impossible thing.

A Tidings of Magpies

1. *Gregarious birds, magpies are intelligent, opportunistic, and bold.*
2. *The magpie is viewed by some cultures as an omen of bad news; other cultures consider the bird a messenger of good tidings.*

During my senior year, I missed Alden so, and I sought out distractions. In September, Kitty, Red, and I saw Bette Davis marry an older man to save her brother from embezzlement charges in *Mr. Skeffington*, and Mother wrote that she was canning peaches. October had one of the most beautiful harvest moons I'd ever seen, a rich, gold disc hovering ripe over the horizon. As a surprise for Alden when I next saw him, Kitty and Red borrowed a car so they could teach me to drive, and we sweet-talked everyone we knew into donating gasoline ration coupons so we could refill the tank with ethyl.

Alden couldn't break free for the holidays, and the weather was so awful that I left Mother in the capable hands of her many Somerset County cousins while I stayed in Chicago, sharing Christmas with Mrs. Hudson and the other boarders who had no place else to go. A small part of me secretly hoped that Alden would appear on Christmas

Eve, make a big surprise of it, but I was wrong. I chastised myself for having harbored such little-girl wishes.

We slipped into 1945, and Alden's letters became increasingly sparse—his work was frantic, the pressures great. I continued to write to him, although at times it felt as if I were sending letters like fragile paper airplanes out across some abyss. We weren't communicating—not really. My letters to him were more like journal entries or lists of what I'd done in any given week.

I began to feel as if I weren't truly married, not in the sense of any marriage I'd ever seen. I told myself that other women lived alone while their husbands were fighting overseas, and I suspected they didn't receive regular letters, either. Still, no matter how much I rationalized the situation, tried to talk myself out of a funk over Alden's relative silence or berated myself for being selfish, the truth was that I felt sorry for myself. Poor, poor Meri.

In January I applied to graduate schools, and that brought me back into a sense of a life with potential, a future. Professor Matthews kept his gentle, guiding hand at my back, reviewed my applications, and wrote the most beautiful, laudatory letters of recommendation. I couldn't wait to see Alden's face when I revealed acceptances to him, to share my happiness with him, to make him proud.

JERRY CAME BACK, OUTWARDLY unscathed, and returned to his pre-med studies. We exchanged awkward waves but otherwise made every effort to avoid each other. He seemed subdued, less the bon vivant. And then, within a few months of returning, he ran his car into a telephone pole and was killed. I don't know if it was an accident; no one knows. Maybe at that point even Jerry didn't know an accident from a purposeful release.

Then, by May 8, 1945, Hitler was dead, and Germany had surrendered. *Soon*, we all thought. *Soon*.

ALDEN DID NOT ATTEND my graduation ceremony. He said his work had now reached a fever pitch, that in the early summer of 1945 he could not be spared. Instead, Professor Matthews and his wife gave me a small party in their backyard. Mrs. Hudson brought a spice cake with precious wartime raisins and just the right amount of cream-cheese frosting. Red and Kitty came with potato salad in hand. Mother, who had been given guest accommodations by the Matthewses, was blessedly silent on the topic of Alden's absence. She loved the Matthewses and could not stop talking about their kindness, how highly they must think of me to go to such trouble on my behalf.

Before we took our seats at a lopsided wooden table set beneath an enormous, spreading oak tree, Mrs. Matthews led me and Mother on a botanical tour of her gardens. We extolled the beauties of her abundant peonies.

"They attract so many ants," my mother said.

"Oh, we spray for them."

"They come over from my neighbors'. I can't do a thing about them." Mother, unlike me, was tall, broad with strength and physical labor. She stepped carefully on the rough paving stones that bordered the Matthewses' flower beds.

"Mother, what neighbors?"

"The Kowalskis. You know how awful their yard is." My mother reached to scratch her ankle.

"I don't remember."

"Because you haven't been home."

I took a deep breath, let the jab go unanswered.

"Let me show you my bleeding heart," Mrs. Matthews said, taking

Mother's arm and leading her off. She turned her head and winked at me over her shoulder.

We sat until it was dark and the fireflies came out.

"There are no fireflies in New Mexico. And not nearly so many mosquitoes," I said, scratching my forearm.

"Tell us about it," said Mrs. Matthews. "Give us the pros and cons."

"Pros: your stockings dry in seconds, since there's no humidity." I took a sip of lemonade. "I like that there are fewer people, less hustle-bustle." I paused. "And it has my husband."

No one knew how to respond, and I felt a need to reassure them. "But maybe soon I'll have him back again."

"Let's hope so." Mother put a flat hand between my shoulder blades and rubbed a circle. "She's our wee brown sparrow, you know. Daddy would be so proud, honey. So proud."

In the dusk of that night, I looked at her—really looked at my mother for the first time in a long while. Her dear, clunky black pumps, thick support hose wrinkled about her ankles, her homemade cotton dress. She'd sent me an apron that winter, made of remnants of the same material she'd used to make the dress she was wearing. White, jagged rickrack trimmed the pockets and waistband of a garment I had yet to wear due to the absence of any kitchen in my life.

I felt my love go out to her, stretch across the universe of the tablecloth to where she sat, solid, immutable, the only steady fixture in my life. My mother, who loved sticky buns and used words like "smearcase" and "davenport" and "goosebumps," who made me root beer and ginger ale in the damp of the cellar, and who commandeered my services on laundry day. I remembered one spring day in particular, helping her to move the laundry tub from the cellar to the backyard, filling it with the hose, feeling a frisson of fear when she repeatedly warned me to keep my fingers far from what she called "the mangler," where the pressure of the rollers squeezed nearly every drop of moisture from the clothes. The wooden clothespins that could be made into dolls with tiny painted faces, my straining to reach high enough to pin things to the clothesline. Black dots of flies come to drink moisture on the white sheets where they hung listless in the air, yearning for a breeze. A tiger swallowtail dancing scallops across the backyard. The taste of heavily sugared iced tea sipped while rocking gently in the porch swing, *Jane Eyre* in my lap. The smell of her Pears soap, her mint-green bedspread. Her stable bosom, her amplitude of figure, of love.

Her home, though. My mother's home, no longer my home. I felt acutely the fact that I had no home, had not had a home for years. And then I realized that I had begun to need a home, that transience would no longer do.

To:	From:
Meridian Whetstone	Alden Whetstone
1225 Waverly Ave.	PO Box 1663
Chicago, Ill.	Santa Fe, N. Mex.

July 17, 1945

Dear Meri,

I know it's been too long since my last letter. Weeks—maybe as much as a month? I'm sorry, Meri. One day, you will understand. ██████ was a huge, successful step toward that "some day" but for now I must leave things at that.

We need to talk about your plans for graduate school. Please wait before committing to anything final in terms of acceptance of offers or plans for moving. Admittedly, we should have talked about this sooner, but this is all out of my hands—our hands. Please don't worry or be angry, just give me time.

One more "I'm sorry" and then I'll sign off, as it's 2 a.m. and I am worn to the core. I'm sorry I was not at your graduation ceremony. Again, one day you'll understand, and you'll know that I really had no choice. My love for you was outweighed by other matters—matters that one day will recede and let my love for you take precedence.

Still and always,
Alden

I'd not revealed my pursuit of graduate schools to Alden, but he must have guessed I would be applying, given academic calendars and deadlines. Too, I'd never found what felt like the right time in our sporadic, terse correspondence. I'd already said "yes" to Cornell. I'd tell Alden later, when I could see and touch him. It would be a surprise.

ON AUGUST 6, 1945, the *Enola Gay* dropped Little Boy on Hiroshima, and the entire world changed in a single day. President Truman talked about the "greatest scientific gamble in history," paid homage to the "achievement of scientific brains," and mentioned "an installation near Santa Fe, New Mexico." I knew my mother, the Matthewses, Kitty and Mrs. Hudson—everyone who had doubted Alden, who had failed to understand our necessary separation, would hear those words. I felt a swell of pride when the President characterized what Alden and the others had accomplished as "the greatest achievement of organized science in history."

There were newspaper descriptions of the first test of the bomb in New Mexico on July 16, and I realized that was why Alden couldn't see me graduate in June, why his letters had dried up for a time, and why in his letter written the day after the test, he had told me our being together was coming soon. The newspaper accounts described the vaporization of a huge steel tower on the test site and said that the blast had the power of more than 20,000 tons of TNT. I could not fathom it. Nothing was immediately known about what had happened in Hiroshima, although we knew there were over 300,000 people living there, that it was a port city and a manufacturing center for the tools of war. I could not imagine what must have happened to the city, its inhabitants.

But I suspect Alden could imagine what had happened. Finally, I understood Alden's misgivings and terribly opposing emotions: a desire to put an end to a war that was hemorrhaging untold lives every day versus the incomprehensible destruction of an atomic blast, the unknowable impact of the release of atomic energy on all of our futures.

Later, we learned that in an instant, birds in the sky over Hiroshima ignited in midair.

WE WERE DAZED BY reports of the atomic bomb. It was truly incomprehensible. Still, I felt the bomb had accomplished a great deal in building the morale of the country, and now Russia joined us in fighting against Japan. *It can't last much longer*—that's what I thought, and I know I was not alone in my fervent hope. We dropped a second bomb—code-named Fat Man—on Nagasaki on August 9, and on August 15, Japan accepted the terms of an unconditional surrender. When a two-day holiday was declared, we piled into the streets, shouted "Peace!" and drank, danced. There were no strangers—only fellow Americans, people who felt unadulterated release in the wake of so many years of deprivation and loss. The next day, the government called off ration points for all canned foods and gasoline, and we had even more reason to celebrate.

At a newsstand near campus, I bought a copy of the August 20, 1945 issue of *LIFE* magazine, which featured before and after photos of Hiroshima. The article included a fairly extensive description of the role played by Oak Ridge, Tennessee, but there was next to no discussion of Los Alamos—only a tidbit about the first bomb test at the Trinity site. Los Alamos remained largely in the shadows, still a secret.

I sat in Mrs. Hudson's dust-free parlor where a fan whirred nosily, and I turned the magazine pages. A bead of sweat eased its way down my back beneath the wilted cotton of my slip. On a page next to an artist's rendition of the Trinity explosion, there was an advertisement for Poll-Parrot and Star brand shoes, with animated, freckle-faced children touting the virtues of the shoes and a reminder for customers to BUY AND KEEP WAR BONDS. In another ad a man carried a woman in a red and white print summer dress across a stream while she held their two bottles of Schlitz beer. The pairing of the surreal with the mundane, the quotidian and the miraculous.

About a week after the second bomb, when the hoopla began to wane, I at last heard from Alden, who sent me precious hothouse gardenias with the simple message: "Triumph!" The fragrant flowers were beautiful, and to celebrate Alden's contribution to the war's end, I pinned them to my navy blue suit collar and treated Kitty and myself to tea at the Jubilee Tea Room. Afterwards, we went shopping. I bought a new purse for $2.98 and a plain, very smart Stetson hat for $7.98.

As for my future, I did as Alden asked. I put off Cornell, deferring admission until the spring term. Alden had said we'd resolve things by the new year, and so I stayed on with Professor Matthews, who found a stipend to pay me. I read the studies and texts he suggested, outlined my graduate studies, and began to refine the list of possible hypotheses for my master's thesis. Still feeling as if I were caught at sea, becalmed without even the most minuscule breeze to fill my sails, I waited for Alden.

"YOU HAVE A NUMBER of choices, Meri." Alden was in Chicago for the Christmas holidays, and the two of us were seated in Mrs. Hudson's parlor. I'd lived in her boarding house for going on four years. This week we had four inches of new snow on the ground, and I actually longed for the New Mexico heat, the intense, relentless, summer sun. I remembered the bottoms of my bare feet burning as I ran across a flagstone patio to meet Alden as he pulled up in front of my rooms on Walter Street.

Alden was flipping through a red-covered booklet, *This Week in Chicago*. He held it up for me to see: "Danny Thomas is at the Chez Paree. Ted Weems and his orchestra are performing 'Sun Fun' in the Boulevard Room." He showed me the advertisement. "At the Tropics, there's Sam Bari and His Men of Rhythm and Red Duncan, billed as a 'famous blind pianist.'"

I was thinking about the startling red clay cliffs of the Jemez Valley.

"I'm assuming you're going to veto 'Scan-Dolls of '46' at the Playhouse." This ad showed a drawing of a woman in nothing but heels and a swathe of material strategically placed across her lap. "And you're going to pooh-pooh 'O-le-o-lay deeeeeee' at the Heidelberger Fass, right?"

"No lederhosen, you're right about that," I said, snatching the booklet and reading. "You didn't mention Devi-Dja and her Bali-Java Dancers at the Sarong Room."

"No use wasting my breath."

"But you never know. I might want to expand my cultural horizons."

"All right, then. It's settled." He took back the booklet. "Oh, joy to the world! We'll see their 'Mystic Balinese Temple Ceremonies' and hear the 'Primitive Jungle and Tribal Rhythms'—all while sipping cocktails. Good choice, Meri." He chucked me under the chin, and I could feel a bubble of happiness surfacing.

I was the awestruck, besotted student again. I studied him through a swirl of cigarette smoke, tried to fathom what he'd done, what he and the others had conceived and made reality atop that distant mesa. The pull of his breathtaking intellect again had a hold of me; the force of the attraction I felt for what he could do with that head of his made my heart quicken to the point of dizziness.

The vinyl seat of the taxicab crackled with the cold when we left the supper club, and my legs in their much-mended stockings began to tremble. I curled myself into Alden's side, wondering if I'd ever be warm again. *I'd move to New Mexico in an instant*, I thought, just to escape the sharp, penetrating Chicago wind. My jaw hurt from clamping my teeth, and although I knew that relaxing my muscles would help, I only grew tenser, more knotted, as the cold permeated my coat and gloves. Alden had the cabbie take us to a hotel.

I took a hot bath and crawled beneath the covers, lit a cigarette, and watched Alden as he sat reading, pipe smoke wreathing about his head. He closed the book, and I read the spine: *The Physics of Flight*, by Alfred Landé. *Well, well*, I thought, pleased.

"At least you've stopped trembling," he said, climbing into bed.

"But isn't that exactly what you want from me in bed? Trembling?"

He laughed and then reached toward the night table for the oversized nail he used to tamp down his pipe tobacco. He relit his pipe, and I inhaled a vicarious sampling of the mixture he always bought—Scottish Mist.

"You said you wanted to talk with me."

He puffed several more times to ensure the pipe remained lit. I watched his cheeks cave in, release, cave in, release. I knew that he sometimes used this ritual to buy time.

"I've put this off, this conversation," he said.

"Obviously."

"Well, it's difficult."

"Just tell me. We can talk to each other, can't we?"

"Sometimes," he said, and I was struck by the honesty of that statement. He laid his pipe across the ashtray and turned to face me, plumping a pillow to hold his head at the right angle. "Here's the thing." He brushed some hair from my forehead. "The plan is to keep Los Alamos functioning, make it into a real research facility. There was a bill introduced in Congress—just last week. The McMahon Bill." He rubbed his eyes. "Oppenheimer, et al., have been on Capitol Hill, discussing what the country's atomic energy policy should be, how the bulk of scientific knowledge should be handled. We need to keep our science out of the hands of the military and the politicians."

"All right."

"We're hopeful the bill will pass, and we really think it will."

"What does it *mean*, Alden?"

"Los Alamos could be a top-notch research facility—like Berkeley or other spots. But it wouldn't be academia—and not privatized, either. It would be run by a new government agency, the Atomic Energy Commission."

"You're telling me you want to stay there."

"I am." Now his eyes lit up, the hesitation in them subsided, replaced by excitement, animation. "I could work there, without the inevitable restrictions and distractions. No teaching duties—just pure research. Meri," he cupped my cheek in the palm of his hand, "I can have a freedom there that I can have nowhere else, and, frankly, the pay is better—much better than what I can make if I stay in academia."

"But what would I do? What about my studies?"

Now he reached to hold my head in both of his hands, to keep my gaze focused on his. I felt an Alden promise coming.

"Maybe you could work there, too, with your laboratory skills. Part of the mission would be to find peacetime uses for atomic energy."

I sat up, moving his hands away from my head. "But that's not what I want. It's not ever been what I wanted, you know that."

"I'm saying it could turn out to be what you want. I'm telling you about the enormous potential of the place, of all of this. Of what we can build there, with the ongoing interaction of so many intriguing, challenging minds."

"Crows, Alden. Crows are what I find intriguing and challenging."

He closed his eyes briefly, reopened them. "You could move as soon as next month, start the new year living with me. After so long, we could be together—really together. Why don't you think about it, sleep on it. We can talk more tomorrow." He turned from me to flick off the bedside light, as if darkness would alter my vision of my future, make me more compliant.

In the gloom I heard his breath deepen, watched his shoulders release their tension. He'd said his piece at long last, and now he could relax. For me, any chance of sleep had vanished, and so I took my book, a blanket, and a pillow into the bathroom and climbed into the empty tub, just as I had when I was a girl. The hard sides of the bathtub seemed an appropriate place for me to lay my body that night—unforgiving and nonmalleable. I couldn't concentrate, though. Finally, I pulled a hand towel from the rack, bit down on it, and used it to muffle my sobs. I let my shoulders spasm, felt the muscles of my lower back tighten into fists of pain.

I could understand why he wanted Los Alamos, what it represented to him, what it could do for his future, his career. Were my needs less important than his? More trivial? Or were my needs great enough to overshadow what Alden might accomplish if he could continue to pursue research that literally changed the course of man, of history? I couldn't be that selfish, could I?

By morning, I'd found a place of compromise. I agreed to a one-year trial period. I'd still do what I could in terms of crow observation, and then I'd use that research as a foundation for my master's degree.

A Descent of Woodpeckers

1. *Woodpeckers do not sing to attract a mate, they drum.*
2. *Sacred to Mars, the Roman god of war, woodpeckers guarded a woodland herb used for treatment of the female reproductive system.*

It was February of 1946, fortunately a snow-free day. The Studebaker was packed with my two suitcases and box upon box of books—that's all I brought to New Mexico—clothing and books. Really, that's all I owned. Headed north out of Santa Fe on a wet, hissing highway, we descended into a valley and encountered Tesuque Pueblo. I tried my hand at pronunciation: "Tea-soo-key."

"Teh-*sue*-kay."

"Tesuque."

"Right."

The wind cut across the highway, and condensation on the windows distorted my view. I wiped the passenger window with my woolen coat sleeve and looked out at undulating, pale pink-brown hills studded with daubs of dark green piñon. Remnants of snow from a storm earlier in the week iced the dips of the hills like skillfully applied makeup.

The horizon was vast, open, and I had a sense of how that openness could help to create a sense of freedom, of possibility. I reached my hand toward Alden's, and knitted glove to knitted glove, we held hands as he drove toward several more amazing words: Cuyamungue, Pojoaque, Otowi, Totavi, Tsankawi.

The climb toward Los Alamos began just after Tsankawi. The narrow road wound through outstretched fingers of mesa with surprisingly flesh-colored ascents pockmarked with hollowed-out openings that Alden told me had been Anasazi cave dwellings. Many of the caves had soot-blackened ceilings, and he called the rock *tuff* or *tufa*, saying it was pyroclastic, the result of a giant volcanic eruption in the Jemez Mountains just northwest of Los Alamos. I thought about how the firelit caves would have looked at night, blinking constellations embedded in walls of rock. The clouds dissipated, and I was struck by the sensual beauty of that flesh-colored landscape against a pure blue sky. I imagined people scaling the edifices, reaching for foot- and handholds, trying not to fall into the brush below. I closed my eyes, felt a thrilling sensation of vertigo.

The dropoff grew enormous as our Studebaker chugged up a rutted, muddy road that lacked the comfort of guardrails. I looked out my window over the edge of a perilous cliff to the floor of the valley below, looked back over my shoulder to see the Sangre de Cristo Mountains above Santa Fe. This part of New Mexico was so much greener than Albuquerque, and I could see clear changes in vegetation as we gained altitude, approaching Los Alamos at over 7,300 feet. Alden said Wheeler Peak, farther north, was over 13,000 feet—effortlessly dwarfing my father's proud bens of Scotland. I thought of all my father had missed, his short years on the earth, and how much he would have loved trying to put his arms about this vast landscape.

Armed MPs stopped us at the East Gate, which looked like a typical highway toll station with several lanes. A nine-foot security fence surmounted with triple strands of barbed wire encapsulated the site. Above it all stood a formidable guard tower. We parked and went in to fill out paperwork that would gain me entry on a temporary basis; later, I'd have to apply for a permanent identification card that I'd be required to carry with me at all times. If I wanted to leave, I'd have to surrender my pass, which had to have Alden's signature on it as my host. Two tanks flanked the entrance. In Los Alamos, it seemed, the war had not ended.

As we drove into the town, I saw parked cars with tires sunk in mud, dirty mounds of snow, a few wooden sidewalks built beneath clotheslines strung across puddle-pocked mud, and ramshackle, temporary wooden buildings of army green. Alden pointed out landmarks that, at least for now, were meaningless to me.

It was a dreary setting, one that failed to inspire. But then the crows came: a benediction. First one or two, and then in increasing numbers, swooping to land on fenceposts or rooftops, setting up gruff choruses in the bare branches of trees. Clustering on the edges of trash barrels, their entire bodies bending and stretching with each vocalization. Stridently pacing across the frozen ground, tilting their heads to look up, then down, their eyes alive with curiosity. I rolled down my window and was greeted with their croaks in bursts of three to four serial *Caw!*s.

They told me I would be all right in Los Alamos. They told me they would protect me, keep me company, that they had not deserted me any more than I had deserted them.

OUR FIRST HOME WAS a Morgan Area house with a pitched roof, wooden siding, and a white picket fence—a decided contrast to the usual pueblo-style architecture of the region. We used Alden's Brownie camera to take photos to send to Mother and other friends and colleagues so that they could see what our lives were like in this exotic, foreign land. In one photo, Alden stands in front of our Studebaker, parked in our dirt driveway. He has a cigarette in one hand, the other hand in his pocket, and on his chest is his omnipresent security badge. In another, Alden slouches on the couch, the light glinting off of his new wire-framed glasses and rendering the expression in his eyes one of blurry boredom. I'm close beside him, my thin legs in oversized trousers and saddle shoes, and behind us are the flower-printed paper curtains that covered all of our windows. A droop-leafed plant rests on an end table. One of our first purchases, a red, white and black Navajo rug, hangs on the wall behind us.

At twenty-two, I am small, inconsequential, girlish next to Alden's forty-three years. My smile is nascent, still in its formative stages.

I'D MADE A RUDIMENTARY shopping list and was sweeping the living room floor when the women knocked on the door and announced: "Welcome Wagon! Welcome Wagon for Mrs. Alden Whetstone!"

They wore bulky winter coats and stamped their feet as if that would remove the thick coating of mud and ice adhered to their boots. Each of the four women carried a tinfoil-covered plate, and they held them out to me so that they could free their hands to remove their galoshes. They stepped into our home in their stocking feet.

"Marge," said an ample, big-breasted woman with bright red lips and a homemade knitted cap with ear flaps. "Banana bread."

Madeline wore a man's flannel shirt and dungarees, Jillian had a short dark blonde pixie haircut, and Marcy handed me a casserole of noodles with tinned beef in gravy. "Don't knock it," she said. "It's the best I can do with the limited offerings of the commissary." She exchanged a look with the others, who nodded. "The end of the war hasn't yet meant much improvement in groceries."

"Please call me Meridian," I said, finding room for their plates on our small wooden dining table. "And thank you. Thank you for all of this."

They occupied the couch and single reading chair, instantly making themselves at home. The women had a sense of oneness about them, of a unit with a common cause.

"Oh, honey, we didn't leave you a spot!" Marge seemed to be the leader of the group. She tugged her red sweater over her round belly and scooted her wide hips closer to Madeline. Patting the Naugahyde cushion, she said: "Plop down here. Tell us about yourself."

"I can stand, let you have the room."

"Nonsense," she said and pointed at the cushion until I obeyed. "Tell us what a sweet young thing like you is doing in all of this mud and squalor." Marge laughed too loudly.

"My husband," I began.

"Oh, we know. We all know," Madeline said. "Alden's been at our dinner tables. Poor man needed a decent meal or two."

"You missed all of the fun," Marge said. "You missed the impossible furnaces, the water shortages, the cracks in the walls. From now on, it's a piece of cake."

Was this some kind of competition? If so, I'd be happy to let them win.

Marge continued, "For those of us who were here from the start, during the war, things have been pretty tough. We've had to make do," she said, slapping my leg so hard it stung. "One hell of a change from Princeton, I can tell you that."

"Never thought I'd live in tenement conditions, that's for sure," Marcy said, picking lint from her navy blue wool skirt. "But, we were glad to be here to do our part, to take care of our men, right girls? The hours they put in!"

"But we're doing all the talking," Jillian said. "Let's give Meridian a chance."

What to say? Where to start? "It's such a pleasure to be here at last," I said. "I've waited so long."

"For *this* place?" Marge said, laughing. "Oh, girl."

"I mean, to be with Alden. Not to be separated."

"He bragged about you—all the time," Marge said, softening.

"He told us you study birds," Marcy said. "Ornithology, right?"

"Crows in particular."

"Well, you'll have plenty of opportunity to watch them here. They're all over town, all through the canyons. They're so bold. They even challenge Bitsy, our cocker spaniel, in his own backyard!" Jillian said.

"They're not afraid of much—if anything," I said.

"Darn it." Madeline was searching the pockets of her trousers. "I forgot it. Our little handout."

"You can bring it by later," Marcy said, standing. "I have the feeling we caught you off guard when we just showed up, didn't we, Meridian? But we were just so excited to have another gal join us, that we forgot our Ps and Qs."

Marge stood, too. "Girls, we need to let Meri be for a bit, now that we've said our hellos."

"Oh, but it's all right," I said. I'd actually begun warming to the company.

"It's a little handout we made, with tips and pointers," Madeline said as she struggled to buckle her boots.

"You'll need it for baking," Jillian said. "We did all the calculations for high-altitude, what changes you'll have to make to your recipes. We made a chart."

"Remember your basic science," Marge said. "Higher altitude, less air pressure—so you have to add more flour, alter the liquids, change the oven temperature. Up here, gases expand more, liquids evaporate more quickly."

"Not bad for an architect." Marcy winked at Marge.

"This architect designed one heck of a fort for her boys!"

"When is spring?" I said by way of commiseration and farewell. "Soon?"

They laughed. "Comes and goes. Pretty uncertain," Marge said. "But maybe May."

"You'll get a scattering of nice, warm days before then," Madeline said reassuringly. "Don't despair. But don't hang any laundry on the clothesline, either."

I waved as they headed down the muddy road toward their houses, and then I went to look in the bathroom mirror, wanting to see what they'd seen: a few curls escaping from the kerchief I wore over my hair when I cleaned, a smudge of dirt across my left cheek, but soft, moist skin and an earnest smile. *Pleasant enough*, I thought.

In their wake, the house was still. I thought about how good it would be to find friends here. Someone other than just Alden. Women to share things with—even something as prosaic as high-altitude baking tips.

THAT FIRST YEAR OF 1946 was an active one—establishing a home, exploring. Alden and I went on adventures to Indian ruins and natural attractions. We'd roll up our pant legs and wade into the bone-chillingly cold, dark-green water beneath the falls at the soda dam, a Yellowstone-type rock formation on the back side of the Jemez Mountains. We drove to the valley below Los Alamos, climbed to the top of Black Mesa, a thick, stubby black column of rock that rises dramatically alongside the Rio Grande on the San Ildefonso Pueblo lands. We knelt at the praying stone on top of the mesa, placed our weight upon our forearms along the top of the rock, and wished, prayed, hoped. We hunted for potshards, and once Alden found a small turquoise carving of a frog.

I skated in the bottom of Los Alamos Canyon on a rudimentary frozen pond of ice fashioned by the private boys' school that preceded Oppenheimer's city. I loved the bubbles trapped in the thick, uneven ice, the shadows of pine and fir trees, the tautness of my cheeks reddened by wind and cold. Some nights the men lit bonfires so that we could skate with piñon smoke scenting the air. From time to time, Alden would come and watch me try to teach myself to twirl. He didn't like to skate but would sit on a rock and plant the tread of his galoshes on packed snow. More often than not, though, he stayed home to smoke and read, and I'd head out by myself. I didn't mind going alone—it meant I wouldn't have to worry that he was bored or getting too cold. I'd throw my head back, look up at Orion's Belt, and think of things I wanted to discuss with Alden when I got home. I thought about the distance of the stars, the tilt of the earth's axis, and Galileo's trial for heresy.

I realized this was a place that would help me grow healthier, that permitted me wholehearted access to nature away from the noise and fumes of a big city. I quit smoking, and my lungs thanked me by quickly adapting to the high altitude and greater physical demands I was placing on my body. I missed the university library but found I did not long for supper clubs or dinner shows. Many of the scientists played instruments, and they'd give small, informal performances of classical music that really were quite enjoyable. We had a movie theater with a green monster of a machine that for a nickel dropped a paper cup and filled it with cold, foamy Coca-Cola. On Friday nights, we joined other couples at the bowling alley next to the movie theater, afterwards crossing to Sparky's soda fountain where I could order a vanilla egg cream and Alden could get a scoop of ice cream with chocolate sprinkles and a flourish of whipped cream.

While Alden worked long hours, I set off on adventures, much as I'd done during my solo summer in Albuquerque. Although Alden protested loudly, sometimes I'd drop him off for work and then take the Studebaker and head off the Hill. I'd drive in the dust to San Ildefonso and Santa Clara pueblos and buy round loaves of bread baked in humpbacked *hornos*. I bought black glazed pottery from Maria Martinez and Teresita Naranjo, my best-loved piece a wedding vase, shaped with two spouts so that bride and groom could each drink from a different side. There were times when rainwater came so quickly that the desert sands could not consume it all, creating flash floods that ran in sudden red rivers as deep as my knees. I had to be careful easing the car across those torrents, especially around the deep arroyos of Totavi. I learned how to remove a distributor cap and wipe it dry, to get the car to start again and take me away from the gushing waters.

For me, those times were divine adrenaline. I knew I was in New Mexico for a short time and so felt I should take advantage of all opportunities. Besides, I quickly grew bored sitting in our small house, sweeping floors that were instantly, redundantly covered in red clay dust or thumbing through magazines in search of the latest Jell-O recipe.

We got along, Alden and I. He had his work, which consumed him, and I found so much to learn from New Mexico's nature, its history and cultures, that my mind was sated. In the evening, Alden and I would settle deeply into conversations, and I thought that domestication suited me just fine.

I BEGAN MY CROW journals about two months after arriving in Los Alamos. At first, I explored all of the areas where crows tended to congregate. I wanted a spot where I could be certain I was looking at a stable population. Alden found an army surplus canvas backpack for me, and I loaded it with warm drinks in the winter, cool water in the summer. I carried a waterproof poncho, matches, toilet paper, a pocketknife, several sharp number 2 pencils, and a beautiful, blank book with rich, cream-colored paper—far too lovely for tromping about in the woods, but something I'd found in a stationery store in Santa Fe and knew I must have for my first crow journal.

Ultimately, I settled on a length of Los Alamos Canyon, alongside what became the Western Area housing development. I could hike there easily, perch on a rock high on the north side of the canyon, or climb down through pines and scrub oak to the stream that ran the length of the canyon. I did not have the equipment or assistance I'd need to band birds, so I wouldn't be able to track individuals. Instead, I was forced to look at group behaviors, to see, for example, how the community of birds dealt with food in abundance or shortage. I listened to hours of their vocalizations, tried to ferret out meaning, to see and hear patterns, to look at body language and displays.

I believe they came to know me, that they learned to inform each other of my presence. They seemed able to rapidly assess my nonexistent threat level and to engage in mutual observation with me. Always, of course, I had to think about how my sitting, standing, or walking might alter their behaviors, whether I should be building blinds so as to escape their notice. But I knew that my constructing a blind wouldn't fool them—these birds were too smart.

And so I decided my study would have to include me—that I would have to observe and carefully record my own behaviors, including the colors of my clothes, any perfumes or hats, what noise I made.

Those were quiet, respectful, contemplative times for me, the days I spent in the woods with the crows. The breezes that traveled the canyon raised the hairs on my forearms and held the crows aloft, hovering over prey, arcing coal-black through blue skies, toward burgeoning thunderheads.

THE LAB BEGAN TO take on a more permanent shape, eating its way across the mesa top, digging its way into the canyons. Temporary buildings were razed, and solid structures that signaled Los Alamos' new-found permanence rose in their places. Still, there were frightening setbacks, like Louis Slotin's accident in mid-May of 1946. Word of what had happened to the Canadian physicist/chemist spread through the research facility quickly, and Alden and his friends met at our home that evening. Slotin had been at the University of Chicago with Alden, and so the whole event hit Alden particularly hard. The men who sat in our living room were sober, shocked, reminded of the dangers of tickling the dragon's tail, as they called it.

Alden had made it clear that some of their talk would involve classified information, so after I served coffee along with bakery pastries and cookies, I would have to step out. I acquiesced, but found myself hovering in the hallway, eavesdropping. One of the men said that Slotin had been engaged in a demonstration that included creation of some of the first steps in nuclear fission. The experiment involved bringing a hollow hemisphere of beryllium around a mass of fissionable material that was resting in a similar, lower, hollow hemisphere. Removing the spacers between the hemispheres that usually kept the experiment subcritical, Slotin then brought the shells together slowly, using only a screwdriver to keep the spheres apart. When the screwdriver slipped, the experiment went to a critical phase, with a resulting blue glow and heat wave. Slotin quickly used his hands to separate the spheres and halt the nuclear reaction, preventing expansion of the chain reaction and, ultimately, a much greater release of radioactivity.

When Alden climbed into bed, I reached to hold him.

"What did you hear?"

"Nothing," I said, nuzzling my face into the side of his neck.

"Meri," he took my chin in his hand. "What did you hear?"

I touched the tip of his nose, feigning playfulness. But I was a terrible actress. "Enough to scare me. Horribly," I admitted.

"Your feet are ice."

"I'm cold all over."

He rubbed my hands. "You don't have to be afraid for me."

"But . . ."

"Things went wrong, Meri. Mistakes were made."

"And we all make mistakes. Even you, Alden."

"That's why we met tonight. To talk about what happened and figure out how to do things better. It's clear that criticality experiments can no longer be hands-on. We'll come up with ways to perform them remotely. More safely than with screwdrivers and slippery hands."

"What will happen to Louis?"

"He's dying. It's a matter of days."

"Oh, God."

"He was irradiated. He received a lethal dose and will die of radiation poisoning—there's nothing that can save him." Alden took a deep breath. "We don't know exactly what the dosage was. Not a one of them was wearing a dosimeter."

"You . . . ?"

"I wear mine. Always. And we all just got a goddamned good reminder not to get sloppy."

I pressed my hands to his chest, and Alden kissed the top of my head.

"Meri," he sighed, "I have you, and that's plenty reason to be careful not to be bitten by any dragons I may wrestle."

"Please," I said. "Please."

Louis Slotin died nine days later. He was thirty-five.

THE PAIN HAD BEEN getting worse. I felt it in my lower back and most sharply in my pelvis. At times it took my breath away and caused me to double over. When the bleeding began, I told Alden.

"Are you sure it's not something you ate? Gas from last night's Brussels sprouts?"

"Gas doesn't cause vaginal bleeding, Alden."

"Well, no, of course not."

It was the fall of 1946, and I was seated in our reading chair, bent at the waist, using my forearms to hold myself together.

"Are you sure you need a doctor?"

"I just know something's wrong. That's what I know." I stood slowly and then fainted.

I regained consciousness on the brief drive to the hospital, which was a small, single-story wooden building staffed by former army doctors who continued to practice medicine as if they were working under battlefield triage conditions. When we arrived, two young Indian men who worked as orderlies helped me out of the car and through the hospital door. From the waiting room, I could see the single operating room. Framed certificates and diplomas thickly populated the walls, apparently as a means of proving to scientists that the physicians really were fully qualified to practice medicine.

Dr. Lowden was about forty-four, Alden's age. He spoke to Alden.

"She looks pale. Has she been getting enough sleep?"

"I think so."

"What else is going on?"

"She says her gut hurts, and she fainted. That's why I went ahead and brought her in."

Dr. Lowden unceremoniously pulled my blouse from the waistband of my trousers and began probing my abdomen. "Let me know when it hurts," he said gruffly. He used both hands to press on the right side of my pelvis. I cried out, and then he released the pressure, which eased my pain. "Not appendicitis." He raised his voice as if speaking to a child or deaf person. "You still have your appendix, right?"

"Yes."

"She's had some bleeding, too," Alden said. "Lower down," he motioned, the physicist who could not bring himself to name parts of his wife's anatomy.

"How much?" Lowden asked, putting his stethoscope to my belly and listening.

"How much, honey?"

"Spotting," I said. "Just today."

"Bowel sounds are normal," Lowden said. "When's your next period due?"

"I'm not sure," I said. "I write it on a calendar so I don't have to remember. But I may have missed the last one."

"Meri, you didn't tell me that. Why didn't you tell me?" I saw Alden make a quick fist. "Is she pregnant? Is that it?"

Lowden opened the door to the exam room and called out, "Belle? Belle, will you come in here?"

A statuesque woman with jet-black hair piled under a starched nurse's cap stood in the doorway. She looked over at me, smiled, and winked. "Hiya," she said, addressing me before glancing at either of the men.

"Belle, I need her temp and BP." Lowden turned to Alden again. "How much does she weigh?"

"I'll bet she knows that better than he does," said Belle, moving to my side and putting a reassuring hand on my shoulder. "Howya doin', hon?"

"OK," I said.

"Not particularly convincing," she laughed. "Tell these old men how much you weigh." She wrapped the blood pressure cuff around my bicep.

"One fifteen."

Lowden was making notes. "Height?" he asked.

"Five foot six." I was getting dizzy again.

"Hold on, hon." Belle put an arm behind me, braced me in a sitting position. "You gettin' woozy?"

I nodded, making the dizziness worse.

"Let's lay you down then, she said, propping my head on a thin pillow. "How's that?"

"Better. Thanks."

My blood pressure was slightly elevated, my temperature normal, my pulse seventy-two.

"Any other symptoms?" Lowden asked.

"I don't think so," Alden said. I looked back and forth between the two of them, then looked at Belle, who again smiled.

"My shoulder hurts," I volunteered.

"Which shoulder? Any injuries to it lately? Maybe bump it against something?"

"I don't think so. My right shoulder."

He lifted me to probe my shoulder blade. I gasped with another pain in my gut.

"Describe the pain."

"It's tender most of the time. But then it's like it cramps, a gripping pain."

"Uh-hunh," he said, easing me back onto the exam table. "Belle, let's loosen her trousers, let me get a better look at her abdomen . . . . Actually, on second thought, let's get her in a gown. I should do a pelvic." He motioned to Alden. "Why don't the two of us step out for just a minute. Belle will let us know when she's ready."

I could hear their murmuring voices in the hallway.

"Hell's bells," Belle said, helping me unbutton my blouse and then stand so that she could pull off my trousers and panties. Her movements were unhurried, gentle. "That man has the bedside manner of a pea-brained cow." She held the gown for me and then tied it closed. "He's used to soldiers, not pretty young women." She leaned in close and whispered, "And between the two of us, he's going to be far more nervous about a pelvic exam than you ever could be—he's probably only ever done about six of them, counting medical school."

"That doesn't make me feel any better," I whispered back, suddenly her co-conspirator. She had crystal-blue eyes, Liz Taylor eyebrows, and I could smell mint chewing gum on her breath.

"Oh, he'll be fine. I'm just saying that when he turns beet red, you shouldn't take it personally."

She looked back at me before signaling to Lowden. "I'll stay here with you. Anything hurts, you just squeeze my hand, OK?"

I'd never had a pelvic exam and could not believe that he was going to insert that medieval-looking metal thing into me. He'd told Alden to wait outside, and I could see why—it wasn't something a husband should see another man do to his wife. The metal was cold, the lubricant inadequate. I began to sweat.

"Relax your legs, let them fall open," he said, and all I could see was the top of his head, a bald spot the size of a softball.

Belle held my hand. "You'll be fine." Although she spoke to me as if I were much younger, I guessed that she was about twenty-eight or so. She had pierced ears with little pearl studs and perfectly manicured nails varnished a bright red.

"I see a little bleeding from the cervix." Lowden's voice was slightly muffled. He used his hand to move my cervix. "Does that hurt?"

"Yes. But not as much as the pains I've told you about."

"Breasts tender?"

"Maybe a little." I hadn't realized that until he asked about it.

"I don't feel any masses." He removed his hand and stood, turned to wash his hands at the sink. I saw him look at himself in the mirror.

"Go ahead and sit up, honey." Belle helped to pull me upright. I dangled my legs off of the edge of the table. I was clammy, getting cold.

"You can go ahead and get dressed, Mrs. Whetstone. I'll step out and speak with your husband."

Belle helped me get dressed, and then Alden opened the door.

"All set?" he asked.

"For what?"

"Home."

"But . . ."

Alden looked at Belle, who had her back to us. She'd begun to clean up after Lowden, shrouding with a white cloth the tray that held the speculum. Alden opened the door for her, and she turned to me.

"You take care, kid," she said and smiled. "I'll see if Dr. Lowden needs me to do anything else for you."

"Thank you," I said.

"Yes, thank you," Alden said, helping me to stand.

"But, Alden, what's going on? What's wrong with me?"

He led me to the door. "We'll talk about it in the car."

"But I hurt. I'm not making this up. There's something wrong with me."

"Meri, let's just get you to the car, all right?"

My knees felt as if they wanted to buckle. I held onto Alden, gripping his forearm with both hands. The orderlies reappeared and eased me gently into the passenger seat, closing the door once I got my feet into the car. Alden started the engine and waved his thanks.

"We'll get you home and into bed," he said and then paid an inordinate amount of attention to the road, as if we were battling intense Chicago rush-hour traffic, not the sparsely populated roads of Los Alamos during the dinner hour.

"Tell me what's going on. Please."

He sighed. "All right, then. Dr. Lowden thinks you've got a false pregnancy— pseudocyesis."

"What?"

"Your body thinks it's pregnant when it's not," he said, pulling into our driveway. He turned off the engine and turned to face me. "He says it happens sometimes, when a woman wants to be pregnant but hasn't been able to conceive."

"This is a joke." I opened the car door and looked over my shoulder. "That man didn't say ten words to me, and he's comfortable diagnosing me as a crazy person? A hysterical woman?" I stood but was so weak that I fell into the door, bumping my head against the window frame. I began to cry.

"Let's get you into bed."

I slapped at Alden's hands. "Don't touch me!" I wobbled to the screen door and threw it open with all of the drama I could muster. Why not? I was a hysterical woman—might as well play the part. When I tried the front door it stuck, swollen with the humidity of recent rains. I kicked at it.

"Stop it. Let me help you."

"You've already helped me plenty. You let a doctor who knows nothing about me call me a liar. A crazy person."

"That's not what he's saying. Not at all."

"And did he think I was stupid? A moron or something?"

"Of course not."

"Seems that way to me," I said, heading into the bathroom and slamming the door behind me. I sat on the toilet. It hurt to pee, and there was more blood. Another cramp took hold of my gut and caused me to cry out. I began weeping, out of control. The weeping made the pain worse.

Alden opened the door and knelt beside me. "What can I do for you?"

"Believe me."

"I don't disbelieve you, sweetheart."

"You didn't stand up for me with that man."

"He didn't do anything wrong. Why are you acting this way?"

"Belle said he's got next to no experience with women or gynecological medicine."

"The nurse?"

"Yes, the nurse. You say that as if I shouldn't trust her."

"I just think a man with a medical degree deserves a little more respect than a nurse."

"But maybe she's right."

"Or maybe she's getting you all riled up for no good reason."

"*She* didn't get me 'all riled up.' The man who thinks that I'm an imbecile, that I've lost touch with reality—*he's* the one who got me all riled up." I fastened my pants, washed my hands at the sink. The pale woman I saw in the mirror had a red bump on her forehead, hair that flew every which way with static electricity. There were dark shadows beneath my eyes. I was worn out, tired to the core. "I'm going to bed," I said to myself in the mirror, and over my shoulder I saw the reflection of Alden's relief.

BRUTAL PAIN WOKE ME at two A.M. I was too weak to stand and must have looked even worse than before, because this time Alden moved swiftly to the phone to warn the hospital we were on our way. He left me in my nightgown, wrapped a blanket around my shoulders, and carried me to the car.

Dr. Schumann had replaced Lowden for the night shift. I heard Alden tell him about our earlier visit and Lowden's diagnosis. Dr. Schumann stood over me and put a reassuring hand to my forehead.

"Mrs. Whetstone, do you have pain anywhere other than in your pelvis?"

"My shoulder," I said, my breath coming quickly now, in little pants.

He felt my abdomen. "It's a bit distended," he said, looking across my body to Alden. "A little rigid." He opened the door and called out for the night nurse. I saw Belle appear at the door. "I need the operating room readied. Put in a call to Bingham, tell him we need him for anesthesia." She nodded and moved briskly down the hallway.

"Mrs. Whetstone, I disagree with Dr. Lowden." Dr. Schumann was older than Lowden, the stubble on his face was mostly gray, and the curly hair at his temples was salt and pepper. He took my hand and held it. "I think you've got an ectopic pregnancy, one that's ruptured." He looked at Alden to include him in the conversation. "The shoulder pain indicates that your peritoneal cavity is full of blood. The blood collects in the abdomen under the diaphragm. I need to get in there to stop the bleeding."

Belle opened the door. "Bingham's two minutes away," she said. "I'll get her ready."

"And I'll get ready to operate. Mrs. Whetstone," he said, still holding my hand, "I'll take very good care of you. Very good care."

"Thank you," I said, and I could hear how weak I was, my voice nothing but a thread.

Alden kissed me on the forehead. "Sweetheart, I'm sorry," he whispered. "I'm so sorry." I saw he was about to cry. He left the room.

"Well, I for one am glad I worked a double shift," Belle said, all efficiency. Her hair had come down some from the upsweep she'd worn in the daylight hours, but otherwise she looked no worse for wear.

"Me too," I croaked. I was nervous but also relieved that at last something would be done to help me. As Belle prepped me for surgery, I handed her my trust, and she made me feel safe.

A Charm of Hummingbirds

1. *Hummingbirds display exquisite flight control and are even capable of flying backwards.*
2. *Various cultures view the hummingbird as a symbol of resurrection, a messenger, or stopper of time.*

I was in the hospital for two weeks, including my twenty-third birthday, November 11, 1946. I nearly died from the loss of blood. The pathology report showed infection and inflammation of my fallopian tube where an embryo had mistakenly implanted itself.

Alden came to see me nearly every day. He brought me a bunch of daisies in a green glass vase and a small suitcase with things I'd asked for from home—my own nightgown, a hairbrush, nail scissors, and a hand mirror.

"I should have believed you," he said on that first day.

"It's OK." I recognized his penitence in the bright daisy faces.

"You were pregnant," he said needlessly and lowered himself into the chair beside the bed.

I'd thought about it, of course—my misbegotten child and the fact that Alden and I would have been parents. And yet, I didn't feel as though I could mourn the loss of a child, because in my mind there had never really been a child.

"Are you all right?" Alden asked.

"I am," I said with certainty. There were too many things that came first on my to-do list, before children. I still had Cornell on the horizon, and it wasn't time for a baby. I didn't want my plans disrupted any more than they already had been.

For my birthday in the hospital, Alden brought me a gift-wrapped book. Anticipating some treatise on bird behavior or maybe a Darwin first edition, I eagerly removed the paper.

The dust jacket was a sickly whirlpool of green with *The Snake Pit* written in lowercase, yellow letters.

"It's on the bestseller list," he said proudly.

I looked at the book description: a woman with schizophrenia and her experiences in an insane asylum. Bewildered, I looked up at Alden.

"The critics love it, and psychiatric experts agree that it's well done—honest." Excitedly, he took the book from my hands, read about the author. "It's part fact, part fiction. She really was institutionalized for a time."

"Alden," I said, trying to interrupt his misplaced enthusiasm, but he was undeterred.

"She studied at Northwestern, Meri. Another Chicago girl," he said, continuing to pair me with a woman who'd literally been put away.

"And here I thought you were sorry," I said when he finally took a breath and set the book on the blanket next to me. "Silly me," I continued. "I thought you regretted disbelieving me, characterizing me as a crazy woman. Hysterical."

"What? That's not what I'm saying!"

"It's exactly what you're saying."

"Sometimes you purposefully misunderstand me, Meri." He shook his head, the put-upon husband. "You're overly sensitive." I felt my jaw lock as Alden continued his defense: "Quite simply put, it was a book I saw in Santa Fe. A new book, a book that is supposed to be good. That's all," he sighed. "I thought you'd find it intriguing, especially while you're laid up."

I closed my eyes. I didn't want to feel this way; I didn't have the energy to feel this way. When I looked once more at his face, read his expression, what I saw there was honest confusion. He really had intended to bring me a birthday gift that would be something I'd enjoy. I loved books; Alden loved books. On one level, it made perfect sense.

"Alden," I said and waited for him to stop staring out the window and look at me. "I'm a little touchy on this subject, that's all," I said, trying to bring him back to me, choosing to focus on his intentions, not his obtuseness. "Sit here a moment." I patted the edge of the bed, scooted myself over, feeling the stitches in my abdomen grab, pull.

Gingerly, he sat next to me. "I meant well, Meri."

"I know you did, sweetheart." I put my hand on the small of his back.

"Sometimes, I guess I miss the boat."

I laughed and again felt my sore belly. How perfect some clichés are, I thought. Alden would literally miss a boat, a plane, a train. He would walk in front of traffic, lost in some conundrum of theoretical physics.

"That's what you have me for," I said, smiling. "To keep you on board."

Alden picked up the book and set it on the nightstand. "I'll get you some fresh water," he said, taking the water pitcher and heading for the hallway. "That, I think I can manage successfully," he winked.

"Prove it," I said, grinning.

DURING THE WEEKS I was hospitalized, Belle was a frequent visitor. She brought me Russell Stover chocolates, *LOOK* magazines, and exuberant conversation. She swore with great aplomb, and she seemed to say exactly what she thought with little to no filtering. I swam in her freedom, her liveliness. I don't know if it was because of that shared pelvic exam or if she would have done so anyway, but she spoke freely about sex—not in a vulgar way, just naturally, as if talking about sex were no different from sharing recipes for chicken cacciatore. I half fell in love with Belle Jordan.

"You'll like this," she said one day, hanging her legs over the side of the single visitor's chair. The walls of the room were painted with an ineffectual coating of thin, white paint, and my pillow was so stingy that I had to use my arms to cushion my head. A stark black cross hung above the bed, and I imagined it falling one day, impaling me. "My original Texas girl's name? Watling!" Belle waited for me to catch on. "Belle Watling!"

"As in the good-hearted whore in *Gone with the Wind*?"

"Yes, ma'am. Margaret Mitchell stole my name!"

"It is a pretty name. I like 'Belle.'"

"Sure, me too—but even though the book came out after I was born, people think my parents named me after a madam."

"A madam who never really has sex, though. She just drives around in her carriage delivering gold coins discreetly wrapped in handkerchiefs, donating funds to help the war wounded. She's a beneficent whore." I looked at my fingernails, thought I saw dirt beneath them. I was dying for a hot shower.

"Oh, that's me all right! A beneficent whore!"

"You're good to me, Belle."

"I like you, Meridian. I have a sense about you. Still waters run deep and all that."

"Oh, I might just bore you to tears."

"Honey, you ever let loose, you're not coming back. That's my prediction. You will break out of this pretentious little hellhole, that's where I'm putting my money."

"You may have me confused with someone else."

"I don't think so." She stood, looking at her watch. "Women gotta fight hard to be free, my friend. Daily. Pitched battle." She smoothed the sheets and kissed me on the cheek. "Wait until you get better. I have plans for you."

"Secret plans?"

"Anarchy. Rebellion. And probably a lot of booze."

"My my my."

"So get better. Start eating more of the food they bring you."

"It's awful. Can you identify even half of the entrees?"

She stood in the doorway next to a sign that listed visitors' hours. "Tuna salad?"

"Love it. My husband won't eat it, though, so I no longer make it."

"Well, we're not talking about his culinary demands, are we? The question was whether *you* like it."

"I do."

"Then tomorrow I will bring you a tuna salad sandwich. Maybe a slice of coconut cream pie, if I get my ass in gear this evening. I warn you, though," she paused for effect, "if the cocktail hour extends beyond seven, I may not get around to the pie." She blew me a kiss.

BELLE WAITED SEVERAL WEEKS after my discharge before introducing me to horseback riding. Dr. Schumann owned horses he no longer had the time to keep properly exercised, so he was grateful for Belle's enthusiastic plan to get me out and about. The first time I tried stretching the still-healing skin of my incision up, over, and across the saddle I cried out with the sudden pain.

"Nothing's going to come apart at this point," Belle said from where she'd stood to help into the saddle. She mounted her horse gracefully. "The time is past for you to be sitting in a chair. The way you'll get better now is to exercise."

She showed me how to hold the palomino's reins, to use my knees and thighs to grip the horse, and afterwards how to groom Heathen. I loved the smell of the barn—alfalfa hay and manure. There was something real, essential about it. I learned to feed Heathen carrots and quartered apples without risking my fingers, and I felt my strength returning as we rode along the frosty January ground amidst dried stalks of mountain wildflowers.

I think Alden was glad I'd found a friend, although he never asked much about Belle, didn't seem to want to know her himself. I didn't mind his apparent disinterest; Belle belonged to me. She was my reprieve, my secret hillside of laughter. And, increasingly, she was my only real companion. At night, when Alden and I used to talk, he used to work at engaging me. Now he disappeared into his book, his smoke, and the deep, soft cushions of his chair. It was as if, with relief, he could leave the job of entertaining me to someone else.

In the spring, the male towhee spends between seventy and ninety percent of his mornings singing. Nearly as soon as he mates, however, the percentage of time spent in song drops to five percent.

WE NEVER TALKED ABOUT it, not even once—the fact that my exploding ectopic pregnancy and convalescence meant yet another year's delay of my graduate studies, a bonus year added to Alden's Los Alamos research plan. I wrote a letter begging accommodation of my situation, pleading my unforeseen health problems, and Cornell agreed to give me just one more deferral until the spring of 1948. After that, the admissions office made it clear, the offer for a scholarship and a spot in the graduate school would expire. The fates had intervened, tamped me down like the tobacco in the bowl of Alden's pipe. I wasn't going anywhere.

I TOLD BELLE ABOUT my crow journals, about my chance at graduate school slipping away.

"I'd like to know what's stopping you," she said one day while we sat at the edge of the stream in Frijoles Canyon, letting the water flow over our bare feet. We wore the Los Alamos outdoorswoman uniforms of crisp white blouses, heavy cotton dungarees, and leather belts with silver and turquoise buckles. I'd been letting my hair grow, and at last I was able to wad it all into a ponytail or spin it into a French twist when I wanted to feign elegance. I wore my favorite pair of sunglasses—Wayfarers with dark green lenses and near-pink plastic frames. We were finishing a lunch of apple pie, accompanied by a Thermos of coffee white with cream.

I picked up a decaying alder leaf, held it up so that I could see its skeletal remains, the fine lace of venation. "I'm like this leaf," I said, showing it to her. "This is what's left of me. The flesh is gone, the meat of me is gone."

"Only if you let it be."

"What am I supposed to do? Tell me. What do I do?"

"Get back to the writing. Get back to the birds."

"There's no point, anymore."

"I think there is." She took the leaf from me, leaned over the stream and let it go. We watched it, an inconsequential weight on the stream's current. "You cannot give up, Meri. You just can't. There's too much of you, too much that you are and can be." I saw debris stuck between her toes, wondered if we'd remembered to bring a towel to dry our feet.

"Was. The operative word is *was.*"

"I don't believe that. Don't squander your gifts. Don't let yourself waste away in this fucking place."

We were quiet for several minutes.

"Tell him that you need more than this." She gestured to the trees around us, but I knew she meant Los Alamos. "Tell him he made you a promise. You can give him an ultimatum."

"Oh," I sighed. I could not imagine any positive reaction Alden would have to an ultimatum. And would I leave him if he didn't accede to my wishes, whatever they were? Would I have the courage to draw a line and stick to it?

"Give it some thought, kiddo," Belle said, and stood. "As someone who cares for you, I can't watch this much longer." She brushed leaves from the seat of her pants and walked toward the car.

I looked once more at the surface of the stream, saw many more alder and cottonwood leaves traveling downstream, lodged against stones or submerged, signaling for help from the depths like drowning swimmers.

"I'VE BROUGHT YOU SOMETHING."

A couple of weeks later, I stood at the kitchen counter slicing the fresh zucchini I'd bought from a valley farmer.

"Come outside," Alden continued. "It looks best in the sunlight."

I dried my hands on a dish towel and followed him to the driveway. He unwrapped something heavy from a chamois cloth. There was a rounded brass base, about three and a half inches in diameter, with two lines incised for decoration, and on top of it nestled a disk of thick plastic, the bottom of which was painted a deep, indigo blue. He held it in his palms like a priest offering a sacrifice to the gods. "Step closer and look."

Floating in the plastic disk was a piece of the moon—tinged green, sparkling, glowing, pitted. I could distinguish some grains of sand embedded in the rock. I took the plastic disk from its base, held it up so that I could see the thin crust of rock from the side.

"It's Trinitite. Desert sand fused to form glass, heated by the first blast at Trinity site. A fellow I know, plastic chemist, he made some of these. One was sent to Truman, sits on his desk."

"If I were a girl, I'd swear you'd been to the moon and chipped off a piece." I moved it in the sun, let it catch the light. "It has the dark side of the moon trapped in it, too."

"Well, it's for you. For you to know what our sacrifices mean."

I looked at him. "Sacrifices?"

"During the war. How long we had to be apart." He put his arm about my shoulders, squeezed. "But now that's all over."

"The sacrifices aren't over."

He released me, stepped back. "I'm not sure I know what you mean."

"I mean my sacrifices. They are not over, they are not encased in a hunk of plastic and on display." I handed him the Trinitite. "And you know that." I realized I'd planted my feet further apart, steadied my stance. Was I really going to do this, now? Confront him, with so little planning?

"I meant this as a gift. It was just a gift."

"I know that, and I appreciate it. But you cannot pretend that I am not still, always, giving up my dreams so that you can have yours."

"But we've talked about this. I'm not going back to Chicago. This is where I want to be, and I am doing what I need to be doing."

"And me?"

"You've got your crow observations, you can do something with that—maybe publish, if and when you reach some conclusions, prove your thesis."

I blew out a breath. "Which is what? What's my thesis, Alden?"

He was folding the chamois cloth, carefully.

"You don't know it. You don't know what my hypothesis is."

"All right, Meri, it's true. I don't know." He shoved the chamois into his back pocket. "But I strongly suspect that you don't know what it is, either. I've seen you do very little in the last several months that has the remotest connection to your crow research."

"Would you notice? Would you even notice?"

"I think I would. I'm not obtuse. I try to talk to you—you're the one who has stopped talking to me."

"I'm talking now."

"No, you're fuming. What is your point, other than complaint? You cannot seriously propose that I give up my job, that we leave Los Alamos and live in some student's turret in upstate New York while you write a master's thesis."

"I was thinking about compromise."

"Which would look like what? What do you envision as compromise in these circumstances?" I could see he was trying to keep the tone of his voice even, measured. "What do you *want*, Meri?"

But there wasn't a viable compromise. Nothing I could see or imagine. And he knew it. I tightened the sash of my apron. I left him standing in the evening sun, walked back to the kitchen, and finished slicing the squash.

I'D NEVER BEEN A drinker. Belle, on the other hand, kept an inviolate cocktail hour, and she found inventive ways to include alcohol in most of her off-duty pursuits. She wasn't alone—a good number of the women (and men) in Los Alamos drank. They drank to adjust to life in a small, isolated mountain community after having lived in European cities and America's university campuses, where they'd had access to theater, live music, restaurants with innovative chefs—fulfillment of all desires.

Belle was the first woman I'd known who let loose so easily, and in placid Los Alamos she was my good-time friend. I started drinking primarily because she practically demanded it of me, but also so that I could feel as free as she seemed to be. Trying to keep up with Belle, the effects of alcohol more intense in my small frame, at times I drank until I stumbled, bruised my arms and legs, slurred my words. For a time—the time with Belle—drinking was the anesthesia that made my life endurable. Alcohol lulled to sleep the resentment that lived inside of me, stilled its petulant voice.

Still, I could take it or leave it. I was not an alcoholic; I didn't need the booze to function. I drank in context—that context being my drinking buddy, my "bad influence," as Alden called Belle.

"Fuck all of them," Belle said as we sat in one of our favorite spots in the canyon near the Quemazon Trail.

"Yes. Yes!" I shouted.

"Say it, Meri—you have to say the word." She nudged my shoulder, her lipstick smeared far beyond the lines of her beautifully curved lips. "Say THE word, Meri."

"Fuck."

"Louder."

"FUCK!"

"One more time!" she cheered.

"FUCKFUCKFUCK!" I roared into the twilit woods and heard deer skittering away across dry pine needles.

"Well done," Belle said and lay back on the huge block of rock where we sat. Soon, she began to snore. I put my palm to the granite, felt the last remnants of the sun's warmth emanating from the stone, traced the outline of a thunderbird chiseled into the rock by some long-ago Indian. What was the Indian legend about the thunderbird? Something about the beating of its enormous wings creating thunder and wind. I couldn't remember. But who cared, anymore? Certainly, not I.

"PLEASE TELL ME YOU did not."

"I did. Belle and Butch are coming for dinner. Tomorrow night." I enunciated each word clearly, the knife's edge of a dare in my voice.

"Did you think for a moment that I'd enjoy an evening with a bellicose, gum-smacking drunkard and her plebian security-guard husband? A man who calls himself 'Butch'?" Alden was tossing magazines and books off the end table. The pages splayed, crippled and awkward, when they hit the floorboards.

"What are you looking for?"

"Matches."

"Use the lighter. It's on the coffee table."

"I don't want to use the lighter. I want matches."

"What's the difference?" I walked toward the coffee table, prepared to plant the lighter in his palm, but Alden stepped into my path. He held my upper arms, looked me in the eye.

"You reek of booze."

"That's your imagination. I am not drunk."

"Meri." He shook me, once. "Meri, this has to stop. You have to stop this."

"Give me one good reason why. Just one." I felt my eyes narrow, my gaze harden.

"Because I asked you to."

"You ask for far too many things. That's just it." I shook myself free of his hold, headed toward the refrigerator. I was going to make a shopping list, figure out what to make for the Jordans.

"What's that supposed to mean—I *ask too much*? What are you talking about?"

I shut the refrigerator door, turned to face him. "You have to ask me? You don't have a clue?"

"I don't."

"But you should."

"But I don't."

I looked at my husband. His shoulders slumped, and he still had his security badge attached to his left shirt pocket, just below the plastic pocket protector in which he carried his mechanical pencils and a fountain pen that invariably bled blue ink. Alden had gained fifteen or more pounds since he quit hiking and going on adventures with me. I didn't pity him, though. He looked weak, pasty, doughy. I closed my eyes to him.

Belle's husband Butch had light blond hair and a prominent cowlick at the front where his hair parted, deep brown eyes, and the narrow waist and wide shoulders of an athlete. The night of my dinner party, he'd come from work and hadn't had time to change out of his security guard uniform. The lightning bolt insignia on his sleeve, symbolic of atomic energy, kept drawing my attention. It seemed appropriate to the atmosphere in our living room—thick with ozone, tension building before a storm. He removed his revolver from his belt and put it on the coffee table. I saw Alden grimace.

Belle wore a blue and white gingham summer dress cinched tight at the waist. She carried a straw purse, and a charm bracelet jingled on her wrist. When she put her arm around my waist and gave me a kiss on the cheek, I could smell bourbon. She put a glass pie plate on the counter alongside the copy of *Tender Is the Night* that she'd promised to lend me.

"Oh, wonderful!" I said, adjusting the scarf I'd tied around my neck. I felt as if I were choking. "I've been wanting to reread it, now that I'm so much older and wiser."

"I like it better than *Gatsby*. And that's one of those banana cream pie things—you use vanilla wafers for the crust." I could see how neatly she'd lined up the wafers, made a pretty pattern along the sides of the pie.

"It's a pleasure to meet you, Professor Whetstone." Butch put out his hand toward Alden, and Alden slowly put his hand into Butch's.

"Alden. Just Alden is fine."

"Alden it is, then." Butch took a deep breath and looked around our living room. "You folks sure beat us on the point system."

There weren't enough houses for everyone who needed them, and so people were assigned points based upon seniority, job criticality. Alden's status easily beat that of a security guard, and so the Jordans had to make do with temporary, inferior housing.

"I earned this place," Alden said, clearly defensive.

"Well, sure, buddy. Don't get me wrong. I take my hat off to you guys. The brains behind the operation," Butch laughed.

I could see Alden's jaw muscles tighten.

"Cocktails?" I intervened.

"A beer will do me just fine," Butch said, lowering himself onto the couch. "Belle, you help out Miss Meri and get me a bottle, all right?"

"Yes, master," Belle said, teasing. "Alden? What can I get you?"

"Meri knows what I want," he said and sat in his reading chair across from Butch. He reached for his pipe.

After dinner, it felt as though Belle and I were performing a circus act—maybe a finely timed trapeze sequence. We struggled to cover our husbands' pointed silences. Finally, Belle hit upon what she obviously thought was the perfect conversation starter.

"Meri, I've been trying to describe your crow research to Butch, but I know I haven't done it justice. Tell us about it, will you?" She plumped up one of my maroon velveteen pillows to put at Butch's feet, where she then sat.

I jostled my glass, tried to free the last quarter-inch of scotch from the maze of ice cubes. I looked at Belle, pleaded with my eyes for her to take another tack. I could feel Alden's gaze as he waited to hear what I'd say.

"I'm looking at the collective behavior of the community," I said, and sucked the rest of the liquor from my glass. "Over in Los Alamos Canyon."

"Like what?" Butch asked. He rested his hand on the nape of Belle's neck, began massaging the muscles there. Her eyes closed for a brief moment, and I looked away, not wanting to see any more of their intimacy. I'd lost track of when Alden and I had last made love.

"Nesting patterns. Whether a nest is reused, and by which birds. If and when the birds share food, in particular carrion."

"Sounds a lot like what I do," Butch laughed. "Observing the locals, checking out where they land, whether they get along. Helping the drunks get home to the right bed," he said, winking at me. I blushed.

Alden stood and stretched. "Well, folks, it's late." He upended his pipe and banged out the ash. "Call it a night," he murmured, as if to himself.

I was stunned, and Belle and I locked gazes. "We should be going anyway," she said, putting the pillow back on the couch. "C'mon, old man." She offered a hand to help Butch stand. He groaned, shook out the muscles of his legs.

"Again, so nice to meet you—Alden," he said, remembering to be less formal. Alden shook the proffered hand.

Alden turned to Belle. "I'm sure I'll be seeing you around," he said, his hands on his hips.

"I hope so." She picked up her purse. "Meri, just keep the pie—I'll get the plate when you finish." She kissed me on the cheek, and Butch gave one of my shoulders a squeeze. From the doorway, I watched him hold the car door for her, heard Alden in the bathroom behind me, the flush of the toilet. I waved good-bye and then began piling the dishes in the sink, waiting for hot water. I liked the ritual of washing dishes, the warm water, the suds. It relaxed me. I heard Alden's footsteps behind me.

"Don't do that again." His voice was cold, commanding. I focused on my chore, kept my back to him. "We have nothing in common with people like that," he continued. "For God's sake, Meri, the man's damned near illiterate, and she's only got a bachelor's degree."

Your wife only has a bachelor's degree, I thought. "She's my friend," I said.

"Then be friends with her, but leave me out of the equation. Do not foist those people on me."

"You were rude," I said, finally turning to face him, letting my wet hands drip onto the linoleum. "You made absolutely no effort. I was embarrassed."

"Me? I embarrassed you?"

"You did."

"The man has all sorts of opinions, but none of them—not one—is supported by any kind of intelligent thought. That should embarrass you, that you, of all people, should choose to surround yourself with people like that."

"He was trying to talk to you, and you froze him out."

"He had nothing of substance to contribute. Nothing whatsoever. The man bored me to tears."

"All I asked was that you be polite, that you make some effort," I said and turned to let the water out of the sink. The drain made a loud, sucking noise. "You couldn't do that one small thing. Not that one small thing," I said, my back to him.

"You are on notice, Meri. Do not repeat tonight. I will not tolerate it."

I rinsed out the dishcloth, made a point of wiping down the countertop. *Or what?*, I wondered. What would Alden do to me? How could my life possibly be any worse than it was—this punishment, this stymied life?

I WENT BACK TO the canyon and the crows. It was the only way I knew to hold on. Alden had spoken of Butch's lack of academic rigor. I didn't have that either, not in the way I wanted or that was expected of me by my fellow biologists—not without being able to band the birds, track individuals. Nevertheless, I told myself I would make do, my father's prescription always resident in the back rooms of my mind.

BY OCTOBER, THE MORNINGS began more crisply, but the afternoon sun was still strong, viable, even in the deep reaches of the canyon. I was watching more than twenty crows sun themselves. They burrowed into the soft dirt, lowering their bellies into the warm soil, and then they spread their black wings to gather the heat. They entered a state of apparent torpor, languid with the sun. They panted, beaks open. It looked as though they'd been decimated by a single lightning bolt, but the snap of a twig beneath my boot sent them all instantly upright, vigilant.

There was one crow I found easily recognizable. He had a withered right foot that hung, bent and locked at the joint, just below his belly. I was impressed with his adaptability, the way he hopped, took off, and landed without wavering. Still, he had a diminished ability to feed himself adequately, to carry heavier pieces of foodstuffs. I saw other crows occasionally attentive, feeding him.

He mated—I saw him engaging in allopreening with another crow. He edged up to the female, used his beak to pick through her feathers to remove parasites, in particular from her head, a place she could not herself reach. I saw them so engaged in the trees, on the ground. At one point, the female used a downed limb to increase her height and make grooming of the handicapped crow's head easier. They were sweet, intimate moments, and I would catch myself grinning with the joy of watching the pair cement their bond.

I thought about the trust inherent in permitting another to groom—and, in the case of crows, to permit a sharp beak to plunge beneath feathers that border vulnerable eyes. The family unit, of whatever composition, strengthens the likelihood of successful reproduction, the passing on of genetic material, of survival. But what if trust within the family disappears, if competition exceeds normal limits, creates insurmountable friction, maybe even peril? Recently, one of Butch's fellow security guards had gone home and shot his wife, then himself. That woman had trusted her husband, thought that he would sweetly groom her and feed her foodstuffs. I knew how harshly Professor Matthews would criticize my expanding tendency for anthropomorphism, my comparisons between *Corvus* and the human animal. Still, I was at last thinking, wondering. It was a good sign.

Crows mate for life, although it does not stop them from mating with others from time to time. I have observed mated pairs interacting throughout the year, not just during mating season. They call to each other softly, and although they are already paired, committed, in the spring I have seen males diving and rolling in the air above their females, still and always trying to impress, to win her over yet again. Crows do not take each other for granted.

A Murmuration of Starlings

1. *Flocks of starlings often fly in tight, cloud-like formations known as 'murmurations.'*
2. *In Celtic mythology, Branwen, who was married to the King of Ireland, taught a starling to understand speech so that it could find her brother.*

Alden was able to get us near the top of the waiting list for one of the new homes being built by Zia Company in the Western Area. The University of California continued to contract with the AEC to perform scientific work, but Zia Company took care of all of our other needs—much like the company towns associated with coal mining I'd known as a child in Pennsylvania. Zia ran the library, was responsible for street maintenance, the school payroll, and construction of the schools. We were like children—wholly cared for, our needs met, but with minimal choices.

Our new home was nicer than anyplace I'd ever lived before. It was composed of concrete block in a pseudo-adobe style, with vigas, hardwood floors, a stuccoed exterior, and a single-car carport. Belle pronounced it "entirely lovely, honey," and then schooled me on the mysteries of paste wax and the heavy buffing machines I'd have to lug from Zia's central offices to keep the hardwood floors in good shape.

What I loved best was the fact that there were two rooms with corner windows that doubled the light. I laid the Navajo rug before our first fireplace, and within a few months we bought another hand-woven Indian rug—this one eight by ten feet in a black, white, and gray geometric pattern. I took a photo of it hanging on our clothesline to send to Mother, who could not understand why I thought the rug beautiful. She came from a world where oriental carpets were the crème de la crème, and my more 'primitive' weaving was a mystery to her.

While I worked about the house, I kept the radio on for company, listened to Dinah Shore singing "Buttons and Bows," danced through my dusting with Perry Como, and dreamed of Chicago nightclubs while swaying to Kay Kayser's "Slow Boat to China."

Cornell had written officially to withdraw its offer, which in the end was no surprise to me. I suppose I had delayed the inevitable for as long as I could. Still, it was hard seeing what felt like a rejection spelled out in businesslike print. Resigned, I chose to see the new house as a fresh start, and I vowed to be a better wife, to create a new start for Alden and me. Like the crow with the withered foot, I would adapt.

"HEY, NEIGHBOR!" A WOMAN crossed the street to where I knelt in the front yard, planting white and magenta pansies in a small bed Alden had spaded for me the evening before. "I'm June, June Jacobsen," she said as she crossed the lawn. "Bob and I live across the street. Bob leads the chemistry division."

"Hi," I said, brushing dirt from my knees. "Meridian."

"You're a gardener?"

"Barely," I said, "but I saw these at the hardware store, and they looked so cheerful. I love the faces of pansies."

"My father was a botanist, so I come by it naturally."

"Maybe you can give me some tips?" I'd written to Mother, but her gardening expertise applied to Pennsylvania, not the high-altitude desert.

"Watch for late frosts, this time of year. Wait for May for more fragile plantings, to be on the safe side. And some things just don't do well in this altitude. I'm still figuring that out, but I have a logbook, and I can keep you posted, let you know what plant species simply won't work. Did you use any soil additives?" June bent and pinched the sandy soil. "The organic composition of our soil is inadequate."

"No. I didn't know."

"I have a master's in chemistry."

"Birds are what I know."

She stood and shaded her eyes with her hand. "I've got a few experiments running so I that can figure out what organic matter makes the best addition to our soil. Organic matter improves both drainage and aeration and also allows better root development. Liberal amounts of organic matter help sandy soil hold water and nutrients," June said, and I felt transported back to the classroom.

"All right then," I said, although she'd already turned back toward her house, was leaving. "Good to meet you," I added pointlessly.

THE FIRST YEAR IN our new home passed quickly. Between establishing a home and keeping up with my crow studies, I managed to keep regret at arm's length most of the time. Alden sent Mother a ticket, and in the spring of 1949 we met her at the train station in Lamy. I hadn't seen Mother in a few years—not since my graduation. Mother had been thirty-five when she had me, and she was sixty when she came to New Mexico. In my photo album she stands on the platform wearing her sensible black low-heeled pumps and a lavender cotton dress she'd stubbornly stitched by hand after her sewing machine broke. Painted on the side of the Pullman car behind her are the words RIO GRANDE VALLEY.

Other photos show her on the climb to the mesa-top site of the Tsankawi Pueblo ruins, where she walks the narrow troughs worn into the white rock by thousands of Indian footsteps. Laughing, she is wedged in between two immovable chunks of rock. How uncomplaining she was about our taking her on a hike in her dress shoes, sand and sharp pebbles sifting into them with each step.

In another photo she balances on a wooden ladder in Bandelier, the dark rectangular opening to an ancient Indian lodge framing her beautiful white hair. Her shoulders in her black wool coat are hunched, her hands grip the side rails of the ladder, and looking at that photograph now I see her fear—the fear I had not seen back then. Maybe I couldn't acknowledge that my mother could be fearful, so great was my need to siphon strength from her.

"YOU'RE SO UNHAPPY." MOTHER and I were sitting on a blanket on a green expanse of lawn outside of Fuller Lodge, near Ashley Pond. She'd made fried chicken the night before, and we enjoyed a lunch of cold chicken and her German potato salad, licking the grease from our fingers. Alden was at work, and it was the day before we were to take Mother to Lamy for her return to Pennsylvania.

"What's the matter?" she tried again, this time putting her hand about my ankle, just above my bobby sock. I saw with some surprise that the skin on the back of her hand had become thinner than I remembered, with a scattering of dark age spots.

Where to start? What to say? How much to reveal without compromising Alden, without destroying her good opinion of him?

"Are you lonely, is that it?"

"Sometimes, yes," I said, my voice surprising me when it broke. I took a deep breath. "I'm lonelier when he's home than when he's at work. I'm lonelier with him than I am without him."

She tightened her grip on my ankle. "But you have your friend Belle. I like her, even if she is a little wild. Still," she said, sighing, "I know that's not what you mean." After a couple of minutes of silence, she released my ankle and brushed crumbs from her lap. "Maybe every marriage has those quiet, lonely times. I don't know," she said. "There were times when your father and I barely spoke, when we lived largely in silence. Those times always passed."

"But Alden and I used to talk all of the time . . . it was everything to me." Then I thought for a few seconds, decided I should reassure her before she left town. "We'll get it back, Mother. I'm sure you're right. Maybe it's just one of those lulls. I just have to try harder. To be happy, I mean."

We watched children picnicking with their mother on a rectangle of bright yellow tablecloth that floated like a magic carpet on the green lawn. The girls' dresses lifted to reveal the edges of frilly white petticoats when they ran.

Mother scooted behind me, began braiding my hair into one long tail. "Remember when you wanted to go to Girl Scout camp?" she asked. "After your father died. I told you we didn't have the money."

"And you let me try; you let me earn it. Mrs. Anthony's sheets!" I said, remembering ironing the neighbor's laundry for a dime.

"You were a determined little girl," Mother said. "And then once you got to camp, you convinced them to let you stay on for a second week, as a scholarship girl."

"We'd sit around the fire at night, listening to the common nighthawks as they dived in the air above us," I smiled. "And I taught myself to swim in the giant scooped-out swimming hole. In the mornings, I'd get up before the other girls and lie in the dew to watch white-tailed deer graze in the wet grass."

"You learned you could accomplish things, if you set your mind to it."

I remembered my pond-scented skin, how camp had solidified my love for wild places.

"I don't know how to stop being angry with Alden." I looked out across the grass to the shadows where robins hunted for worms. "How do I turn it back into love?"

"Oh, boys," she sighed helplessly. I buried my head in her chest, smelled her talcum powder. I could feel her heartbeat against my forehead as I sheltered in my mother's arms.

AS A THANK-YOU FOR the visit, Mother sent me a copy of *The Perfect Hostess*, a publication of The Aluminum Cooking Utensil Company. It was a slim volume, with a purple cover featuring an orchid held fast by a pink ribbon. The table of contents included "Menus With Correct Settings," "Company Meals," "After-Sports Parties," and "Summer Frolics." There were photos of centerpieces the perfect hostess could create for a musical party, graduations, housewarmings. Along with it, she sent a letter.

June 18, 1949

Dear Daughter,

Thank you for showing me your beautiful home, your enchanting New Mexico. It is wild, and so very different from everything I've ever known. I think of you, so far from me in distance but never far from my heart.

I don't know Alden well, but I think you are well suited in many ways. He is as smart as you are. You need a man who is as smart as you are, and there can't be many of those. I know he loves you. He can give you security. He has a good job, an important job. Maybe I didn't teach you enough about how couples get along or about the necessary compromises wives must make. Love does not stay romantic. It changes. Sometimes it's even boring.

No one has all the answers, although I encourage you to go to church, talk to a pastor. Pray for guidance and patience. Don't ask Alden to give meaning to your life. Your meaning will be found in children, in making a good home, in supporting your husband. I wanted for you to have your studies, and you got that in Chicago—you also found Alden in Chicago, and I believe that was a good thing. There must be things other than birds that make you happy. Find those things.

I pray for you, Meri. You can do this.

Love, Mother

Mother's letter led me to realize something: love, the marrow of a relationship, was not something Alden and I could learn in a classroom or comprehend by reading a textbook. Neither of us was particularly well suited to deciphering the other's subtle clues, to understanding motivations and intentions. What had initially held me to Alden—his intellectual prowess—was not what would hold us together in the long term. And, given Alden's particularly inept grasp of social graces, the majority of the work would be mine to carry.

Spurred by my new determination, I decided to experiment with the lessons offered by *The Perfect Hostess*. I began with the Chinese theme from the book's "Round the World Menus." I made invitations with pretend Chinese lettering and sent them to three of Alden's fellow physicists and their wives. In Santa Fe, I found a Simplicity pattern for a belted dress with capped sleeves and a wide, pointed collar, and I bought yardage of green polka-dotted rayon. I also sewed muslin placemats and stenciled Chinese symbols in black on dinner napkins. I even dusted off the punch bowl Mrs. Hudson had given us as a wedding gift. It took me weeks to get ready. When I asked Alden for five dollars extra so that I could go to Santa Fe to find ingredients such as duck gizzard for Ap Chen and Pei Tan, or preserved eggs, he said: "Meri, I'm glad you've found a project, but let's not build the Great Wall of China." Still, he opened his wallet.

I was relieved when the day of the party arrived, because it was the only thing that finally stopped me from incessant preparations and daily improvements upon those preparations. At one point, Alden teased that he was afraid he'd come home and find me painting the walls or reupholstering the chairs, just to be sure the house was absolutely perfect. A half hour before the guests arrived, I tottered about in my new black Naturalizer heels—the ones that featured a decorative swirl of leather curling gently over each open toe. It was fun, for a change, to dress up and feel feminine. Alden emerged from the bedroom wearing his bolo tie with the turquoise and red coral stones.

"I didn't get the crease right on your khakis," I said, inspecting him.

"Let it go, Meri."

"Are you going to wear your sports coat?"

"I'll just end up taking it off."

"Well, the others will have theirs."

"All right, all right." He disappeared into the bedroom.

Georgia Sykes and her husband Gus were short, stocky—they looked like brother and sister, with bulbous eyes behind thick eyeglasses. *Well, at least they found each other*, I thought, taking Gus's jacket and admiring his plain, highly-polished silver belt buckle. I stole a look at Bernadette Lambert's thick ankles, and I thought about Belle's ankle bracelet, the one she'd bought after seeing the way Fred MacMurray looked at Barbara Stanwyck in *Double Indemnity.*

After dinner, the women gathered on the couch with their coffee while the men stood admiring Alden's new Polaroid Land Camera. I could hear Alden detailing the steps in the process, the chemicals and the magic of near-immediate photographic results. The other physicists peppered Alden with questions and posited various theories as to how the camera could be improved.

"Beverly is how old now?" Louise Hamilton asked Georgia.

"Six. Tommy's three and a half. And yours?"

"Didi's seven, if you can believe that. Donny's five. Eve is two."

Bernadette, whose cologne was a perfect, light floral scent I could not identify, chimed in with her children's ages, and then the three of them bustled off to the bedroom to grab their purses so that they could share snapshots. I sat suspended in Alden's chair, trying to look comfortable until they returned.

"Oh, Meri, you have to see," Louise said, scrunching next to me in the chair. "Isn't Didi just cute as a button? Here she is at Christmas, opening gifts from Santa."

"What a sweet little velvet dress!" I said.

"We bought it at Macy's when we were in New York. It's the most gorgeous shade of crimson. But," Louise fingered the silver pin on her blouse, a silhouette of a Hopi flute player. She raised her eyebrows to the other women, who stood around the chair looking over our shoulders, and continued, "The maid nearly ruined the dress."

"She didn't try to iron it!" Georgia said, smoothing the cotton of her sky-blue dress. Her belt was cinched too tight, and soft rolls of fat spilled over.

"She did." Louise grimaced. "And, she used spray starch. On a velvet dress!"

"Oh, no!"

"Well, what can you expect," Louise gestured with a hand. "They live in such poverty and ignorance on that pueblo."

"You have to keep a careful eye on them. My girl, Tomasita, she scorched my silk blouse."

"No!"

"How about you, Meri? Who's your maid?"

"I don't have a maid."

"But how do you manage?" Louise asked.

"She doesn't have children," Bernadette said. "But when you do—*hoo!*," she sang and patted my knee, "Look out! Before we go, I'll leave you my maid's number, just in case."

Was this how women had talked about my mother, after she'd spent the day kneeling at the edge of their tubs, scrubbing soap scum? Did they think my mother was ignorant, had to be watched every minute? And without my housework, what on earth would I do with my time?

"Come, let's sit on the couch," Georgia said, "It'll be easier to see everyone's pictures."

And so it went. Picture after picture, a competition between the women with regard to their children's developing talents, stunning displays of intellect, and charmingly naughty escapades. I honestly found the children cute, admired their beautiful young skin, their happy faces, but my smile felt frozen in place. As the exchange dragged on, I wondered why none of the women asked about my life, my interests, why they thought I should be content to serve as a rapt audience. These were intelligent women; couldn't they find more to talk about? I gave it a try after refilling everyone's coffee cups and circulating a bowl of fortune cookies.

"What do you think about the Soviet Union's test of its first nuclear weapon? *First Lightning*, I think they call it," I asked. "How do you think it might impact work at the Lab?"

They met me with blank stares. Finally, Bernadette answered a bit timidly, "More work for our husbands?"

"Bingo!" Louise said, as if declaring the winner in a game show. "But, Meri, you can't really want to discuss such dreary topics, can you? At a party?"

"I guess not," I said, cowed but not completely daunted. I'd try books, instead. "I just finished *The Naked and the Dead*. Has anyone else read it?"

"I wouldn't have the book in my house," Georgia said. "The language!"

"You mean *fug* instead of, well . . ." I said, wishing Belle were here to say *fuck* for me. Georgia was bothered by *fug*? "I was appalled by his portrayal of women," I said instead. "Rampant misogyny." I added cream to my coffee.

"That reminds me," Bernadette chimed in, "we never finished looking at photos."

We hadn't? Maybe there is nothing more interesting than one's progeny. Maybe that's what I didn't understand. I felt marooned—excluded from the men's technical discussion, marginalized when it came to something "scientific" like a newly invented photographic process—forced instead into a discussion of diapers, the pros and cons of different grade school teachers, and recipes for homemade salt clay. I didn't belong, even in my own home.

At eight o'clock, they began gracious leave-taking, reciting a need to free their respective babysitters. Alden and I stood together in the doorway, handing out jackets and waving good-bye as the couples drove away.

"You did a bang-up job, honey. I think everyone was impressed," Alden said as he emptied ashtrays. "It's good to see you making friends."

I was tired and so I didn't explain to him that those women made me want to put a gun to my head. I removed the pins from my tight French twist and let my hair fall while I ran hot water over the dishes in the sink and tried not to think about how much my new shoes hurt my feet,.

"DON'T LEAVE OUT A single detail," Belle said. "I'm dying to hear about the hoity-toity crowd."

"It was fine."

"Oh, hell, Meri. C'mon! *Dish.*"

"The food worked. Those paper lampshades I told you about? Not a single one caught fire."

"So there were no calls to the fire department. And was Alden wowed by your dress?"

"He liked it."

"OK, this is dull. Was the evening that dull?"

"Well, there was the picture show."

"Oh, lord. Not the baby photo brigade."

"Yes. With the men doing a technical sideshow, dissecting Alden's new camera. A *photographic* theme to the evening, if you will," I giggled.

"Lord."

"The kids were cute, sweet. But only for about half an hour. After that . . ,"

"Half an *hour*?"

"Maybe longer. Seemed longer." I started to laugh. "And they would not be dissuaded. I tried—believe me, I tried."

"Thank you for not inviting us."

It was the very topic I'd tried to avoid—Alden's insistence that the guest list be limited to *his* people. Belle read my face. "Sweetheart," she said, touching my forearm, "I'm serious. I was relieved not to be included. Besides, you can't afford enough alcohol to get me through one of those Lab parties." I smiled at her generosity. "And, Meri baby, you know what's next, right?"

"My next party? Maybe a Scandinavian theme this time?"

"No, sweetie. The reciprocal invitations!" Belle laughed. "Shit, Meri, you've gone and done it now!" She hooted.

Lord, I thought.

"Bone up on the cute-kid talk!"

"Lord," I reiterated.

A Pod of Meadowlarks

1. *The Western Meadowlark has a bold yellow breast and a particularly complex, melodious song.*
2. *Some associate the black crescent shape on the joyful meadowlark's breast with phases of the moon and inward journeys of self discovery.*

On New Year's Eve of 1952, Alden told me he planned to stay home. He wanted to read a bit and then go to bed at his usual 10:30 bedtime. I was twenty-eight years old and not inclined to bring in the year in such a desultory manner. Belle told me I could join her and Butch for pot roast and a New Year's toast, and so I did.

Butch sent the champagne cork flying, and at two minutes till midnight we raised our glasses and made silent wishes for the new year. I watched the two of them look at each other and felt such joy that Belle had that in her life. They turned to me, and each kissed me on the cheek.

The champagne was too sweet, and I took only a few sips before setting my glass aside, making my New Year's wish: *Let me find a purpose, a reason.* I saw Belle mouth "Now?" to Butch.

"What?" I lowered myself onto the floor, my back against a hassock. "What are you two signaling about?"

"We have some news," Belle said. She looked toward Butch, and again I saw something nearly palpable pass between them. She sat beside me, carefully setting her champagne glass on an end table. Her hair was down, loose, and tendrils of it curled along her temples. A deep blush held her cheeks. She smiled at me and reached up to hold Butch's hand where he stood beside her. "Meri, part of this might be hard for you. But I hope you'll be happy for us."

I knew. Had I known for a while? Maybe. "Oh," I said and reached to hug my friend. "You're pregnant," I whispered.

"Yes, darling." When she released me, I saw the deep, vulnerable shadows of her collarbones, and I felt a shiver go through me. Belle noticed. "Be happy for me, will you?" she said, and I could see her fear for me, for our friendship.

"Oh, I am. I am!" And I was. Thoroughly, completely, determinedly happy for her. I raised my glass: "Congratulations! And," I said, miming great solemnity, "you must make me godmother."

"No one else, sweetie. No one else."

"YOU'RE JEALOUS, IS THAT it?" Alden finished carving the roast turkey I'd made for our special New Year's Day meal.

"Of course not! She wants a baby—I'm happy for her."

"All right then." He laid his napkin across his lap. "This all looks wonderful." He touched his water glass to mine and then began ladling gravy over his meat and mashed potatoes.

While we ate, I thought about the chubby, puffed juncos I'd seen that morning hunched in the snowbroth beneath my feeders. I'd wanted to hold them in my hands, warm them, feel their softness. Maybe, I thought, we should get a puppy. I could hike with a dog.

"What do you want to achieve in 1952?" I asked, making conversation.

Ignoring my question, he added more gravy to his plate and asked: "Does it hurt you that Belle's pregnant and you're not?"

"No, it doesn't."

He replaced the gravy boat. "Should we try?"

"Oh," I said, resisting the temptation to stick out my elbows and create room for myself in what suddenly felt like a small broom closet. "Oh," I reiterated, eloquently.

"A baby would be fulfilling, give you a purpose," he said.

No, I thought—being a godmother, experiencing a child through Belle, suited me perfectly. I'd have all of the joys, none of the responsibility, and I could still live my own life. Alden reached across the table and took my hand as if he were courting me. Maybe he was.

"A child might just be the answer you need, Meri." His eyes were soft, the wrinkles of his forehead relaxed. It was one of the few times I'd ever seen him sentimental, blurry around the edges.

I searched for words that would not hurt him. "It's an awfully big commitment for such an iffy experiment," I placated.

"Just because you haven't conceived so far doesn't mean we should give up hope."

We?

"Wouldn't Darwin say it's a natural inclination?" he continued. "Is it so astounding that I'd like for my family name to live on after I'm gone? You have to admit the two of us have some pretty good genetic material. It could be a way of contributing to the world. Meri, we talked about this," he finished.

"When?" I was flabbergasted. When had we discussed having children, ensuring his legacy?

"In Chicago. Long before I left for New Mexico."

"No, we didn't."

"We did. In the café. Remember the mother with the smashed peas?"

"What I remember," I said, choosing my words carefully, "was that you mentioned your wife had a couple of miscarriages."

"Right," he said, nodding. "So I made it clear that I wanted children."

"Oh, Alden." Were we really that bad at talking with each other? "I didn't take that from our conversation—not at all." I pulled my hand back from his, closed my eyes briefly. "I'm delighted for my friend. I love Belle, and I think she will have a beautiful child, a baby I'll love as if it were my own." I hesitated and then looked him in the eye. "But I don't want my own. I don't," I said as gently as I could.

He shook his head. "Sometimes," he pushed his chair away from the table, "sometimes, Meri, I get the feeling you're just a little bit unnatural."

"*Unnatural?*" I couldn't keep anger from narrowing my eyes.

"Women want children. Your position is unnatural." He held a single index finger in the air, a Roman emperor dictating to the senate.

I stood and pulled my napkin from where static electricity had glued it to my skirt. "Don't you understand?" I asked. "I'm lost, Alden. Lost. I can't find my footing. I have no business trying to guide a child!"

"What I see but you cannot see, Meri, is that having a child would give you the direction you need. Your *footing*, as you say. Look around this house," he gestured expansively. "It is filled with half-finished projects. Your hat making. Whatever happened to that? There are boxes and boxes full of material, wooden heads, pins and God knows what else. And how many unfinished sweaters? Hmm? Yes, I can see you're floundering. That's why I am, quite reasonably, suggesting a wholly viable solution to your problem."

With an air of finality, he picked up his plate. I followed him to the kitchen and watched as he put his plate in the sink and then stood there, inert, staring at the floor's linoleum as if he could observe electrons orbiting, spinning off.

"Alden." I moved to put my arms around him, but he stuffed his fists into his pants pockets. "I don't think you understand what I mean when I say I'm lost. I don't think you've ever been lost. Not for a day, not for a moment."

"Lost? Found? Oh, hell, Meri. What's the point? I give up." He turned and walked away, and I heard his match flare as he lit his pipe in the living room. Outside the kitchen door, the sky was a deep gray, and the juncos had bedded down in the interstices of the bushes. I breathed onto the door's glass pane and pressed my palm into the moisture, thinking about the clay handprints I'd once helped the kindergarteners make for their mothers, when I volunteered at the grade school. Tiny handprints, fired in a kiln, preserved for posterity.

Children are the future. They are hope, possibility, and they let us believe in immortality and potentiality. But why couldn't I have those things without a child? How many times did Alden expect for me to bow to his pressure, accede to his inflexible wishes? I pressed my forehead to the glass and tried to cool the burning.

IN THE WAKE OF our standoff, I felt an intense need for change and so made my first-ever appointment at the beauty parlor, next to the new savings and loan. I carried with me an ad I'd torn out of a magazine in which the model wore a "twirler" dress that was cinched to a tiny circle of a waist, high necked, sleeveless, with a full skirt that had fun, oversized diamonds of pockets sewn on in contrasting material. What caught my eye, though, was the model's modern, short haircut. All but the very tops of her ears were exposed, and the top was longer, curled—reminiscent of a sultry Ava Gardner rather than the girlish pixie of Audrey Hepburn. It might not work as well with my lighter colored hair, but it was a striking haircut, and it was different.

"Well, of course, I can do that," Millie Gonzales, the beautician, said, holding the photo and looking between it and my reflection in the mirror. "Sure you're ready for such a big change?"

"Am I ever. Will it look all right on me? I have this odd ear. See?" I said, pulling my hair back from my right ear. "It's deformed, sort of folded over on itself at the top. I try to hide it." I was terribly self-conscious about my ear. Jerry had teased me about it, calling me a Darwinian throwback.

She began tugging at my hair, moving it away from my face. "No one will notice your ear. Your hair will cover the tops of your ears." She continued to fuss. "You have the features to carry it off. Such a pretty face." We both stared at my reflection. "But with your hair, you'll need a permanent wave on top—to give it body. You don't have enough natural curl."

"OK."

"And you'll have to curl the top, set it. Otherwise," she used her palms to flatten my hair, "it will just lie there."

I sat beneath the helmet of hairdryer while the chemicals worked their magic, and I picked up a copy of *Redbook* magazine with an illustration of a blonde, pony-tailed woman wearing a strapless green dress and diamonds, flourishing a cigarette in a long holder. The magazine fell open to reveal a smaller magazine secretly inserted within the pages: *True Confessions*. I looked up at the other women, wondering who might have tucked the magazine within the magazine. I scanned the stories, all of which seemed to be about women who crossed the line, paid for it, and saw the error of their ways—swearing *never again*. Dark, handsome men unbuttoned blouses, unhooked brassieres, and lifted skirts, and repentant women faced unwed pregnancies or the loss of a husband.

I closed the magazine and returned it to the pile. It made me wonder about the secret lives of these women who floated upon the scents of shampoo, peroxide, and nail polish remover. Layers of artifice atop a bedrock desire to transgress.

I stopped by Clement and Benner, the town's only department store, and I bought two pairs of clip-on earrings—one a pair of little gold-plated seahorses, the other round, mother-of-pearl buttons. At the women's foundations counter, the clerk pulled out various plastic drawers and lifted tissue paper to show me slips. I chose a pretty, knee-length white nylon slip with spaghetti straps and wide lace edging the bust. As soon as I got to the car, I put on the big, round earrings. They pinched terribly, but I liked what I saw when I examined my new self in the rearview mirror.

IN MAY I HELD a baby shower for Belle. She gave me a list of people to invite, and her younger sister came from Corpus Christi. I liked Amy immediately—she was just as vibrant as Belle, but with red-brown hair and a thicker accent. We had the usual baby shower fare: crepe paper strung across the ceiling beams, pink and blue balloons, a white cake with the image of a baby carriage drawn on top in frosting, some dreadful pink fruit punch, and those lovely little pillow-shaped, pastel-colored mints in tiny, individual paper cups, mixed with salted peanuts. Alden spent the afternoon at the library, and so we were free to be as silly, as girlish as we wanted—except that Belle and I had agreed: no stupid baby shower games.

That didn't stop the women from reminding Belle of the predictive nature of her every movement. If the ribbon came off of a package in one piece versus two or more, then the child would be a boy. Or a girl—I cannot for the life of me remember which. I do remember that Belle broke a fingernail—the room grew silent for a moment when she stuck the nail in her mouth, sucking away the pain. I got a pair of nail scissors, and when I tried to help her, I saw the nail was broken off to the quick. No wonder she'd cried out.

Amy put me in charge of keeping tally of Belle's loot: several one-piece outfits in gender-neutral tones of green and yellow, a set of very nice glass baby bottles with a dozen rubber nipples, a bottle sterilizer, crib sheets with lions and tigers and bears (Oh my!). I gave her a finely knitted, cream-colored blanket edged in colorful silk butterflies.

She held it up for everyone to see: "Look, girls! Meri made this for me!" She turned and winked at me. "Now, Meri, before you even start, I'm going to tell you to stop—do NOT. I repeat: do NOT be bashful. These women appreciate your talents." I blushed and dutifully logged in the item as "One baby blanket, with butterflies. HAND MADE BY MERI." I drew stars before and after the item and included several exclamation points for good measure.

When everyone had left, Belle and I sat on the couch sipping coffee.

"You never said if Alden liked your hair."

I touched the bare back of my neck, pulled off the eternally painful clip-on earrings and set them on the end table. "After two weeks, I finally asked him what he thought. He hadn't noticed."

"No!"

"He's oblivious to everything but the world inside his head. You know that. But once I asked him, he wanted to know if my neck got cold, without my hair." I rolled my eyes.

"Hah! Well, I like it. Shows off your lovely neck." Belle took a sip of coffee, put a hand to the bulge of her abdomen. "He kicks me. And sometimes," she laughed, "I can tell he has the hiccups."

"He?"

"Well, he or she. Today it feels like a he. Other days, she."

"You promised to tell me names."

"Oh, hell, Meri. We can't make up our minds. But there's still time."

"Then give me the names *du jour*."

"All right then. But keep in mind I don't need a critic just now, even if she is the godmother in waiting." She grinned. "Dementia. Chlamydia. Rubella." We were both laughing, but she kept at it. "Oblivion. Catharsis. Catatonia."

"Perdition. Peccadillo. Paragon. Plethora."

"*Not* Doris. *Not* Brunhilda. *Not* Simon."

"*Not* Alden."

"No, certainly not Alden. No offense to Alden, of course," she said, and we dissolved into laughter.

"I've thought of some names I like," I said, refilling our coffee cups.

"Shoot."

"Olivia. I like Olivia. It's happy."

"Not bad," she said, absent-mindedly rubbing a hand across her belly. "What else? Any boys' names?"

"Aaron."

"Too Biblical."

"Holden."

"Too Salinger."

"I give up."

"So do I," she sighed.

I could tell she was tired. I took her cup and saucer and went to find her sweater.

"The damned thing is practically useless anymore," she said, demonstrating how far it had to stretch to cross her abdomen. "You know," she picked up her purse from the table by the door, "that's what women ought to give each other at these shindigs—clothes to last the rest of the pregnancy. Now that would be practical, useful."

"Sure, but we like to give pretty things, things you'd never buy yourself."

"Oh, don't think I don't appreciate that blanket, sweetheart. You know I love it." She put her arms about my neck, smiled. "Now, take me home so I can put my fat feet up and get Butch to rub them. That man owes me."

JUNE 7, 1952, WAS a Saturday. I got home from the grocery store to find Alden pacing in the living room. His face was ashen gray, and the room was dense with cigarette smoke. He took the grocery bags from me and set them on the kitchen counter.

"Come sit down for a minute." He led me to the couch, disconcertingly solicitous.

"There's ice cream."

"The ice cream doesn't matter right now."

"Why? What's happened? Is it my mother?"

"No, your mother's fine." He sat down beside me, pressed my hand to his cheek, kissed it and then held it in both of his hands.

"You're scaring me."

"I don't mean to. I'm sorry," he sighed. "Meri, it's Belle."

"Her baby?"

"No. Well, yes, but more than that. Look," he said. He lifted our hands together and let them fall back into my lap. "Belle and Butch were headed to Santa Fe. They missed a curve on the Hill Road. Meri, my love, they're dead. The car went off the cliff. They can't even recover the bodies for a while. The rough terrain."

I didn't cry, scream, or yell. I didn't even crumple. I just sat.

"Meri?"

"Alden," I said, a simple statement of fact, without inflection. "Alden," I said again, just to see if I still had my voice.

I couldn't remember the last time he'd touched me tenderly, and I felt his touch, even through the numbing shock that so quickly took hold of my body. There must have been some part of him that liked Belle—even if only because I loved her so.

I stood and walked into the bedroom. It was a quiet, tranquil room, the single window shadowed by a rosebush that had just begun to open into deep, pink blossoms. I cranked open the window, smelled freshly cut grass, heard a house finch singing in the pyracantha bush. A tentative breeze entered the room. I sat on the side of the bed and unbuckled my sandals, laid them side by side on the rug. I lay down on our white chenille bedspread, folded my hands across my belly, and stared at the ceiling. I saw a cobweb in a corner of the room and told myself that tomorrow I'd go through the whole house, take a broom and find all of the cobwebs. It didn't matter that tomorrow was a Sunday—I'd put it on my to-do list. I heard Alden come to stand in the doorway, felt his eyes upon me.

"What can I do?"

"Nothing." I rolled onto my side, facing the wall. I didn't want him there. I didn't want anyone—other than my Belle. I'd never get up. Never again. I'd lie there, whittle away to nothing, end my life in a gray miasma of pain, of lonesomeness.

That's when the tears came, the gut-wrenching sobs—it was when I realized, when I knew in my heart, that I would be lonely for Belle for the rest of my life.

HER SISTER AMY CAME to Los Alamos and packed up everything, took the bodies to Corpus Christi for burial. Los Alamos had no cemetery. No one really believed the town would have a postwar life, that people would spend their lifetimes there, die there. I also suspect the existence of a collective, tacit understanding that the reality of death would not be dealt with—that there had been enough death associated with the place. And so, for years, the dead went somewhere else to rest in peace.

Amy brought me a cedar wood box with some of Belle's things: a handkerchief embroidered with pink rosebuds, a silver flask engraved "Belle Watling," a crow feather I'd given her, Belle's pearl studs and matching pearl necklace and bracelet, and a portrait of Belle and Butch on their wedding day. I put my nose close to the box, smelled the cedar and the musk of Belle. How long before the molecules dissipated, before I'd have only a vague memory of Belle's scent? I closed the lid carefully and stroked the smooth, polished wood.

"She saved me, you know. Six years ago," I said, fighting tears. And then, as if it mattered I added: "I don't have pierced ears."

"You know what Belle would say."

"Pierce them, goddammit, Meri."

I did. I drove to Santa Fe and got them pierced. I didn't care about my deformed ear, if I drew attention to it. I ignored the advice about keeping in place the earrings that came with the price of the piercing and instead pushed the posts of Belle's pearls through the still-bloody holes, fumbling until I got the backs on properly. And then I drove carefully up the Hill Road, never once looking over the precipice.

IN THE MONTHS THAT followed Belle's death, Alden came back to me. I saw his love where I had not seen it for years. I saw him fight the habitual impulse to disappear into a book every night and instead to try to engage me in conversation about the evening news or tales of his coworkers. He took me to dinner in Santa Fe so that I could dress up, wear my nylons, and he paid me compliments.

Belle and I had been friends for six years, and it was the closest friendship I'd ever had. In the wake of her death I felt like a part of me was missing—as if I'd lost an arm, a leg. I thought about the soldiers with their missing limbs, their phantom pain so real and yet so untreatable.

In November, five months after Belle's death, I turned twenty-nine. Before he left for work on the morning of my birthday, Alden actually donned an apron and made pancakes. In the center of the dining table he'd placed a vase of five red roses and a wrapped box. He steered me toward the couch and set the box in my lap.

"Before you open it, I need to say something." He bowed his head and took a deep breath. I noticed that his T-shirt was too tight—I would need to buy him a size larger from now on. "I have neglected you," he began. "I am truly, truly sorry, Meri."

I compressed my lips, determined to let him deliver the speech he'd no doubt practiced. Scientists such as Alden do not ad lib, they do not speak extemporaneously—they plan, refine, practice, and revise.

"I have been an unduly harsh judge of you, of your friends. No one deserved to die the way they did, as young as they were. I did not give Belle credit for her intelligence, and I did not give you credit in your choice of friends." He ran his hand through his hair, and his Masonic ring flashed in a tidbit of winter sun. "I love you, Meri. I want to do better. I want for us to do better."

He stopped. I'd been fiddling with the pale green bow on the package, half reluctant to look at him as he pleaded.

I held my left hand before me, looked at the diamond of the engagement ring we'd bought so long ago in Chicago, when both of us had such strident hopes, when I was naïve and ignorant of the work of love. In that moment, I knew that I needed to forgive him. I set the package aside and stood.

"There is no better birthday gift I could have dreamed of," I said softly, my arms about his neck. I felt the cheese-grater harshness of his as-yet unshaven cheek.

The box was surprisingly heavy for its size. I opened it without tearing the paper, folded the paper and laid it to the side to use again. I slit the taped lid with my fingernail. Resting on top of a thick layer of cotton was a card on which Alden had written:

> Every body perseveres in its state of being at rest or of moving uniformly straight forward, except insofar as it is compelled to change its state by forces impressed upon it.
>
> —Sir Isaac Newton, The First Law of Motion, from *The Principia: Mathematical Principles of Natural Philosophy.*

"I thought I was the one who was always trying to make physics into a description of human behavior." I smiled at him.

"Belle was a force of nature."

"I think she'd like the idea of moving us in a different direction, compelling us to change our state. I think she'd like that very much."

Beneath the protective layer of cotton there was a necklace, which I drew from the box and held before me.

"Oh, my. Oh, Alden." It was an ornate squash blossom necklace, with heavy silver beads and fluted squash blossom flowers. The turquoise was special, veined with black like a spiderweb. Alden must have paid over $200.00 for it. It extended well below the line of my breasts.

"How does it look over my ratty old bathrobe?"

"Perfect."

I let the fingertips of one hand hover just above the silver. "When I wear this, I will think of new beginnings," I said, reaching to cup one of his cheeks in my hand.

After he left for work, I lifted the heavy necklace from my chest and carefully laid it on top of the dresser. The necklace was too expensive. On the other side of the equation of that necklace, that promise of fresh starts, was Belle. The costly deaths of Belle and her baby.

Still, I could hear her voice telling me: "Sweetheart, give it a shot. *Try*, Meri."

WITHIN THE HOUR, I dressed in warm wool slacks and a heavy sweater. I pulled a knitted cap over my hair, being careful to keep it from snagging on Belle's earrings. I laced my boots, packed my rucksack with a Thermos of hot chocolate and graham crackers, a few cubes of cheddar cheese. I put my crow journal in the front pocket and checked to be sure I still had sharpened pencils from the last time I'd gone out, who knows how many months before.

My feet broke through a crust of snow, and the woods were a mixture of shadow and sunlight sparkling on ice crystals. I could hear chunks of snow release and drop as though relieved from the limbs of ponderosa pines. Piñon jays berated me, their dusky blue plumage contrasting beautifully with the green of the pines, the white snow. A male Steller's jay, his black head peaked with that bit of stegosaurus spike, joined the other jays in chastising me. I smiled at them, trudged onward.

I was soon out of breath. It took a great deal of energy to lift my legs out of the heavy snow, and I'd been almost completely inactive for so long. My muscles tired quickly, but in a good way, a way that let me know that tomorrow and the next day I'd feel this hike, know it had been real. I felt snow crystals sift into the back of my collar and then melt instantaneously, closed my eyes, and took a deep breath of the cold, clean winter air.

They were still there, my crows. Once they spotted me, they doubled their caws in quick succession, alerting each other to my presence. I watched their bodies: they announced ownership of the territory by flicking their tails, spreading and then retracting their tail feathers, pumping their upper bodies up and down rhythmically. I heard mates calling and responding to each other across the treetops, keeping track of each other, reassuring each other. And then I swear they recognized me and began instead scolding.

I laughed out loud, found a boulder and used my forearm to clear the snow from it. I sat, not caring that the seat of my pants would be wet for the hike home. I remembered an expression I'd heard once at the university: *colder than a well-digger's ass.* It was something Belle would have said, and it made me smile.

Over the next ten to fifteen minutes, the crows' vocalizations evolved into a mixture of soft chortling, rattles, and low growls. One sounded eerily like a gurgling baby or bleating lamb. I poured myself a cup of hot chocolate and pulled my knees to my chest.

It felt good. It felt clean. It felt clear.

I didn't want to think about Belle being dead. I wanted to think about the future, about possibilities, about potential.

I heard a steady dripping as the snow lacing the pine needles melted in the sun. I'd ask Alden to help me. I'd ask him to be my partner once more, my teacher, my helpmate.

Happy birthday to me, I thought. *Happy birthday to me.*

A Kettle of Hawks

1. *Some hawks are built for soaring, others for agility within the forest, and others, such as the falcon, for speed.*
2. *In Greek mythology, Circe, a goddess of magic known for her knowledge of potions and herbs, is associated with the hawk.*

I decided that what I needed was structure—more than the predictable bread truck on Thursdays, milkman every other day, and Saturday evenings setting my hair with torturous brush curlers held in place with pink pins. I'd make my crow observations on Mondays, Wednesdays, and Fridays; the rest of the week, I'd keep up with the housework and find more hobbies I enjoyed—maybe meet a new friend. I could teach the Girl Scouts birding, swimming, and water safety, and I considered other possibilities such as the hospital auxiliary, the library, and substitute teaching.

My next step was to involve Alden. I broached the subject one morning when he came in from shoveling the driveway. He was breathing hard, and his face and neck were an alarmingly dusky red. He sat down on the kitchen stool to pull off his galoshes, and I resisted the urge to point out how much snow and ice he was leaving to melt on the linoleum. I pulled one of his old T-shirts from the rag bag and picked up his boots, set them on a towel, wiped up the melting snow.

"Sorry," he said, still breathing hard. Alden was only forty-nine, but he lived such a sedentary life. I planned to stop buying ice cream, and no matter how much he loved it, German chocolate cake was going to have to become a near-extinct species.

"Could we try to do some new things together?" I looked for more meltwater to capture with the rag.

"Like what?"

"Things that require activity. I don't know—how about dancing lessons?"

"Uh . . ." He looked at me and stopped himself, switched gears. "Sure, sure. Be happy to. See what the Rec Center's offering, and let me know."

"If you really don't want to . . ."

"No, no. I made you a promise."

And so began what I came to think of as The Activity Years, from the 1950s through the 1960s. I lined up distractions like suitors at a fancy dress ball, picked them off one by one, tried to find at least one that would spirit me away, consume me with a full-throated passion.

Alden bought his version of a dream car, a two-door saloon version of the Morris Minor. It was exotic—black, with red leather upholstery. A tiny, ugly duckling of a car, it made Alden smile when he got behind the wheel and honked the horn playfully. I think it was the first time I'd seen him spend money in a way that approached frivolity.

Without Belle, I had no pressure to drink, no one with whom to drink, and so I gave up alcohol completely. Besides, I had to admit that it had been an incompetent solution to my problem, to wrestling with my resentful self. Los Alamos finally built a community swimming pool, and I began to swim regularly. Swimming, combined with hiking to see the crows, put me in the best physical condition of my life. I felt better—the release following exercise was a tonic.

THE UNIVERSITY WOMEN'S GROUP met in Diane Chamberlain's living room, two streets up from our house. I heard the announcement on KRSN and decided to give it a try, hoping I'd meet someone not like Belle, certainly, but a new friend, someone who could be more to me than the superficial acquaintances I'd accumulated like charms on a bracelet. I set my hair, wore a nice pair of plaid wool slacks, a cream-colored blouse, and a teal-colored wool cardigan that matched the blues in my trousers. I took a plate of chocolate chip cookies, thinking I should contribute something.

I stood on the bricks of the Chamberlains' front porch, waiting for someone to answer the doorbell and looking at the remnants of dry leaves hanging from rosebushes and children's snowflakes stenciled onto the dining room windows. Suddenly, all I wanted to do was hurry back home, skip the entire thing. *What was I thinking?* I'd never fit in here.

"Meridian Wallace?" Diane took the plate of cookies from me. "Now this is a surprise!"

I stuffed my gloves in the side pocket of my purse. "Hi, Diane."

"You're the first to arrive. Let me take your things," she said, setting the cookies on the built-in buffet beside the door. I could smell coffee and cinnamon, warm winter spices. Handel's *Messiah* played at a low volume on the turntable, the chorus voices triumphant.

"I'm early?"

"No, you're on time. You know how it is. Let me get you some coffee. Oops—there's the bell again."

Diane disappeared, and I eased my awkwardness by studying her artwork. I stood before a couple of fine watercolors, women weaving at a traditional Navajo loom, a spotted deer caught mid-leap.

"They're sweetly done, aren't they? Fairly accomplished pieces." The woman beside me had the elongated poise of a great blue heron standing in slim reeds, patiently watching for dinner to swim into view. She was all angles and spiky, sharp edges. "Emma McAllister, newcomer," she said, extending her hand.

Her eyes were hugely magnified with the kind of eyeglass lenses prescribed for post-cataract surgery patients, although she didn't look much older than my nearly thirty years. Her lips were a pencil lead's width of obligatory Revlon Red. "Newcomer to the club or Los Alamos?" I asked.

"Los Alamos. Two years. But that still qualifies me."

"I've been here since '46, just after the war."

"You're one of the originals, then."

"Not quite. Since I arrived postwar, I mean. And believe me, it's been made clear to me that I am not an original." I could almost hear a pinging, my nerves were that taut.

Her bright smile erased the austere aspects of her physicality. "Then we should stick together," she said.

The refreshment table was loaded with freshly baked rolls and chafing dishes filled with scrambled eggs, sausage, and home-fried potatoes. My mouth watered, and I piled the silver-rimmed china plate with servings of everything before I noticed that most women were eating almost nothing; their dainty plates carried only a parsimonious sampling of each item.

"You must not have to watch your waistline," a red-headed woman with a thickened waist said to me. "I envy you."

I smiled at her, found a seat next to Emma in the living room, and spread a bright blue napkin across my lap.

Callie Osbourn, president of the group, called the meeting to order and asked those of us who were first-timers to introduce ourselves. Emma said she'd attended Radcliffe; her husband Vince was the chemistry-metallurgy group leader. I saw several women nod approvingly when she indicated she'd received a Ph.D. in English literature, her focus Thomas Hardy. I gave my background at Chicago and purposefully left out my degree status—simply said I was an ornithologist, now studying crows in Los Alamos.

"Your Ph.D. is in ornithology? Is that correct?" Diane asked.

"That's my field, yes," I said.

"Your graduate degree?" Diane was taking notes. "I need it for the minutes, Meri."

"Oh," I blushed. Why had I thought this was a good idea? It only pressed harsh fingers into my bruise. "Marriage. The war," I said by way of explanation. "I wasn't able to finish my graduate studies."

"Shall I put Ph.D., all but dissertation?" Diane pressed.

My face was hot, and I felt the plate wobble on my knees. "Just a bachelor's," I said. Diane nodded curtly, made her notation, and I saw a couple of the women exchange looks.

How dare they? I thought. At least I was doing something with my degree, even if it was a watered-down version of ornithological study. What were they doing with their Ph.D.s, besides baking coffee cakes? I thought of the long-ago Welcome Wagon women with their high-altitude baking charts, the architect whose name I'd forgotten who was designing treehouses for her kids. Across the street from me, June Jacobsen with her soil studies and knitting classes—what was she doing? I felt a deep well of need for Belle, my savior and champion.

I sat and endured a report on their various charitable activities in the Valley, including clothing drives for Indian pueblos, a Valentine's Day dance the group put on every year to raise funds for library books to donate to small communities in northern New Mexico. I put an occasional hand to my cheeks, hoping my cold hands would speed the blood away from my hot skin.

As soon as possible, I pulled my navy blue car coat from the pile in Diane's guest bedroom, and I made my way to the front door, thinking only about how good a brisk walk home in melting snow would feel. I saw that my plate of cookies sat, untouched, on the buffet, and I felt like grabbing them to take back home.

At the curb, Emma caught up to me. "They're a bunch of snotty, small-town prima donnas," she said.

"The thing is, I knew better," I said. "It was entirely predictable."

"Well, I for one am not going back there. They can have their coconut cake."

"And eat it too."

"Give me a call sometime?" Emma asked.

I nodded, not sure that I would, but glad of the offer.

On the way home, I wondered how they would have treated me, had not I been married to Alden. But I knew—it would have even worse. *Maybe I should study them instead of crows*, I thought, finding my smile as I reached our street. My all-but-dissertation could be on the communal behavior of a brood of old hens.

FOR OUR FOURTEENTH WEDDING anniversary in 1958, I told Alden his gift to me could be to learn to swim. I bought him a plaid pair of swimming trunks and then set about begging, cajoling, and wheedling until he agreed to a first lesson.

I fastened the chin strap on my swim cap with the pink and purple flowers and waited for him in the shallow end, bobbing up and down to keep myself warm. He made his way gingerly down the ladder. Alden was practically blind without his eyeglasses; I thought about how vulnerable he looked and wondered how long it had been since he had tried something new, that he might not be good at. For the first time in our marriage, I was the one with the expertise and confidence.

"Hold onto the gutter if that makes you feel better." I took his hand and placed it on the slick pool tiles. Someone passed us, kicking up a spray of water. Alden winced as if acid had been thrown in his face, but he compressed his lips, stoic.

"OK," he said. "What's first?"

"Why don't we practice the flutter kick?" I took my place beside him, demonstrating how he should stretch his feet behind him. "It should come more from your hips. Don't bend your knees much at all. But don't keep your legs stiff like boards."

He gripped the gutter, straightened his arms and began kicking. The tendons of his neck were taut.

"Good! You're doing a good job, Alden!"

"A little less of the kindergarten teacher enthusiasm," he said, standing and wiping water from his face. I saw him glance at the hook where he'd hung his towel.

"No one's going to take your towel, if that's what you're worried about," I joked, and prodded him in the side with an index finger. "How about we try floating? I'll help you get onto your back." I looked to see if there were a quieter spot in the pool. "Let's go over to that corner," I said, and set off. I looked back and could see his trepidation. "C'mon, Alden. Just hold onto the gutter and walk your way over." He moved slowly, hand over hand, blinking exaggeratedly whenever water splashed him.

I helped him onto his back, kept my arm beneath his lower back as support, and told him to use his knowledge of physics to assess how to alter his body position so that he could maintain the float, adjust for the density and weight of his legs. "Archimedes," I said.

"Displacement!" I showed him that if he put his hands over his head, it would make his body take a different position in the water than if he held them out from his sides, and what a difference it made if he held even just his fingertips out of the water.

"If you can relax, you'll find it really is easy."

"Meri, I am not going to relax," he sputtered. His face was red.

I tried moving my supporting arm out from under him for a moment, and he panicked.

"What the *hell*!" He began thrashing his arms.

I took him by a shoulder and helped him stand. He immediately searched for the gutter and grabbed onto it.

"Why on *earth* would you let go of me?" His hair was plastered to his head like the fur of a scrawny, wet dog.

"Don't you trust me?" I said, teasing, and yet wondering.

"That's enough for today. That's enough."

I knew better than to object—and I could see that he'd never agree to come back and try again.

"Where's the ladder?" He was blinking, blind.

"To your right. Follow the gutter."

"You stay and swim. I'll get dressed and wait in the balcony."

"OK," I said, trying to mask my disappointment. I watched as he toweled off and put on his glasses. He wrapped the towel around his shoulders like a prayer shawl and headed for the men's locker room.

I put in a quick half mile, promising myself that I would work to remember this as a brave attempt on Alden's part. Still, I couldn't help but remember Jerry, our long-ago swim at the lagoon in Jackson Park, and his unabashed leaps from high boulders into dark waters.

I REGISTERED FOR A drawing class at the Rec Center. An artist from Santa Fe drove up twice a week to teach Drawing Figures.

The classes met in the mornings, when the children were safely tucked away in classrooms.

Anorexic Peggy Hillson dressed only in Beatnik black—black leggings, black skirt, black turtleneck, and thick-soled sandals. Her light blonde hair was cut in a pixie, and she was so thin that her knees looked like softballs balanced precariously on the batons of her lower legs. Her fingers were long and tapered, and she carried a miniature cooler filled with bottles of Coca-Cola. While we drew, I would listen for the clink of her bottle-opener against the glass, the hiss of carbonation. We started with perspective, drawing boxes. She talked about our cone of vision, setting the horizon line, and I was intrigued by the concept of a vanishing point. Peggy handed us wooden rulers and rectangles of soft, pink erasers. The hour went by quickly, and I disappeared into the paper, totally focused on my task. I immediately grew to love the process, and it was marvelous to use my brain in a different way. To *use* my brain.

Peggy looked over my shoulder. "You're doing a fine job, Mrs. Whetstone," she said. "I hope you'll continue to work at it."

"Definitely," I said and heard her stifle a little effervescent burp. She moved on to Allison Montgomery, who was erasing with such vehemence that I heard her paper tear. It made me think of Belle—she'd tear the paper, I thought, and then swear a blue streak. I pretended she was there with me, nudging me in the side, calling me teacher's pet. Someday, I wanted to be able to draw a portrait of Belle, to reproduce the contours of her face. A part of me was terrified I'd forget what she looked like, that I'd be unable to close my eyes and see her.

AS THE SIXTIES BEGAN, I continued to take art classes, my favorite being a course on drawing from nature. I started sketching my crows, depicting the communicative body language I'd previously tried to describe in words. I drew my withered-footed male and his mate, the pin feathers of his just-molted head. I drew the pair open-beaked, cawing out warnings, mobbing predators, playing tug-of-war with a stick. I drew nests with striking blue-green, brown-spotted eggs and young crows with their pale-blue eyes, before they matured to brown. I filled the margins of my crow journals with their images, and as time went by, I was surprised at how far the drawings progressed beyond my first, primitive attempts.

Withered Foot was the only individual crow I could reliably identify without a banding system. He was my link back into the science, into reliable, reportable results. Year after year, Withered Foot and his mate nested in the same section of the canyon, losing portions of their offspring to high winds, predators, and disease. I drew naked, featherless baby birds with bulbous, unseeing eyes on spindly, weak necks and watched Withered Foot and his mate care for their newborns. I drew the dead baby birds.

I drew myself in my increasingly odd but practical outfits, my denim trousers and boots, my pearl earrings and army-green ball cap. I drew myself small, nearly invisible, a tiny human speck in a grand landscape. I drew myself alone, but contentedly so, and purposeful.

THE RINGING OF THE phone woke us. It was late, after eleven. Alden put out a hand to tell me to stay put, and he made his way to the phone in the hallway. I heard his terse questions: "How did they get it?" "Oh, no," and "Oh, sweet Jesus." I turned on my reading lamp.

He returned, rubbing the furrow between his brows, his glasses slightly askew.

"It's awful, just awful." He sat on my side of the bed, his hands clenched in his lap, almost prayerful. "You know the fenced land along the new road? With the barbed wire, all of the no-trespassing signs and warnings about explosives?"

"Where they used to test rocket launchers and bazookas?"

"Right. Well, someone was there early this morning." He looked at the alarm clock. "No, yesterday morning—Saturday."

"OK."

"He took his nephew—just ten years old. They found an unexploded bazooka shell."

"Oh, God, no."

"They took it home—put it in the trunk of the car and took it home, if you can believe that."

"Oh, Alden."

"Wait—it gets worse."

I pulled up the bedcovers. It was mid-July, but I was suddenly cold.

"He gave it to his nephew and some of his nephew's friends—five kids total. They played with it, and one of the children either dropped it or hit it with a hammer—that part's not clear—but it exploded." I put my hand to my mouth. "One child was killed outright. One little boy lost both of his legs. God, Meri. Little children with a bazooka—little children with live, unexploded munitions."

Alden removed his eyeglasses, set them next to my glass of water on the nightstand. His face was ashen. His voice was a whisper, his face in his cupped hands. "This place is still killing people. Children. Babies."

"Alden," I said, taking his hands from his face. "Look at me. You know this is not your fault. You cannot make that connection—it's completely invalid."

"I've never gotten past it. I've tried." He tilted his head.

"The bomb?"

"The damage done."

"It had to be done. Even in retrospect, you know it had to be done. Alden," I said with all the firmness I could muster. "Listen to me. Hear me. Really hear me." I paused. What could I say that would give him absolution for a sin he believed he'd committed but that I would not admit was a sin on any level? "You're making a connection between the war, the bomb, Japan, and the foolhardiness of someone who should have known better. An adult who lives in this community and who could read the warning signs but who—for whatever reason—call it hubris or pomposity or just sheer negligence, call it whatever you want. My point is that what happened today—as tragic as it is—it's not your doing."

He took a deep breath, and it caught somewhere in his chest. His shoulders slumped.

I went on. "I'm not going to argue the merits of the atomic bomb tonight—not at this hour. We can do that ad infinitum at some point, if you'd like," I said, refusing to condone his train of thought by commiserating. "You're a scientist, Alden, not a philosopher. Use your science. Apply your knowledge."

He kissed me softly, and I ran my thumb beneath each of his eyes.

"I love you," he said, and then reached for his eyeglasses.

"Where are you going?"

"To make myself some warm milk."

"I'll do it for you."

"No. No, Meri, you go back to sleep. I'll probably read for a while." He left the room, closing the door softly behind him. I heard the pan when he placed it on the burner, the whoosh of the burner's flame.

I closed my eyes and saw five children in a totemic circle, taking turns ritualistically pounding on a bazooka shell. The empty sound of the metal when the hammer head hit, the percussive rhythms. A flash of light, a boom, like lightning in the forest cracking the length of a giant pine. Arms and legs and hands and bellies and faces shot full of scrolled metal shavings. I smelled burned flesh. Burned hair. I saw multicolored ribbons blown from pigtails descending softly to the ground. I saw the incinerated birds over Hiroshima.

Where could we bury all of our sorrows, our regrets, our guilty responsibilities—deserved or undeserved? How deeply could we burrow into that place of oblivion? The scent of Alden's pipe tobacco made its way to where I lay and, worn out from crying, I fell asleep breathing that calming aroma.

One of the children—the boy who lost both legs—lived in our neighborhood. Some time after the accident, I saw him first in a wheelchair and later learning to walk with crutches on two false, plastic legs. A few years later, his parents moved from Los Alamos, spiriting their son away from the nightmare, but every time I drove along that stretch of barbed wire, saw the signs that said DANGER—EXPLOSIVES, I thought of that circle of children.

IN LATE AUGUST OF that summer of 1962, Bessie, my mother's neighbor and longtime friend, found Mother lying dead, her head pillowed in a mass of full-throated, deep red peonies, her feet in their sturdy black work shoes awkwardly splayed. Mother's wet laundry lay scattered in twisted clumps beside her, and angry red insect bites covered the tender skin of her arms and neck.

Bessie and members of Mother's church helped me to make the long-distance funeral arrangements. Alden's reasons for not accompanying me were all rather vague—he needed to meet some deadline for an experiment. He did agree to drive me to Albuquerque for my flight, and once in Pittsburgh, I'd rent a car for the trip to Greensburg.

I felt a pleasant tightening at the base of my throat as we taxied down the runway, the plane gained momentum, and the wheels let go of the earth. Although I was nearly thirty-nine years old, it was my first plane ride. I enjoyed the tiny salt and pepper shakers that came with my meal, the efficiency and perfect fit of the puzzle pieces of food on the tiny plate, the cup and saucer with their red TWA logo, the crisp presentation of the fat-free stewardesses.

And then there were the clouds. It was magic to be above them, to see their uppermost contours, the way they caught the light and held it, their vast shadows moving upon the face of the earth. I wished I could open the window and know what the world sounded like at that altitude. I thought about the solitude of that world, how it must be inhabited by the voice of the wind, only. I put my head back and closed my eyes. I thought about what my crows saw as they flew above canyons and treetops, the birds-eye view of life. They would recognize specific trees, perches, and nesting sites from a completely different perspective than I could. Their maps differed from mine; they knew the topography, the contours of the landscape, on a much grander scale.

I stretched my neck muscles, kneaded them with my fingertips. Mother was gone. She had not ascended into the clouds, knocked on any pearly gates, or donned any gently curved angel's wings. She did not walk the streets of a land of milk and honey, of jeweled lampposts, and she did not dine upon airy tidbits of meringue and chocolate. I hoped she'd found her God, the God that had bolstered her when my father died. I hoped that regrets hadn't tugged at her between the time when the vessel in her brain exploded and she fell to the ground, dead.

For the remainder of my life, I would not be able to ask her questions about the things she'd done or thought, how she felt about me. I'd not be able to ask her to help me remember some childhood event, some part of our family's history. My link to the past was gone, and my link to my father and his history gone with her. I'd never had more than superficial connections with Mother's treasured Somerset County cousins, and I knew they'd fade after the funeral service, that at most we'd exchange cards once a year. I wouldn't feel the reassurance of Mother's encompassing embrace, smell her Pears soap, or unwrap her Christmas gift of homemade tea towels and dresser scarves. Without her, I wondered if centrifugal force would be powerful enough to keep me from spinning off like some errant planet, or if I would become lost in the cosmos.

IT TOOK ME NEARLY three weeks to go through Mother's home and find a realtor to sell the house. I said goodbye to the banister I'd polished as a girl, the kitchen that had held the delicious memories of stuffed cabbage and apple butter, my father's reading spot in the light of the front window, and last of all to their bedroom, which still smelled like Mother.

Alden picked me up at the airport in Albuquerque, and on the drive back to Los Alamos I related the details of those busy weeks, the complicated logistics of getting into Mother's safe deposit box, my discovery there of the booklets full of war stamps I'd sent her for safe keeping when I was in college.

"If the house is in the hands of a qualified realtor, I don't know why you're worrying," Alden said as we at last pulled into the driveway and walked to our front door.

"It's more than a house or a real estate transaction, Alden. I'm talking about my memories," I said as he unlocked the front door.

"But this is your home," he said, stepping inside.

"Of course it is. It's just that I feel as though I'm giving up my father in a more final way. Giving up Mother forever. Giving up Pennsylvania and all that it has meant to me."

"You've lived in New Mexico for over sixteen years, Meri. You're not a child anymore."

"But Pennsylvania's the place that formed me. And," I paused, feeling a fist of pain in my chest, "my mother gave me such unadulterated love. I'm losing that."

"I don't?"

"Of course you do. I didn't mean that. But a mother's love is different, irreplaceable. She comforted me. She loved me fiercely, Alden."

"I give you comfort. I love you. You have a good home, a good life."

I put set down my purse. "I'm not talking about physical things or solutions to problems like who's the best realtor and what's a reasonable sales price. I'm talking about softness, tenderness. Sometimes, all I want for you to do is to hold me. If you'd just—right now—hold me, acknowledge that I've lost my mother, that it is a significant, painful loss to me. You don't have to agree or even understand, Alden. Just listen to me when I try to talk about it. Hear me when I say that I've lost a pivotal person in my life."

"So, you want for me to hold you."

"Yes. That's it, Alden. It's really that simple."

"Before dinner?" he asked.

A COUPLE OF MONTHS after Mother's death, Emma and I drove to Santa Fe for a decadent lunch of French fries, hamburgers, and root beer floats at Bert's Burger Bowl. In the Santa Fe Book and Stationery Company we went our separate ways, but when we met up at the cash register we discovered that we'd both picked up a copy of Doris Lessing's *The Golden Notebook.*

"Synchronicity!" Emma smiled.

"Shall we read it together, meet over coffee and discuss it? What do you think?" I asked as we walked along Marcy Street back to her car.

We put our packages in the backseat, and then Emma sat behind the wheel, turned the keys in the ignition. "A book club of two?"

"No," I said, watching an elderly Indian woman who was stopping cars, holding up a handful of necklaces to sell. "Not a book club. What if we start a decent version of the University Women's Group?"

"I'm not sure I understand."

"A discussion group. Of women, for women. We'd talk about things—other than gossip. Things that interest us, inspire or nourish our minds."

Emma nodded. "And the book is our jumping-off point?"

"I think so . . . . It just came to me. I don't have all of the angles worked out." We passed the absurdly bright pink Scottish Rite Temple on Paseo de Peralta. "But definitely more than a book club. Closer to Oppenheimer's famous Berkeley discussion group—something like that."

"Good. I like that better. For a minute, I was worried."

"That we'd have to invite Diane Chamberlain to take notes and humiliate anyone who didn't measure up?" I laughed and rolled down the window so that I could smell the desert sage.

Later that night, I tried to share my excitement with Alden.

"You're starting a coffee klatch?" he asked, barely raising his eyes from the book he was reading.

"It's a discussion group for women. About women's issues, things that interest us."

"I thought all that talk about diapers and report cards and Brownie troops bored you to tears." He set his book in his lap, reached for his pipe.

"Intelligent, thoughtful discussion amongst intelligent, thoughtful women," I countered.

"A coffee klatch," he smiled, taunting me.

"Maybe you haven't heard . . ."

"What?"

"They're talking about letting us have the vote."

He smiled again and beckoned me to sit in his lap. I leaned back against his chest, took his hands in mine, and for the twelve millionth time admired their shape. They were perfectly proportioned, his fingers those of a pianist who could run through scales flawlessly.

"I'm just yanking your chain, Meri. It's a hobby of mine."

"Don't I know it."

I turned and kissed him, holding the kiss and feeling fledgling joy, possibility. It felt good to lie in his lap, to nestle there with his arms about me, contented, peaceful.

I RAN INTO EMMA on the sidewalk outside of Mesa Public Library. "I've called Barbara Malcolm, Judy Nielson, Dawn Hendricks," I said. "And let me think . . . Betty Van Hessel, Margo Whiting. I don't want for it to get too big."

"And they'll come?" Emma asked.

"When I told them it's a serious women's discussion group, that we'll discuss books, current issues, things that matter to us as women, every single one of them jumped at the opportunity. I mean it—it was wonderful to hear the enthusiasm in their voices."

"And it's wonderful to hear the enthusiasm in *your* voice. I've never heard you sound this excited. Well, with the exception of when you're talking about your crows."

"I was thinking that we could rotate through the group. Each person comes up with a topic, leads the discussion, and we meet once a month. Or maybe every six weeks." Emma nodded. "Oh, and one more thing," I added.

"What's that?"

"I am done with girdles."

Emma laughed loudly. "Meri!"

"I've had it, trying to squeeze into those things."

"You don't need one, anyway."

"For some styles, I do. But I'm not wearing them anymore. I quit."

"Anything else, oh Woman of Change?"

I tugged at the curls on the top of my head. "See these? They're going too."

"You're getting a crew cut like Alden?"

"I'm going to grow it out. I'm sick to death of permanent waves and bruising my scalp just to be beautiful."

"Well, well." Emma shaded her eyes with her hand. "What does Alden have to say about all of this?"

"He minimizes. With humor, but he minimizes."

"Then show him."

"I will."

An Exaltation of Larks

1. Literature celebrates larks' melodious, extravagant song.

2. "Exaltation," derived from the Latin exaltare, means to "raise aloft."

It was Vietnam, finally, that reminded the world of the existence of Los Alamos. With the immediate threat of World War II forgotten, Los Alamos was transfigured. It was no longer the place where extraordinary minds and talents had converged to put an end to war.

Wearing a petal-pink cotton shift, my hair grown out nearly to my shoulders, I came out of the Safeway one early summer afternoon in 1968 to stand with other housewives who were watching a parade of hippie buses traveling down Central Avenue. Scruffy kids emerged carrying signs that called Los Alamos an "atomic proving grounds." They beat drums and chanted something I couldn't make out, and then they concluded their protest beside Ashley Pond, where they lay on the grass playing wooden flutes and shaking tambourines.

They either conveniently forgot or determinedly ignored what Los Alamos had accomplished in terms of lives saved—maybe even the lives of the fathers of these self-same hippies. I didn't mind that they protested, but I did mind their overly simplistic, self-serving analysis. I minded purposeful, nearsighted ignorance.

I wondered what Belle would have had to say about it all—if she would have sat cross-legged with the kids or if she would have yelled back at the protestors, ridiculed their signs and banners.

In the end, I rather think she would have swirled the ice in her cocktail glass thoughtfully and then said: "Thank God it's not my son dying over there."

The Los Alamos antiwar protests were sporadic, but hippies and protest marches seemed omnipresent on television. As 1970 arrived, I watched the parade of young men and women, their wild, creative explosion of clothing and hair, and I wondered what it would be like to talk—really talk— with some of them. Could we have a genuine conversation? Or would they dismiss me as someone over thirty and thus irrelevant?

I WAS PERCHED ON my favorite observation post, blank pages of my crow journal before me. I watched Withered Foot's son, a crow with a patch of remarkable white flight feathers near the tip of his left wing. White Wing was trying to win a mate as he dove, circled, hovered, and soared above me. Two females perched in the uppermost boughs of separate ponderosa pines, and both were clearly interested in White Wing. This year he would inherit Withered Foot's territory and establish his family in that portion of the canyon. Although snows were rare this late in the year, they remained a possibility, and I wanted to see if young, inexperienced crows such as White Wing and his mate could outwit the variability of spring in northern New Mexico.

All at once, the crow community began cawing an alert, signaling the presence of an intruder. I closed my journal and looked about me. Across the canyon, I heard rock falling followed by a distinct, effortful grunt. I moved so that I could see through an opening in the trees, and I focused my binoculars.

A man clung to the vertical outcropping on the opposite side of the canyon. Pebbles loosened as he climbed with bare hands, bare feet. Despite the cool spring temperatures, he wore a sleeveless undershirt, and his dark blond hair, woven into a French braid, hung down the middle of his back.

The crows quieted until more rock fell, and then they again sent out their alert. I kept my breath shallow, held the binoculars steady. The climber was lean, the striations of his muscles pronounced. Over the course of about fifteen minutes, I watched him contemplate each hand- and foothold, the wisest course. At last, he boosted himself onto the top of the ridge. He turned and looked directly at me, and I self-consciously lowered the field glasses. I saw a flash of white teeth, and then he raised a hand and waved. I held up my hand, wiggled my fingertips, and blushed at having been caught.

I had not ever before been so struck by the power of a man's body, the sheer beauty of an animal in its prime. Was this what the human male's wing display looked like? Why had I never before taken it in so acutely?

I closed my eyes and felt my leg muscles twitching as if I had been the one scaling cliffs. When I opened my eyes, he was gone.

The entry in my journal bore only the date and time, nothing more: May 11, 1970, 1:15 p.m. There were no crow descriptions, and I made no sketches. I merely sat until the warm sun eased me back into my usual rhythm, until I knew my legs were again strong enough to carry me out of the canyon and safely home.

THAT NIGHT, MY SLEEP was fragmented. I tried to pretend that it was because of Alden's snoring, but I knew better. I was forty-six years old, and I'd never felt such a primal stirring in my gut. It was exhilarating. It was frightening.

The next day was a Tuesday, not one of my usual crow days, but I went back anyway. I justified it by thinking that I had to make up for the previous day's lack of observation and my need to keep on top of White Wing's mating choice.

He wasn't there. I tried to focus on White Wing, and for a few minutes at a time I managed. Still, my efforts were inconsistent, haphazard. Finally I removed my windbreaker, took off my ball cap, and tilted my face to the sun. My hair had long ago grown out, and it hung past my shoulders. Most of the time, I kept it bundled into a ponytail to avoid the insistent tangles that bred at the nape of my neck. When I ran errands downtown or walked to the library, I wore skirts, dresses—simple things. Once a year, I convinced Alden to let me splurge on a high-quality Pendleton suit, bought at a store in Santa Fe that carried a good variety of the lovely wools. But when I worked with the crows, I still wore boots, khaki or denim trousers, and a practical blouse.

I leaned back against the rough, vanilla-scented bark of a ponderosa pine and began to doze, knowing that the crows would tell me if he arrived. Minutes later, the crows and I heard him at the same time—the snap of a twig, the crunch of gravel. I turned and could see him making his way down the path to my spot. He began whistling a tune I didn't know. I heard him laugh in response to the crows' hoarse calls. I stood, self-consciously removing the rubber band from my hair and loosening it to cover my misshapen ear.

He stopped a few feet above me and smiled. He was wearing faded jeans embroidered with flowers and peace symbols, and I could see a frayed slash across one thigh. I wanted to touch the worn material of his jeans, to feel the exhausted softness in my hands. I also wanted to leap away, like a deer in flight.

"Hi," he said, simply.

"Hi," I mirrored.

He took a few careful steps toward me as if he knew I was primed to flee, and then he held out his hand. "Clay Griffin."

"Meridian Wallace. I mean Whetstone."

"Having an identity crisis?" His grip was strong. I liked that he didn't shake my hand as if I were frail or weak.

I laughed. "I don't know why I said that. It's Meridian Wallace Whetstone."

"Quite a mouthful."

"People call me Meri."

"May I sit with you for a bit? I don't want to intrude."

"No, no, it's fine." I shifted my gear to make room for him.

"So, what is it you do out here? I'm assuming the Lab security forces are onto you."

"Right," I smiled. "They spy on me, and I spy on the crows."

"You're a birdwatcher?"

"An ornithologist wannabe, is more accurate."

He slipped his arms from the straps of his backpack, and I saw him glance at my open crow journal, the columns of field notes.

"Why wannabe?"

"I never made it to graduate school."

"Looks as if that didn't stop you," he gestured toward the journal.

"Well, it's all rather informal. Less than immaculately scientific."

"Immaculate science? Really?"

"Well, I don't know." I put my ball cap back on, thinking about sunburns, my forever peeling nose in the summer. "I don't know why I used that word."

"I like it. *Immaculate*," he said, pensive. "Words are fun. I like a woman with a rich vocabulary."

I could hear the murmuring of White Wing, and I tried to see if I could tell which female he might have chosen.

"You're watching one crow in particular?"

"White Wing." I pointed. "He's in that tree. Fourth branch down."

"Is that unusual? That feather coloration?"

"Yes. And mercifully so." I felt more at ease, now that we were on a comfortable topic. "It lets me track him."

He shaded his eyes with his hand. "So what's White Wing up to?"

"Picking a mate. Well, more accurately, attracting a mate. He's got two possibilities." I pointed. "Check over there, and then go to your right two trees, and you can see the other female."

Clay followed my directions. "So, what's the determining factor? How will they choose, and what happens if both of them want him? Or if both of them reject him?"

"That's what I'm trying to figure out."

"Fun."

"To me, it is."

"That's all that matters, isn't it?"

We were quiet again.

"You draw, too?" he asked, picking up my journal. "Do you mind? I don't want to intrude." It was the second time he'd used that word, and I liked that he seemed so sensitive.

"It's all right," I said, and, surprisingly, it was. Not since Belle had I let anyone look at my journal—not even Alden, although truth be told he'd never asked.

Clay turned the pages carefully. "You're good," he said. "Really, these drawings are beautiful."

"What do you do, Clay?"

"Geology. Rocks. Layers of rocks. The formation of rocks. Upheavals. Events of seismic proportion. I'm working on the new geothermal project in the Jemez. For a few semesters, on an internship. The plan is to mine heat from the earth's crust. The rock is still hot, still retains the volcanic heat from the formative days of the earth." He fingered the loose threads that bordered the slash in his jeans, pulled one and broke it off. "Geologic time. Fascinating concept, fascinating perspective on the smallness of human history." He paused when one of the crows let out a loud series of caws, four sharp beats.

"Darwin started out as a field geologist," I said. "He used geology to get to his theory of evolution, working off of his observations and the theories of Charles Lyell—mostly about the true age of the earth."

"I remember reading something about that. Wow," he said. "I love that you know that, Meridian." He squeezed my knee and I flinched, surprised by the intimacy. He withdrew his hand and placed it next to his hip on the boulder. "But you asked about the geothermal project. The plan is to pump water into the crystalline rock, inject it to a depth where it becomes superheated. Then we'll pull it back out and extract the heat from it. It's an ecological way to generate energy."

"I didn't know. About the project, I mean."

"Well, it's not as though we hit the front page of the *Los Alamos Monitor*."

"What hits the front page of the *Monitor*, in case you haven't noticed, is hardly newsworthy. The best part is the Police Blotter. My husband reads it just to find out how old everyone is."

"Husband?"

"Husband."

"Too bad."

I was stunned. I was old enough to be his mother, surely.

"How old are you?" I asked.

"Twenty-six in just a bit."

"Oh my."

"You can't be that old."

"Oh, but I am."

"How old do you think 'old' is?"

"Forty-six."

"Geologically speaking, it's a heartbeat, Meridian."

"Really, Meri is fine."

"Meridian is too beautiful, too unusual, not to be used." He stood and picked up his knapsack. "Will you be here tomorrow?"

"I don't know." I stood; I didn't like looking up at him.

"I will be." He touched my shoulder lightly and then turned, walked the zigzag path back up the side of the canyon.

I listened to the crows bidding him good-bye, until their voices turned to soft murmurings, until I could hear the susurrant breeze as it sifted through the tops of the pines.

His eyes were blue, a light blue captured in a ring of darker, almost navy blue. He smelled of Irish Spring soap, the hair on his forearms shone gold in the sun, and I knew that if I pressed my lips to his chest I would taste salt.

I TOLD MYSELF I would not go back the next day. I felt too eager, too giddy, and it wasn't right. But more than that, I was afraid Clay would sense those things in me, perceive me as ridiculous.

I stood behind Alden as he shaved. "Do you want me to trim your eyebrows?" With age, Alden's hair follicles seemed to have gone into overdrive—his eyebrows grew wild and curly, hair sprouted from his nose and ears. Several years before, he'd given up on his mustache—he could not keep it clean, and it made it nearly impossible for him to eat ice cream cones with any semblance of grace.

"Maybe later," he said, preoccupied.

At the door, he looped the lanyard for his security pass over his neck, and I handed him his briefcase. He gave me a perfunctory peck on the cheek and climbed into the mint-green Corvair he'd bought in 1969. The Morris Minor was now my car—the first car I'd had to myself so that I could go where I wanted, when I wanted. When Alden had turned over the keys to me, he showed me that he'd put together a safety kit, including flares, a tire pressure gauge, and jumper cables. I had felt like a child going off to camp, fully loaded with both her father's fears and his blessing.

I used all of my willpower to keep myself out of the canyon. I distracted myself by standing at the M&S Market meat counter waiting for the butcher to wrap my ground chuck in nice, white waxed paper. I performed mundane household tasks, and then I drew in my crow journal. In the early afternoon, I pulled out the volume from the previous year and flipped through it until I found a drawing I'd particularly liked of Withered Foot. I used *Webster's* to prop the book open, and then I got out my watercolor paper and paints.

KRSN played "Bridge over Troubled Water" and "Raindrops Keep Falling on my Head" while I copied the drawing as a watercolor. I decided to paint Withered Foot in the topmost branches of a pine, his beak open, his neck outstretched as if calling to his mate. When I finished, I set the watercolor to dry on the windowsill in the dining room.

I pretended that the painting was intended as something other than a gift to Clay. I lied to myself for the rest of the day and throughout the evening, as Alden read *Bury My Heart at Wounded Knee* and I watched *The Carol Burnett Show*. Occasionally, Alden would look up and shake his head.

"What?" I asked, taking the bait despite my better judgment.

"I don't know why you watch that crap."

"Because it's funny."

"Really, Meri? Really?"

"Yes, Alden. *Really.*"

CLAY WAS SITTING ON my boulder.

"I thought you worked," I said, setting down my pack.

"A student intern has flexible hours. I missed you yesterday," he said, scooting over to make room for me.

"Well . . ."

"Are you scared of me, Meridian?"

"Yes." I could smell his soap again, and I sneaked a look at the tear in his jeans. I felt a burning in the center of me—pure, unadulterated lust. I was afraid my skin would betray me, and I made myself look away.

A boisterous jay emerged from beneath a scrub oak with an acorn in his beak and then flew deep into the woods.

"I have something for you," I said at last and pulled my journal from my pack. I opened it to where I'd inserted the painting. "This was Withered Foot, White Wing's father."

He followed the curve of Withered Foot's back with his fingertips. "What happened to his foot?"

"As far as I know, he was born with it, always had it."

"Hmm. Do you think," Clay paused. "Do you think it could have been a birth defect caused by radiation or chemicals?"

"I honestly don't know. I doubt radiation. But chemicals—during the war they weren't at all careful with those, didn't think anyone would ever live here, and so they just dumped a lot of it in the canyons."

"I could just be paranoid," he said. "But, I guess to take it a little further, I'd wonder about White Wing, about the aberration of white feathers. A genetic mutation?"

"It's been so long since I took genetics. Since I took anything. There must be all kinds of advances I've not kept up with."

"You seem to think you're ancient or something."

"I feel it some days," I said, laughing

"Well, Meridian, let's do something about that." He took off my ball cap and then stroked my hair lightly. "Do you mind?" he asked, keeping his hand in my hair, resting it at the nape of my neck.

"I wish I did, but I don't." I thought I heard a high-pitched humming in my ears.

Clay threaded my hair behind my misshapen ear. I put my hand up to cover it, self-conscious.

"What?"

"My ear. It's disfigured."

He removed my hand, looked carefully, and pinched the odd bump of cartilage.

"No, it isn't."

"It is."

"Who on earth told you that?" He paused. "Maybe more importantly, why did you believe them? You think you're old, you think you're disfigured. Good grief, Meridian. I have to say that's just plain stupid."

He pronounced "stupid" as "*steeeeeeeeeeeeeeeew*-ped." I laughed again and then closed my eyes, listened to a breeze moving high in the pines. Then I felt him kiss the tip of my nose like the single raindrop that comes sometimes minutes before the rest of the raindrops in a thunderstorm—that first raindrop that is an explorer.

I STAYED AWAY FOR a week. I knew I must be his perfect prey—a lonely, middle-aged woman, somehow signaling her availability, a perceived waft of pheromones. How presumptuous he was; how presumptuous I'd let him be. He was too young to be so self-assured.

I slammed about the house, broke three glasses while washing the dishes, knocked over a lamp and tore the lampshade, and bruised my arms and legs by turning too sharply and hitting walls, thudding my shins into furniture. I even managed to burn my arm while ironing Alden's shirt, so lost was I in thought.

I climbed into bed, crossed the middle line, and ran my fingers down Alden's back, kissed him between the shoulder blades.

"What?"

"I just wanted . . ." I fumbled for words. I rarely came out and asked Alden for sex, but I was filled with longing. "I want to be close to you."

"Not now, Meri." He kept his back to me and sighed. "Look. I'm exhausted." Finally, he rolled toward me, took my hand from his body and patted it twice, the Alden dismissal signal.

"I really hate it when you do that," I said.

"What?"

"The tap-tap that says 'go away, Meri.'"

"Please let's just get some sleep tonight," he said and turned his back to me once more.

I'd been rebuffed—completely. I was glad of the dark. It hid my shame.

Alden had told me before that he no longer needed sex the way I did, that he'd "gone past that," as if he'd evolved beyond me, ascended to some Dantean stratosphere of perfection. But it was more than sex that was missing, that left me aching, lonely. We'd lost the core of our relationship. Alden and I no longer reached deeply into each other, no longer strived to know and understand each other. Genuine intimacy had been supplanted by boredom, lassitude.

I got out of bed and went to sit out back in one of the metal lawn chairs. Wrapped in a blanket, I listened to the pulse of crickets, interrupted by the strident yowl of a tomcat. "You and me both, buddy," I said. "You and me both." I sat there, inert, until the sun came up.

AFTER BREAKFAST, I HEADED for the canyon. There was no sign of Clay, but I found a dark, imposing stone about the size of my fist purposefully placed on my boulder. Beneath it, wrapped in several layers of plastic wrap, was a note.

> May 23, 1970
>
> Dear Meridian,
>
> If you think I want something from you, you're right. I want to get to know you.
>
> I know you don't trust me, but I'd like to convince you that I would not ever purposefully injure you.
>
> I also know this: life is short. LIFE IS SHORT. I have seen my friends die. I have killed people, too many people. I know the smell of flesh burning, and sometimes at night I hear screams, cries. LIFE IS SHORT.
>
> Flight is possible, but we have to take flight—it has to be a decisive action, a purposeful, brave act.
>
> Clay
>
> P.S. I picked up the rock at Glencoe, in the Scottish Highlands and have carried it with me ever since—apparently so that I could give it to you. Look closely—do you see the red specks in it? The blood of your ancestors, encased in stone?

He'd killed people. I shivered despite the warm morning. I'd never known anyone who'd killed, had I? By the time Jerry had been through the war, he and I no longer spoke. Well, there was Red, Kitty's beau—but somehow for Red Guadalcanal had been another lifetime, cut off, dissected from the man he was when he returned. Then I felt my gut clench: Alden had killed—not face to face, not in person, but as much or more than any bomber pilot. Alden had killed on a massive, impersonal scale. Death achieved by theory, invention, and the calculations of esoteric formulae.

Clay wrote of screams in the night and the smell of burning flesh. He was on intimate terms with death. For reasons I couldn't articulate, that drew me to him.

And, he was right—we have to *take* flight. It's not given to us, served up on a pretty, parsley-bordered platter. We have to *take* wing. Was I brave enough to do that? Or would I be content to remain earthbound? I pulled my knees to my chest, laid my forehead on them, wrapped my arms about my legs, breathed in the darkness I'd created, and rocked myself, gently.

I thought about the bird's progression toward flight. A fledgling's plumage, the feathers of her wings and tail, are much shorter than the feathers of her parents. Although the fledgling is capable of flying, due to her inexperience she may be reluctant to try. She'll likely have difficulty with takeoffs, landings, and covering any distance. Gradually, though, her feathers continue to grow, and as she practices, she gains greater skill. Eventually, her plumage will no longer differ from that of any adult bird of her species, and she will venture farther and farther from the nest, become less dependent upon her parents for food. Finally, she rides the canyon thermals, looking down at the treetops, skimming the sharp edges of mesas.

I tore a page from the back of my journal and wrote: YES. Then I reused his plastic wrap to shelter my note and placed it beneath the solidity of Glencoe.

NEXT TO HIM ON the boulder, he had a bag of trail mix and a Thermos of coffee with nesting cups.

"Are you really that certain of yourself?" I asked.

"I'm that hopeful." He stood but stopped himself from touching me. "And it was my birthday wish. Yesterday," he said before I could ask.

"Happy birthday."

He motioned. "Join me for breakfast?"

I wore a deep, rose-colored cropped sweater that brought out the pink in my cheeks, and I'd bought new button-fly 501 jeans at the men's store. I hadn't yet washed them and could feel that they were still stiff with sizing, but I knew I looked good in them. I saw him quickly look away when he realized I'd caught him staring.

"Clay."

"Yes."

"Thank you."

"Trail mix is nothing, Meridian."

"No, I mean the note. Your words." I smiled tentatively.

"You're welcome," he said.

"I would like to know you," I said, finally joining him on the rock. "But I won't pretend that I'm not absurdly nervous about all of this." I touched the rough surface of the boulder, thought about the Indian thunderbird cut into the rock Belle and I had sat upon so long ago. The truth was, I was scared but elated, shot through with adrenaline. I felt unprecedented need. Wanton. I was guilty—guilty of betrayal I'd never suspected I had in me.

"I don't usually pursue married women."

I put my hand to a facsimile of a monarch butterfly that hovered at a flower, just over his right shin. "No, you go for girls who embroider."

"One girl. She was at New Buffalo when I was there," he ran a fingertip along the tendons that lifted across the back of my hand like carefully cultivated rows in a farmer's field.

"New Buffalo?"

"The commune. Up by Taos, at Arroyo Hondo."

"Oh."

"Now you're more scared, aren't you?"

"Well, free love and all of that. Hippies. I just—we only see hippies once or twice a year here." I paused. "They come to protest."

"So I've heard. But, Meridian, I left the commune." He touched the nape of my neck where secret curls tangled. "The communal thing doesn't work," he continued. "At least it didn't work for me." He withdrew his hand, poured coffee, and brushed hair from his forehead. "Too much time spent talking things to death, not enough doing. An idealistic concept about going back to the land—without ever once thinking that their college educations don't prepare them for working in, with, and against nature."

"And you know those things, about working in nature?"

"I spent my childhood on a ranch near Missoula. Some of these people come out of Radcliffe or Columbia or whatever, and they apply for food stamps, take handouts from the same government they reject." He let out a long sigh. "There's also always the option of getting your parents to send money, and then talking about how square they are, how obtuse. In the end, I couldn't take their brand of hypocrisy any more than I can tolerate what comes out of D.C."

I thought about dashed hopes, burst bubbles. The lure of utopia. "How long were you there?"

"Not quite six months. I got back home, after Asia, and after a few months at my parents' in Missoula, I headed for New Mexico."

"And school?"

"Initially, the University of Montana. But then I joined the Marines, made my father proud." In an instant, he was silent, staring off into the woods.

I sipped my lukewarm coffee and watched his face. All that he chose not to say was there in his eyes.

"You have one hell of a vocabulary for a ranch-fed boy," I said, trying to lighten things, bring him back.

"Don't be such an elitist," he poked my arm. "We have books, too."

"Touché," I said, smiling.

"I'm at Berkeley now. I didn't fit in as a Montana Grizzly. Not anymore."

"So were you in on those student protests, at Berkeley?"

"No. That's a hostile crowd for a guy coming back from Nam."

"Wouldn't the commune be just as bad?"

"I actually hid my service, didn't want to be branded a baby-killer." His eyes were narrowed, his jaw clenched.

"And they never caught on?"

"Nope." He pulled a necklace made of tiny green and purple seed beads from beneath his blue cotton work shirt and fingered it absentmindedly.

"That's a pretty necklace. But maybe you don't call it a necklace, for a man, I mean."

"They're love beads. The same girl who made these pants gave them to me."

"What was her name?"

"Marion."

"Another Mary."

"Hardly." He was quiet. I wondered if she had jilted him, or how that worked in a commune with free love. What did they do with jealousy and competition? Envy? What happened with all of the natural parts of the Darwinian world, of intraspecies battles for genetic propagation?

He tucked the beads back beneath his shirt collar. "Too much about me. Your turn."

And so I told him. Pennsylvania, Chicago, New Mexico in the 1940s. Crows. More crows. Hiking, horseback rides, skating. Cooking, cleaning. Volunteering. Not Belle, specifically not Belle. Not yet. And finally Alden, meeting him as an idolizing student, morphing into banality. I didn't complain about Alden or disparage him, —I'd promised myself I'd never do that, as if somehow that were a greater sin than betrayal of him with another man. What I said was that relationships die a slow, incremental death of boredom, resentment, and lassitude. When I finished, I thought surely Clay would see how sad my small life was.

"I'm sorry about your father," he said, frowning. "But I don't like the 'wee brown sparrow' bit. Same thing with calling you 'Meri'—doesn't do you justice."

"No one's ever said that to me."

"I can tell."

"What makes you think you can?"

"See?" He smiled at me.

"No, I don't see," I said, growing more defensive by the second. "And I don't see why you're mocking me."

"Because you have a backbone, even though you have convinced yourself of the contrary. You can fight."

He must have seen something in my face, because it was at that moment that he took my chin in his hand, pulled me toward him, and kissed me with an open, luscious mouth.

"Well," I said, finally pulling away.

"Well, well," he said.

"I could do that again," I laughed and quickly suppressed a vision of Alden's familiar face in concentration, his hands cupped about his pipe and the pilled gray sweater he wore in the evenings while he read.

I wanted this man. The way he made me feel. I wanted the unprecedented, relentless pull in my gut. I was tired of saying *no* to myself, of feeling forever deprived. I wanted to stop reflexively obeying all of the rules. So very many rules. I could see myself unfurling my wings, easing them open in the bright sun.

THAT EVENING, I SAT beneath the buckeye tree I'd planted in the backyard when we first moved to our home twenty-three years ago. It was now nearly twenty feet tall, with a generous spread of shadow. This time of year, it bloomed plentifully, with stacked, pinkish-yellow blossoms.

In my hand, I tilted a tumbler with gin and tonic back and forth, back and forth, like a clock's pendulum. It had been eons since I'd had a drink, eighteen years since Belle's death, but tonight I needed it. I smelled the juniper in the liquor, and a robin skipped through the branches above me. I wanted Belle's voice. I wondered if she'd try to talk me in or out of this thing with Clay.

I stayed there, drifting, until I heard Alden's car in the driveway. When I stood, I felt the impact of the booze. My limbs were loose, my back muscles had unknotted themselves. I was sufficiently numb.

I'd made meatloaf, baked potatoes, and lima beans, one of Alden's favorite vegetables. I hated lima beans passionately. For me, eating them was like swallowing dollops of paste.

"White Wing has mated," I said, passing Alden the butter for his potato. He chewed silently. "I think I'm going to name her Beacon." When he remained unresponsive, I added a fake lilting tone to my voice, "What an unusual name, Meri! Tell me more!"

He looked at me, his face set in a derisive expression.

The gin and tonic—and I was now on my second—told me to keep going. "Well, since you ask, *Beacon* came to me because I am hoping that she and White Wing will be a *beacon* for me, lead me to new insights."

He set his fork upside down on the edge of his plate, wiped his mouth, and laid his napkin beside his plate of barely touched food. "I'm so glad you've taken up drinking again. It brings out the nicest aspects of your personality, your most winning ways."

"Why thank you," I said, mimicking the accent of a Southern belle, purposefully using the sound of the ice in my glass for emphasis. "God knows, I try," I said, feeling that I had been trying to share something with him.

He calmly took his plate and carried it to the kitchen. I pursued him.

"You're not going to eat?"

He kept his back to me while he scraped his food into the trash can and said "I'm not hungry."

"Alden." I wanted for him to turn around, talk to me. I wanted to see the tension leave his back. I wanted for his shoulders to stop their progressive curving inward, like an old woman trying to keep the heat beneath her shawl.

He rinsed his hands, picked up the dish towel to dry them, and turned to face me. "How many is that?"

"Two. Just two."

"Why?"

"Why what?"

"Don't pretend stupidity. Why are you drinking?"

"Because it's spring and it sounded good."

"And now for the real reason?"

All right, he'd asked for it. "Maybe it's because otherwise I have to sit through another silent meal. That is, unless I do a song and dance and shoot off fireworks, hire a brass band to march through the room, just to try to get your attention. All I want is for you to *talk* to me, take an interest in me."

He shook his head, turned and folded the dish towel carefully, setting it on the countertop. "So," he said as he left the kitchen, "I'm to be treated to a rerun of the 'Poor Meri' show?"

I heard him close the bathroom door. Then I heard the click of the lock. We did not lock doors in our house, not against each other. Not in the twenty-six years we'd been married. Not until now.

When I came into the kitchen the following morning, Alden was reading the newspaper, his breakfast plate pushed to the side. He quickly drank two cups of coffee and then lit a cigarette. I poured myself a cup and sat with him, silently nudging the little beanbag ashtray closer to him as the ash on his cigarette grew in length. From the radio parked on top of the refrigerator, Paul Harvey reported the news, signed off with his catch phrase, "Paul Harvey . . . good day!," and then KRSN began playing its morning theme, "The Syncopated Clock." I yawned and rubbed my eyes.

He folded the paper back so that he could more easily read a story and said: "Ludicrous."

"What?"

"Princeton. They've given an honorary doctorate to that singer."

"Which singer?"

"Dylan. What's his name? Bob Dylan, that's it."

"Oh." I'd heard some of his music. While I thought his voice was awful—surprisingly awful—and he mumbled half the time, his words nonetheless drew me in. I rather thought he qualified as a poet, even if I didn't understand all of the lyrics.

"Tell me how that does not degrade those people who've actually earned Princeton degrees. Tell me that." He lowered the paper and looked at me.

"You're asking me to defend Princeton? To justify some decision Princeton made?"

"I'm trying to have a conversation with you. It's what you asked for, isn't it? So here I am. Talking."

"I see."

"Forget it, Meri. Just forget it."

"I don't want to argue with you."

"I'm not arguing. I'm trying to have a coherent conversation, to discuss a topic with you."

"No, you're not. You're arguing."

He slapped the paper onto the tabletop and stood behind his chair, resting his hands on the back of it as if it were a speaker's podium. "If you don't care, then I don't care enough to try. It's that simple." He glared at me.

"All right," I said, keeping my voice as even as possible.

"Oh, good. The kindergarten teacher's voice is back."

"What do you want from me? What?"

He struck the tabletop with his fist, and the plates and cups rattled.

I flinched but kept quiet. Anything I said would be fashioned into a weapon, taken as an insult. He wanted to be insulted.

Daring me with his eyes, he said: "So this is it? Now you're going to mope, to pout? Give me the silent treatment?"

I carried our coffee cups to the sink. He followed me, said loudly: "Don't walk away when I'm talking to you!"

I faced him, my hands on my hips. "What's the fucking point? I don't want to fight; you do. But I will NOT let you goad me into a fight!"

"Not in my house, Meri. Not in my house. You do not use that kind of language in my house."

"Your house? *Your* house, Alden?"

"Anywhere, come to think of it. No wife of mine talks like that."

"Well then, I have news for you, Professor Whetstone," I sneered. "*Your* wife, as you say, will talk any way she wants, wherever she wants." I picked up a coffee mug, raised it high, and dropped it. It didn't break but instead bounced and rolled in a wholly unsatisfying way. It disappeared beneath the serving cart where I stored electrical appliances.

I couldn't help it; I started laughing. I'd never had much of a flair for dramatic gestures.

"It's not funny," he said, his voice low, almost a growl.

I put my hand to my mouth, willed myself to stop laughing. I took a deep breath, but by then he'd turned on his heel and was headed for the door.

I stood at the front window and watched him back out of the driveway.

I walked into the bedroom and made the bed. Then I opened the closet doors and stared at Alden's side of the closet.

He kissed me on the forehead now, never on the lips. Like a pontiff or *paterfamilias*.

I walked into the closet, pulled the door shut behind me, and sat on the floor. Then I crawled deeper, pushed my head into a corner, wedged my body as far into that cave as I could. I cried until my sobs caught, my lungs stuttered.

That evening, Alden brought me a single red rose. I was in the kitchen, boiling noodles to go with a roast chicken. Safeway had a sale on French-cut green beans, so they were simmering on a back burner. The grocery store was all I had managed that day. I felt wrung out from the fight with Alden, and I hadn't the energy to face the confusion of

Clay. I hadn't even felt up to sitting with my crows. Now, I took judicious sips from a tumbler of scotch. I'd decided to allow myself just one drink, although admittedly there were several inches of liquor in the glass.

Alden laid the rose on the counter and stood beside me. I saw him glance at my scotch and refrain from comment. "I shouldn't have raised my voice," he said.

I turned and leaned against the counter. "The pounding on the table was what upset me most, I think," I said, watching his eyes. "It frightened me a little."

"I did not pound the table."

I couldn't believe he was going to deny it. "Alden, you did pound the table."

"That's not something I'd do."

It was if he'd been in an altered state, oblivious to what he'd done in his rage. I was dumbfounded.

"You may not remember it—you were pretty angry."

"I'm saying I'm sorry. Can't we leave it at that?"

I took his hand. "I'm sorry, too," I said, searching his eyes.

"Just let bygones be bygones." He pulled his hand from mine. "And don't let's talk this to death, Meri." He flicked his eyes over to my drink. "Not when you've been drinking."

"Please don't use that as an excuse. I've had a few sips, that's all."

"I don't understand why you'd start drinking again."

"Because I'm worried, distressed. About us."

And I was. I'd never suspected myself to be the kind of woman who would betray her husband—a *hussy*, my mother would have said. Still, separate and apart from my undeniable attraction to Clay, was the issue of our deflated marriage.

"Alden?"

"What?"

"Aren't you? Worried about us, I mean."

"Friction is real, inevitable, Meri. Part of the physical world, and part of relationships."

"But I want to ease that friction."

He sighed. "This is exactly what I was afraid of. That you would not let this go. I thought I apologized. I could swear I heard you accept that apology."

"I did. I do. But I want to understand why you seem so dismissive of me. Why you're so angry with me."

"Good *God*, Meri!" He shook his head. "You're relentless, you know that?"

I felt near tears. But I wasn't making any progress, and I was afraid that if I didn't give in, let this go—at least for now—then Alden would begin pounding his fist again.

I poured the noodles into a strainer, took a deep breath, and steadied my voice. "Dinner is ready, if you want to wash your hands," I said, dumping the noodles into a serving bowl and adding a hunk of butter.

"Are we finished, then?" he asked the back of me, and I could hear relief in his voice.

I thought, *Oh, that is exactly what I'm afraid of*, that we are finished. Instead, I said, "Apologies accepted, and time to move on."

He patted my back. "Good. And it all smells wonderful, Meri."

I took one final sip of my drink and set the tumbler on the countertop. It was as if Alden's reticence were a prodding hand at the small of my back, propelling me toward an affair with Clay.

I HADN'T BEEN TO see my crows for nearly a week. I felt my legs shake with nervous anticipation as I looked down from the canyon edge to the boulder, wondering if Clay would be there. He wasn't, but there was a neatly stacked pile of notes under Glencoe, all folded into the plastic wrap.

I unwrapped them carefully. They were not the personal notes I expected; they did not plead for my return or ask about my absence. They did not ask anything of me. What Clay had done, instead, was to carry on my crow observations. He'd used the same format he'd seen in my journal—date, time, weather conditions, and then he added what he was wearing, the crows' response to his presence, the crows' exchanges, their reactions to other animals or canyon events. No one had ever given me such a perfect gift.

Before I left, I wrote to him: "How grateful I am to you for your kind gesture. How overwhelmed by your thoughtfulness." I was careful not to make him any promises.

THE NEXT DAY, CLAY was back.

"Meridian." He waited for me to turn and acknowledge him. I stood, took him in. He was an animal in his prime, built for instant speed, a hunter, fluid. I walked to him, reached for him, and we held each other. He kissed the top of my head, and I heard him inhale.

"The smell of you," he said.

"What smell?" I asked with my face buried in his chest.

"You have a scent. It's better than any perfume."

We sat together on the boulder that had been mine alone for so many years. A downy woodpecker worked its way up the trunk of a tree, digging insects from the bark.

"They've built a nest." I pointed. "White Wing and Beacon."

"You named her."

"Yes."

"That's a positive step."

"What?"

"The female gets a name this go 'round."

"I'm too old for you," I said, apropos of nothing.

"That again."

"I think it needs to be said."

"And I'm old enough to make this decision without parental guidance." It was the first time I'd heard even a tinge of annoyance in his voice. I felt chastised. "Meridian, look at me, please."

I rubbed my thumb on the beginnings of two strident vertical lines between his brows.

"Give me some credit. I am not looking for a mother or a caretaker. That is most decidedly not what I want from you." When I said nothing, he continued, "I can't stop thinking about you."

I looked at him, at his clear blue eyes, and I realized that I was going to do this—be with Clay—because I wanted to be with Clay. I wanted the life in him, and I wanted to be wanted. Desired. My need for this ran deeper than I had realized. I boldly took his face in my hands and kissed him.

"Not here. Not the first time." He stood, brushed needles and decaying leaves from his jeans, and helped me stand. "Will you come to my apartment?"

I told myself this was the moment to act. To be. To be alive in a way I'd not been alive for more years than I could count.

"Yes," I said.

WHEN HE PUT THE key in the ignition of his pickup truck, he didn't press the accelerator but instead reached over and, with his palm to the back of my head, kissed me deeply. I felt heat, desire, such as I'd never felt before. A riptide of lust.

Clay lived in the Sundt Apartments north of Bathtub Row, where Oppenheimer and the other top scientists had lived during the war years. He parked in the shade of a maple tree and led me to an end apartment. I could hear scratching on the other side of the door.

"Get ready," he said.

A furious mound of black fur threw itself at his waist, and a cloud of deep barks surrounded Clay where he stood. "Come in if you can. "Down, Jasper. Down," he said, nearly wholly ineffectually.

I stepped into his living room and waited until the dog had settled before I began scratching his chest where there was a tiny patch of white hair in the shape of a heart. "Hello, sweetheart," I said.

"Jasper found me about two weeks ago." He scratched the dog between the eyes. Jasper's eyes narrowed in pleasure. "Something to drink?" he asked.

I checked my watch. "I think 10:30's too early."

"Not booze, Meridian. Something refreshing. I have sun tea."

"Sun tea?" I started to look around. "What's that?"

"You brew it using the sun's heat—not a stove."

"Sure." It must be part of the hippie thing. And I was in my first hippie home. Well, at least I thought Clay was a hippie. Was he a hippie?

Jasper followed him to the kitchen, and I toured myself around the living room: awful green shag carpeting, bookshelves made from cinder blocks and unpainted boards. A scattering of candles, and a black and white poster of a young man of leonine looks wearing terribly tight leather pants and caressing a microphone. The tip of his nose was slightly upturned, and love beads hung from his neck beneath a white silk shirt.

"Jim Morrison," Clay said, handing me a cold glass. "Do you know The Doors?"

"The Doors?"

"The rock group. Huxley's *Doors of Perception*. I'll play some for you," he said, walking toward a turntable. He squatted and started flipping through the albums that were lined up against the baseboard. "No, not Jim Morrison. Something mellower." He selected a purple album with a portrait of a woman's face gazing upward, counted and put the needle on the fifth song. There was static, simple acoustic guitar, and then a voice like a pristine silver bell filled the room. "Judy Collins." He led me to a pile of pillows, a variation of a couch.

Her voice was unspoiled, one of the purest I'd ever heard. I thought I remembered seeing her perform once, on the *Smothers Brothers Show*. I'd never done this before—sat with someone, just listening to the words of a song. I let myself sink into the pillows and was surprised at the ease of being there with him.

When the song finished, Clay stood and lifted the needle. "That song needs to stand alone," he said, "although the one before it is really great, too." And then he came back and knelt beside me.

"My body isn't what it used to be," I said. "I wish I had a better body to offer you."

"Stop."

"Then show me your bedroom," I said, feeling myself bold.

He led me to his room and closed the door behind us so that Jasper was confined to the rest of the apartment. There was a mattress on the floor with an Indian-print cotton bedspread in cream, yellow, and red paisley. An alarm clock sat on the floor next to the bed, along with a gooseneck lamp, a pile of books, and a small carved wooden box with swirls of pseudo-ivory inlay. A series of hooks with a pair of jeans and a few shirts ran in a line along one wall. I liked that his room was devoid of clutter, the accumulation of years of the superfluous. He didn't carry the weight of things.

The first thing he did was to unfasten my barrette, let loose my hair. It hung past my shoulders, straight, soft and fine. He reached beneath it, lifted it from my neck, and held my neck with one hand. He kissed me.

No one had ever used his tongue the way Clay did. I mimicked him, swallowed the sigh that he breathed into my mouth. He unbuttoned my blouse, assigned it a hook. I began to unbutton my jeans, but he grabbed my wrist and stopped me.

"Slowly," he said. "Let me show you what it's like to take forever." He laid me on the mattress and kissed the tops of my breasts above my utilitarian Playtex Living Bra. He lifted me, unhooked my bra and slid it down my arms.

"Oh," he said, and I closed my eyes. I wanted to feel all of this, to deny any visual input that might dilute things. I felt his teeth, a soft nibble that raised my nipples, set them erect. He drew a moan from deep inside me where, somehow, it had survived in the dark.

He stood and removed his clothing, and I noticed he didn't wear any underwear. Another hippie thing, I guessed.

What was I doing? I was *thinking*. I had to stop that.

We kissed again, skin to skin. I felt the heat of him, the muscles, saw the contrast between tanned and protected skin. He cupped my breasts one at a time and continued kissing and caressing me, moving down, past my waist. When he put his mouth to the center of me, pushed his tongue inside me, I sat up on my elbows, suddenly.

"No. What? What? What are you doing?" I was mortified.

"Oh, no. Meridian. No." He traveled back until he was lying with his face next to mine. "I'm so sorry," he said.

"You just caught me off guard." I knew I was blushing. God, this was horrible.

He shook his head, confused. "Please tell me . . ." He tried again: "This is new to you?"

"What you did?" I asked.

"What I'd not even begun to do."

"I don't understand."

"God. That's sad."

"What? What? Am I inferior somehow?" I started to look for my blouse. "I know I'm not like the girls nowadays."

"Stop it." He held my shoulders in a tight grip. "Meridian. Stop for a minute and listen to me."

I took a deep breath.

"It's pleasurable. It's not something to be afraid of."

"It's disgusting."

"No, it's not. *You* are not." I heard anger in his voice. "Let me show you. Trust me."

"Never trust a man who says 'trust me.'"

"This isn't a game. It's not a war of wits."

I looked at him, really looked. I touched the lines at the corners of his eyes. "Crows' feet," I said. "You have the beginnings of crows' feet, just like me." Then I took a deep breath and said: "Show me."

HE LET ME OFF on Fairway so that I could walk home. I didn't want June to see his truck dropping me off at my doorstep.

I stood in the shower, letting the warm water run over me. It was as though every pore of me was open, alive, taking in sensation. I thought of Milton and *Samson Agonistes*—how Samson despaired that eyesight was limited to the "tender ball" of the eye rather than being housed in every pore so that the world could be seen from every pore.

It had never happened to me, before Clay. Never. Never before had I experienced a climax. Sex had been fine, enjoyable, but I'd never before lost control, cried out, felt myself levitate.

Afterward, I'd cried. Not sobbing, not a bereft weeping, but instead warm rain on a summer night. I'd thrown one leg across Clay and sheltered in the hollow of his neck. I wanted to be there forever, to take up residence.

What was I going to do? *What?* I told myself to focus on the here and now. I dressed and headed for the grocery store to find something quick to make for dinner.

IN THE PRODUCE SECTION, I exchanged hellos with Doris Beecham, who was testing the ripeness of peaches, and I wondered: *Did Doris know?* She had a Ph.D. in mathematics and taught at the high school. Did her husband take her to the places I'd been that afternoon? Had she ever floated in a world of blues, from insubstantial pastel to bold cobalt?

I perused the meat display and responded appropriately—at least I think I did—to Alice Van Fleet's greeting. Her son had rejected all of his Los Alamos education and was reportedly studying to be a cobbler. A *cobbler*, in 1970. Her other son was a welder in Santa Fe. Did her sons know what Clay knew? Did Alice know what her sons knew?

I held a can of peas before me, failed to see the can, its label, or even my hand holding the can. What did Bob and June Jacobsen know and do in bed? What did June feel with Bob?

I put the can of peas in my basket and pushed the cart toward the checkout stand. It wasn't until I got home that I realized I'd bought fish. Alden hated fish.

AFTER DINNER, I SAT beneath the buckeye tree where I could drift and listen to the evening songs of robins and finches, the Mozarts of the bird world. I wasn't drinking. I knew I should feel guilty, but I didn't. I let part of myself be Alden's dutiful wife—albeit with secret misgivings—and I let the other part of myself dream, *live*.

I'd seen pink and mauve scars on Clay's lower back, his buttocks, his upper thighs. More than a dozen of them. I'd kissed a few but had not asked about them. *The war.* It had to be.

A TYPICAL CROW'S NEST contains between three and nine eggs, and crows sit the clutch for about twenty days. The time for Beacon and White Wing's young to hatch was coming soon, and I needed to go daily, to check nest activity and listen for the sound of baby birds.

I went early the next morning. I'd not slept long, but I'd slept deeply. Clay arrived quietly, but not so quietly as to escape the crows' notice. He grabbed the bill of my ball cap and whisked it from my head. "Beautiful Meridian," he said, plopping the hat back onto my head so that I had to lift it again, cram rebellious hair beneath it.

"Shall I tell you about crow sex?" I squeezed his hand. "They're like most birds—there are pregame displays and rituals."

"Like what?"

"Crouching with drooping, spread wings, vibration of the tail, up and down."

"Males or females?"

"Both—the females seem always to do it; the males are hit or miss."

"Sounds about right." He jabbed me in my ribs, and I flinched, laughed.

I felt younger. But not naïve—no longer naïve.

I continued: "They'll vocalize, before. Then," and here I looked down, blushed, "there can be screams—really loud ones—during copulation."

"Oh my," he said, mockingly shocked.

"Keep in mind that copulation lasts less than thirty seconds."

"Now that's just sad." He kissed me lightly on the lips and then reached for his backpack and pulled out a folded blanket.

Decades of needles cushioned us, although a few odd ones poked their sharp tips through the blanket. “Let me be underneath,” he said, “it’ll be easier on you.”

That position forced me to be the more active partner, and I was nervous, but intrigued. I straddled him, but before lowering myself onto him I reached down to encircle his erect penis in my fist. I squeezed, lightly but firmly, enjoyed the velvet of his skin, the purple monk’s hood.

He bucked once so that he was more fully, deeply inside me, and the crows chortled above us, seemingly contented.

“YOU’RE NEXT UP TO chair the meeting,” Emma said.

“I know.” We were headed for lunch at a tiny Española restaurant that served the best red chile. I was thinking about enchiladas versus chiles rellenos, maybe guacamole and sour cream.

“So, what’s your discussion topic?”

“Not now. I have to focus on driving,” I said, smiling.

“Oh, Meridian, please. Surely you can walk and chew gum at the same time.”

“Sex.”

“Sex!”

“Not bodice ripper stuff. I’m talking about lust, the sex drive, the part it plays in evolution, propagation of the species.”

“Well, gosh . . .”

“See what I mean? You’re my guinea pig, Emma, and if you question it, I probably shouldn’t do it.”

She was thoughtful, staring out the window at the landscape dotted with yellow rabbitbrush. “What brought this on?”

“Just thinking. About the role women’s desire plays. Men get all the press, and they pretty much control things. Well, maybe we let them think they’re controlling things. It’s complicated,” I finished, ineptly.

"Mmm hmmm."

"I'm not talking about sitting in a circle, looking at our genitals with mirrors."

"Well, thank God for that. Even Vince has only ever seen me in my slip."

I hid my surprise at the quick glimpse into the McAllister bedroom. "Honestly, Emma. I'd never suggest some kind of encounter group—or whatever you'd call it. It's not like we're not in San Francisco." We'd passed Santa Clara Pueblo and were nearing the outskirts of Española. "Maybe now is not the time," I said.

"I think that's a wise choice."

"I'll think of something else." I worked to keep disappointment from my voice.

"And I'll buy lunch," she said, compensating.

CLAY AND I HIKED to the Reservoir. In the deep shade along the dirt road, I bent often to touch soft, green moss.

Someone had gutted trout, and crows had descended upon the offal. They bickered and leaped about, played tug-of-war in a battle for fish intestines that stretched and then broke, leaving each crow to some extent the victor. I caught sight of White Wing, no doubt gathering food to take back to Beacon at their nest. I'd write it all down when I got home.

Clay was by the water, stripping off his clothes.

"You have got to be kidding," I said. "The water's freezing!"

"It's called *invigorating*. Don't be chickenshit, Meridian."

No one had ever before called me chickenshit, and I wasn't about to lose a match to Clay. With a dramatic flourish, I tossed my ball cap into a thorn bush. "Shit," I said and then pulled my T-shirt over my head. It felt good to stretch my arms high in the sun.

Clay jumped in, feet first, and let out a loud whoop. "You're right," he said, treading water and slightly out of breath. "It's fucking-ass cold in here."

I'd been unbuttoning the fly of my jeans and stopped.

"No no no no," he said. "Get in here."

"Well . . ."

"I double-dog dare you, Meridian Wallace Whetstone."

I pulled off my jeans and then, tucking my thumbs beneath the waistband of my panties, I surveyed the sides of the reservoir to be sure no one was lurking. Climbing onto the boulder from which he'd jumped, I leaped. I felt my hair lag above me as I plummeted deep into the algae-green shadows of the water. I looked up at my air bubbles as they caught the sun, became gold and mercury. I used my arms and a single, powerful scissor kick to raise myself to the surface, coming up about ten feet from him. It was my turn to whoop—a war whoop of glee.

The crows lifted off, cawing, only to return within less than a minute.

"We're disturbing them," I said, shaking water from my ear. The scent of fish hovered just above the surface. I treaded water and then flipped onto my back, felt the sun on my bare skin, heard the sound of the waves we'd made as they pulsed over and under my suspended body, rocking me.

I felt time slow to a crawl, felt myself enter the minutes, the seconds, expand into the present as if it were infinite. I saw my belly rise with each breath, watched a dragonfly speed across the surface of the water that buckled with my softly kicking feet. I sculled figure eights with my fingertips.

I liked how I was—alone, but with him, deep in the moment, sensing time and space on every possible layer—from atom to molecule to liquid. I thought I could feel the tickling eyes of fish below me as they calculated the meaning of my body's shadow above their world. I thought of the microscopic animal and plant life that was suspended in the water, just as we were.

I was younger there with Clay, in that grand accumulation of rain water, than I had ever been. Time collapsed at the same time as it expanded, and I became Clay's contemporary. His partner. His lover. I don't think I've ever been happier—before, or since.

A Deceit of Lapwings

1. *Lapwing chicks run within minutes after hatching.*
2. *Chaucer wrote of the "false lapwynge, ful of treacherye" in his poem, "Parlement of the Fowles."*

"I'll be leaving in a couple of weeks, gone for the last week of June, going into the first few days of July," Alden said.

I looked at the 1970 Sierra Club calendar that hung on the kitchen wall next to the phone. "You'll be gone the whole week?" I asked.

"The conference lasts from Monday through Friday, so yes, the whole week—including travel time."

"The Fourth of July, too? I thought we were going to Emma's for a barbecue and fireworks."

"Sorry. I fly back on the fifth."

"I don't understand why I can't go with you."

"Because it's a *scientific* conference."

I shook my head. "Do you even think before you say things like that?"

"Here we go," he sighed.

I lowered the heat on the Brussels sprouts. "You know I've always wanted to see Niagara Falls—you know that. I could do other things while you're speaking. I could see the sights on my own."

He shook his head dismissively. "This isn't negotiable."

"Why not, Alden? Why not? Give me one good reason—just one."

"Because I said so."

"That's the kind of answer you give a child."

"Well, you're acting like one."

"Fuck you, Alden."

I'd never said it out loud. His upper lip trembled, and he came at me. I'd picked up my tumbler of ice water, started to take a sip, and he struck it from my hand. The glass flew into the wall, splintered, and sent shards of glass flying.

"I cannot believe you." My jaw was tight to the point of pain.

He advanced toward me with a raised hand, this time as if to slap my face. Then I saw by his eyes that he'd stopped himself. Instead, he walked to the door, picked up his car keys, and left without a word.

I lowered myself to the floor, breathing hard. During all our years of marriage, Alden had never once raised a hand to me. Now, he'd progressed from pounding his fist on the table in a rage to hitting my hand hard enough to send glass flying.

My heart was racing. I scooted until I could lean against the wall, and I felt the back of my dress getting wet. I realized that it was the water, running down the teacup wallpaper. I needed to clean up, turn off the stove.

I knelt and started to gather the fragments of glass in the palm of my hand, and that's when it happened. I misjudged the sharpness, the length of one shard, and it sliced into my right palm. I froze, looking at my hand, seeing the shard rising from my palm like some misbegotten stalagmite. There was very little blood—the glass plugged the hole.

Then, something shifted inside of me, something I cannot explain. I contemplated that shard, the power of it, its potential—and rather than removing it carefully, I squeezed my hand about it, purposefully pushed it deeper than it could have gone on its own. I wanted the pain. I wanted a pain other than that of my heart. I wanted a pain that could be bandaged, anesthetized, and eventually healed.

The pain was burning, instantaneous, and I dropped all of the other pieces of glass I'd collected. I ran cold water over my hand. Once I pulled out the glass, there was a surprising amount of blood. I tried to assess the gash and nearly fainted when I saw the extent of what I'd done. The cut was deep, very deep.

Then, I felt a queasy sense of panic. What were the layers of skin? *Epidermis.* The lucidum—that layer showed up only in the palms of hands or soles of feet. Then what? I needed to remember. It would help to calm me, surely. Granulosum. Or was the spinosum next? Hell, I couldn't remember.

The bleeding would not stop. I wrapped my hand in the dish towel, as tightly as I could. I needed to get to the hospital, get it stitched, but I knew I was too dizzy to drive.

Hell.

June. I could call June. Or Bob.

But then they'd know. They might even already have seen Alden storm from the house.

Hell.

Clay. I wanted Clay.

I found the piece of paper he'd tucked into my wallet. The blood had already soaked through the towel, and I was getting it all over everything. My hands were shaking, and I couldn't tell if I was weak from fear, adrenaline, or blood loss. The blood flowed more quickly when I released the pressure to dial the phone.

"I need you," I said when he answered. That was it—just that.

"Where are you?"

"Home."

"You want me to come to your house?"

"Yes. Now. Fast." I was panting. I leaned against the kitchen wall. "My address is—"

"I know. I know where you live. Five minutes, Meridian. Five minutes or less."

I hung up and slid to the floor. I should stand up, get another towel, check the burners on the stove. But I didn't; I just sat there, numb. The TV was still on in the living room, and I could hear David Brinkley reading body counts. Killed. Wounded. Captured. And the competing counts for North Vietnam. Were we winning or losing today?

I cushioned my wounded hand in my lap and could feel the blood beginning to seep into my dress. It was a light linen dress, a pale celery green. Soon, I could feel the blood on my thighs, beneath the fabric.

I heard Clay's truck door slam, his footsteps as he ran up the sidewalk. He rang the bell. Jesus, he rang the bell.

"Here!" I yelled as best I could. "Clay!"

I heard him open the door. "Clay!" I said again, and I could hear him follow my voice.

He stood for a moment, taking in the situation—the smell of ham, the blood and glass. And me, faint against the wall, my hands limp in my lap, my eyes pleading, frightened.

"Baby, what the fuck?" he said and knelt. "Let me see." He looked around the kitchen. "Where are your towels?"

"Third drawer. By the stove. And the stove."

"I'll check it." I heard the click of a knob and then heard him slide open the drawer. He picked up half a dozen towels, came back and gently unwrapped the blood-soaked one.

"Tell me."

"Later," I breathed more than said. I wanted to sleep. To fall asleep. I felt my body sliding to one side, headed for the floor.

"No, Meridian." He pushed me back upright. "I have to get you up, get you to the hospital." He got the towel wrapped very tightly, and the pressure took away the pain. "Can you stand?"

I tried, but I was too weak. I wanted to sleep, still and always. Just to rest, to close my eyes.

"Baby, stay awake." He reached one arm beneath my knees, the other across my back, and I felt him lift me.

"Purse," I said.

"You don't need your purse." He got to the door, struggled to get it open wide enough to accommodate my legs, and then was down the steps of the front porch and to his truck in a surprisingly short amount of time. Next, he struggled to get the passenger door open. I knew I should help, but I couldn't. I thought about the towel and squeezed it.

"Ow!"

"Did I hurt you?"

"I hurt me." It was true, so true, and so I said it again. "I hurt me."

When he started the engine, the radio blared to life, a lilting pop song melody.

They were kind to me at the emergency room. The only painful part was the shots the doctor spaced about the wound to numb my hand so that it could be stitched closed. My hand felt puffy, bloated, as if it were no longer a part of me.

I didn't cry—not until the nurse brought me a set of scrubs to change into and I remembered Belle, all of those years ago, helping me with my clothes. That's when I cried, as softly as I could.

• • •

THE NURSE SAID MY "friend" had gone out to his truck to clean up the blood, and she offered to go get him. I thanked her, but I wanted to walk, to prove to myself that I could.

The soft island of light from his cab led me to his truck, a refuge in a sea of asphalt. They'd put my arm in a sling to keep my hand from jiggling, and it felt secure, protected, as I held it against me. For the time being, I was going to have to learn to do a number of things left handed, although the doctor said he thought there was no nerve damage.

We sat silently in the dark. I leaned against the door, exhausted. The doctor wanted to give me codeine for the pain, but I'd declined. Besides, I still rather wanted the pain. It seemed appropriate somehow, a lesson—the ramifications of which I needed to sort out, maybe over a long time. My whole arm ached, as if not just the palm but my entire limb had been traumatized. I wondered if the pain would travel farther into my body, if it would scrape out a hollow in the dirt of my heart until it made itself a bed, a dog's burrow beneath a bush.

"Did he do that to you?"

"Not really."

"Please do better than that."

I could see his profile in the muted silver glow of a distant parking lot lamp. He was angry with me. He let out an exasperated sigh. "What happened in that kitchen?"

"My side or his?"

"Why would you even ask me that?"

"Why are you angry with me?"

"Oh for God's sake, Meridian, don't be ridiculous!" He turned to face me, but I couldn't see his expression, just a halo of light behind him that lit up curly pieces of hair that had escaped his braid. "I'm not angry with you! I'm angry that you were hurt, that your husband was not there to take care of you." He paused. "I'm angry because I'm afraid for you—can't you see that?"

I waited a few seconds before responding. "We had a fight about a trip he's going on. He won't take me." I smelled antiseptic wafting from my hand.

"And so *what happened*?"

"He knocked the glass out of my hand. It broke, and I was cleaning up the pieces—that's how it happened."

"And where was he?"

"He'd left."

"That's mature."

"I think he did that rather than hit me. I think that's how he stopped himself from hurting me."

"Jesus *fucking* Christ."

I heard the siren of an approaching ambulance and then saw Clay's face awash in flashing red lights, a lurid Christmas display. It made me think of the blood that waited for me at home.

"What happens next time?"

"Next time?"

"The next time he says you've pissed him off. The next time, when he's unable to stop himself from hurting you."

"Alden would never . . ."

"You're going to defend him?"

"No. It's not that. I'm just saying he won't hurt me."

"He's escalating, and you're changing, whether you realize it or not. He sees it, and it threatens him." He gripped the steering wheel with both hands, so hard that I thought I saw the wheel flex. "A man threatened is not something to minimize. You can't close your eyes to this." He paused. "*I* can't close my eyes to this."

What could I say? I didn't believe that Alden would ever contemplate hurting me. At the same time, the Alden I'd seen wasn't contemplating anything. He wasn't thinking—he was raging, a hair's breadth away from losing control. Tonight, I'd completed his work for him. That's how efficiently, after such a long marriage, we worked in tandem.

Clay reached across the seat, picked up my left hand, and kissed the back of it. "Come home with me."

"I can't." It was reflexive—I didn't even think about it. I could not go home with Clay. "It's the wrong way."

"The right way being . . . ?"

"I don't know yet. I don't know yet, Clay."

The ambulance driver turned off his lights, submerging us in shadow once more. I just wanted to go home, get into bed, sleep, forget. I was tired of thinking. My hand hurt.

"I hate this," he said and sat for a minute, clearly struggling with whether or not to say what he said next: "I hate thinking of you lying next to him. He's a fucking bully."

"I'll ask him to sleep on the couch."

Clay let go of my hand and struck his forehead with the palm of his hand. "Perfect! That'll solve everything! Why didn't I think of that?"

"Don't be insulting."

"Don't you be naïve. Don't be purposefully blind and stupid. You're far too bright to believe a word you just said."

He started the truck, let it idle, and then said: "I'll come inside, let him know that I'm looking out for you."

"You'll only make things worse."

"Then tell me what the FUCK I'm supposed to do!" he yelled.

"Don't, please," I said. "I've had enough yelling for one night."

He sat there, shaking his head, looking down into his lap. When he turned to face me, the dashboard lights revealed his face. He was crying.

"How can I love you and take you back there? How am I supposed to reconcile those two things?"

I laid my head in his lap, moved my arm in the sling until it didn't hurt and bent my legs so that they fit on the seat. He turned off the truck engine, turned off the headlights. He bent over me, kissed the cartilage bump of my funky ear. He brushed my hair gently back from my forehead, my temples.

There was no good solution. No clear way out, no approach that would earn the Good Housekeeping Seal of Approval. *Why*, I wondered, had I even chosen to challenge Alden about Niagara Falls? Wouldn't I rather stay home, spend more time with Clay—a man who'd just told me he loved me? I'd fought Alden at the wrong time, over the wrong thing. Or maybe the fight was inevitable, the context irrelevant—as unstoppable as a rockslide that requires only the slightest amount of rainfall before it loses its grip on a hillside and tumbles.

ALDEN KNELT ON THE linoleum, the plastic bucket I used to mop floors next to him, an old bath mat cushioning his knees. He looked up at me when I stood in the entryway. Splashes of water darkened his khakis like a weak abstract painting. I sat on the kitchen stool and saw that the suds in the bucket had turned pink with my blood.

"You cut yourself on the glass," he said, matter of fact.

I didn't think his statement necessitated a response.

"How bad is it?"

"Twelve stitches."

"I wondered. It's a lot of blood," he said, surveying the kitchen. "It's on the walls, the living room carpet, just about everywhere," he said, suddenly a perturbed housekeeper.

"Sorry."

"That's not what I meant." He moved a few feet and started working on another section of the floor. "I was thinking about how hard it must be to clean up all of the evidence after a murder. The blood goes everywhere." He grunted, leaning over to reach beneath the kitchen cabinets. "It must be impossible to get it all."

"Out, out damned spot."

"I'm sorry you cut yourself," he said, and I thought about how neatly he had circumvented even a hint of his own responsibility.

As I watched him, I wondered how many times a heart can heal. Are we allotted a specific number of comebacks from heartbreak? Or is that what really kills us, in the end—not strokes or cancer or pneumonia—but instead just one too many blows to the heart? Doctors talk of "cardiac insults"—such a perfect turn of phrase—but they know nothing of the heart, not truly.

In bed, I listened to the sound of Alden emptying the pail and refilling it, to the slop and swoosh of the rag as he mopped the remainder of the floor. As I drifted off to sleep, I wondered if Alden realized my cut was more than a cut, my wound much deeper than twelve stitches could remedy. He'd failed to ask me how I managed to get to the emergency room. Did he even care?

I'D FINISHED MY SHOWER the next morning and was standing, staring out the front window, numb. I realized I should call Clay, let him know I was all right. I had looked everywhere, but I could not find the bloody slip of paper with his phone number. I doubted that in those moments of chaos I'd had the wherewithal to put it back in my wallet, but I searched there anyway, finding nothing but a few dollar bills. I looked under tables and furniture, hoping that it had somehow escaped Alden's notice. But it was gone.

I felt sick. Maybe he hadn't read it; maybe he'd simply seen the state of it, the blood, and thrown it in the trash. I opened the cupboard beneath the sink and pulled out the trash can, began digging through it with my good hand. I couldn't find it; it wasn't there.

The phone rang at close to eleven. I'd dozed off on the couch, reading Puzo's *The Godfather.*

"Good, you answered." It was Clay. "I wasn't sure about calling, but I hadn't heard from you."

"I can't find your number. I think Alden must have found it when he cleaned up."

"Well, nothin' we can do about it now. Tell me how you are. Talk to me."

"We're doing what we always do."

"Which is?"

"Ignore it and hope it goes away."

"Sounds productive."

I laughed humorlessly. "He's sixty-seven, Clay. He's not about to change. Not much, anyway, and certainly not in the realm of personal relations."

"And you find that fulfilling?"

I ignored him, rubbed my forehead with my one good hand.

"I want to see you," he said.

"I can't drive."

"Duh. Look, I'll park further up the loop, walk to your house.

"Well . . ."

"I won't stay long. I just need to lay eyes on you." His voice deepened into a broad baritone. "Let me have this, Meridian. I'll leave out the back door if I have to. I'll be your backdoor man."

I smiled. I had a backdoor man. Well.

HE CAME IN THROUGH the kitchen door and held me, gingerly.

"I'm resisting the reflexive hostess offer of a cup of coffee," I said, and sat on the kitchen stool. I don't know if Clay heard me; he was staring at the bulletin board over my shoulder, and he raised his hand, pointed.

"It's right there," he said.

I spun on the seat. In the center of the bulletin board, stabbed through the middle with a silver tack, was the bloodied chit of paper with Clay's phone number.

Clay reached to remove it, but I put my hand to stop him. "Leave it," I said.

"But why?"

"Because he wants for me to see it. If I take it down, I'm admitting something."

Clay should have known then to run, fast and far—from me, from Alden, from us. We were toxic, worse than any radioactive dump. We were sick together, so long sick together.

I told him the dates several weeks from then, when Alden would be in New York, and Clay decided to take the week off of work. He began to plan things for us to do together. He called it "Liberation Week."

"We'll go on liberty!" I shouted.

"That's the navy, Meridian. The Marines don't go on liberty."

I looked at him, standing awkwardly in my kitchen, realizing with sudden clarity how much he hated being there. Being in my home made my marriage palpable, unavoidable. I swore then that I wouldn't ever again have Clay in my home. It was as dangerous and wrong as mixing ammonia and bleach to create a wildly toxic domestic gas.

MOTHER ONCE GAVE ME a tapestry valise shaped like an oversized bowling ball bag. Within an hour of Alden's departure for the airport, I filled it with toiletries, underwear, extra socks, sandals, a thin cotton robe, the book I was reading, and a spare pair of jeans. I packed a picnic of simple cheese sandwiches and fruit—what I could easily fit in my knapsack—and then I remembered I had a frozen Pepperidge Farm cake that I could set to thaw on the seat between us while Clay drove.

While I sat on the couch waiting for Clay and watching the sun filter through the venetian blinds, I thought about Marilyn Monroe on the edge of Niagara Falls, the way she glowed in every scene, how I would forget to listen to the film's dialogue or notice anyone else, so riveted was I by her presence. Her red dress, her slow, seductive dance in the motel courtyard, Joseph Cotten grabbing her record from the turntable and smashing it.

I wanted to be near that massive, voluminous torrent rushing headlong to a death-certain plummet. I wanted to feel the cool spray of the water, to become dizzy while standing close to the edge.

When Clay pulled up in front of the house, I rushed out to meet him. He opened the truck door for me.

"After this, let me do it myself," I said. My hand no longer hurt—I just had a jagged red scar, a talisman that would remain with me for the rest of my life.

"Sure," he grinned. His teeth were so white, beautifully squared and even, like the meticulously placed stones of Incan builders. It made me wonder if some of them were false, if he'd lost his teeth in Vietnam. They were too beautiful.

He turned up the volume on the radio. "This is just out. You need to hear it. It's Neil Young. The Kent State massacre."

Massacre? It was awful, what had happened—I wouldn't argue for a moment about the incalculable shock of the National Guard killing unarmed students—but my context for "massacre" was vastly different. World War II had featured so many massacres, of proportions entirely incomparable to what had happened in Ohio. I kept my thoughts to myself and instead said: "Neil Young?"

"Crosby, Stills, Nash and Young. A group."

"Oh," I sighed.

"Don't, Meridian. Don't focus on the age thing again."

I laughed. "Are you a mind reader?"

"All I have to do is look at your face. Look," he said, checking the rearview mirror, "this is our week. *Our week.* Do not screw it up."

I saluted. "Yes, sir!"

"At ease, soldier," he said automatically, and I looked at his profile, pictured him with a short haircut, the Marines dress uniform of brass-buttoned jacket, pants with red piping running down the leg.

"Your parents must have loved you in uniform."

"Probably my father's proudest moment—me in costume."

"It's a lot more than that. Aren't you proud?" I asked.

"Of what?"

"The legacy of the Marines, being a part of that."

"That I'm proud of. The discipline. But don't ask me to be proud of what I was ordered to do."

He drove on in silence, and I was afraid to take the conversation any further.

After nearly three hours, we reached the Malpaís—bad country—outside of Grants. It was the most forbidding landscape I'd ever seen. Conquistadors searching for gold were unable to traverse it because their horses' hooves would have been lacerated on the sharp, unforgiving chunks of black lava.

"It's part of the Mount Taylor volcanic area," Clay said animatedly. "You know that's one of the biggest volcanic regions in the U.S., right?"

I saw the little boy in him—the part not lost to the war—whose early passions had framed who he would be, how he would be in the world. He was an only child like me, a loner playing in solitude in the high grasses of his parents' ranch, turning rocks in his grubby, scabbed hands, puzzling over remnants of stars embedded in mundane rock.

He stopped the truck several times so that we could get out and walk across some of the frozen, other-worldly rock formations. Hardy, adaptive plant life managed to wedge itself into dust-filled cracks in the lava, and there were bluffs where rainwater collected in shallow pools. In some of those pools, tiny fish darted about the surprisingly clear water. Darwin was omnipresent in my thoughts, the miracle of fish eggs hovering in suspended animation until merciful rainwater opened the way to a full, swimming life.

Finally, in the distance we could see an enormous sandstone bluff rising two hundred feet above the valley floor.

"El Morro. Also called Inscription Rock." Strands of his loosened hair were whipped into arabesques by the currents from our open windows. "You are going to love the calligraphy," he nearly shouted. I reached across the cab, tucked his hair behind his ear, where it rested for less than a minute before again taking flight. He grabbed my hand and bit my index finger in his enthusiasm.

"There's a deep basin at the foot of the cliff. It fills with rainwater, which is really why the rock was so popular. Beale, who was with the U.S. Army, watered camels there."

I hooted. "Camels?"

"He was testing them for the army. Is that cool?"

"Very," I said.

We picnicked beneath alligator-skinned junipers, bathed in the warm scent of decaying needles. I listened to the tiny, tinny castanet sounds of beetles, but Clay insisted he couldn't hear them. "Too many close-by explosions."

I unwrapped the sandwiches, white bread slathered with plenty of butter and heaped with thick slices of Colby cheese.

"Clearly, you are not a health nut."

"What's wrong with a cheese sandwich?"

"White bread? It's like eating cake, pure sugar."

"Oh, no it is not," I said dismissively. How could anyone compare bread with cake? I'd take cake over bread any day.

"Whole grains—that's what's healthiest for your digestive tract, for decent blood sugar levels."

"Mmm hmm." I'd been eating like this for nearly fifty years, and I was neither fat nor decrepit. "There's fruit cocktail, unless you consider that unacceptable too."

"As in Libby's? Eh gods, Meridian. That shit's packed in syrup."

"How can you have a problem with fruit?"

"It's pallid, diced, fiberless fruit. It's disgusting."

"Then don't eat it." I was picnicking with a finicky child. I tossed a crust of bread into the grass and wildflowers. A crow landed in the lower branches of a juniper a few feet away. *He knows good food when he sees it,* I thought. To Clay, I said: "Are you going to have a problem with cake, too?"

"Cake?"

"It's in the bag on the seat in the truck. Probably thawed by now," I said, my mouth full of bread.

"Oh, for fuck's sake, Meridian."

I ate my fruit cocktail in silence. In some ways I had to admit that he was right—the grapes looked pallid and slimy. Now he'd ruined fruit cocktail for me, but I wasn't going to let him know that. I choked it down, snapped the lid back onto the plastic container.

"Meridian?"

"Yes."

"I'm sorry."

"It's OK."

"No, it's not. It's not OK for me to make you feel bad about yourself."

"I don't feel bad about myself. I just am bone-tired of having men *pronounce and presume.*"

"Again, I'm sorry," he said, reaching for my hand.

"Bygones," I said and actually meant it. I knew I had a hair trigger when it came to feeling insulted, criticized. Finally, I said "So, who wants cake?" and then dissolved into laughter.

We walked toward the base of the bluff. Three crows arced through the warm air that flowed up the face of the cliffs, their echoing voices rasping and loud. We stood there, squeezing our hands together, feeling the otherworldliness of the crows as their shadows raced across the canyon walls.

WE GOT BACK TO Clay's apartment late that afternoon. Jasper gave his usual frenetic greeting, and I took him on a quick loop of the apartment grounds. When I returned, Clay was pouring tea. He touched the tip of my nose.

"Red," he said.

I put my hand over my nose. "Aw, hell," I said. "Sunburn, peeling, a couple of my more attractive traits."

"I unpacked for you." He motioned for me to have a seat on the cushion-laden floor alongside Jasper. "Are you going to tell me why you're reading *The Naked Ape*?"

"Oh," I said, suddenly embarrassed. "I thought maybe I could learn something."

"What?"

"Well, he's looking at human behavior in the evolutionary context." It was a decent dodge.

"Mmm hmmm," he said.

"Oh, all right then. I checked it out of the library so that I could read the chapter on sex."

"Jesus, no," he said, laughing and nearly spurting tea from his nose. He coughed.

"Don't make fun of me."

"I'm not." He tried to regain his composure. "But, Meridian, honestly. You're going to *The Naked Ape* for sex advice?" He wiped tears from his eyes. "I'm not laughing at you. It's just so insane, what lengths people have to go to, to learn about sex. Why not just talk about it?" When I chose to stand mute he continued, "What do you want to know? We can teach each other, help each other."

A man who wanted to talk about sex? I was mortified. But, this was Clay. After everything we'd already done together, it seemed silly that a simple conversation would be so daunting.

"I wanted to learn about oral sex. How to do it for you."

"Fellatio."

"Well, the book told me what to call it, but nothing else. Just that the human animal does it—nothing about how to do it."

"And you can't talk to your friends?"

"Women of my generation don't talk about these things." I had a fleeting vision of Belle, the exception to the rule. Then I tried to imagine inviting June Jacobsen over for coffee so that we could trade sex tips.

He finished his tea and stood. "I already had something in mind for tonight, and now that I see what you're thinking, it might help. Are you game?"

"I need more information than that."

"That's fair," he said, opening the refrigerator and holding up the pitcher to see if I wanted more tea. I shook my head.

He returned to sit by me, patting Jasper on the head. "I make a great spaghetti sauce."

I waited, wondering what on earth spaghetti had to do with fellatio techniques. Was it the sucking in of strands of pasta?

"I made two versions. One has pot, one just has oregano."

There it was—the drug thing.

"You've never tried it, right?" He wiped the condensation from his glass onto his jeans.

I looked around the room, mimicking nervousness. "Assuming the Lab does not have your apartment bugged, I can tell you this: Alden and I smoke marijuana every night. Usually during *The Johnny Carson Show*." I giggled. It really was a fun scene to imagine.

"Didn't know Alden stayed up that late."

"Hah! But what does this have to do with oral sex?"

"It will loosen you up, let you feel more. Well, more accurately, I think, it will make you aware of the things you ignore, the sensations—all of them—that you bypass every minute of every day."

"I thought it just made people stupid."

"Depends on the person," he said. "And, Meridian, you can never be made stupid. Never."

"All right then. Let's have the super-oregano spaghetti."

"Bravo, baby. Bravo." He squeezed my shoulders, and then he adopted a serious countenance: "But do this one thing for me."

"What?"

"Return Desmond Morris to the library."

THE SPAGHETTI SAUCE WAS good, although I could still taste something slightly off. Clay told me that as far as disguising the taste of marijuana went, his sauce was as good as anything else he'd discovered. I took his word for it—it seemed to be a topic he knew thoroughly.

After we ate, he took me on a musical tour of his albums: The Doors, Joni Mitchell, Bob Dylan. I liked Janis Joplin best; I had not ever before heard a woman's voice so freely express heartbreak and keen devotion.

I kept waiting to feel different. Maybe I was immune to the drug's effects.

"Just be patient," he said, and when the sun was nearly down he led me onto his meager front stoop to sit beside him in the cool air. Robins in the treetops bid each other goodnight while Clay swatted at invisible mosquitoes and Jasper chased grasshoppers that ricocheted away from him across the lawn.

A few minutes later, I felt my face grow slack, as though my jaw muscles just let go. I leaned back on my elbows, felt an ache in my lower back and an overwhelming desire to stretch every portion of my body, to release each joint. I was smiling—an unbidden, easy, summertime smile. I thought of Joplin's rendition of "Summertime," the yearning in it, how her voice itself took flight when she sang about spreading wings, taking to the sky.

And then I felt my mind shift, lift. I closed my eyes, rose above the ground, left behind the robins, the treetops. I could feel a wind in my face, my hair blown back, and I drifted slowly over rooftops, headed for a canyon edge, where I thought I might find a thermal to ride.

"Not at this time of night, you won't."

It was Clay's voice. Was he responding to my thoughts? I'd not spoken out loud, had I? I opened my eyes and turned to the indistinct, twilight Clay who sat beside me.

"I was talking out loud?"

"You were." He traced my lips with the tip of his tongue. "The grass hit you."

Jasper gave a great sigh and lay at my feet. His tranquility passed into me by osmosis, from his skin and fur across and through the membrane of my skin. I wanted to curl up beside him, to sleep beneath the stars, awaken beneath the canopy of a tree, to feel dew slide from my brow.

Clay was massaging my neck. I leaned into his hand, moaned. So this was what being stoned felt like. Long strings of thoughts. Had I been thinking for a long time or a short time? Did time grow under the influence of marijuana?

"Meridian," Clay whispered, so close that I could feel his voice cause the tiny hairs in my inner ears to vibrate. I tried to remember how sound made its way into the human ear, how it was translated by the brain.

I'd again gone off on some obscure pathway of thought. Where were the mile markers, the directional signs?

"Let's go to bed," he said, helping me to stand. "You are gone," he said. "Gone."

I held my scarred palm close to my face, stretched the hand open and closed.

"Does it hurt?" he asked.

"I don't know." I laughed. "I can't decide."

"Cool," he said, and we went inside, closed the door to the world, and turned off the lights.

I don't possess adequate words to describe the majority of that night, what happened to me, how I felt—except to say that each minute sensation ran along the nerve fibers to my brain in a more direct, potent way than ever before, that I registered and took in every sensation. Fellatio, an act that in concept had disgusted me, turned out to be a joy. It was a joy to give, to taste and smell, to listen and to sense which of my experiments were met with the most enthusiasm, pleasure.

The boundaries that had defined me for four decades dissolved. I began to believe I could be anyone. Anyone.

It was my choice.

I TOOK IN THE MAIL and the newspaper, smelling some mustiness in my home, seeing a patina of dust on everything. I'd been gone less than twenty-four hours—hardly enough time to make the place seem unlived in, abandoned. It felt that way, though.

Maybe no one had lived there for a very, very long time.

Alden considered long-distance telephone charges unendurable, and so I knew he wouldn't call while he was in New York. The only thing I had to watch out for was neighbors—nosy, ever-watchful neighbors named June.

I stopped by the library and returned *The Naked Ape*, wishing Desmond Morris well. Then I stood in front of the bank of card catalogs and stared at the petite wood drawers with their brass pulls and hand-lettered alphabets.

Clay had asked me something in bed the night before—he wanted to know if I'd ever climaxed by masturbating. I knew he'd been trying to hide his surprise, that it was something he'd clearly been thinking about since I told him that the orgasm he'd given me had been my first. I wanted to know if I were the freak I'd begun to think I might be. Men masturbated—I'm not sure how I knew that, but I did. But women?

I knew there was a report on human sexual behavior, a scientific report that was based on interviews with men and women, the first compilation of human sexual behavior. It was there, a tickle in my brain's storage system; I just had to access that memory. The author's name began with a "K"—that much I remembered, and so I thumbed through the cards as quickly as possible. Finally, I had it: Kinsey's

Sexual Behavior in the Human Female, published in 1953. These women were my peers; surely I could learn from them. I found a well-thumbed copy, the edges of the pages grimy with dirt. That made me smile—I could see the Los Alamos scientists with their heads down, eyes averted, claiming it was job-related research.

In the shadows of bookshelves, hidden away from prying eyes, I found what I was after: sixty-two percent of women reported that they masturbated. So, I was in the minority—the sad thirty-some percent.

But not anymore.

NEXT TO HIS STOVE lurked a bowl containing an ominous dark brown liquid and pale, beige cubes of some unidentifiable matter.

"This is dinner?"

"Tofu. I'm marinating it in soy sauce."

"What?"

"Tofu. It's bean curd, or coagulated soy milk."

"You can't afford meat? I could have brought some steak or chicken."

"I'm a vegetarian, Meridian. I don't eat meat."

I stood there, flummoxed. Now I was involved with a *vegetarian* hippie.

"Don't take it personally, OK? Don't get offended," he said.

"I'm not. I'm just thinking. But I don't see how you can get enough protein. Fish? Will you eat fish?"

"Nothing with a face."

"Oh." This was getting awfully complicated, this dietary thing with Clay.

"Aw, Meridian, stop it. Try something new."

"This looks miles from palatable." I poked a finger into one of the mushy cubes. "You put up with this, Jasper?" I asked, grinning.

"Let's smoke a number before dinner," he said, moving toward his bedroom. He returned with the carved wooden box, set it on the counter, and pulled out a miniature wooden pipe. He unrolled a plastic baggie and used his fingertips to gather a small amount of pot that he then tapped lightly into the bowl of the pipe.

"You don't worry about your neighbors, that they can smell it?"

"Frankly, my dear, I don't give a flying fuck what other people think."

I laughed. "That's a new one."

"What is?"

"Flying fuck."

"Well, then you'll really like this one. *Why don't you take a flying fuck at a rolling doughnut?*"

"Oh, my," I said, laughing.

Clay laughed, too, and let out a burst of smoke. "Let me light it for you—it's basically a one- or two-hit bowl."

I had no idea what he was talking about, but I followed his lead. The smoke instantly burned my throat.

"Try to keep the smoke in as long as possible. You'll get higher, faster. Remember, there's no filter. It's hotter than cigarettes," he said, ever helpful. I imagined him teaching a roomful of Lab scientists the finer points of getting high, and that only made me laugh and then cough harder. "You're off and running," he said.

"Lord," I said, trying to catch my breath. "Tell me, my love, when do we eat this absolutely scrumptious banquet you've prepared?" And then I laughed so hard that I was afraid I'd lose my balance. I moved to the cushions, watched Clay knock the ash from the pipe and reload it.

We laughed without reason or reference. We laughed until our faces hurt, until we had to work cramps out of our jaw muscles, until the tears ran, until our sides hurt. I don't think I'd ever really played, even as a child. It had always seemed to me that smart people didn't play, and they certainly never nearly peed their pants with uncontrollable laughter while seated next to a vegetarian hippie veteran who instigated wholesale abandon.

I AWOKE WHEN I FELT the mattress moving. I rolled over, attempted to go back to sleep, and then Clay began kicking, waving his arms. It progressed to shouting, yelling, and then he awoke on his own.

He was eel-slick with sweat, breathing hard, and I could feel the rapid beat of his pulse where my hand circled his wrist. He switched on the bedside lamp and leaned against the wall.

"You had a nightmare."

"Yeah." His breath was shallow but slowing quickly.

"Do you want to tell me about it?"

"Do you want to hear about it?"

"Of course I do."

"Don't be so sure." He used the hem of the sheet to wipe the sweat from his face.

"Water?" I asked, tossing back the covers and pulling his T-shirt over my head.

I took one of the tall glasses from the dish rack and filled it at the sink. A full moon silvered the yard and trees. I nearly tripped over Jasper's water bowl when I turned to go back into the bedroom.

"Where's Jasper?" I asked before I spotted him cowering in a corner of Clay's bedroom. "Oh," I said.

"He's not used to it."

"How could anyone get used to that?"

"I was that loud?"

"You were that frantic," I said, handing him the water glass. He drained it. "More?"

"Yeah." He rubbed his forehead. "Meridian?"

"Yes."

"I'm sorry."

"Don't be." I returned to the kitchen sink and let the water run longer this time, hoping it would be cooler, buying myself some time. I could feel that my heart rate was rapid, too. Grains of sand stuck to my bare feet as I walked across the wood floor.

I handed Clay the water and sat cross-legged at the foot of his bed, watching him. He drained the glass and set it on the floor beside the mattress.

"Come back here," he said, patting the mattress next to him.

"Not yet." I shook my head. I wanted to see his face clearly, and that would be impossible if I were next to him in bed. And then I waited, which is easy, in concept. In practice, it's difficult to resist the impulse to fill silence, to let the person you love off of the hook, to let them be.

It was then, while I waited and before he told me his story, that I first knew I loved Clay, truly loved him. Not as a boy, a man, a lover, but as a person—another person struggling in life's paisley swirl of ugliness and blinding beauty. When he reached a big toe to touch my folded legs I took his foot in both of my hands and held it, looked him in the eye.

"I'm strong enough to hear this. Don't protect me any longer." I began rubbing the arch of his foot. "I want all of you. ALL of you, Clay. Good, bad, ugly, sad, black, gray, boring, funny, loving, angry. All of you." I kept my distance, did not go to him to comfort or hold him. Had I done so, the story would not have emerged; he could have kept it inviolable.

"It's pretty much the same every time," he said. "Fuck."

"What happens?"

A couple of minutes passed. Clay held a forearm across his eyes, and I wasn't sure he was going to speak again. Finally, he lowered his arm and looked at me.

"My buddy dies. Steps on a fucking landmine and gets blown to pieces."

I picked up his other foot and began massaging it.

He stared past me, over my shoulder. "He was just a few feet behind me, on patrol. I heard the click, and I know he did, too. And then that was it. He was gone, and I was down." He took a breath. "Couldn't hear a fucking thing, burst my eardrums; the blast took the air out of my lungs, just sucked it right out. And I lost consciousness—went out like a light." He paused. "Could have been me, Meridian. I just didn't step on it when I went past. Roger did. Roger took the step." He put his hands to his face and hid from me.

Now I moved up to be beside him, to pull his hands from his eyes, kiss his eyelids. I rested my head on his chest, above his heart, and thought of how it was to my great, good fortune that he had not misstepped those many miles from home, that his chest was percussive, alive.

He wound his hands in my hair, tugged at it gently.

Neither of us slept any more that night. We held each other in silence until Jasper, who had at last crawled to the foot of the bed and curled into sleep, awoke and begged to go out.

JUST AFTER NOON, I went home to bring in the mail, dump my dirty clothes, and pick up some clean ones. When I returned Clay's apartment, there was loud music blaring from the open front door. Myriad young people sat and stood on his stoop, floated in and out of the front door, letting the screen door bang like intermittent gunfire. I parked next to a couple of unfamiliar cars and a VW bus with "Love Machine" painted on the side. I sat in my car until Clay spotted me.

"What are you doing?"

"Who are they?"

"Friends who dropped in on their way up to New Buffalo. They're crashing here tonight. C'mon," he said, opening my car door. I held onto the handle from inside, began a tug-of-war with him. "Come meet my friends."

"Maybe another time."

"Don't be such a downer."

"I didn't know . . ."

"Well, neither did I. But they're here, so come inside. Join us."

I hated this. Hated it. But finally I grabbed my purse and a bag of groceries. I'd also bought him a couple more drinking glasses so that we didn't have to do dishes every five minutes. He took the bag from me as we crossed the lawn, and I watched the hippies eye me.

"Everyone, this is Meridian. Meridian, this is everyone. I'll let you introduce yourself," he said, ducking inside the apartment with the grocery bag.

He was going to leave me here, abandon me to stand stupidly in this group of kids?

"I'm Sunset," a blonde woman with dirty feet hugged me, and I could smell sweat and marijuana smoke trapped in the fabric of her peasant blouse.

"Hi," I said, and stepped onto the porch.

"There are some wicked magic brownies in the kitchen," Sunset said, "if there're any left."

People were either propped up against the walls of his living room or lolling in the pile of pillows. There must have been at least twenty of them crammed into Clay's tiny living room. They passed a tall vaselike object around the room. When they inhaled, it made watery, gurgling noises. One of the men dropped a lit cigarette onto the carpet and then reacted slowly, finally flicking it off of the fibers and toward the baseboard with an "Aw shiiiiit."

"Are you sure it's out?" I walked over, picked it up. He ignored me, and then I heard him whisper snidely to the guy next to him: "Thanks, *Mom*." I wanted to kick him, see if he'd even notice he'd been kicked, but instead I went to find Clay. The bedroom door was drawn partway closed. I rapped softly and opened it.

There were three bodies on the mattress, moving beneath and on top of the sheets. I saw breasts and butts and legs and arms and hair—lots of hair. Busy mouths.

"Oh, sorry!" I said and shut the door as quickly as I could. The bathroom door was open, and a woman sat on the toilet with her skirt lifted while two men perched on the edge of the tub, passing a joint between them.

"And, it's like, you know . . . ," she said. "Rousseau. *The Dream*. That painting? His jungle. Colors, man. Green, green, green. And water. Sweat. Dripping wet." She picked up a paper cup from the edge of the sink and drank thirstily.

"Wet . . ." One of the men grinned lazy, wide. "Right on."

"And then," she continued, "it rains. Jungle mist. Wetter and wetter. And she's naked, and her body takes it all in. All the moisture. She's sooooooo wet. So the jungle fucks her. She fucks the jungle. They're one. *ONE*, yeah?" she asked the men.

"I could fuck a jungle," one of the men said. "LET ME AT IT!" he roared. I turned and left.

"Hey!" Clay said, six people deep in his kitchen. "Meridian! Over here!"

I shook my head and pushed through to the front door, stepped over a couple kissing on the steps, not sure if they were man and woman, woman and woman, or man and man. I wondered where Jasper was, but all I wanted to do was to get home, take a shower and be rid of all the filth.

Halfway across the yard, someone grabbed my arm, and I spun, ready to strike.

"Where're you going?" Clay asked.

"Home."

"But you should be with us."

"No, I shouldn't."

"Don't be so uptight, Meridian. Let me roll you a number," he said, tugging at my arm.

I shook myself free. "You let people—several people from what I could tell—have sex in *our* bed, on *our* sheets?"

"I have another set of sheets."

"Not the point." I opened the car door, threw my purse onto the passenger seat, and climbed inside.

"Stay," he begged now, a softer, less demanding tone to his voice. "I want you here, with me."

"I don't participate in orgies. This is hardly the way I enjoy myself."

"You could. You could learn. Open up." He looked back at his lawn, and then he winced, seemed to see it all differently. "Baby, I'm sorry. They just showed up. Don't be this way."

"There's no dignity," I said. "It should be private. What I have with you is intimate." I started the car. He stepped back from the car door so that I could back out. I glanced in the rearview mirror as I drove off, saw him standing there, separate from his friends, separate from me.

Would he go back in, climb onto the mattress with Sunset or Sunrise or High Noon or one of the other beautiful girls with questionable hygiene? It made me heartsick. And it frightened me—that I needed him, that I cared, that I couldn't be in his world. That his boundaries were so permeable and that mine were so stridently defined.

• • •

THE NEXT MORNING, I went to my crows for solace. I both hoped Clay would be there, and hoped he would stay away. When my crows told me he'd arrived, I steadied myself.

He circled around in front of me, looked up at me where I perched on my boulder. He shoved his hands into his jeans pockets. "I don't really know what to say."

"Me either."

"They're gone."

"I knew this wouldn't work, Clay. I told you."

"Don't give up on us."

I shook my head. "What's the point?"

"The *point*, Meridian? Really? You don't know what the *point* is?"

"We're too different."

"No, we're not." He took a deep breath, let it out. "You saw the old me last night. That's not who I am now."

"That did not look like ancient history."

"It's what we do. We welcome people. We don't plan every fucking second of every fucking day."

"Neither do I."

"You—" he said, a false start. "How can you experience life if you don't let it happen? Break a few rules?"

"But there's a limit. And I can make choices—I don't have to tolerate behavior that's personally offensive."

"Wow. Personally offensive. What's that?"

"Sitting on a toilet with two men watching while I urinate. Carelessly burning someone's home and not caring about it."

"It's just a different way of being."

"Precisely. And it's not my way. Those people have no boundaries."

"And they'd tell you that's exactly what they're after—total freedom."

This was it. Our worlds could rub shoulders, but we couldn't meld.

"What if I tell you they won't be back? What if I tell you that I told them they can no longer crash at my pad. Off limits."

"One of them called me *mother*."

"Then he's an asshole."

The writhing bodies were in my head, again. "Clay?"

"Yeah?"

"Did you . . . Did you sleep with those girls last night?"

"No."

"And I can believe you?"

"You can choose to believe me."

"It's just that . . ."

"The sheets are hanging on the line as we speak. And I'll finish cleaning this afternoon."

"Good. Open a few windows, too."

He laughed. "Already done. So this evening? A fresh start?"

"I'm not sure."

"Think about it." He stepped up onto the boulder, bent and kissed the top of my head. "Don't kill this. Don't run away."

I watched him as he climbed out of the canyon, and I knew I'd go back.

HUMBLY, I COUNTED AND kissed each scar. I measured their spans with my fingertips and let my index finger ride up and over the bumps. Some had shattered, starry outlines; they gathered to form galaxies of remembrance. I drew dot-to-dot lines between them, tried to see what images the combination of wounds revealed. I rubbed them with my thumb, thought to erase them.

I could not see his face, buried in a pillow. I licked the salty sweat in the crack of his ass, trailed my tongue down the backs of his thighs and counted a second territory of wounds. He lifted his head and cushioned it on his forearms, his face still hidden. He took several deep breaths, one of which caught in his throat.

In the corner, Jasper licked his paws, relaxing into his nighttime ablutions.

"I'll be back," I said and padded into the kitchen. I wrestled with the ice cube tray until I had a bowl of ice, and then I returned, touched an ice cube to the sides of his neck, beneath his ears.

"Cool," he sighed with pleasure.

I began to illustrate his body with lines of meltwater. I drew his wings. I followed the striations of his muscles, the lines of his tan. I used the cubes as erasers, worked once more at trying to remove the scars.

"Turn over," I said, choosing a new ice cube. I began with his face, his resolute cheekbones, the wells of his closed eyes, and I moved down to the twin caverns of his clavicles. I crisscrossed his chest, toured his dark red nipples, detoured into the darkness of his armpits. I left what remained of the ice cube to melt in the bowl of his navel.

"I want to make them disappear," I said softly. "I want to make it as though none of that happened to you."

He opened his eyes and shook his head.

"I can try," I said. "I can try." I pressed my palm to his forehead, wanting to siphon off the memories that lodged in his brain. I wanted to take them into myself. I wanted to free him.

"Roger's inside of me, too," he said, taking my wrist and removing my hand. "And if you're thinking of trying a lobotomy, don't." He turned his head to look out the window at the stars.

"I think I understand."

"No, you can't."

"I know I can't, not really, but I think I can."

"Meridian, I'm not speaking in poetic terms. Not about Roger."

I straddled him, held his face in my hands. "Then tell me," I said. "Help me understand."

"Take my word for it. You do not want to know. Once I tell you, you won't be able to forget. It will sicken you." He used a rougher voice than I'd ever heard from him. "*I* will sicken you." He rubbed his face with both hands and then sat up, holding my hips to keep me in place.

"I swear to you," he said looking into my face, "you will be sorry."

"Let me be the judge of that."

He kissed my scarred palm. "Shrapnel." He took a deep breath, looked down at our hands and then back at my face. I felt my head tip to the right, knew my eyes had opened wider, that tears were already pooling in my lower lids. "It can be metal or wood, Meridian."

I began to cry. He hadn't even said it yet, and I was crying. "Please," I said and waited.

"It can be human, too. Human bone."

"Oh, God," I said. "Oh, God."

"Shards of Roger's bones were shot into me, buried inside of me."

I felt a shudder go through my body. I wasn't helping him at all—not like this.

"Oh, for FUCK'S SAKE!" he yelled and moved me off of him, got out of bed. The bowl of ice tipped over, spilling a pool of water onto the sheets. I set it upright, tried to decide if I should follow him.

He was standing at the bathroom sink, staring into the mirror. I stayed in the doorway, uncertain as to how far to push him, fearing I'd already gone too far.

"So much for lowering your inhibitions," he joked half-heartedly. "No more grass for you."

But he wasn't smiling, and he wasn't looking at me. He was staring at himself, still.

I pressed my hands against the sides of the door jamb, isometric exercises in self-restraint. "I'm sorry," I said.

"Nothin' to be sorry for."

"Oh, I think there's a lot to be sorry for."

"It's not a war you had anything to do with." He leaned his weight on his arms, his hands on the sides of the sink, and I could not help but admire the bulk of his triceps muscles, the way the muscles of his back moved, tensed.

"You're so beautiful," I breathed. "So beautiful."

He turned and looked at me. "I'm not ugly to you? Now that you know?"

I shook my head. And then, while I looked at that still-boy, I felt bile rise in my throat. It was anger. Pure, visceral, acidic anger. How could anyone have taken such beauty, such faith, and sent it half a world away to be so irrevocably damaged? How many lives were we damaging, destroying? And why? What could possibly justify what I beheld in the dull yellow light of that tiny bathroom with its fractured linoleum floor?

"So," I said, locking eyes with him. "I'm fucking pissed off."

He laughed—a big lungful of a laugh. "Fuckin' A! Meridian gets righteous," he said, letting go of the sink and enfolding me in his arms.

And then, in the softest whisper possible, he wove these words into the strands of my hair, tattooed my scalp with them: "Bless you, baby."

OTHER THAN LETTING JASPER out periodically, we stayed in bed the entirety of the next day. We showered together—something I'd never before shared with anyone. We smoked pot, the ashtray balanced on the flat of Clay's belly. Talked. We ate leftover spaghetti, cherry popsicles for dessert.

I rode him, and when I climaxed, my entire body shuddered repeatedly.

"Nine point seven on the Richter Scale," he said. "I'd like to feel that time and time again. Forever." He smoothed my hair back off of my forehead, out of my eyes.

"Me too," I said, breathless. "Me too."

"HOW COME YOU'VE NEVER been to the Gorge Bridge?" It was the last day of Liberation Week, and we were headed north, toward Clay's old stomping grounds. He'd given me my choice, and I'd picked the new bridge that spanned the Rio Grande, northwest of Taos. Except it wasn't that new—it had been completed five years earlier.

"Alone?"

"Why not? If Alden won't go with you, why not go alone?"

"I used to," I said, thinking.

"Why'd you stop?"

"I don't know." This conversation was making me sad. "Today's for fun, Clay, so let's drop it."

"OK."

"I'm not mad."

"I didn't think you were."

"Good."

We rode in companionable silence, and eventually Jasper grew bored with the scenery and curled up to sleep between us. I rested my hand on the top of his head, feeling the wonderful solidity of his skull beneath my palm. Tom Jones came on the radio singing "Daughter of Darkness," and I turned up the volume, sang along. I slapped my hands against my thighs, pinched Clay's thigh.

He reached over and switched off the radio. "You have got to be fucking kidding me."

"What?"

"Tom Jones?"

"I listen to your music!"

"I have taste."

"A matter of perspective," I said. "You could use a more open attitude, you know." I switched the radio back on. "Don't be so *uptight.*" I grinned. "He has a fine voice, better than Dylan."

"Everyone has a better voice than Dylan. It's what Dylan says, man."

"Well, I get a kick out of Tom Jones."

"Please tell me you don't watch his show. Those pants! The guy's ridiculous."

"Those pants are one of the major reasons women watch his show. We pretend it's about his voice, but where else are we going to see something like that? Men have their magazines and strip clubs."

"He stuffs. I guarantee it."

I giggled. "Tube socks?"

"Probably." He glanced over at me, a sly grin on his face. "The striped variety."

I dissolved in laughter, picturing Tom Jones backstage, trying to get the zipper closed over a wad of socks. I put my feet up on the dashboard.

"Tom fucking Jones." Clay shook his head, smiling and checking his rearview mirror.

"I should give you money for gas," I said, suddenly remembering that I'd meant to make the offer a few days ago. I'd used up all of the cash Alden had left for me under the salt and pepper shakers. Fortunately, I had a cache of bills I'd hoarded in the toes of some heels I no longer wore.

"What is it with you and money, anyway? Alden has to make a good salary."

"I don't know. Well, I know he makes a good salary . . . ."

"You don't know how much money your husband makes? How old are you, Meridian?"

"It's the way we've always done it."

"And it doesn't piss you off?"

"A little."

"A lot?"

"I don't know."

"Where's your anger? Haven't you heard of the women's movement? Women's lib?"

"I've heard of burning bras, which seems incredibly wasteful to me." I took my hand from Jasper's head; it had grown uncomfortably hot.

"You have a right to the money, too—it's your money, both of yours."

I laughed. "Tell that to Alden."

"I might."

"Don't you dare." I gave him a light slug in the arm.

"Tom fucking Jones," he said, shaking his head. "The woman has no taste. None whatsoever," he grinned.

WHEN CARS PASSED US, the suspension bridge vibrated, sending delicious shivers up my spine. I stopped about a third of the way across the bridge and leaned out to look down at the ribbon of river over six hundred feet below. The Taos Gorge is relatively narrow, darkly shadowed basalt, and so completely impassable that a 1950s-era car remains stranded amidst the boulders. A breeze cooled us as we stood there, only our upper arms touching. Jasper put his nose in the air, sniffed.

I contemplated the last thoughts of those who hoisted themselves up and over the railing and then leapt from the bridge to their deaths.

Then I thought that in a way I was getting some of what I'd wanted from Niagara Falls—the edge of oblivion, the proximity to easy, dramatic destruction. Freefall.

Clay was thoughtful too. Eventually, I asked him what he was thinking about as he scanned the length of the gorge.

"I was thinking about the rift, technically a passive rift, that it's the only active one in the country. I was also thinking about time." He wound Jasper's leash tighter around his fist. "Then, I was thinking about flying away with you."

"So let's fly," I said and took off running, headed for the center of the bridge. "Last one there . . . !" I shouted.

" . . . Is a rotten egg!" he yelled, easily overtaking and passing me, with Jasper barking excitedly. When I caught up to him, I jumped up and wrapped my legs around his waist.

And there he held me, suspended on a cantilevered truss bridge designed to withstand ninety mile-per-hour winds (or so the placard said). We hung there, locked together above the dizzying depth of the world.

WE ATE AT A sidewalk café in Taos where we could keep Jasper beside us. I slipped chunks of my green chile cheese hamburger to Jasper and said "Who do you love, Jasper? The carnivore or the vegetarian?" He thumped his tail enthusiastically.

I don't think of myself as a jealous person. I'd never really felt jealousy over Alden or Jerry. But it came on violently, powerfully, when the young redheaded woman did a double-take as she passed our table.

"Clay!" she shouted. I saw him reach unconsciously for his love beads. He pulled them from beneath his shirt and fingered them as she approached our table.

He stood, reached a hand to shake hers. She ignored it and hugged him. "Where've you been?" she asked, glancing my way but pointedly ignoring me.

"Around," he said. He picked up my hand, held it. "This is Meridian. Meridian," he said, "this is Marion."

Marion of the Sacred Heart of Embroidery. Marion of the Perpetual Love Beads. Marion of the Holy Love-Ins and Communal Free-for-All. She was beautiful—perfect skin, long limbs, superbly tanned, her teeth unstained by decades of caffeine. I noticed a Chinese character tattooed on the inside of her left wrist. Her breasts beneath a sapphire tank top were perky, brazenly free of Playtex girding.

I let go of Clay's hand and reached to shake her hand. "Hi," I managed.

She looked from Clay to me. "You two . . . ?" she said, exaggerating her bewildered state as a gratuitous insult.

"Yeah," Clay said, smiling.

"Well . . ."

"Very well," he said, and I smiled.

I watched her hide her disappointment. "Where are you these days?"

"Jemez," he said, purposefully avoided the Los Alamos topic. So, Clay wasn't as bold, as independent as he preached. He wanted to dodge any allegations that he was contributing to nuclear annihilation.

"Cool," she said. And then she looked at me. "And you?"

"Crows," I said.

"Wow. Cool. The indigenous people have been so wronged."

The Crow Indians?, I thought. As far as I knew, the Crow reservation was in Montana.

"Meridian studies crows. She's an ornithologist," Clay said, sitting back down. Jasper was sniffing at Marion's moccasined feet. I wondered what she'd walked in and could only hope it had been something nasty.

"Hunh," Marion said. *She doesn't know an ornithologist from an orthodontist,* I thought.

"Well, good to see you." She looked only at Clay. "Don't be such a stranger."

"Yeah," he said, and reached for Jasper's ears, pulling them softly.

"And good to meet you," she added.

I had to give her credit for that. I smiled.

I watched her cross the street, and when I turned to look at Clay, I saw him watching her, too. I felt a flame burn in my gut. His gaze left the back of Marion and returned to his plate of tofu scramble.

"She's beautiful," I said, picking up a French fry and feeding it to Jasper.

"She is," he said.

"Wrong answer."

"Accurate answer. I'm not going to pretend differently."

"Not even for the sake of my middle-aged vanity?"

"She doesn't begin to compare with you."

"Bullshit, as you would say."

He shook his head. "I knew this would happen."

"What? What would happen?"

"You'd start this again. The age thing. On our last day together, you have to do this."

It was impossible. I knew—had always known—that I'd never hold Clay to me. He would leave me. I tilted my head back, looked at the clouds, and he sighed in frustration.

"I just don't know why you want me," I said. "I've never understood that. Why would you be with me when you could have Marion? A dozen Marions?"

"My mother would say that the heart wants what the heart wants."

I found a Kleenex in my purse, blew my nose. I stared across the street to where the ghost of Marion lurked in the shadows of a portal. I imagined how much lighter her spirit was, how much less work it would be to traipse through life with her. "You should be with her. Or someone like her."

"Fuck this, Meridian."

Jasper put a paw on Clay's knee, begging for a little tofu scramble. I dug in my purse for another tissue and then found the Trinitite I'd wrapped in a handkerchief and tossed in my bag when I'd made a quick trip home that morning. I sat for a minute with my hand in my purse, the Trinitite cupped in my palm. And then I took it out and set it on the table in front of Clay. He picked it up, held it up to the sun just as I had so many years ago when Alden brought it to me with such pride.

"It's Trinitite," I said. "From the first atomic blast."

"I've heard about this. I've heard people have it, that if a helicopter flew over Los Alamos with a radiation detector it would go bananas from all the Trinitite in all the houses."

"It's yours," I said. "A geologist should have one of the rarest rocks on earth."

"The colors are amazing." He set it in front of me. "But I can't keep it."

"Why on earth not?"

"It's not what I want from you."

"But it's a gift. It's my gift to you."

"I can't keep it."

"Because of Alden?"

"Right on."

I hadn't thought about it from that angle. He could take me—Alden's wife—but he could not take Alden's rock, his science, his achievement. I'd been a fool to offer it.

"Baby," he said, leaning closer to me. "I love the thought of it, the love behind it. But I want for you to find something else to give me. Something that's purely you."

I rewrapped the Trinitite. He was right. Whatever I gave Clay had to be of me—of the hopeful, dreaming and driven girl I'd once been. Of the woman I was becoming.

NESTLED AGAINST CLAY'S NAKED body and drifting off to sleep that night, I thought about what Clay had told me about geologic rifts. That they were the earth pulling apart, like wounds opening. I wondered at the depth and mystery of it, a crack in the earth, in myself. Part of me recognized it as a potentially dangerous breach of my skin; another part of me relished the possibility for change that it posed, the powerful forces at work.

I closed my eyes and imagined the spread of Clay's war wounds like shards of glass across my kitchen floor. A girl like Marion could never face those. He'd not told anyone but me about the bone shards, the talismans of his friend he'd carry for the rest of his life. I think that's the closest I ever came to fathoming his love for me—as inexplicable as that love might remain, as mysterious as it still was to me.

An Unkindness of Ravens

1. *Smart, dangerous predators, ravens are larger although more slender than the crow, with a thick neck and shaggy throat feathers.*
2. *Because legend dictates that if the captive ravens at the Tower of London ever leave the Tower the British Empire will crumble, the Tower's ravens' wings are clipped.*

Alden was due back from Niagara close to dinnertime. I left Clay's at dawn to return home to a house that seemed oddly unfamiliar. The air was stale, close, and so I stepped outside to have my morning coffee in the backyard. I wanted to sit in the cool air and listen to the hummingbirds' staccato cries as they disputed territory. A pair of robins chased a sharp-shinned hawk from their nest, berating it and repeatedly dipping within a few inches of the bird's talons and beak.

I was going to miss Clay, the closeness we'd developed, the luxury of having an expanse of time to be with him, to sleep and dream together. At the same time, I was exhausted, and I wondered how much longer I could have gone at Clay's speed. Surely, eventually we would not have been so greedy with each other, forever aware of the limited time we had together. And I did believe our time was limited. He would grow tired of me or simply leave to return to school. As for me, I would return to . . . what? I couldn't go back to my former life; it no longer existed.

I dressed in my scruffiest outfit and began cleaning. I wiped the Trinitite clean of smudges and returned it to the shelf, and I stood before the bookshelves, glancing through the spines with their familiar titles. I could remove them all, blow the dust from the valleys atop each volume, reorganize things. I could get rid of my college textbooks—the majority of them were anachronisms, and how likely was it that I would ever again refer to them?

I retrieved old boxes from the shed and began emptying the bookshelves. It felt like an unburdening. I turned up the volume on the radio, listened to Brook Benton's rumbling "Rainy Night in Georgia." Then I began on the closets, loading the bed with teetering mountains of clothing neither of us had worn in ages. In the kitchen, I pulled out pots and pans that had gone ignored for years. I weeded through my recipe books, tossing aside the ones Alden had brought me when he returned from business trips to New Orleans (*Southern Cooking at Its Best*), Boston (*Baked Beans and Other Traditions of New England*), and San Francisco (*Sourdough Delights*).

I'd meant to shower before Alden returned, but when his fellow traveler dropped him off, I was caught covered in dust and sweat, trying to jam more boxes and bags into the backseat of the Morris Minor.

Alden set his suitcase on the front walk. "Are we moving?"

I laughed. "No, I'm cleaning. Debridement." I gave the backseat stockpile a solid kick and managed to slam the car door. I went to Alden and put my arms about him. "Welcome home," I said. He kissed my forehead, and while he did so, I unintentionally compared the soft flesh of his back to Clay's.

"I started dinner." I followed him up the walk. "Stuffed pork chops baked in milk."

"Mmm," he said with the requisite modicum of enthusiasm.

"You've always liked those, and Safeway had a sale."

He opened the front door and stood surveying the disarray generated by my wild day of weeding. "It looks as if a bomb went off in here," he said, heading for the bedroom to empty his suitcase. He stopped in the doorway, looked at the surface of the bed strewn with clothing, belts, dilapidated shoes. "What on earth possessed you?" he asked.

"It began with the bookshelves, and then it just kept going."

He looked at the shelves. "Where are all the books?"

"In boxes in my car."

"Not my books."

"Just some of your books. Ones you haven't looked at since Chicago."

"You got rid of my books? Who told you you could do that?"

I stood there. *Please, not a fight.* Not on his first night back, his first half hour back. Not over some old books.

He set down his suitcase and sighed. "I'm tired, Meri. Really tired, and I don't feel particularly well. But before I sit down to dinner, I need to know which boxes have my books and where you put them in your car."

"But isn't it nice to see the shelves with some openness, some potential for new books, new ideas?"

"You didn't even ask me," he said, a slight petulance to his tone.

"I didn't think I had to. Not about old, unused books."

"Well, you thought wrong."

I was tempted to block the door, prevent him from undoing so much of my day's work, but it wasn't worth it. "I'll bring them back in," I said, running a hand across my forehead, noticing a patina of grime obscuring the scar on my palm. "You sit and relax."

He gestured toward the cluttered living room furniture. "Where?"

I stopped by the couch, moved the boxes, turned on the television on my way out the door. It was as if I were entertaining a child so that I could get my work accomplished.

In the driveway, I arched my back to take some of the tightness from it, and then I opened the car, took out two boxes of books, piled them on top of each other and stumbled back into the house.

CLAY WAS WAITING FOR me the next morning at the boulder, the toes of his tanned bare feet splayed across patches of sage-green lichens.

I stood beside him and pulled his head toward me until it touched the outside of my thigh. He leaned into me, much as Jasper would lean into a friendly human.

"I missed you," he said needlessly. "Happy reunion?"

"Fairly even-keeled." I sat down, put my knapsack at my feet. White Wing called from a lower branch and was answered from a tree several feet away. On the forest floor, a rufous-sided towhee busily lifted dry leaves, hunting for insects.

"I didn't sleep," Clay said. "Couldn't get it out of my mind." His voice had quickly taken on a heightened tone.

"Couldn't get what out of your mind?"

"Did you fuck him? A welcome-home fuck?" White Wing took off, winging away from us.

"No."

"Will you?"

"I don't understand."

"You don't *understand*?" He stood, took a breath and tried to regain his equilibrium. "The woman I love sleeps with another man. How difficult is that, Meridian?"

"What I don't understand," I said, keeping my voice measured, even, "is how you reconcile your days in the commune with what you're doing right now."

He stared at me. "OK," he sighed and let go of some of his outrage. "I'm just going through Meridian withdrawal, and I hate it."

"What can I do that will help?"

"Do I really have to tell you?"

"What?"

"Leave him."

There it was.

"Please sit back down," I said. "I want to talk to you about this. To be as articulate, as honest as I can be."

"You're saying no."

"Not in the way you envision."

"How many ways are there to say *no*?"

"Oh, Clay." He hadn't lived long enough yet to know the infinite ways in which *no* becomes manifest in the world. "You have to finish school."

"So? What's to stop you from coming to Berkeley with me?"

"You need to do this part of your life alone, without the weight of me."

"Fuck that, Meridian. Alden may consider you a weight, but I do not."

"Focus on your studies. Don't throw your life away on me."

"So someone who loves you is throwing their life away?"

This time I raised my voice: "I'm telling you *exactly* what someone should have told me. To set my career, not to give it up for some man, for anyone. Don't you see that? I only wish someone had loved me that much."

"I think you've forgotten what real love looks like."

"Real love looks like this."

He was quiet for a beat or two, formulating his argument, and then he said: "I'm offering you a new start. You could finish your graduate studies."

I laughed, picturing myself on the Berkeley campus I'd seen on the news, the student protests, yet again ensconcing myself where I would never fit in.

"This is bullshit," he said.

I took his hand, and we sat for several minutes beneath the breeze that rifled the tops of the pines, listening to the occasional watery murmurings of White Wing and Beacon.

"You're not saying never?" he said, finally calmer.

"I'm saying not yet."

I rested my head against his shoulder and was glad he couldn't see the fortitude it took for me to say "no" and to maintain the hope that he would keep loving me.

A FEW DAYS LATER, Alden announced over dinner that beginning in the fall he would be teaching Physics 101 at the University of New Mexico's burgeoning Los Alamos branch. He was more animated than he had been in years.

"You're retiring?"

"No, no. This is in the evenings—Tuesdays and Thursdays."

The following morning, I drove to the library and picked up UNM's course catalog. I read the listing with Alden's name and then left the catalog on the passenger seat of my car when I went to Clay's.

We made love with unprecedented ferocity, like two animals who had not copulated in decades. We sweated and grunted and cried out. Clay authoritatively moved my legs into various positions, some of them extreme; he pushed me up against walls, pinned my arms above my head. I bit him, sucked and bit at the tender flesh of his inner thighs until he gasped and I left bruises. "I'm marking you," I said. "Branding you as mine. I'm feeling just a tad possessive."

He seemed to like that.

CLAY WAS RIGHT, I could go back to school. I decided take one of the courses I'd seen in the UNM catalog, and I went to the bank to withdraw cash to pay my tuition.

I drummed my fingertips on the countertop while the teller counted out the bills. I was pulling out more than I needed, taking some of *our* money for *my* needs.

"There's one more thing you can do for me," I said. "I'd like to know the entirety of our holdings, current balances."

"Certainly. If you'll wait just a bit longer, I'll retrieve that information for you."

She returned with a Photostatted ledger and identified various items.

I was stunned. We had a checking and savings account—fine, that made sense to me. But there were also five certificates of deposit.

"You're earning good interest on these," she said, pointing at the eight percent interest rate figure.

"I see," I said, trying to hide my surprise.

Over the course of twenty-six years, Alden had squirreled away over $1.5 million.

In the bank parking lot, I sat in the Morris and rolled down the window. I had done without so many things, scrimped, saved, endured the infantilizing humiliation of a minimal household allowance. A few months ago, I'd moved furniture and painted the house myself, not hired anyone. I'd stripped the teacup wallpaper in the kitchen, painted the walls a bright, cheery yellow. And then I'd asked Alden for a refrigerator—one of the new avocado green ones. I wanted a color television, a dishwasher—just a few things to make my life easier, to bring us into the current era. I had secreted cash around the house just to have a few dollars of my own to play with—"play" being something so wild and crazy as a new crow journal or a pair of Dearfoams slippers. I touched Belle's pearl studs. I didn't buy jewelry or expensive clothing; I didn't have June Jacobsen's wardrobe, her shoes. I bought meat on sale, never paid top dollar.

I watched other Los Alamos wives enter and leave the bank, their children's hands held tightly, protectively. We had no children's college funds to build. We'd never gone anywhere. We rarely ate out anymore.

I had nothing. Nothing. And yet I was a millionaire. A millioinairess.

I hit my fist against the steering wheel, on my way to a full-blown explosion, and then I stopped myself. It was my own damned fault. I'd allowed Alden to do this. A child says *Screw you!* and throws a fit or holds her breath until she passes out. An adult does something about it.

I drove to the UNM administrative offices and plopped down my tuition payment. I would take expository writing, sharpen my skills in preparation for writing my thesis one day.

"GOD *DAMN*, MERIDIAN! I am so proud of you!" Clay waltzed me around his living room. Jasper nipped at our flying heels.

My hair came loose from the clip, flew in the air as he twirled me.

"Wait a minute," he said and stopped. He pulled the rubber band from his hair, loosened his braid until his hair hung free, longer than mine. "Whirling dervish!" He began spinning, his hair flying.

We spun until we were dizzy, out of breath. I dropped into the cushion pile. Every cell of my being effervesced.

He stood there staring at me so intently that I grew uncomfortable. "What?"

"I'm memorizing you. I love seeing you like this."

"Thank you."

"Not my doing, baby. You did this. Take credit."

"IT'S A GREAT IDEA, Meri." Alden was loading his pipe for an after-dinner smoke. "I applaud your decision."

"I'll go Monday, Wednesday and Friday nights," I said. "We won't see each other much during the week."

"Worth the sacrifice," he said, his cheeks working like a bellows to get the tobacco to ignite. "Kudos, wife of mine."

I chose not to tell him about my trip to the bank. I was armed with the knowledge, and that's what mattered. I'd also long ago observed that if a smaller, weaker bird is challenging a predator bird—a raptor, a crow—then it is best to fly above the predator. If I flew just over Alden's back, he wouldn't know I was there unless and until I cried out. For now, I intended to hold my silence.

DURING WHAT REMAINED OF the summer of 1970 and into the fall, I saw Clay at our crow spot and in the evenings when I told Alden I was swimming.

I tried to enjoy each moment, not to project myself into the future, but every time Clay and I made love I felt I'd eaten another chocolate in a box of candy—that soon enough, all I'd have was paper wrappers and the ephemeral memory of sweetness.

"HIROSHIMA AND MY LAI," I said, handing my first expository writing assignment to Emma. "We were supposed to use the technique of comparison/contrast."

"Aren't you brave," Emma said, beginning to scan the first page of my essay. I looked out her kitchen window as she read, and I sipped coffee from a mug that read CAPE CANAVERAL—something Vince must have picked up while working on some space project. I could hear her dryer tumbling clothes, and I smelled fabric softener and furniture polish.

She finished reading and looked up at me.

"Your honest opinion," I said. "Show no mercy—you're the expert, and I want to learn."

"The putative permission to kill granted to those in Vietnam by what took place in Hiroshima and Nagasaki, the comparative 'guilt,' the way American society has reacted to the two events . . ."

Oh dear. I knew I'd chosen a topic that might offend; now I realized I'd done exactly that.

"I know it was—" I began.

"It's well done," she said, her eyes swimming behind the bulbous lenses of her eyeglasses.

"I was afraid I'd offended."

"You didn't offend me, although you may offend your professor. But, Meridian, if you really want to write, if you really want to speak through your writing, to communicate anything of value, anything worth saying—well, you have to be fearless. Sometimes, to get people to think, you have to offend, get them riled up. My advice is don't anticipate what people will or will not think about what you've said, how it might alter their perspective of you." She reached behind her back to adjust the elastic of her belt. "Define yourself—don't let your imagined reader define you. Say what you have to say. Or," she paused, "you are wasting your gift."

"Gift?"

"Gift. You're good." She smiled. "The person who wrote this essay interests me. Has interested me since the day I met her." She tapped an index finger on my paper. "And you know I do not flatter needlessly or engage in puffery."

"Emma?"

"Yes?"

"Thank you."

"I'm proud of you." She reached across the table, patted my hand. "I think you are, at last, donning your seven league boots."

"I may need them."

"I suspect you will."

ALDEN FINISHED READING MY essay and flipped it face down on the dining room table. He removed his glasses and rubbed the bridge of his nose.

"Well, I don't know what you expect from me in terms of a reaction, but it's not a good one—just know that," he said, using a napkin to clean the lenses of his glasses.

"You don't think my points are valid, the questions I pose are appropriate?"

"The entire exercise is *in*appropriate." He put his glasses back on.

"That we impose rules on war is absurd," I said. "Isn't the point of war to win? And if it is, then why not win at all costs? Why do some wars have certain rules, other wars have different ones? Isn't war like evolution, the goal being survival? Those are all valid questions. They're *ideas*, Alden—and you of all people should not be threatened by ideas." I paused, but just for a moment—I was driven, and I didn't want to let his reaction stymie me. "Just think of the British in their red coats, their inability to adjust to circumstances, what great targets they made marching in line across open fields—it was behavior wholly inapposite to survival, to evolutionary success. Was it a war crime to take advantage of their ineptitude?"

"But you didn't write about the British, Meri. You wrote about *me*, about the men in this town. You compared us to teenage boys in Vietnam who failed to exercise any moral restraint, who stood face to face with women and children and killed them for the sport of it."

"I don't think that's fair."

"What *you* did is unfair. You cannot compare the unenviable, necessary use of scientific theory, scientific advances of a monumental scale, to the kind of wanton slaughter that took place at My Lai."

"I *can* compare them. I can compare and contrast, which was the purpose of the writing exercise."

"Well, it's offensive. It's insulting. I am not a war criminal."

"No, never! I am not saying that at all! I'm saying *none* of the people are criminals—not you, not Bohr, not the boys in Vietnam!"

He looked peeved, exasperated, but he lacked the characteristic Alden fire I'd known for so many years. I felt sorry for the fading, flat man who sat before me, and pity deflated my anger.

"I'm sorry if I hurt your feelings. That was not my intention."

He stood up from the table. "Do me a favor. Don't show that to anyone else," he pointed an accusatory finger at my essay.

I'd planned to present the paper to my women's discussion group after I turned it in to my professor, but I realized that Clay was the only other person I really needed to read it.

"All right," I agreed.

What I wanted to say was that it sickened me that my country was asking boys to make split-second decisions in a hellish landscape—decisions that would haunt them for the rest of their lives, if they were lucky enough to have lives that lasted more than a few more humid, insect-infested months. I wanted to know what Alden felt, now decades distant from his work on the bomb, but I couldn't remember the last time we'd had a substantive conversation, the kind that had fueled our early love, those long-ago expansive talks that had kept me awake at night, abuzz with ideas, with the perspectives he offered. I missed the respect he'd once shown me as an intellectual sparring partner.

Now—now that I was rediscovering the person I'd once been, he no longer wanted to know that person. He did not have the energy for that person. Just as I was reemerging, Alden was disappearing.

CLAY LEFT A NOTE with his reactions to my essay on my crow boulder.

> Baby,
>
> No matter what I say, what anyone says, especially including that asshole sometimes known as Alden, you keep saying whatever it is you have to say. I don't agree with everything you wrote, but I don't have to. No one does.
>
> The thing for me in Nam was that there was no PURPOSE. Nada. Your war had a reason, and it still does, even in hindsight. Nam has no purpose other than political football bullshit. There is no valid reason for this country to ask us to do what we did, for killing us, maiming us, fucking us up. I bought a line of shit, but I was young, dumb and full of cum.
>
> The other thing I think you left out is the dehumanizing part of it all. You can't think your enemy has feelings, a family, that he loves his kids or his wife, that a gook mother loves her baby as much as your mother loved you. They're animals, man, GOOKS—and it's ok to kill animals. It's why I don't eat meat anymore—I just don't see life as expendable as I did when I was there. But when I was there, I had to do what I had to—we all did. And now we have to do what we have to, to end this fucked-up bullshit war.
>
> You keep getting stronger. Don't let them mess with your mind. Take no prisoners, Meridian.

You made me FEEL—and that's the whole bag, isn't it?

OK. That's all that matters right now. Except this: I'M PROUD OF YOU. I LOVE YOU. KEEP ON KEEPING ON.

—Clay

LATE IN THE FALL of 1970, once-gold aspen leaves lay brown and decaying on the forest floor. Although the mornings were prickly-sharp with frost, I huddled in a blanket on the back patio and watched dollops of sparrows scurrying beneath my feeders. The slightest thing sent them racing for cover in the bushes. It was amazing that they managed to consume any food, as skittish as they were. They were flighty—a word used so frequently to describe women.

Actually, I thought, the small birds' behavior made perfect sense—they were so low in the pecking order, so vulnerable. Their predators were bountiful, between the roadrunners, crows, raptors, dogs, and cats. The entirety of a sparrow's world was peopled with threats. Of course women are flighty, I thought. We have more predators than men; we have to operate constantly with greater wariness. Women alone in parking lots can be singled out, mugged, or worse. Our own mates can beat us, kill us.

I wanted to talk with Emma about it, make it the topic for my next essay. I was eager to begin.

IT WAS A SURPRISE, when I arrived at Judy Nielson's house, to learn that one of the discussion group members had invited June Jacobsen as a guest. I was leading the discussion that day, and I'd decided to stay away from any discussion of war crimes. Instead, I wanted to talk about the women's strike held in New York a few months earlier. It was, in part, a commemoration of the fiftieth anniversary of the Nineteenth

Amendment and women's right to vote. Betty Friedan, the strike organizer, highlighted the problems women still faced: in some states they still could not make wills or own property, except through a husband.

"Women can have the same education, the same work experience as a man, and yet we're paid only about half what a man is paid to do the same job," I said.

"I've seen it at the Lab—exactly what Meri's saying," Barbara Malcolm added.

"But those women in the protest," Judy began. "Why do they have to act so ridiculous? It turns me off of their cause. It embarrasses me."

"It's your cause, too—as a woman," Barbara said but was ignored.

"And what they were saying, that women are sex objects? I, for one, like to have men look at me," June interjected. "Bob likes for me to wear pretty things. He likes that I'm a woman, that I wear frilly things." She tugged at her purple polyester skirt, which was short. On her right hand, she wore an oversized cocktail ring of rubellite, tourmaline, and diamonds. "I don't see anything wrong with serving my husband breakfast in bed. He works hard!"

As June spoke, I tried to comprehend the fact that this woman was the same person who had once so expertly lectured me on organic soil additives.

"Those women look like men. Short hair, jack boots. And so angry," Dawn Hendricks said. She was wearing a baby-blue polyester pantsuit with white topstitching and white leather pumps. She held up her frosted pink nails, as if to demonstrate. "What's wrong with looking like a woman? I don't want to be a man."

"Bob says they're dykes," June smirked.

"Lesbians," June whispered while Dawn tittered.

"Wanting to be treated equally, fairly, does not mean I want to be a man. Or that I'm a lesbian," I said, feeling a blush growing across my chest.

"Well, not you, Meri," June said, a saccharine smile on her face. "We know you're a girl." She stared meaningfully at my Levis and the comfortable suede desert boots I'd recently begun wearing. I'd reduced my makeup to a bare minimum—foundation and a light shade of lipstick—and I wore only Belle's pearl studs, my wedding rings, and a turquoise and silver ring in the shape of a flower. The heavy squash blossom necklace felt more like one of those old-fashioned horse collars, and so it lived in a box on top of my dresser.

"What I think they're saying is that we should have a choice," Barbara said. "About how we want to dress, to be, as women. June can dress up, and Meri can wear her jeans."

"The news coverage was biased," Emma said, trying to steer the conversation in another direction. "They belittled women's legitimate concerns. Does anyone here honestly believe women shouldn't serve on juries? And yet, in some states women can't be jurors. How is that a jury of your peers, if you're a woman sitting in the defendant's chair?"

"Murder trials? Rapes?" June said. "Leave me out of it. We women don't want that kind of responsibility, Emma. It's too stressful, deciding someone's fate."

"Women decide the fate of their children every day!" I said.

"And women have an important, different perspective to lend to a jury's decision," Emma added. "What about female empathy?"

"I say let the men have it," Judy said, standing. "Now, who wants carrot cake?"

"Only a tiny piece," June said, joining Judy. "I have to watch my weight or Bob says he'll divorce me," she giggled.

I looked at Emma, who rolled her eyes.

• • •

NOVEMBER 11 WAS MY forty-seventh birthday, and I told Alden that Emma and I were headed to Santa Fe. Instead, I met Clay at his apartment, where he'd made brunch, complete with champagne and a white sheet for a tablecloth, laid over a card table where he usually kept his bills and schoolwork. A huge cardboard box wrapped in the funny pages sat in the middle of his living room, with Jasper as its guardian. I knelt on the floor to open the box. Inside was a copy of Simone de Beauvoir's *The Second Sex*. Clay had underlined Chapter XXV, "The Independent Woman."

"Oh my," I said, looking up at him. "You have high expectations of me."

I dug deeper in the box and found Janis Joplin's *I Got Dem Ol' Kozmic Blues*, the album cover a blurry picture of her head, hair whirling, the frenzy of her movements and her energy so perfectly captured. Next came a wide, floppy-brimmed black felt hat with a beaded hatband in pinks, greens, and blues. I set it on my head and wondered if I'd have the courage to wear it anywhere—other than canyons or isolated mountain trails.

"Beautiful," he said. "Keep going."

A photo postcard pictured the Campanile at the entrance to Berkeley, and on the back he'd written:

> "Picture yourself in the hat, walking arm in arm with me here. Happy BIRTHday, Meridian. You are reborn. You got NO time to waste. LOVE.

"THERE'S ONE MORE GIFT," he said when, mid-afternoon, I finally made myself rise from his bed and dress.

"It's too much." I turned to him while I fastened my skirt. "Don't forget, I have to explain all of these things."

"Jasper." The dog lifted his head, ready to come if needed.

"Jasper?"

Clay helped me tug my sweater over my head, ran his fingers through my hair to smooth it.

"It was OK when I could take him to work at the site, but now that the weather's changed and I'm stuck at a desk, writing reports, analyzing data—well, it's not fair to leave him cooped up in this apartment all day."

"You want me to take him home?"

"Until we head to Berkeley, yes. Can you do that? You know he loves you. And, there's this, too," he said, clearly reluctant to go on. "I'm going to Montana for a month. To spend Thanksgiving and the holidays with my folks."

"Oh," I said, smelling our lovemaking, the scent of us melded together. I would miss him so.

"Meridian?" He rubbed his thumb across my cheekbone. "You must have noticed the same thing I have," he began. "My nightmares. I don't have them as often, and they're less intense when they happen. You did that. There's no one else on the face of this earth who could have done that for me."

"Oh," I said, "I rather doubt that."

"Just for today, give up on the self-deprecation, OK? You know it's true," he said, and I had to smile a tentative smile of agreement. "The peace you've given me is what's going to let me spend time with my parents—without worrying that I'll scream and yell in the middle of the night, scare them half to death."

I put my forehead to his chest and held it there for several seconds. In that moment I felt such hope for Clay, for his future. I thought about what strength he possessed, to survive what he had seen and done. And I'd managed to give something meaningful to him; our relationship was a true exchange.

I stepped back at last and beckoned to Jasper. "Will you come live with me, boy?" I asked and felt Clay's arm go about my shoulders.

THAT EVENING ALDEN PRESENTED me with bakery cupcakes and a box wrapped in pink flowered paper. I'd left Clay's gifts in the trunk of the Morris Minor.

I stood at the dining room table and started to open the package carefully, so that I could save and reuse the paper. Then I remembered we were millionaires and that I was supposed to be intensely alive, so I ripped the paper with a dramatic flourish, and Alden applauded. I felt how heavy the box was when I lifted it to remove the wrapping paper stuck beneath it.

"You have me guessing," I said, smiling at him.

He grinned. "It is exciting. Really, at this point, a prototype—they won't come out officially until next year, but I knew someone who knew someone . . . . Well, you'll see."

It was good to see him eager about something. I muscled open the top of the box and found a heavy glass lid. I reached around the sides of what appeared to be crockery—the old brown crockery similar to what Mother had used to make pickles. I lifted the entire thing from the box. It was orange, with a single black dial and an electric cord.

Alden was irrepressible. "It's called a Crock-Pot. You use it to slow-cook food. In the morning, you put a meal in it—say chicken or ribs or something—and then you go about your day, check on your crows, write your essays, even go to class in the evenings—and the meal will be ready when you get home."

I crossed to his side of the table and kissed his cheek. "It's very thoughtful," I said and tried with all my heart to mean it.

ON THE AFTERNOON BEFORE Clay was to fly to Montana, we made love one last time, as if our touch were prayer. He used his fingertips to tap out secret messages along the soft, inviolate skin of my inner thighs.

"I never used to cry." He ran a hand along the outside of my thigh, thoughtful. "It's not manly. You do anything not to cry. You laugh. You fight. But you don't cry, man."

I ran my knuckle along his jaw.

"You get brainwashed in boot camp. Hell, you get brainwashed from the moment you take your first breath. Be a man. A *man*," he spat.

I reached behind his neck, put my hot hand to the atlas that crowned his backbone.

"Roger. He was my brother, dig? I couldn't cry for Roger or for any of the pieces of Roger that got blown into me. He was black. I don't think I said that before. He had my back, and I was supposed to have his." He rolled onto his back, stared at the ceiling. "He turned me on to grass, Deeeetroit, the Temptations. The Four Tops, for Christ's sake." He laughed halfheartedly. "Fucking bullshit." He wiped tears from the wells of his eyes.

After some time I went to the kitchen to get us a glass of water, and I pulled the small jewelry box from the depths of my purse. I handed it to him.

"What's this?"

I'd found it in Santa Fe—a slim lace of supple brown leather. Onto it, I'd threaded milagros I'd found in a shop off of the Plaza.

"You know about milagros, right?" He shook his head. "They're religious folk charms, for healing. The legs are to cure your war wounds."

I motioned to the charms as he moved them along the length of the necklace. "The bird is for my crows. The sun is for New Mexico, and the heart is for obvious reasons."

"A guy's version of a charm bracelet," he said, pulling the love beads from around his neck and laying them aside. He lifted the hair from the back of his neck. The milagros fell in the center of his chest.

"I have something for you, too." He reached beneath the mattress and handed me a similar jewelry box. Inside was a key.

"The key to your heart?"

"I rented a post office box in my name. So we can write to each other while I'm away. Your name's not associated with it in any way. I'll address letters to myself; you go pick them up."

"You're about ninety steps ahead of me, you know."

He tapped the side of his head. "Always thinking, baby, especially when it comes to you."

"Devious," I said and reached to tickle him.

"Oh, no you don't." He pinned me to the mattress and locked eyes with me.

"And you're taking Jasper home tonight. I have his box packed."

"Something I've been meaning to ask forever. Why *Jasper*?"

"It's a common stone, but mythology—I forget whose—says that jasper has the power to protect from fears in the night."

"Oh."

"He's a good talisman, but I prefer you."

Now it was getting hard. He saw it in my face.

"It's not forever," he said, stroking my temples as if soothing a fevered child.

"I know," I said and closed my eyes to it all.

• • •

JASPER BOUNDED TO THE door to meet Alden when he came home from work.

"Meri?"

"His name's Jasper. A friend of mine at the pool was moving, and she needed a home for him at the last minute."

Surprisingly, Alden knelt and let Jasper lick his chin. I stood there, amazed. "You don't mind?"

"It would have been nice if you'd asked, but if it was a last minute thing . . ." Jasper put a paw on Alden's shoulder, instant comrades in arms.

"He really likes you," I said. Jasper had never responded this enthusiastically to me.

"Dogs tend to like me."

"I never knew that."

Alden put his briefcase on the side table and headed toward the kitchen. "C'mon, boy, let's see what we have to feed you."

They left me standing in the middle of the living room, my hands clasped tightly at my waist, entirely befuddled.

WHILE HE WAS ALONE with me, Jasper was purely my dog, and we hiked the trails in and around the Los Alamos canyons and Jemez Mountains. He looked handsome riding on the Morris Minor's red leather seats, and he gave me someone to talk to as we clambered up and down hillsides or crossed streams. I sewed a little backpack and made him carry his own kibble and water, and he shared the crusts of my cheese sandwiches without complaint about their relative lack of nutritional value.

At home, however, Jasper was Alden's faithful sidekick. He began sitting in the front window waiting for Alden about fifteen minutes before Alden's punctual arrival, and it was Alden who fed him his evening meals. While Alden read *Khrushchev Remembers*, he kept a palm on Jasper's head, and Jasper curled for warmth against Alden's leg. He slept on the floor beside Alden's side of the bed.

Jasper forged a link between Alden and me, a demilitarized zone. He gave us a safe topic of discussion. I wondered what Clay would think of this unintended result of his gift, and I hoped he would be glad that Jasper lent some peace to our home, that he eased tensions somewhat. I think Clay loved me enough to be that generous.

"IT'S BEEN A WHILE, so refresh my memory."

Just after Thanksgiving, Emma and I were seated at a booth in the soda-shop portion of Anderson's Pharmacy. There were few places in Los Alamos to go for coffee and conversation—unless one wanted to frequent the American Legion or the B.P.O.E.—and we didn't.

I set *The Second Sex* on the tabletop. "What she says is that with D. H. Lawrence, a wife derives her justification for existence from her husband—Lawrence's women have to adopt their mates' values, his universe."

Emma took a sip of her coffee and watched my face.

"It's precisely what I've done," I said. "I've submitted to Alden, with some small flurries of rebellion that quickly melted. Coming here, staying here—he required that of me."

"Without discussion?"

"With minimal discussion. I glanced at the countertop where three big, yeasty doughnuts rested beneath a glass dome.

"Just because I won't doesn't mean you shouldn't." Emma smiled.

I nodded at the girl behind the counter, who took a pair of tongs and selected one of the doughnuts, brought it to our table, and refilled our mugs. "Thanks," I said.

"I know about the minimal discussion," Emma said. "But let's talk about why it was minimal."

"Because my compliance was pretty much assumed."

"Sure. Mine too. But you're not blaming Alden for the whole thing, are you?" She took a breath. "What I mean is that the entire culture assumed, right along with our husbands. It was *understood.* And while they might well respect us, love us, sometimes even be a tad less intelligent than us, by marrying them we tacitly agreed to a contract in which we would sublimate. They did not have to subjugate—we did that for them."

"So I'm just as guilty as Alden?"

"Maybe even more guilty. You put the bridle in your mouth, your neck in the noose, your head on the chopping block—whatever metaphor you'd like to use."

"And you?"

"*Mea culpa.*"

"So why are we still here?"

"I love Vince."

"It can't be that simple."

"For me, it is." She stirred her coffee for no reason other than to give herself time to think. "I think I've given up fretting about it. Vince loves me in the best way he can. We've made a life here, and there is no longer any other life I want more than this one."

"You've settled."

"Yes."

"But should we settle?"

"The real question is should *you* settle, because I'm not the one who is tortured by all of this."

I began shredding my napkin into strips. "Maybe that's one difference between us. You finished your Ph.D. Maybe that permits you a level of contentment that I can't find."

"You think you still have something to prove."

"Maybe." I paused in my dismemberment of the innocent napkin.

"You're telling me that you don't already know how bright you are? You don't know that you could have finished if you'd chosen to do so?"

I blew out my breath. "At the start, Alden was . . ." I spread my arms wide, " . . . he was so big in my life, such a massive intellect, such a compelling mind."

"And now?"

"He hasn't lost his intellect, but he doesn't share it with me anymore. Does Vince still talk to you?"

"About?"

"Work. The one thing they love, what consumes them."

"But they can't—not for the most part. They can't discuss classified work with us." Emma waited while the waitress refilled our coffee mugs and took away my empty doughnut plate. "Vince and I talk about books. We talk about the news, politics, about the people at his work. But never his work, Meri. It's verboten—you know that."

"But even the *ideas* of work—quantum physics, *something* that interests him. He used to be so animated, talking about wave propagation, particles. He was glorious, Emma. *Lit.* But not anymore. The other day, he was reading Khrushchev's memoirs. So asked him about them, what he thinks."

"And?"

"First, he said *Read it yourself, Meri.*"

"Oh."

"Then he said he had no intention of joining my ladies' coffee klatch."

She reached across the booth for my hand, halting my paper shredding.

Her kindness deflated the balloon of my anger. "I had you all wrong," I said, squeezing her hand.

"Meaning?"

"Your reserve."

She laughed. "Don't you know? Still waters run deep. Cold hands, warm heart. Truthfully, I've grown careful over time. It's living in this small town," she said, looking out the plate glass window onto Diamond Drive. "It's one way of maintaining some modicum of privacy in a city where people will talk if you make an excessive number of lane changes in less than three minutes." She let her voice fade and again stared out the window, thoughtful, before turning back to me. "Do something for me?" she asked, and I nodded. "Take another look at your husband, try to see him with fresh eyes. See if he's really an unfeeling ogre." She folded her napkin precisely, used her thumbnail to sharpen the fold. "If he is, then that's one thing. If he's not, then talk to him. I'd do that before I walked away from all those years."

AT FIRST, I FAILED to notice the difference, but within minutes I realized that the crows had not alerted to my presence. The woods were silent, but for my footsteps and Jasper's panting.

As we descended to the boulder, I saw them—at least a hundred crows, lining the pine branches or clustered in groups on the ground, their focus a single crow lying inert in the center of the gathering. They stood together, not quite a huddle but with their backs to the world, for once oblivious to intruders. I heard murmurings, understated crow voices, and I felt intensely their black coloration, their seeming mourning dress. There were a few punctuations of squawks when one crow jostled another, but for the most part they remained eerily quiet.

I whispered to Jasper to sit and stay, and then I focused my binoculars on the inert crow.

I drew a quick, audible breath, startling some of the birds.

It was White Wing, and he was dead.

I lowered the binoculars, but not before I glimpsed Beacon just to White Wing's left. Her head was bowed.

One by one, they approached White Wing and either stopped short of him by a few inches or touched him with their beaks, as if placing a hand on a closed casket, bidding farewell.

I was seeing a crow funeral, as impossible as that seemed. They'd gathered for White Wing. To say good-bye? To honor him? I couldn't make sense of it.

I squatted on the ground beside Jasper, leaned my head against him as we watched the crows bid adieu and then take off. When the departing crows had flown some prescribed distance from the setting, each one called, two to three brisk caws.

Eventually, the only birds remaining were Beacon and her dead mate. I left my pack with Jasper and made my way slowly, respectfully, to where White Wing lay.

His eyes were gone, shot out with BBs. I knelt beside him, touched him for the first time in my life, in my head saying *holy, holy, holy.* Then I picked up a fist-sized stone that lay near his body. I screamed and threw the rock as hard as I could. I heard it ricochet off of another stone and then roll.

Beacon answered my call from her perch, and then we both sat, bereft and empty.

A Murder of Crows

1. Among the smartest animals on Earth, the American Crow is highly adaptable.
2. "Murder of crows" may have come from the belief that crows circle in large numbers above sites where people are expected to die.

December 15, 1970

Happy Christmas, Clay.

Do you recognize the feather that comes folded so quietly into this letter? Did you hear Beacon calling for her mate?

Someone shot White Wing with a BB gun. I watched the crows hold a funeral; it was extraordinary. Beacon looked awful, but I guess she should—she's lost the mate she'd made for life. And then they left—all but Beacon. Here is my theory about the crows' disappearance: They learned that the canyon is a dangerous place—they touched him and saw his wounds, and knew that they had to abandon their territory or risk extermination. I'm certain they are that smart, that evolved. I know it.

I wanted for a part of White Wing to be with you. I want him to go beyond this place, to float on a new horizon, and he'll have that, through you. I kept another feather—I put it in a cedar wood box that was given to me when my best friend Belle died. It's where I keep precious things. I haven't told you about Belle, but I want to, now. I will tell you when I can touch you and see your face. I want to show you the same level of trust you showed me when you told me of Roger.

One more death—then you can put this letter away or burn it and somehow get rid of its weighty sadness. Beacon is dead. You are the only person I can tell, who really, really knows how this feels. I went back to the canyon this morning, and she was lying on top of the snow. I unfolded her wings, stretched out her feet that had drawn up close to her belly in death. I couldn't find a single wound on her, no reason for her to be dead. I swear to you—she died of grief. Her heart broke and could not mend itself.

When I got home I read from a book a professor gave me long ago—a book from 1923 by Townsend. He described how he'd seen a crow in a tree with one foot entangled in a piece of string—it could not escape. When Townsend returned to the site an hour later, the entangled crow was still entangled and alive, but a second crow lay dead on the ground beneath the tree. Townsend dissected the dead crow but could find nothing wrong—he said he was tempted to say the second crow had died of grief for the imprisoned crow.

I believe that our minds, our hearts, control our bodies—by chemicals or whatever, we can bring on our deaths when no other reason for death exists. Beacon did that. Beacon decided to do that.

I am sad. Just so sad. Hold me in your mind, your heart, as I do you.

Meridian

I WENT TO THE canyon every day for over two weeks, but the crows were completely gone. All of the years I'd spent there—and now, nothing. I wrote up observations of the funeral, Beacon's grief-stricken death, and of the crows' abandonment of a long-term home ground and breeding site. I closed the journal and packed it away on top of the journals of previous years, in a box in the back of the hall closet, next to the sheets and blankets, the towers of embroidered and crocheted dresser scarves and doilies Mother sent me over the years.

The heart had gone out of me with the crow deaths, and although I told myself that in the spring I'd set up a new research site and continue my studies with another crow community, I wondered if I would. Or if I were finished.

I felt the passage of time, counted the years I'd been living in Los Alamos and was surprised when I realized I'd been living there for half my life. I noticed that the lines that ran in curves from Alden's nose down past the outer edges of his lips had had deepened into ravines, that his eyelids sagged under the influence of inescapable gravity. I inspected my face carefully in the harsh light of the bathroom, saw the beginnings of tiny commas of wrinkles in my cheeks, generated by forty-seven years of smiling.

The holidays came—Christmas cards, decorations, holiday baking, shopping, and Alden's numerous work-related parties. I bought white linen at Dendahl's, just off the plaza in Santa Fe, and I sewed new drapes for the entire house. I had Alden's reading chair reupholstered in a nice, bright fabric of gold, green, and oranges. I sent my usual annual card to Professor Matthews, told him about Beacon's death, thanked him for his prescient gift of Townshend's book. Two weeks later, the postman returned the card. Someone had drawn a single line through Professor Matthews' name and written in blue ink: DECEASED. My crows receded further.

CHRISTMAS WAS QUIET, AS was New Year's. Alden took off for a few days, spent the time in his chair, reading and smoking. On a couple of occasions, he got up from the table during our evening meal and ran to the bathroom. I attributed his gastric distress to the rich holiday food.

I listened to Nat King Cole, baked cookies, put on a midi-length denim skirt, and drove the cookies to El Mirador, a state-run facility for the elderly in the valley north of Española. I hung the stockings I'd sewn years earlier—made of red, white and green felt, our names spelled out, faded gold sequins now popping free of exhausted glue and dotting the floor in front of the fireplace.

And I thought about Clay—wondered if he went into the Montana woods and cut a fir tree for his parents' home, if his mother baked, what he told his parents of his life in New Mexico, if away from me he'd reevaluated his love. I was certain I'd lose Clay next August or September, when his internship ended and he headed back to Berkeley. Or would I lose him sooner?

I put off decision-making, thinking there was, as yet, no decision to be made other than what to make for dinner, what themes I'd choose when my poetry class began in a few weeks.

I USED THE KEY Clay had given me, started a pot of coffee, and unwrapped the tinfoil from one of my homemade fruitcakes. Despite the cold, I left the front door cracked open so that Jasper could keep a lookout. I was nervous and thrilled, happy and frightened. I wore my new wool jumper in forest green, a beige turtleneck sweater, and chunky Frye boots with a two-inch heel. I'd pulled the sides of my hair back into a barrette, and I'd dabbed Maja perfume behind my ears. Alden was at a planning meeting for the university faculty, so I only had a three-hour break.

I heard his truck door slam, opened the screen door so that Jasper could race to him, and then stood in the doorway, taking in the sight of Clay, his backpack slung over one shoulder, a heavy Irish cabled sweater all that stood between him and winter.

"God," he said, when we finally separated and looked at each other.

"Your hair," I said, touching his short locks. "It's curly!" He'd grown a beard as if to compensate for the loss of head hair, and his beard grew in with red curls nestled amongst the blond. "I like it," I said, grinning. "You look wonderful."

"I decided it was time to let go of some things," he said, stroking my hair.

I pointed at my temples and turned my profile to him. "Do you see?"

"What?"

"Gray."

He kissed the few gray hairs I identified, and we laughed when Jasper squeezed in between us.

"So, first," he said, "your crows. Are they really gone?"

"Completely."

"What will you do?"

"For now, I think I'll keep trying to write poetry. Keep drawing, painting."

"Wow."

"I know. I'm surprised, too." I thought a moment and then said, "That's not right. I'm not surprised. In a way, for years I've been drifting away from science, into poetry and art. Maybe that part of me was always there, just biding its time while science held the reins . . ." I petered out, then said: "Maybe the birds left me at the right time." As soon as I said it, I knew it was true.

"You know what they say about adaptation, right?" Clay gripped my shoulder. "That IQ is actually a measurement of adaptability—the more adaptable, the higher the IQ."

"So we're both adapting. You, in the facial hair category, me in the realm of literature and art."

"Thanks a lot," he said, poking me in the ribs. "Such a compliment. *Laudatory*," he said drawing out the first syllable.

I laughed, then sipped my coffee and lay back on the cushions. I felt I'd found sanctuary, that everything would be all right. He'd come back to me.

"How was it?" I asked. "With your family, I mean."

"Actually, it felt good. It made my parents so happy to see me, especially for more than a couple of days." He used his thumb and index finger to move the curls of his beard away from his mouth. "Mom cooked, and Dad and I split a mountain or two of firewood."

"And your sleep? Any nightmares?"

"Some, but they were quiet, I think. But, Meridian, you know we didn't talk about any of it. The war. Talking about it is not how my family does things."

"It's not a topic people know how to talk about," I said, realizing my coffee had grown cold.

Clay took a bite of the fruitcake and grimaced.

"What?" I asked, propping myself up on my elbows.

"I can't decide what I've missed more," he smiled. "Making love with you, or your cooking."

"Asshole!"

"Let's go, Meridian. I need you."

The pieces of my world clicked audibly into place, the long winter darkness and miasma of death that had consumed me surrendered, and I thought: *Now I know why loons call only in the summer.*

• • •

I STOOD IN LINE, waiting to pick up a refill of Alden's blood pressure medicine. Ahead of me, I overheard Lisa Morrison tell the pharmacist she needed cough medicine for her daughter.

I felt a light touch on my forearm and turned to see Clay standing beside me in his faded jeans and turtleneck sweater. Lisa glanced at Clay; I saw her eyes widen briefly, her nostrils flare as if she needed extra oxygen.

"What's happening?" Clay asked.

"Picking up a prescription," I said, my voice as matter of fact as I could make it.

"Well," he said and then touched his fingertips to my waist, an intimate gesture that quickly registered in Lisa's expression. I looked away from her, and Clay added, "Be seeing you."

"Take care," I said, wanting to disappear.

"WHAT WAS THAT?" I asked Clay over the phone.

"What?"

"At the drugstore."

"Saying hello?"

"Touching me."

"I didn't touch you."

"You did. You put your hand to my waist."

"Well, it was automatic. And what's the big deal?"

"The big deal?"

"Yeah. What's your problem?"

"This is my community, Clay. You can't expose me that way."

"You need to mellow out."

"I'm hanging up."

"Jesus, Meridian."

"Don't do that again. Don't mark your territory, assert your rights in public that way again."

"You think that was what it was about? I can't be friendly? People can't know that you even know me?"

"Lisa Morrison saw you. What if word gets back to Alden?"

"I got no problem with that."

"Well, I do. This is my life. It's my risk to take—not yours. You don't get to decide for me."

"OK."

"All right."

"I love it when you get all riled up."

"I'm hanging up."

"Promises, promises."

I hung up.

I READ MY POEM "Recipe for Crushed Hope" to the women's discussion group:

Take one Naïve Girl.
Bring to room temperature in the Big City.
Add three cups Academia.
Sift in one cup Encouragement.
Fold in two drops Love.
Sprinkle with one teaspoon Adoration.
Mix thoroughly.
Spoon carefully into greased Pan of Matrimony.
Bake in Desert Heat for 25 years.
Test doneness with Careless Toothpick.
Let cool on Wire Rack of Inertia.
Serve with generous dollops of Benign Neglect.

When I finished, I saw sympathy in Barbara's face, confusion in Judy's. Emma leaned over and kissed my cheek. Margo Whiting pulled a tissue from her purse and blew her nose.

"Well, I'm just going to say it," Betty Van Hessel said. "Meri, you just made me look in the mirror, and I don't like what I see."

"Ditto," Marge said.

"I don't get it," Judy said. "Will somebody please explain it to me?"

Emma burst into laughter, and then, one by one, we all joined her—even Judy.

"Aw hell," I said, wiping my eyes and grinning at my friends.

"Misery loves company!" Betty shouted. "Let's break out the mimosas."

"I still don't get it," Judy said.

"I DON'T WANT TO nag." We were lying on Clay's mattress in a haze of post-coital bliss. Our affair was ten months old, and yet I would still nearly tap-dance my feet with impatience to see him.

"Nag?" I asked.

"I want to know your thoughts. What are you thinking, Meridian?"

"About?"

"Us."

"More than I can say."

"Well, then let me be more specific." He turned my head so that I faced him rather than the cracks in the plaster of his ceiling. "About coming with me to Berkeley."

I took a deep breath, let it out slowly. "It's a dream."

"Meaning?"

"Dreams can come true." His face lit up. "But not yet, not yet," I said, stroking his eager cheek. "Although I feel I have less and less reason to stay—now, not even my crows." I ran my index finger over his lips. "I have to find the strength to leave a fading man."

We lay there, looking at each other. I was afraid—contemplating the ramifications of leaving Alden, how it might change my definition of myself, were I to abandon the man who had, for most of my life, held my hand and set my course.

IN THE MIDDLE OF breakfast, Alden rushed to the bathroom. Jasper pushed his nose as far beneath the door as possible, whining.

It had begun happening more often—Alden's having to leave the table during a meal or ensconcing himself in the bathroom after a meal. I could not use onions in anything—they produced excessive gas, diarrhea. He could not eat much fiber, and so I stuck to white rice, white bread, pastas, and left out broccoli or salads. Spices made him ill, so I quit making Mexican food.

I knocked on the bathroom door.

"Don't come in," he said, a tinge of panic to his voice. "Finish your breakfast."

I stood there, silently tracing the grain of the wooden door with my thumb.

"Meri, just go."

"You need help."

"Just go."

"Go see Dr. Philips. Please."

"Go away."

"I'm going."

"Good."

THE WEEK-LONG PROTESTS IN Washington, D.C., by the Vietnam Veterans Against the War took place in April of 1971. There was Clay, front and center, on our new color television. He'd told me he'd be gone for a week, but he'd kept his destination, its purpose, a secret. I watched him march alongside Gold Star mothers, shook my head when the government incomprehensibly locked the gates of Arlington Cemetery, kept the women from laying wreaths on their sons' graves. Listening to John Kerry's testimony before the Senate Foreign Relations Committee, I heard *rape* and *telephone wire taped to genitals*. And then, on Friday, Clay and more than eight hundred other veterans threw their medals and ribbons on the steps of the Capitol.

I left the living room in tears, hiding from Alden in the bathroom until I was certain the news was over. The courage of Clay's convictions—that's what I saw when I watched Clay amongst the other veterans. But I worried for his job, his future. He'd probably just lost any chance at a security clearance; he'd be drummed out of the Lab. He'd risked so much to say what he felt needed to be said and to be the person he wanted to be. How could I not match him? How could I not rise to the challenge?

I LEFT A NOTE on Clay's kitchen counter.

April 30, 1971

Oh, Clay. I saw you.

Do you know what H.L. Mencken said? He said that while it's noble to die for an idea, it would be much more noble if men died for ideas that were true.

I've decided. I will come with you to Berkeley.

Yours—Meridian

"HOW ARE YOU GOING to tell Alden?"

"I don't know."

"When will you tell Alden?"

"I don't know," I said.

Gliding along in Emma's new, plush, living-room-sized Cadillac, we were returning from a day in Albuquerque. Each month, I'd been removing twenty to fifty dollars in cash from the checking account and, thus far, Alden had chosen to ignore my little financial rebellion. Emma and I had gone to Paris Shoes at the Winrock Shopping Center, tried on a dozen pairs a piece, taxed the salesman who kept disappearing behind curtains and reappearing laden with boxes, and then each bought two pairs.

I was particularly excited about the bone-colored wedge heels—strappy things that were almost like stilts. I had no idea where I'd wear them—but in California, surely there would be more opportunities. I'd been daydreaming about living near the sea, the kindness of humidity. In my head, I was recreating myself—wearing long cotton skirts that floated gracefully in a breeze off of the bay, colorful tank tops. I loved what I'd seen of the kids' creative hodgepodge of Victorian lace and pop colors—that form of self-expression that marked Clay's generation. He promised we'd hunt through San Francisco's antique stores and used clothing shops, that he'd buy me a feather boa and long strings of pearls.

"Let's stop at the La Fonda for dinner," I said as we neared the southern outskirts of Santa Fe.

Emma hit her turn signal. "Will Alden be all right?"

"He can stick a Swanson's TV dinner in the oven. How about Vince?"

"He can open a can of soup."

As we climbed the steps of the west entrance to the La Fonda Hotel, a crow called out an evening message from the top of a nearby building. He had an unusual rasp to his voice, and I felt a twinge of desire to be back in the scientist's role. Inside, an ammonia-tinted cloud of permanent wave solution floated down from the beauty parlor on the second level, and I saw exhausted tourists sitting on the deflated leather cushions of the lobby's heavy wooden furniture. A few panhandling hippies, one of them using an old black top hat as a collection plate, quietly solicited handouts from the tourists.

"Do you miss them, your birds?" Emma asked when we were seated in the restaurant.

"I do. All the time."

"Will you go back to ornithology at Berkeley; is that part of the plan?"

"Not immediately. I'll miss the fall semester, even assuming Berkeley will have me. Clay will go out first in September, find us a place to live, and I'll go later—once I get a divorce, pack my things." I sighed—what I was contemplating was daunting.

We were quiet while the waiter, in a cropped turquoise jacket holding a silver pitcher, filled our water glasses. He lit the tabletop candle and brought Emma a clean fork.

"May I ask you an extremely intimate question?"

"I'd say I opened that door, Emma."

She steeled herself. "Are you leaving Alden for Clay or for your birds? Why are you leaving? Why Berkeley and not someplace else? What do you think a divorce and move will do for you that you can't do here?"

"That's more than one intimate question."

"Sorry."

"No need to be. Oh, Emma, I'm just stalling because you're asking me hard questions I can't really honestly answer, questions I've been asking myself." I overloaded a chip with salsa and tried to keep from dribbling tomato juice down my chin.

"Will you try to answer even a few of those questions before you take this irrevocable step?"

I finished chewing. "Let me say this . . . . I can say this: it's not just lust. It's not just Clay. It's that if I don't do this, if I don't take this risk, then I'm afraid I will live with such enormous regret, such a sense of failure for never having tried. Does that make sense?"

"Abundant sense. I just . . . I'm not sure how to put it, how to say what I'm feeling, but let me try." The waiter delivered her tostada plate with extra sour cream, and Emma eyed my chiles rellenos.

Holding her fork above her plate, she delayed the first bite. "Make sure this is your dream, no one else's. The risk should be for you, not to please yet another man. Don't follow another man because he asks you to—don't repeat your previous error. This should be for you."

We ate in silence except for commenting on the delicious food. Finally, I said: "I'm not doing this just for Clay."

Emma looked at me, nodded solemnly. "That's good." And then, in an attempt to lighten the atmosphere, she said, "And don't stay because I will miss you so."

"I know," I said, looking at her across the table, seeing the flickering candle reflected in the lenses of her eyeglasses. The waiter cleared our plates, brought us *sopaipillas* with honey and coffee. I poured a generous amount of cream into my cup and then remembered: "I brought a poem for you to read." I handed her a folded piece of paper. She read it out loud:

> Men do.
> Women make do.
> We wait, patient Penelope at the hearth.
> We conform, good girls in girdles.
> We serve, suppressed sighs growing stale.
> We meld with oblivion,
> Flying ever in his slipstream.

"Remind me about slipstreams," she said, folding the page and handing it back to me.

"Migratory birds make use of the slipstream. Alden calls it 'vortex surfing.' Wingtip vortices generated by the lead bird donate a sort of lift force so that the birds following the leader don't have to work as hard to achieve lift. The trick for the subsequent bird is to achieve optimal adjustment of distance between herself and the lead bird so that she can obtain the benefit of added lift. The follower also has to adjust her wing flapping to that of the lead bird."

"Wonderful. Now in my variant of English, please."

"I can benefit from flying in Alden's slipstream if I adjust my position and speed, the timing of the flapping of my wings, to his. If I don't do that, there's no benefit to flying in formation, and I might as well be on my own. He also determines where we fly." I closed my eyes for a moment. "Crows don't fly in formation; they do not vortex surf."

"All right . . ."

"The slipstream is an illusion. It's a trick, a deceit."

"For some women. For some couples."

"Granted."

ON THE NIGHT OF May 8, I awoke to the noise of Alden retching into the toilet. I tied my cotton robe about me and stood in the doorway to the bathroom. He'd thrown off his T-shirt, and I could see the vertebrae of his spine etched in his flesh like the fossilized remains of a fallen dinosaur. He straightened, wiped his mouth with a length of toilet paper, and saw me standing there.

"Go back to bed."

"Something you ate?"

"It's been going on for a while," he said, using the edge of the sink to help him stand. He ran cold water, rinsed his face and mouth.

"What does 'a while' mean?"

"Several hours. But don't let's start with the interrogation."

The retching began again, and Alden knelt once more on the floor. This time I saw the result—dark, green-brown bile. When he moved into profile, I could see his belly: It was the size of a bass drum, blown up like some sort of aberrant creature in a carnival freak show. I knelt beside him, touched the taut skin.

"There is something terribly wrong here."

"I'll be fine."

"No. I'm taking you to the emergency room," I said, assuming greater authority than I had. "This is dangerous, Alden."

"No."

"You're being foolish. Foolhardy. Your body is speaking to you."

He turned and looked me full in the face, peevishly imitating me: "*Speaking to me*, Meri? Where in the hell do you get that kind of language?"

"What does it matter where I got it?" I fumbled. "It's obvious to anyone who looks at you—you are ill."

He flushed the toilet and almost immediately sent another torrent of brown liquid into the bowl as it slowly refilled.

I stood. "Your choice. Either I take you in, or I call an ambulance." He motioned for me to leave the room and then his legs gave out, and he sat hard on the floor. I was already untying the sash on my robe and slipping it from my shoulders: "I'm going to put on some clothes and start the car. Stay here until I come get you." He was wearing his shearling slippers and blue cotton pajama bottoms—that would be enough, if I grabbed a blanket. I'd get the mop bucket and a roll of paper towels so he could throw up in the car on the way to the hospital. Because I wasn't sure how long we'd be gone, I filled Jasper's bowl with extra kibble and made sure he had plenty of water.

Alden was like an obedient, chastised child by the time I held the door for him and handed him the bucket, stowing the paper towels at his feet.

MILES OF SAGE-GREEN WALLS and pine-toned linoleum. Starched white uniforms, crepe-soled shoes squeaking on polished floors. The purgatorial wait for blood tests. Reports of bowel habits coaxed from the reluctant, private, dignified scientist who'd never once even mentioned the existence of bowel movements to his wife of nearly three decades. A man who was used to being in charge and plotted all contingencies in advance, was now reduced to a helpless state. When Alden began to hallucinate, asked me about the "white stuff all over my legs," they started an IV to keep him from becoming further dehydrated. Finally, interpretation of X-rays of Alden's abdomen: intestinal blockage, a growth of some kind. It was most likely a tumor, cancer.

In two terse sentences the doctor altered the course of our lives, like a lightning-felled tree suddenly damming a stream, sending the flow skittering across tender green fields.

They decided to send him by ambulance to Albuquerque for surgery, and I was to follow in my car, as he'd probably be admitted for some time.

I stopped by the house, hurriedly packed a bag, turned on some lights, and called Clay, asked him to come get Jasper, and then to lock up our house. To all of his questions, I said "I don't know," including his questions about me, how I was doing. There was no time for the luxury of contemplation.

THE SURGERY TOOK OVER six hours, and although at one point the nurse came out to tell me that Alden would not have to endure an ostomy, in the end, they created a mouth in the soft flesh of his abdomen that pursed its lips and emptied the contents of his bowels into a bag.

The cancer, they said, had set up shop in several areas of his intestines and had likely spread to other areas of his body, including his liver. His body was shot full of rampaging, mutinous cells, although Alden didn't yet know any of this. He'd be sleeping off the anesthesia for some time. With the exhausted surgeon seated next to me in the waiting room, the nurse encouraged me to find a motel room and get some sleep.

"But what's the prognosis? What does all of this mean in terms of his life?" I asked.

The doctor removed his surgical cap, fiddled with it in his lap, slouched, and relaxed his long legs. Dr. Bridges had been on his feet most of the night, his hands in Alden's guts. I thought with some amazement that he'd seen parts of my husband I'd never seen, that, in a way, he knew Alden on a more intimate level than I ever could.

"It's hard to say, Mrs. Whetstone. It's highly variable, highly individualized. Your oncologist can give you a better idea, a bit further down the line."

"All right," I said, exhausted, benumbed.

"He could have months, maybe a year."

"Ten years, maybe?" I bargained.

"Probably not."

I checked into the Trade Winds Motel, called Emma and Clay, and then slept for a few hours. I hadn't yet cried; I didn't panic but instead focused on listing what needed taken care of: bills to be paid, Alden's work to be notified. I was focused on Alden, how he would handle the news, how he would respond to plans to treat his cancer. I guessed that he'd first defer to the medical experts and then make himself into an expert, too—that he'd learn it all, manage his fear with his fierce intellect.

"THERE'S MONEY," ALDEN SAID, his voice hoarse from the tube they'd slid down his throat during surgery. "Enough to take care of you when I'm gone. I've made arrangements. Everything's been arranged."

A brutal, chain-stitched incision ran from the top of his pubic hair, around his belly button, and up to his sternum. I gripped his hand, hard, and said: "Just focus on getting better."

He put a hand to the base of his throat. "The top left drawer in my desk has the safe deposit box key. My will is there." He winced and touched the thick gauze over his incision.

"All right." I put my fingers lightly to his brow.

"Meri."

"Yes."

"I'm sorry."

"Oh, Alden, don't."

"I let you down."

"This isn't your doing."

"But it is. It is. The doctor was in this morning. I should have paid attention to the warning signs."

"It doesn't matter now. Don't go down that path."

"But I made you that promise."

A promise? What promise?, I wondered. Then I remembered. There had been one night, lying in the dark with Alden, just months into our New Mexico life, when I'd made him swear that he would not die on me as my father had, that he would not abandon me, leave me alone.

Seated beside Alden's hospital bed, watching him as he slept, I realized something: I'd chosen crows for my research because of their intelligence. I'd not chosen a bird with interesting feather coloration or displays, a songbird or a bird that migrated to exotic climates. I chose the smartest bird, a bird with complicated language and behaviors.

I chose Alden's boundless intellect, the complexity of his language. I should never have expected him to step outside his species, to dazzle me with reds, greens, blues, and yellows, or to sing me into serenity.

I kissed the back of his hand, next to where the IV needle dove into his vein. How could I have thought about leaving this man? A man who had loved me as best he could? He was apologizing for unwillingly dying and abandoning me—when I had intended to abandon him quite willingly.

I cried then. For Alden, Clay, for the three of us, my face buried in the rough hospital sheets stamped "BCMC" in bold black letters—as if any person in his right mind would steal the Bernalillo County Medical Center's horror-stained linens. Alden rested his palm on the top of my head, and I thought I smelled his pipe tobacco, that the smoke of his pipe circled the two of us, settled warm and comforting next to Alden's hip, laid a protective, comforting head lightly on him.

I RENTED A FURNISHED apartment near the hospital. Soon, I had a routine: first thing in the morning, I climbed the hospital stairs to the sixth floor. A kiss on Alden's forehead, a series of questions about what the doctors had said when they made their rounds, and then downstairs to the cafeteria for coffee and biscuits, a piece of fruit. Playing Chinese checkers and Parcheesi with Alden in between his being whisked off in a wheelchair to one section of the hospital or another for one treatment or another, sitting with my sketchpad and drawing while he slept. He'd never been willing to pose for me, but now he was captive, and I chronicled the emergence of even more of his bones as the chemotherapy took its toll, as they took him to the edge of death in an effort to heal him.

At the apartment complex, I met my next-door neighbor, one of the soldiers forced on the Bataan Death March when we lost Corregidor to the Japanese. Berto had been sent to Bataan with a large contingent of New Mexicans, mostly Hispanic. He showed me his mess kit one hot summer evening as we sat on the steps sipping iced tea. The pitted metal dish bore the scratched names of his fellow prisoners of war, many of whom had not survived the lack of food, the heat, the disease, brutality, and haphazard machine gun fire. He touched his fingertips to the sacred names and told me he'd never washed it—that it might still have microscopic remnants of rice, rotten chicken, blood. Berto's other souvenirs of Bataan included malaria, beriberi, nightmares, an inability to feed his dog without retching at the smell of the dog food, and a promise to himself never again to go barefoot—not even at night when he got up to go to the bathroom or to check the locks on his doors.

When the bombs were dropped on Hiroshima and Nagasaki, an eighty-pound Berto was on a boat, barely alive and being taken to Japan as slave labor. He said men in the hold of the ship were killing their fellow prisoners, just to be able to drink blood and slake their thirst. He held my hand and told me that the atomic weapons created by Alden and his fellow scientists had saved his life.

In that moment, I knew that I would not leave Alden. The Meridian I wanted to see in the mirror would not leave him to die alone—that was not who I knew myself to be.

CLAY WAS TO HEAD for Berkeley in a week. He was still following our original plan—that he would go first, find us a place to live. During Alden's hospitalization, we'd talked sporadically on the phone, but we hadn't seen each other at all since I'd made my decision. Now, I'd asked that Clay come to Albuquerque for the day to see me. I had to tell him.

Just after dawn, before the September heat had a chance to intensify and leach the minerals from our bones, we threaded our way through the petroglyphs on the mesa west of the city.

"Here," I said, pointing to some shadowed chunks of black lava next to a petroglyph depicting a family of goats grazing near water.

A student pilot circled his small plane slowly overhead, and the sound of the plane's engine reverberated off of the rocky escarpment. A pair of juvenile turkey vultures landed on a nearby escarpment.

"It's probably stating the obvious," I began, "but I'll do so nevertheless." I reached for Clay's hand, and he gripped mine.

"You're not coming."

"I'm not coming."

"Ever?"

"I'm sorry," I said.

He tossed my hand from his and stood with his back toward me so that I couldn't read his expression. "If he gets better?"

"I don't think he will, Clay."

He faced me once more, his jaw set, challenging. "If he dies?"

I gripped the sharp edges of the rock where the lava had been sheared off. I wanted to cut myself, slice my palms, release and so end the pain, avoid hurting this man whom I so loved. "I'm so sorry, Clay. So, so sorry."

"Everything we talked about, all of the things we planned. Your new life. Your *full* life, Meridian. What was that? Lies? Just talk? Did you mean a single thing you said?"

"You know what I wanted. You know how *much* I wanted."

"But you're going to give it all up, just like that." He snapped his fingers.

"No, not just like that," I stood and snapped my fingers in response. "Do you think for one moment this is easy for me? God," I spat, "what am I supposed to do? How do I live with myself, no matter which way I turn? This is untenable. I can't win, don't you see that? I've lost *everything*, Clay. *Everything!*"

"You're really doing this. You're really going to do this, aren't you?" He kicked at broken pieces of rock. It was then that I saw the coiled rattlesnake just inches from his feet, lying in the shade of a chamisa.

"Snake!" I yelled.

Clay leapt backwards, nearly falling. "Shit!"

I grabbed him from behind, encircled him with my arms and buried my face in his sweaty back. I breathed deeply.

"Fuck!" he said. "Fuck fuck fuck fuck fuck," he finished.

CLAY HAD TO COME through Albuquerque on his way to California, and so I met him in the hospital lobby. We sat in a line of gray molded plastic chairs as far from squalling babies as possible.

"For you," he said, handing me a wrapped gift. I could feel a binding. "But open it later, when I'm not around."

"If Alden weren't so sick. If he weren't dying."

"I know, Meridian. I know. I understand, OK?" He patted my knee. "I don't like it, I don't agree, I hate this beyond belief, but I get it. I know why you're doing what you're doing. I just . . ." He stopped and cleared his throat, gained control of his voice. "I just can't do this anymore. It's too painful, this teeter-totter of hope. And," he paused, clearly considering whether he should verbalize his next thought. "Maybe if I leave, maybe if I go, you'll change your mind."

There it was again, that beast of hope without which life would be so much easier.

"I love you. I swear."

"Baby," he breathed into my hair.

And then he stood and walked away, leaving me in that roomful of strangers, his gift clutched to my chest as if it could protect me.

THE BOOK WAS *The Painted Bird*, by Jerzy Kosinski. In the front, Clay had written: "To my love, Meridian—named for an imaginary line, but so real to me. PEACE. LOVE. Fare *well*." He'd marked a page with a crow feather, and a penciled star told me where to begin reading.

It was a passage about a wild hare, a spectacular hare that had been caught and caged. At first, the hare rebelled against captivity, threw itself against the walls of the cage. But eventually the hare's captor could open the cage door, and the hare would not attempt escape but instead would only move inches outside of the opening, briefly smelling freedom but finally choosing to turn its back and return to the hutch. Clay twice underlined Kosinski's beautiful words about the rabbit having taken the cage into himself.

A Fall of Woodcocks

1. *This solitary, superbly disguised bird is almost impossible to discern as it forages on the forest floor.*
2. *Woodcocks are widely hunted, with about a million birds killed annually.*

Alden and I paid obeisance to the god otherwise known as five-fluorouracil, 5-FU. We drove back and forth to Albuquerque for treatments, Alden suffering even more indignity by having to ride in the passenger seat while I piloted the Morris Minor. The drug's side effects were horrific necessities: agonizing joint pain, ulcers in his mouth and throat that further decreased his ability and desire to eat, volcanic eruptions of the skin on the backs of his hands, and—worst of all, given his ostomy—diarrhea. One by one, he lost his toenails; his beautiful, thick, curly hair thinned until I could see the vulnerable pink skin of his scalp. He was tired all of the time and could not get warm, no matter how many layers of clothing we dressed him in, no matter how high the level on the heating pad that accompanied him everywhere.

He endured it all, mostly silently. Often, his throat was so sore that he couldn't call to me for help, and so I gave him a little silver bell that he could ring. Even that he did reluctantly, as if he shouldn't ask anything more of me.

In November of 1971, just before my forty-eighth birthday, the brown-bile vomiting began again, and his gut blew up to the size of a dirigible. This time, he didn't fight me—we headed straight for the hospital and then were sent to Albuquerque for another surgery.

The BCMC waiting room where I sat was packed with impoverished people from distant parts of rural New Mexico who had moved in for the duration, accompanied by pillows, blankets, and shopping bags full of food. I watched one woman who barely fit between the arms of her chair eat an entire bag of Lay's potato chips, washed down with a can of Tab. Her thick black hair was matted on one side, and dingy gray bra straps escaped from her short-sleeved top. A toddler crawled at her feet, pushing a Matchbox car back and forth on the linoleum while a television bolted near the ceiling spewed a soap opera.

An elegant black man pressed his wife's shoes to his chest and stood, staring silently out a window at the variegated pigeons that intermittently wheeled on and off of the rooftop. His posture was stalwart, dignified, and he wore a light gray suit, a purple silk tie. The low heels he held were cream colored, with precise bows decorating open toes. I resisted an impulse to pull him from his isolation and comfort him. I could do nothing for him.

This time Alden's operation took eight and a half hours. Dr. Bridges walked me down the hallway in an attempt to find some privacy, and standing next to a display case filled with meaningless, self-congratulatory placards the hospital had undoubtedly awarded itself, he told me he'd removed three more tumors from Alden's intestines. There would be no 5-FU miracle.

"Meridian," he said—because after all, by this point we knew each other better than we'd ever wanted to know each other—"it can't be long, now. It's unstoppable."

I said I understood, but I didn't. There was no sin Alden could have committed that would justify this slow, torturous death.

"I'll speak with your oncologist, but I don't see any reason to continue putting your husband through chemotherapy or radiation. At this point, it should be palliative care. We'll do our best to alleviate his symptoms."

"Yes," I said.

"His pain."

"Yes," I said.

"Meridian, is there someone who can drive you? Are you staying in Albuquerque?"

"No and yes for now," I said. "But I'll be fine."

"If you're certain."

"Oh, I'm not certain of anything anymore," I said.

I walked back to the waiting room. A baby had the collar of my coat stuffed in his mouth, and I could see a wide, hydra-headed sheen of saliva coating the navy-blue wool like a freeway system of snail trails. The child's mother paid no attention as I pulled the material from the baby's tiny fists and he began to wail. I used a tissue to remove what I could of the slick spit, and when I searched for a trash can, I saw the elegant man once more.

He curved his body so as better to hear the diminutive nurse who was speaking to him. The leather of his wife's shoes crumpled as he clutched them tighter. The nurse put a hand on his elbow, and he buried his face in the shoe bows. As I watched the stranger's drama play out, I felt the beginnings of tears. For the man, his wife. Not for Alden or me—we were now old hands at this business of pain, of hope and despair.

CLAY'S BOX OF BIRTHDAY gifts was waiting for me when we returned. Bob and June had been watching the house and keeping Jasper for us, and when Bob took Jasper into the bedroom to greet Alden, I slit open the tape on the box.

On top, there was a sandwich bag in which Clay had rolled an index finger of dope and written *For Alden—good for nausea.* Then, nestled in a small black box was one of the brass buttons from Clay's Marines uniform. He'd threaded it through a leather thong so that it became a bracelet. I ran my thumb across the button's eagle, globe, and anchor, and noticed that on the reverse he'd had it engraved: *Nemo me impune lacessit.* It was the phrase my father had loved, the one that adorns the Scottish pound coin: *No one wounds me with impunity*. I didn't read it as angry or vengeful. What it told me was that Clay was going to fight; it told me he wanted for me to fight, too. Not for us—we were done, over, and my skin was stitched to Alden's slow death. But for life, for hope.

In an envelope at the bottom of the box there was a photo showing the inside of Clay's left wrist, now tattooed with a replica of my painting of Withered Foot, bordered by an elaborate, twisted oval that made me think of Clay's long braid. On the back of the photo, he'd written lines about a man, a woman and a blackbird from Wallace Stevens' "Thirteen Ways of Looking at a Blackbird."

Indelible, I thought, *he made us indelible*, and I began to cry.

I did not respond to Clay's gift box, as beautiful as it was. I thanked him in my heart, just as I told him every night that I loved him, missed him. I also wrote to him, in my journals. Notes about crows, birds, my thoughts, drawings, poems. What I would tell him, were he seated with me before the fire or lying next to me in bed. In my journals, we had wild, animated conversations. On good days, I knew he could feel me, that he understood.

ALDEN AND I TOASTED 1972 quietly, the reality of his impending death left unacknowledged. His weight had dropped to less than 130 pounds, and although palliative care had been promised, the doctors were stingy with their prescriptions for pain meds. Alden remained stoic, but I was desperate to relieve his anguish, and Clay's gift of marijuana was long gone. My desperation bore no fruit—nothing that would let Alden float above relentless bone pain, for now the cancer carved byzantine catacombs through his bones.

In April he fell from the edge of the bed, and I was unable to lift him. I called Bob, who carried Alden to the car and drove us to the hospital. Alden's left femur was broken, and he was admitted for observation. Then, in the chain reaction that had become Alden's life, he developed pneumonia. He spent his days sleeping in a fetal position, an oxygen mask over his nose and mouth, tubes extending from his frail remnant of a body, and one leg encased in plaster, an anchor weighting him to this life.

For a week, his body put up an ineffectual battle against the pneumonia. I listened to his moist, labored breathing. He had not spoken for days, had not eaten in over a week, and his eyes, on the rare occasion they opened, were unfocused. Alden had stepped back from the world; I could feel his departure, could almost glimpse the stark white bottoms of his bare feet as he ran briskly away from me, down a long, dark hallway.

On the 21st of April I climbed onto the bed, fit my body to his back. His love for me had been clumsy, at times wholly inept, but it had been solid, unwavering. And, I realized, my love for him fit the same description. I had never once stopped loving Alden Whetstone, not in the entire twenty-eight years of our marriage. I whispered: "Tomorrow is our anniversary. But you don't have to stay, my love," I said, my voice breaking. "You can go now." I reached around him, took one of his hands in mine. I kissed his medicine-scented neck. "I can do this. I'm strong enough."

I doubt it was in response to anything I'd said, but he took a deep breath, and I could hear it crackling in his lungs. His legs jerked a few spasmodic kicks, and I put my index finger between my teeth and bit until I tasted blood.

WHEN I ASSURED ALDEN that I was strong enough to survive, I was sincere. I was also naïve. Surviving his actual death, making it through writing his obituary, funeral negotiations, the well-meaning telephone calls and deliveries of flowers and food, the thank-you notes—that was nothing. I made my lists, crossed things off. It was after the rituals were past, when the house was ominously quiet, the phone silent, when people no longer knew what to do with me, what to say to me, and so chose instead to avoid me—that was when depression arrived to sit in my lap like an obstinate bowling ball.

For more than a year, I'd had such a singular, driving purpose to my life—to care for Alden. Now that was gone. I no longer had a *reason*. I imagined it must be like losing one's lifelong faith in God; there was nothing but a wide swath of desolate desert before me. Too, I think that Alden's drama had delayed any real knowledge of the finality of Clay's absence. Every supposition I'd made about how my life would be, its definitional boundaries, had been obliterated.

Some days, I found myself sitting on the couch for hours, lost in thought, immobile. Repeatedly, I'd tell myself to stand up, *STAND UP!*, but still I sat. My to-do lists lost their power to motivate. I thought about hiking, losing myself with movement and sweat in the summer woods, but still I sat. I left the radio turned off and the television inert, a hollow, cold eye. The refrigerator hummed, the kitchen clock ticked—at one point I considered silencing them, too, but the mountainous task of rising from the couch was too overwhelming in anything other than concept—so still, I sat.

Clay must have heard of Alden's death, because he sent me Emily Dickinson, the page with "Hope is the thing with feathers" dog-eared. I read the poem, immediately dismissed as pabulum Miss Dickinson's little bird, and put the book aside to gather dust. I would not open the door to hope, no matter how exquisite her feathers, how promising and sweet her song. I was done with hope.

GABRIEL SALAZAR SAT IN his high-backed black leather chair in the offices of Salazar, Salazar and Dabney off of Old Pecos Trail in Santa Fe. A glass wall looked out on a stand of white-barked aspen trees and a piñon-dotted gully. The other office walls bore several bland western landscapes meant to be innocuous but offending by their very fungibility. I hadn't known of the existence of Gabriel Salazar the probate lawyer. I had no last will and testament of my own. I'd always assumed that when I died, anything I had would just go to Alden—but Alden had met with this man and created what the lawyer was calling an "estate plan."

"Mrs. Whetstone, your husband directed that all assets fund a trust. He appointed the bank in Los Alamos to administer the trust and disburse funds to you in accordance with the terms of the trust." Salazar paused to be sure I was following.

So this was what Alden had meant when from his hospital bed he'd told me everything had been taken care of, that everything was "set." "What are the 'terms of the trust'?" I asked.

He turned pages in his file, running an index finger along the margin, "It's here, in Article VI, Section 4." He read silently and then looked up. "You are to be provided with a monthly allotment of $450. In addition, once a year you'll receive $2,000. Otherwise," he read again before continuing, "you would need to apply to the trustee, the bank, with a documented request for any extra funds. For example," he looked into a corner of his office for inspiration, "let's say you needed a new roof. You would make a written request for funds, including estimates to prove the necessary costs."

I was stunned. Alden's version of caretaking had put me in shackles. I took a deep breath, imagined my anger rising like water in the gully outside the lawyer's window, pictured brown, churning water full of sharp sticks, roiling, rotted tree trunks; I saw the water reach Gabriel Salazar's window and pummel the glass until it broke, dirty, cold water rushing over his tasteful carpeting, obliterating the carefully worded provisions of Alden's trust.

"You're saying I'm to have an allowance."

"The trust will disburse funds."

"An allowance. And a pathetically small one at that," I said.

The lawyer nervously adjusted the knot of his tie. "I can understand that this might come as a bit of a shock to you, but please don't kill the messenger. I'm only effectuating your husband's wishes."

"Understood, Mr. Salazar." I stood. "I'd like a copy of that file before I go."

"I really wish you'd stay a few more moments, let me explain."

"What else is there to explain? Maybe there's a provision indicating that if I go over budget I'm to be sent to bed without supper? Oh, *I* know," I said, following his gaze to the hallway where a secretary passed, "If I'm very very very *very* good, I can get a year-end bonus, maybe a box of candy or a new doll."

"Your husband just wanted for you to be safe, for you to be provided for."

Now I was lit. "You're wrong, Mr. Salazar. If Alden had wanted to provide for me, to care for me, he could have left what is *our* money—

not just his money, *our* money—to me to do with as I see fit. He could have remembered that he married me largely for my intellect, my abilities, and he could have chosen to acknowledge those abilities. He could have treated me with respect, but that's not what he chose to do." I walked to Salazar's doorway and paused while he half stood as a good-bye gesture. "I'll wait in the lobby for my copy," I said and walked away trying to project more assurance than I felt. I'd so few skills when it came to confrontation, but I had a vocabulary and a brain, and I was determined to learn to stand up for myself.

THAT NIGHT, I REMOVED my engagement and wedding rings. I tied them together with a length of gray satin ribbon from my sewing basket, and I buried them at the bottom of my jewelry box.

Over the course of the next few weeks, I talked with Emma, Bob, and June, and they all recommended the same law firm in Albuquerque. In the meantime, the Lab notified me of the existence of a life insurance policy—the proceeds of which had escaped the hungry jaws of Alden's trust plan. All I had to do was fill out forms and present a certified copy of his death certificate and—*voilà!*—I received a check for $100,000. It was more than enough to pay my limited expenses and fund a lawsuit to break the trust. I would take my jesses from Alden's tightly clenched fists at long last. If it took every penny of the $100,000, I would do it.

"GOOD. GOOD FOR YOU, Meridian," Emma said when, several months later, I finished updating her on the legal proceedings—my attorney had beaten back the bank's motion to dismiss my lawsuit, and so my case could continue. Emma and I were hunting for a parking place in Santa Fe, headed for lunch at the Pink Adobe. I was eagerly anticipating green-chile chicken enchiladas and a cup of dark coffee. It was early December 1972, and the air was heavy with the divine scent of piñon smoke feathering gently from chimneys. Most of the snow from two days earlier had melted, but a few inches coated the round-shouldered tops of adobe walls. Broken, dry staves of hollyhocks rattled in a cold breeze.

I watched a hippie couple wrapped in bold-patterned blankets. They held a toddler by the arms and kept him suspended between them, bouncing him and whooping each time they raised him high. The boy's giggles were infectious, and I grinned, blowing warm air into my gloves in an attempt to thaw my aching fingertips.

At the same time, I ignored the quick, responsive pain in my chest. It had been nearly a year and a half since I'd felt Clay's touch.

We found a corner table away from the tourists, their numerous shopping bags and their gaudy, post–ski hill attire. I didn't think I'd ever before seen so much down-filled nylon in one place, and I wondered how many geese it took to plump so many tourists.

"It's good to see you smiling again." Emma's cheeks were flushed from the cold, and she cleaned the condensation from her eyeglasses with hem of her purple turtleneck.

I unrolled my silverware from the cloth napkin. "It feels good to smile again."

"So, do you think you're coming out of it?"

The waitress poured coffee and took our orders. I held the mug in my cold hands, blew on the surface before sipping.

"Coming out of grief?" I asked.

"Yes."

"I do. But more out of the flatness, the lethargy. I think the grief continues—on some level or another, in one way or another, forever. And it continues despite my anger," I paused. "But yes, yes, Emma, I am pulling out of my tailspin."

We sat quietly for several minutes, both of us people watching.

"Have you thought about what you're going to do with yourself?"

I waited while the waitress put our plates before us. Emma was having a stuffed *sopaipilla* filled with shredded beef. I could almost hear Clay's commentary on the rampant carnivores. Emma lifted a forkful of her entrée.

"For a while," I said, "I thought I might travel." I pictured Alden's penurious savings spent on a trip to Niagara Falls, complete with a symbolic, rebellious ride on the *Maid of the Mist*, my face covered in a cold spray. "But then I realized I don't have a strong desire to travel—not the way I used to."

"More school then?"

"No, not that either. At least not now, at this point."

"Please tell me you're not going to move."

"I'm not going to move," I smiled at her.

She looked at her plate when she next spoke, avoiding my gaze. "Have you heard from Clay?"

"A book of poems. Gifts on my birthday."

"And?"

"And nothing." I fought to keep my voice even.

"What have you told him?"

"Nothing. Emma, if I respond, we'll start up again, and that's just wrong." I paused. "I know that sounds odd, probably makes little sense, because I still love him, will always love him. It's just that . . . well, I don't really know how to articulate it. I don't believe it would be a good thing—not anymore. He needs to live his life, and I need to find my way alone. It's one of the few things I know these days—that I need to make my way on my own."

I was pretending a greater ease with all of this than I actually felt. I fought a daily, sometimes hourly temptation to call or write to Clay, to pack a bag and fly to California. I could only hope that over time what felt like the insistent pull of an addiction would subside and let me relax into some level of forgetting.

"Bravo, Meridian. That's what I say—that, and that it is a privilege to watch you bloom. Especially," Emma winked, "in the middle of winter."

Later that afternoon we stopped by Payne's Greenhouse to walk through a giant room packed with plank tables full of poinsettias—pink, traditional red, creamy, candy-striped blooms. The air smelled of living, growing things; it was warm, humid, and I felt slightly drowsy, languid. What I hadn't said to Emma and had barely admitted to myself was how much I knew I would miss a man's touch, being held and comforted. Sex.

I walked outside to stand in the parking lot. An arrowhead of noisy ducks passed overhead. I counted them, was glad when I came up with an uneven number—it meant that they would accommodate the loner duck, like me.

Emma met me at the car with a flamingo-pink hibiscus. "For the exotic Meridian Whetstone, to commemorate her new life." She surprised me with a kiss on the cheek, and then held the door while I climbed in and set the beautiful plant on the floor next to my feet.

I hope I can keep it alive, was what I thought.

ONE AFTERNOON AFTER THE New Year, I returned home from a brisk winter walk and found a plain white envelope nestled within the curve of the handle on my front door. The lettering, which read MRS. WHETSTONE, was exaggerated, the letters drawn with great flourish.

I fixed Jasper his supper, lit a fire, and sat cross-legged on the couch before opening the envelope to read:

January 14, 1973

Dear Mrs. Whetstone,

My parents suggested that I contact you about a senior research paper I"m beginning this spring. I plan to write about birds,, and my parents say you are the person to talk to. Would you be willing to help me? I"d be forever grateful.

Sincerely,
Marvella Bennett (555-7710)

I watched the fire eat into a thick hunk of cedar. Flaming drops of sap fell from the log, hissing beneath the grate. Jasper stared me down until I patted the couch, giving him permission to join me—something I only dared do since Alden's death. He curled his rear next to my thigh, kicked a couple of times to inch me ever so slightly out of what he'd determined was his spot on the cushion.

"Comfortable?" I asked, pulling gently on his ears. "What do you think?" I held up the note, but he merely sniffed a few times and then buried his nose in his front paws.

I'd seen the ghostly Marvella from time to time—walking to school, picking wildflowers in Mesa Meadow. The Bennetts lived at the end of the cul-de-sac. Over the years, I'd seen Marvella's name in the *Monitor*, with references to her running the hurdles, winning at the regional level of the science fair competition. She'd grown tall, with an intensity to her expression that was remarkable.

"Of course I'll help her," I told Jasper, whose ribcage swelled with a deep, easy breath.

"TELL ME PRECISELY WHAT you've determined will be the premise of your paper," I said, sounding more like a schoolmarm than I intended. Marvella sat on the front edge of Alden's reading chair, her palms pressing on the outside of her thighs. She wore blue jeans—the straight-legged Levis I favored, not the hip-huggers I saw on most high school girls. Her legs were coltishly long; I could imagine her effortlessly stepping over hurdles as she rounded the track. She'd removed her down jacket to reveal a dark green crewneck sweater softened by age, and over her long straight pale-white hair she wore a cotton scarf patterned with spring flowers and a navy-blue border of curlicues. She possessed a serene, really rather extraordinary beauty.

I liked her. Immensely. Immediately. And that was before she answered my question.

"I want to study bird behavior and weather. How birds' behavior changes—if at all—just prior to certain weather events."

"Perfect!" I said, not quite believing the warm surge of joy I felt in the presence of this half-formed girl.

"I put out feeders, at home, and when it's about to rain or snow, the birds feed voraciously. They just go crazy. The sparrows, especially." She'd removed her hands from her thighs and they fluttered in the air around her. "Clouds of them, on the ground, on the feeders and in the bushes. I can't imagine where they all come from!"

"That's a good, concrete example. You should also consider any changes in flight patterns, what relationship they might have to changes in atmospheric pressure." She was nodding, wide-eyed and attentive. "Think about this, too," I said. "Do you want to observe variations in bird behavior in an artificial or natural setting? Or maybe you'd like to compare behaviors in two settings."

"I hadn't thought about that."

"Feeders create an unnatural environment. If you choose to observe them in that setting, it would be easier, but you would need to make that distinction in your paper."

"What do you think?"

"It's not my project, not my idea," I smiled at her.

"I don't know . . . ."

"What would stop you from watching them in the woods?"

"I don't know," she said, but it was clear she did know and was choosing not to say, that she was holding something back.

"Let's have tea," I stood to go into the kitchen. "Do you drink tea, Marvella?"

"Herbal?"

"Sure. Peppermint?"

"My favorite."

I put the kettle on the stove and leaned in the kitchen doorway, looking into the living room. Marvella had walked over to the set of bookshelves beneath the front window, and she picked up a miniature I'd done of a crow's nest filled with eggs.

"This is cool," she said. "Really cool."

"Thank you."

"You did this?"

"I did."

"Wow. And you're a scientist, too?"

For a moment, I couldn't decide what would be an honest answer. Finally, I said: "I was. Am. I am a lot of things, just as are most of us."

She put the piece back in its spot and turned to me. "Most of us?"

"Women. Men, too, but I was thinking of women."

"Not my mother."

"Your mother is a bright woman, Marvella."

"Oh, no doubt about that. But she's a housewife." She spat out the final word as if it were poisoned.

"Didn't she study astronomy? That's hardly something to dismiss so readily."

"But she quit! She doesn't even mention it, and you wouldn't even know she ever did anything that great."

The kettle began whistling, but I didn't want to turn away from this girl. "Your mother is like a lot of us, honey," I said. "That part of her isn't dead, it's just in shadow. She's still a smart woman deserving of your respect." I filled two mugs and set them on the coffee table, along with a bowl for the spent teabags. "Things are not as simple as they may seem." I watched her pinch the teabag and dunk it up and down. I inhaled the peppermint. "Some of us had to make some very difficult choices."

She set her mug down and looked at me. "Like what?"

"Like loving someone, wanting for him to have a good life, and giving up some of our plans."

"Did you?"

"Yes." I could tell she was waiting for me to go on. "I gave up my plan for a Ph.D. so that I could stay here with my husband, so that he could continue his research at the Lab."

"But didn't that piss you off?" She put a hand to her mouth. "Sorry." She blushed.

"It's OK. I'm not afraid of a little profanity. If we work together, you'll hear plenty of it from my lips."

"Would you? Would you consider working with me?"

"I'd be delighted, Marvella," I said, sipping my tea. "On many levels."

"Oh," she said, beaming. "Oh, thank you, Mrs. Whetstone!"

"You're welcome. Now, let's get out a pad of paper and start an outline."

• • •

I HAD THE CLERK in the photo shop show me all of the portable cassette tape recorders (there were two). I picked the one with the best microphone, and once home I wrapped it carefully in glossy white paper. I used plain old brown twine as ribbon, and I drew silhouettes of birds in flight. Marvella's research project was complete, her paper turned in—and this was my graduation gift to her. Although I knew she'd also use it to play music—I'd been hearing a lot from her about Cat Stevens and Gordon Lightfoot—I wanted for her to be able to record birdsong.

She showed up half an hour early, in tears. I sat her on the couch and tried to find out what had happened.

"Didn't Mr. Drummond like your paper?"

"No. No, I got an A+."

"All right then." I grabbed the Kleenex box from the kitchen counter and set it beside her. She blew her nose, flipped her hair behind her shoulders.

"My parents," she said.

"What about them? Weren't they proud?"

"Yes, they said it was great," she sniffed. "And I know they meant it."

"So, what?"

"My dad says they're putting their feet down."

"Meaning?"

"No Santa Cruz."

Marvella had been thrilled when she received her acceptance letter from the university. "They won't let you go?"

"No."

"Why on earth not?" The Bennetts had the money, it couldn't be that, and besides—employees of the Lab paid in-state tuition rates for California schools. "Marvella," I said, holding her shoulders and forcing her to look at me. "Why not?"

"Too far. Too liberal. And," now she scrunched her face, spoke mincingly: "If a New Mexico school was good enough for your brother Stirling, then it's good enough for you."

Stirling Bennett, the prodigy, had dealt his parents a near death blow when he turned down scholarship offers at the University of Chicago, Berkeley, and Yale and instead headed off to a New Mexico community college only one hundred miles down the road in Albuquerque. He'd not merely cut off his nose to spite his parents: He'd mutilated himself.

This was absurd. Just because Stirling had chosen to throw his life away didn't mean the Bennetts should punish their daughter. After all her hard work—to crush her spirit, to so gratuitously dismiss her immense thirst for knowledge, her lively curiosity. I hugged Marvella to me. How did one name a child "marvel" and then so incongruously deprive her? I could not let this girl go to waste, not without a fight.

I ASKED THE BENNETTS to meet me on neutral territory, in a place where they'd be reluctant to behave badly—so a restaurant. In Los Alamos, there were not many choices, and we ended up at Casa Luna, which made mediocre pizzas and enough other entrees so as to be good at none of them. I ordered fried chicken, which always took so long that Alden joked they first had to raise the chick from pullet to adult, then kill and dress it before making my meal. It bought me time.

"I've enjoyed working with Marvella," I said, focusing on her mother. If either was going to understand, it was the woman who'd had her own trajectory irremediably altered.

"She's been so happy, so enthusiastic," Rebecca said. "It's been a great experience for her."

"For me, too," I said, taking a sip of water.

Rebecca Bennett was an obese woman. The buttons on her blouse strained against untold tensile pressures, and her cheeks were heavy, soft, oversized peaches. Her skin was beautiful, and I could see how pretty she once must have been, before she'd decided to cloak her charms in an immense coat of fat. I imagined her struggling to climb the steps of the bleachers to watch her daughter run, fleet of foot. Her knuckles were indentations rather than mounds of bone, and her fingernails were immaculately manicured, a perfect bubblegum pink. It made me want to tuck my chipped fingernails beneath my thighs.

Mark Bennett sighed. "She's going through an awful teenaged rebellion just now, though. Pretty impossible. Screaming and crying fits." Rebecca looked to her husband.

"I think she's in a lot of pain," I said.

Now Rebecca scanned my face. "She's talked to you about it?"

"About Santa Cruz," I said.

"Non-negotiable," Mark announced, and I watched him curl his wife's fingers away from the fork handle she'd gripped tightly. He patted the back of her hand once he'd managed to get her to release the utensil. *Good dog*, I thought.

"May I tell you a story?" I asked.

"Feel free," he said, out of politeness rather than any genuine desire. I watched Rebecca slip her hand from beneath his and fold her hands in her lap—undercover prayer.

"I once knew someone like Marvella. Bright. Industrious. On her way," I said, holding my hands up before me. "The world in her hands." Mark was eyeing me suspiciously. "Her mother had invested heavily in her—sacrificed for her to have an education that could take her beyond the provincial town in which she'd grown up. She wanted for her daughter's life to be big—as big as she deserved." I was leaning forward now, trying to mesmerize Rebecca. "She wanted her daughter to have all of the opportunities she never had: to use her mind, to find the challenges that would keep her alive, bring her fulfillment. She wanted her daughter to achieve her potential."

"Marvella can achieve her potential at the community college," Mark pronounced, intending to end the discussion.

"No," I shook my head. "No, she cannot. And forgive me, but I have to say this: She will not have the peers she needs there. Marvella deserves to have to fight for A's, not to be handed them because she has, half asleep, written the best paper in the class. She deserves to have top-notch professors push her, delight in her, grade her harshly, reward her appropriately. She deserves the connections those professors can give her, the doors they can open for her. I swear to you, if you send her to a mediocre school, if you take this dream from her, everything she's capable of achieving will be lost. Your daughter will know how little you think of her." I stopped myself, feeling I was getting a little overdramatic but nevertheless wanting so badly to get through to them. I looked at Rebecca, saw true pain in her eyes.

"Are you finished?" Mark asked.

"I only want to ask that you reconsider your position. Please—for Marvella's sake. And for yours—it's a decision I fear you will regret one day, and that's a weight no one should carry."

"We appreciate what you've done for our daughter," he began. "I assure you that we love our daughter and only want the best for her."

"I don't doubt that," I said.

"And you have some brass balls, lady."

"That I do," I smiled. I caught a fleeting smile on Rebecca's face, too.

"I did not intend a compliment."

"I know that."

"I'm not sure I have any appetite remaining." Mark stood and held his hand out to his wife, who looked over at me.

"I think I'll stay," she said in a near whisper, ignoring his hand.

"You're not coming?"

"I think I want to have a meal with Meri," she said, her voice still barely above a whisper. But she said it; she did it.

"Fine." He took out his wallet and laid bills on the table.

I'd forgotten what it was like—the man paid; the woman likely didn't even have any cash on her.

I MADE A NEW friend that evening, a bonus I'd not anticipated. Rebecca Bennett took my hand and held onto it, tears running down her face. We sat together silently, and I actually began to wish the cook would hurry my chicken along.

"Are you all right?" I asked.

"Better than I've been in a long, long time."

I smiled at her.

"I wanted for Marvella to be able to go. To Santa Cruz, I mean." She took a deep breath. "I just couldn't say the things you said to Mark. I wanted to, I really did. But his temper." She looked into my face, searching. "Where did you get your courage?"

"First of all, he's not my husband. That makes it easier." I pressed my lips together. "Secondly, I really don't care if Mark likes me. And I had some good teachers. Some people who loved me enough to encourage me. Finally, life, its events."

"Alden's death?"

"That. And some other things. People. One hugely precious person."

"Well, I envy you."

"Don't," I said. "Really and truly, don't envy me. Don't envy how I got here."

"I love Mark."

I waited. She didn't need for me to comment on her marriage.

"It's just that sometimes . . ."

The waitress came and lit the candle on our table. "Soon," she assured us.

"He's a little rigid."

I couldn't help but laugh, which made her smile broadly.

She fidgeted with her wedding ring, and I could see that it had been cut in the back to accommodate her larger finger.

"Mark thinks she'll get hurt out there. You know," she said, "it's *California*."

"It's opportunity. And, if you've done your job well—and I think you have—then she will handle that opportunity, that freedom. She will make you proud. More importantly, she will make herself proud."

"When I hear you say that, I believe you."

"Believe your daughter. Remember who you were long enough to trust your daughter."

It was enough to start her crying all over again.

"THANKYOUTHANKYOUTHANKYOU!!!!" Marvella danced in my living room a week later.

"You'rewelcomeyou'rewelcomeyou'rewelcome!"

"I've never been so happy!"

Bravo, Rebecca, bravo!, I thought.

"I HAVE AN IDEA I want to run by you," I said, just as the heavy raindrops began. It was July, a few weeks after Marvella's graduation, and Emma and I were hiking side by side on the nature path in Bandelier. Burgeoning towers of black clouds rumbled.

"Let's head for the portico," Emma shouted, and we ran. We found a spot for two on the wooden benches that lined the long, roofed porch of the Visitors Center. Twenty or more people packed the benches, all of us made instant friends by the drama of the storm. We looked toward the flesh-colored cliffs, and I closed my eyes and took in as much of the ozone-filled air as possible, listened to the booming thunder. Within minutes, the hail came. It pounded so hard on the tin roof that it was impossible to hear anything else, and so we sat, simply enjoying the concert.

A piece of hail bounced across the flagstones to my feet. I picked it up and slipped it down the front of my blouse. I looked up in time to catch the eye of an older man, likely in his seventies, who'd seen me. He was smiling at me, slightly dumbfounded, and so I smiled back. A rivulet of warmed water flowed between my breasts, down my belly and into the waistband of my jeans. It made me want more hail, more rivers, but the storm was over quickly.

Emma and I lingered. The storm had cooled the air by a good twenty degrees, and I shivered once.

"So, talk," she said.

"This idea I have—borne of events with Marvella and her parents."

"All right."

"I'll have the check in a week." The lawsuit was over at last, and all of the funds from Alden's estate were soon to be deposited into a bank account that bore only my name. I would have nearly two million dollars. I stretched my legs, thinking that now I'd allow myself the luxury of a new pair of hiking boots. "I want to start a group for girls."

"Los Alamos girls?"

"Initially. But I have bigger plans. Eventually, I'd like to open it up to girls throughout northern New Mexico."

"What kind of group?"

"To encourage girls in their dreams, support them in pursuing their dreams. Increase their exposure to the multitude of possibilities that are opening up for women. Help them find out what their dreams are."

"Careers in science?"

"Careers in *whatever*. But not just careers—I'm thinking of lives of independence. Strong lives. Brave lives. How can a girl who's only lived seventeen or eighteen years fully evaluate the ramifications of her choices? I want for girls to see what they have in terms of potential, where their talents lie, and then I want to provide them with role models, support in terms of practicalities—how to go about making any given dream manifest. An actual plan for life."

"And you think they need this in addition to parents?"

"There are girls whose families will give them all of this, although in my mind any family could use supplementation—no one knows it all, can be everything. And there are girls who just need an outsider, a sounding board."

"Women's lib."

"Well, somewhat—but I'd call it quiet resistance to subterranean chauvinism."

"Lovely—*subterranean chauvinism*. How do you anticipate presenting this, getting parents to let their daughters participate?"

"Through the high school. The Girl Scouts, 4-H Club—even the rodeo club. Churches. A youth center, if the county ever gets one going. *Home ec classes*," I said, meaningfully.

"Ha ha!" Emma clapped. "And you'll do this all alone? Or will you hire people?"

"I've talked to my attorney about forming a nonprofit corporation. I'll do it that way. But this is the best part," I said, sitting taller. "I want the women of Los Alamos—all of us, our generation—to be mentors to these girls. All the women you and I have known for decades, everyone I know from the pool, women from the grocery, TG&Y. Clubs, the choral society. Think about it!" I was nearly shouting. "Our women's discussion group! Barbara Malcolm—you know she has all of that public health experience." Emma nodded. "Judy Nielson—she's got a Ph.D. in math. Dawn Hendricks—she volunteers at the Museum of the Palace of the Governors—her degrees are in history and anthropology, I think. Betty Van Hessel—botany. *Rebecca Bennett—astronomy.*" I smiled widely.

"Meridian Whetstone—biologist, artist, poetess, and more. Margo Whiting—sociology. And me—don't forget me," Emma grinned.

"Would you?"

"Try and stop me."

I was so happy, so shot full of adrenaline that my hands shook.

"I want to get it up and running by the fall."

"Give me assignments."

"So you think it will work? You like it?"

"Meridian, it's inspired. Two birds with one stone, I think—you help the girls, you help the women feel they can make a valuable contribution to the future."

"I have a name for it." I drummed my hands on my thighs for effect. "Wingspan."

"Glorious." Emma hugged me. "I knew 1973 would be your year. I just knew it."

AT FIRST, I HAD far more mentors than mentees. Talented women came out of the woodwork, eager to contribute to the future of girls.

The girls came—slowly at first. I increased my efforts to get the word out, printed brochures and left piles of them in the offices of guidance counselors. I managed to get articles about Wingspan printed in the *Santa Fe New Mexican* and both Albuquerque papers. I drove to San Ildefonso and Santa Clara pueblos, to Española and Pojoaque. I wore my nice Pendleton skirts and blazers, got my hair cut so that it fell in layers to just beneath my chin, and spoke at luncheons, conventions, and in classrooms. On my lapel I wore a silver pin in the shape of a feather—one Alden had given me for our twentieth anniversary—and I went through any door I could wedge open with my foot, anywhere people would have me. I sought out the eyes of the girls in my audiences, preached as if I'd found Jesus at last.

We had ten girls the first year. Ten girls who were able to tap into the wealth of experience and wisdom offered by the women of Los Alamos, and who thereby expanded their peripheral vision.

CLAY SENT AN ENVELOPE for my fifty-first birthday in 1974. It contained a copy of a letter from the University of Washington in Seattle, confirming his acceptance as a Ph.D. candidate in geology. Folded within that letter was a check for fifty dollars, made out to Wingspan.

He knew.

When I deposited the check, I drew a heart with wings beneath my signature. I hoped he would see my joy when the canceled check made its way back to him.

A Flight of Sparrows

1. Although difficult to keep alive, sparrows have been kept as pets since the time of the Romans.

2. The Wee Brown Sparrow takes flight.

Nearly eight hundred girls have taken part in Wingspan between 1973 and now, the final days of 2011. My generation has faded, although others have come to fill our places, and I've made sure that Wingspan is well funded, that it will continue when I'm gone. I also created the Belle Jordan Scholarship, which is awarded to one girl each year who goes into medicine. Melody Mason, a Wingspan alumnus, took over as executive director two years ago. As for me, I'm content to climb onto my pile of Albuquerque phonebooks so that I can see over the steering wheel to drive my little Subaru Forester at just over twenty miles an hour—maximum—to downtown Los Alamos to put in an appearance at Wingspan luncheons. I no longer struggle with pantyhose, and so I wear my tried-and-true Pendleton wool pantsuits and have just enough energy to participate as a member of the audience but not to take the stage.

My eighty-eighth birthday arrives shortly. I cannot fathom that number of years. I admit to seeing an old woman when I look in the mirror—the short, wispy, flyaway white hair that it is evident I cut myself, the thick population of brown spots on the backs of my hands and forearms, the still-vibrant blue eyes—and I am surprised, always, because inside, where I live, I am at most forty, still eager for change, still hungry for learning, still curious, still yearning.

LAST WEEK, I DROVE willy-nilly around town, just to get out of the house. The Lab has added new security measures since 9-11, and after I crossed the bridge that spans my crow canyon, I ended up stuck near a check point. I started to make a U-turn, and the guards stopped me, asked for identification. I played the silly old woman so that they wouldn't make me get out of my car and explain myself, and then I listened while they doled out a gentle lecture and wrote down my license plate number. The whole thing wore me out, made me wonder if it's time for me to stop driving.

CLAY, MY FAITHFUL CLAY, has not missed a single one of my birthdays in forty years. I took a moment just now, repeated that mental arithmetic, and still came up with the same number: 40. Astounding. He has sent me so many wonderful things—a partial list, a sampling:

- A copy of his Ph.D. thesis, "A Comparative Study of Archean and Post-Archean Granitic Rocks Over Time and Observations Concerning the Geochemistry of Subduction-Zone Magmas";
- A mix cassette tape (that forced me to go buy my own cassette tape player) with songs like Tim Buckley's "Once I Was [a Soldier]" and Donovan's "Lalena";
- Jewelry he made from his own rock finds (the breathtakingly intense green, fractured variscite bracelet sits steady on my wrist as I write);

- So many books to keep my mind lively—Robert Wright's book on the new science of evolutionary psychology—*The Moral Animal*; oh, and *Banquet at Delmonico's*, with its behind-the-scenes history of Darwinism, social Darwinism in America;
- Syllabi for each of the first courses he taught as a new professor at Northern Arizona University;
- A T-shirt for a hang-gliding club he started in Flagstaff; and
- A photograph of his family—Clay, looking less sinewy and more domesticated, his surprisingly plush wife (identified on the back as Brenda), and two girls—Elizabeth Meridian and Obsidian Solstice. There was a dog, too—a chocolate lab mix called Ujjayi. The photo lives on the bulletin board in my kitchen.

When it was time for me to let Jasper go, I whispered into the fur of his neck, thanking him for the company, for helping me to ride out my loneliness after Alden. After Clay. I sifted his ashes beneath the pines where Beacon, White Wing, and Withered Foot had fallen. I kept all of my little hearts, my never-children, in one place, where I confess I have often gone, seeking and sometimes finding solace.

MARVELLA HAS COME TO town for the holidays, and I ask two things of her. She drives me to Socorro, the nursing home out near the old East Gate entrance to Los Alamos. I take Emma a New Year's gift of an African violet in a pretty cream-and bronze-colored cloisonné-patterned pot. Her eyes flicker beneath translucent eyelids painted with shattered patterns of burgundy capillaries, and I set the plant on the windowsill where it can bask in the gentle morning light. Marvella moves a chair next to Emma's bed for me, and then she goes to stand in the hallway—near enough to hear me call, but far enough away so that Emma and I can talk. It is a sensitive, diplomatic move, but unnecessary. Emma's Alzheimer's prevents any true discourse, and at most we have meandering exchanges that involve a frustrating level of repetition and a miasma of confusion.

I let Emma sleep, let her hover in a world I hope is better than this room that stinks of urine and shit, where I hear cries of pain and loneliness escaping from rooms down the hallway while indolent, indifferent staff watch television in a front office. I turn Emma's hand until I can see the veins of her wrist, and I run a crooked, arthritic finger along those veins. I wish death for her. I wish it with all my heart.

Marvella can see that I am weakened by the visit, and she takes my elbow as we walk down the hallway to the exit. My walk is now habitually unsteady, although I abjure the use of a cane. I stand in the parking lot and gulp fresh air.

"How about a dish of ice cream before we head back?" she asks, and I am glad of her attempt to erase the past half hour. We sit next to a sunny window in the ice cream shop, and I let my scoops of burnt toffee ice cream melt to the consistency I like best.

"How old are you now?" I ask, taking full advantage of the leeway permitted old people—we have too little time to bother skirting around things and so are blindingly direct.

"Fifty-six," she says, carving her vanilla ice cream with the tip of her spoon. She is drawing elaborate swirls in the surface of her single scoop.

"Impossible."

"I know," she says.

Marvella works as a veterinary medical officer at the U.S. Geological Society's National Wildlife Health Center in Wisconsin. She still runs marathons, an activity that I have opined is crazy. Marvella good-naturedly ignores me.

"Will you come again next year, do a few presentations for the girls?"

"You know I will. You know I'd do just about anything for you, don't you?" she asks, and I can see a surprising uncertainty in her eyes, as if she is afraid I don't know that she loves me.

"I know," I say. "That request is for the girls."

"Is there something else? Something I can do for you?"

"When we get back to the house," I say, prevaricating.

I am fortified by the ice cream, and once we're in my living room I tell Marvella she should toss her coat on the couch. "In here," I say, and she follows me to the bedroom, where I have stacked all of my crow journals on the foot of the bed.

"What are these?"

"They are everything," I say. "Everything," and my voice breaks. I did not think it would be this hard, but it is.

"May I?" she says, and I nod. She picks up one of the earliest journals and flips through the pages. I see my columns, my neat handwriting. Because it is an early journal, there are no drawings, and there is no poetry. It was one of the purely scientific journals. "The others, too?" she says, looking at me.

"They changed over time," I say, trying to marshal my emotions. "They evolved as I evolved."

"In what way?"

"Less objectivity. More subjectivity. More intimacy."

"Your life's story, then, is that what I'm holding?"

"Yes."

Marvella sits on my old, worn cotton bedspread faded to a pale yellow, and she holds the journal in her lap, one hand resting on the cover, the slim fingers of her other hand tracing the bound edge. "This is incredible," she says, taking in the number of books stacked beside her.

"I have empty boxes in the shed." Realizing I still have on my knit cap, I pull it from my head and try to tame my hair. "I want to box these up for mailing."

"All right."

"I'll give you the address and the money," I say, heading toward where I set my purse on the table beside the front door. I hand her a twenty-dollar bill. "I don't know what it will cost."

"Less if we send them book rate. It will take longer, though. Is that all right?"

"They've waited this long," I say.

After she has fitted the books into boxes, and after I have put a benedictory palm to the topmost volume before she tapes each box closed, she lugs the boxes to her car and drives away, waving to me as I stand in the front window, thinking as I always do these days, that it is the last time I will see her.

I smoothe the bedspread that still bears the imprint of all of those volumes, and then I lie down for a nap. I think about the sparking of catalysts, about Belle and Alden and Clay. I think about unseen connections, the forces that beckon birds along their migratory routes, that pull people together and split them from each other. I think about Clay's face when he opens the boxes, the perfection with which he will hold the weight of my history, my love.

Acknowledgments

Writing is an intensely solitary endeavor, but a story isn't truly heard until many hands have held it. I thank my early feedback readers, in particular Frances S. Koenig, Ruth Pregenzer, Teresa Odle, Alan Church, and Tom Mayer. I am forever grateful to Annie Hwang, who literally pulled Meridian from the mountainside of manuscripts at Folio Literary Management and brought my novel to the attention of Michelle Brower, who provides me with the very best representation and remains a vital, steady source of optimism. I owe many at Algonquin Books of Chapel Hill my thanks, especially my astute and sensitive editor, Andra Miller.

Although many sources helped me to interpret the world of the crows, the most helpful was the riveting *In the Company of Crows and Ravens*, by John M. Marzluff and Tony Angell (Yale University; 2005). I nevertheless own any and all errors, on all matters.